Autumn of the

White Woods

JONATHAN LOVEJOY

Armageddon Publishing

Cover: *The Knitter*, 1886
William Adolphe Bouguereau (1825-1905)

ISBN-10: 0692359117
ISBN-13: 978-0692359112

For every Elizabeth

Righteous Heaven

In such Peril

There is no Counsel

And no hope to be found;

Save only weeping and sighing

And begging for your mercy

Righteous Heaven

In such Peril

We beg for your mercy.

MAOMETTO II
Gioachino Rossini

JONATHAN LOVEJOY

1

I am my mother's prophecy.

I am Elizabeth.

2

"*I should have let you go to God when you were born.*"

It is a macabre refrain. A reminder that the pain I came to know as a child had its origin in the womb. A seed nurtured in her body, which broke free on the morning my father was killed. I pushed my way out of her in shrieking, on an icy cold November morning so many years ago.

I cannot stop my mind from drifting to her. Wondering about the Italian Girl in Carolina, though the woman I call Barbara Jean Coletti is Italian in name only. I see her in her hospital bed. Drowned in grief. In mourning over her dead husband. A young widow, unable to hold the thing that ripped its way out of her a month early.

I imagine that she is driven home, holding misery in a baby's blanket, dreading the sight of her country house on that lonely little dirt road. Walking alone, through the front yard to the wooden porch steps. Climbing them, as though ascending a spiral walkway into a darkened hall. Inside she stands in the pale, violet glow of dawn. The baby in her arms begins to move, prompting her to look down at its audacity to claim life. At its presumption to expect growth. She takes this baby to her room, lays it on her bed and sits down. Folding her hands in her lap. Letting her tears fall.

Eventually, the baby cries.

The voice slices cold through the air, then through her, making her draw a breath. I imagine that she thinks of how it was the cause of this new nightmare she is in. The orphan Michael Cole, who reclaimed his birth name Coletti, was gone because it was placed inside her. His body is in a cemetery. Killed because he traveled to work every day to earn money for it. It had come into the world like a parasite, to latch onto her life. To steal from her the light of hope, the glow of living, and all expectation of joy and happiness. The woman turns her head slowly, staring through a haze of tears, through a fog of every emotion, including fear. The beautiful woman moves, creeping steadily as if possessed, onto the bed on all fours. She gathers her hatred nerve—and rests her body on the infant in full.

She feels the baby's muffled voice. Her thoughts explode with possibilities of freedom, perhaps even to leave this place. Returning to the arms of her own mother, after its body is buried deep in the ground. But forces act upon her, striking against her will until she raises up just enough, so that the child turns its head to the side, and breathes its lovely screaming into the walls of its mother's bedroom. But she lays there, taking satisfaction that for now there will be no feeding of mother's milk, but rather the poisoning, the choking on a mother's contempt. There she lays for as long as it takes. Until the baby's energy is depleted. And there is no more sound.

Yes. I imagine that as an infant, I learned—adapted—until the weight of my mother's body became a comfort, rather than a burden of terror.

3

My mind is lifted upon gentle breezes. Drifting through time, until I am one with the winds of my childhood—on a cool summer's day. Cold warnings and premonitions are carried in this lonely breeze. Perceived by few, heeded by fewer still. Through the trees, upward. High over the leaf canopy moves the summer wind. Flowing downward. Fast over the back country roads—

Until it swirls gently around a young traveler. Blowing long, black hair gracefully behind her. A cool, quiet breeze of foreboding. But in ignorance she strolls along, unaware that this is the last day she can hope to feel normal, and that today, she will begin to learn what it means to suffer.

This is the last day of my fifth grade year. The last day of my education. I am a year older than the other children, because I had to repeat a grade. "Emotional immaturity" they called it. I wouldn't talk to anybody, and had cried almost every day. But the teachers have been so kind. Always kissing me on the forehead and wiping my eyes, promising that everything will be alright. One of them even said she might steal me and take me home, and adopt me for her very own. But I am wary of them, not because of unfriendliness, but because I am already afraid of other people. And the children all try to be my friend or sworn enemy, but none have succeeded-- because I cannot respond to the friendly little girls drawn to me, nor to the ones who call me names and throw dirt in my long, black hair.

There is one adorable little blonde in particular, who never misses a time to show her fifth grade savagery, as cold as a winter snowstorm. And why do boys yank my hair and my clothes, and trip me on the playground, running away while I stumble to the teacher in tears? Even now, my pink and white dress bears a grass stain. The stain is a travesty, but hardly tragic, being that my thrift store dress already looks like it was made from an old checkerboard tablecloth. And dresses like these do not help my cause. Marking me as not just a country girl…

But a *poor* one.

Your dress looks like my Momma's dishcloths, Sarah had said on the bus, on the way home from school. She wears a pretty shirt or blouse, always. A pair of jeans and the latest high cost athletic shoes. A tomboy doll in Jenny-braids, who will someday tread the sorority path of Ivy.

Is that her mother's blonde prettiness I see?

"All of your clothes are ugly," she says calmly. She blows a big, purple bubble, sucking it back into her mouth. "What are you gonna do this summer?" her gum snapping and popping. "My Dad's taking us to Florida. We're gonna stay in his condominium. You don't even know what a condominium is, do you?"

If I say no, she will laugh. But if I don't answer, she'll pinch my arm, kick my leg or poke me in the eye. I shake my head, and she laughs cruelly. But thankfully, the other girls don't notice.

I know it was Sarah who told the boy to trip me on the playground today.

"You think you have a pretty face don't you?" She leans towards me. "Country Carmen." She puckers her tiny lips like she is going to kiss me, then spits the bubble gum right into my eyeball. Thank God the other children didn't see me cover my eye. They would have torn me to pieces laughing. But Sarah stands up as if nothing has happened, chattering wildly with another girl.

As the Italian Girl walks home in Carolina, a twinge of fear pricks me, when I remember Sarah Brown.

I feel pleasant again. That echo of happiness that touches every child on the last day of school. A little melody haunts my mind. A beautiful one that my music teacher had played for me.

Weeks ago, Ms. Ida caught me staring at the piano.

"Have you ever played before, Carmen?"

"No, Maam."

"Its easy to learn. Maybe I can teach you someday." She touches my face. "You look like a lady musician," she says, smiling. "Let's play something…"

She proceeds upon the venerable *Twinkle Twinkle, Little Star*, failing to notice the serious, scholarly look that overtakes me. I am able to repeat the notes very fast. Too fast. It is as natural as walking or breathing.

"Are you sure you never played, Honey?"

"Yes, Maam…"

What forces her to play *Those Endearing Young Charms* next? Is she trying to teach me a lesson for having beginners fortune? A brief, lucky flair for her instrument? No. When she sees my fingers whirl across the keys, I think a chill clutches her both body and soul. Without another word, a few bars of a bagatelle, for someone named Elise. Slowly. And then, a phrase from a little sonata in C major, for beginners. My desperation.

That day, Ms. Ida was in my mother's home.

But Mrs. Coletti, if you could just see her play…

The conversation went nowhere, and I knew better than to mention it again.

I stroll by these summer woods. Humming a few notes of the *Sonata Facile*. Suddenly, the wind whispers louder through the green forest. My mind's piano is whisked away, and the wind breathes the voice of a small *orchestra*--stopping me dead in my tracks, making me look around. Where is it coming from? The orchestra, en masse, is joined by a new piano, and they continue together, to form the beginnings of a small *concerto*.

My compensation.

The color I will need. When the world turns to ashen gray regret.

4

I hurry through the four-roomed country house, to the little space that is my own. My bedroom. Sometimes, a refuge from the storm. My notebook binder is quickly put aside, and I waste no time shuffling out the back door. There are chores to do.

Our house is isolated deep in farming country, a few miles south of Williamston, nestled among the trees down a dirt road. Behind the house is a small, abandoned cropfield, good for being the biggest back yard in town. I have spent so much time sitting or lying in this empty field, a loud yelling distance from the house. Enjoying the trees that border our world, or sometimes gazing at the afternoon sky, watching the clouds float by. I always wonder where they come from, and where above Earth they are going to.

I am a country girl. I know the pain of cleaning the filthy henhouse, and collecting eggs at the crack of dawn. The big chicken coop is high-fenced inside a long area, plenty big enough to give the flock enough space. Especially the lower hens. They can be cornered and cannibalized, if there's nowhere for them to run.

These smelly, noisy things are my responsibility. I ignore them while inside the messy henhouse, brushing the strong smelling poop from around their nesting boxes onto the plywood floor. The droppings make my eyes water, like ammonia. The flock is little more than an echo from another time, when my father had designs on a big egg farm. That was 13 years ago.

There was a time, when the widow had been home all day with her husband. Watching him, helping him. Loving him. But somewhere in the midst of paradise, her pregnancy had begun to show. He took a job, and commuted to work every day. But one night, he didn't come home. When she found out he had been killed, the shock hit the child in her stomach, doubling her over in agony, nearly killing her.

That was 13 years ago.

The hens are pleased with their new house cleaning. I water them, fill their feed trays, and collect the few eggs I see. I leave them to the business of pecking and pooping, and take the eggs into the kitchen. The chores seem to go by quicker today.

Is this the age when children reason what they've suspected? When assumptions become revelations? When every word, every expression, every part of their parents' body language is studied?

But I haven't been punished in quite a while now. And when Mother listened to Mrs. Brooks begging about the piano, it sounded like she was going to give in. Maybe, I should have asked her more about it then.

I am on my bed now, legs crossed Indian style, leaning my chin on my hands. Knowing that I have to play. Hoping it will work out alright.

This burning is not a new thing. Melodies have always called to me. Causing sensations in my body. They are echoes from the River Valley, since before my first day of school. Fragments of song. Visions and dreams, so many lost in my former memory. The sonata Mrs. Brooks played today had caused my vision to haze, and I thought briefly that *colors* had appeared. And though I have never played before, I know what keys are correct. How? It had felt very strange, as though I didn't have control over where my fingers played.

I have to learn.

I have to.

The radio cannot soothe my nerves today, so I go back out in the afternoon sun. The flock is noisy outside. The warm breeze foretells of spring's last days, and summer's early arrival.

The winds of summer blow across the eastern county, flowing through the green forests and fields, whispering promises of warm, hopeful days. The Carolina sky is painted the deepest blue, with tall, fluffy white clouds looming afar off. They are beautiful, but convey a sense of foreboding. Potential for catastrophic power.

Foreboding.

Butterflies. Not the little white ones fluttering here in the backyard. I need to take a stroll, away from the smell of the chicken coop. The breeze blows gently in my face while I wander to the open field, going all the way to the middle, sitting down in the low, thick grass. I lean back on my hands, and gaze at the Azurean Sea. Two airplane trails have made a giant cross in the sky. The house and the chicken yard seem so blissfully, dreamily far away.

My body is boyishly straight—the inherited curves have not yet grown. But some claim that an amazing prettiness is in my face, but I do not know what they mean. I only know the voice of melody, as I breathe in the woodsy air. There is no sweet smell of honeysuckle, though. The summer air only smells green, like leaves of grass. The grass makes my legs itch if I sit for too long.

When I close my eyes, I think of Mrs. Brooks, and how nice she has always been. Her attractive, smiling face and curly dark hair are a pleasant memory. Mrs. Ida Hirshman-Brooks. My angel in crystal.

I hear a calling! A cry of new music, drifting from the air around me! The sound expands on its own, until I can only hear chords of harmony, and not a single other noise in Creation. That is why I cannot respond, if an angry voice screams my name from the house…

With the stealth of a predator, she steps up behind me, raises her right hand, and whacks my face as hard as she can. A loud *smack,* a wallop that sends me reeling to the side. She grabs my hair with one hand, dragging me to my feet. My face burns, and all I can see is her wicked expression.

"Why didn't you *answer* me when I called you! I told you to *never* ignore me!"

She shakes me violently on the "never," then shoves me hard towards the house, making me fall in a clumsy, noisy heap, causing my lip to bleed. She pulls me up quickly, and I feel two hard whacks on my bottom, hard enough to rattle my insides, lurching me forward.

My vision hazes while I stumble away, mouth half open. Trying to swallow the lump in my throat. Trying not to blink.

So the tears won't come.

*T*wilight is the echo of dreams. A scene in violet and deepest blue. Mother is near the open field, staring at bright stars already visible.

Hair as black as midnight silk. A creamy smooth complexion. Her chaste, serious look is pleasant, but there is something about her eyes. Pale gray and piercing. *Witch eyes,* to be sure.

The Lady is in the dusk with her arms folded, watching the guilt form. This day has threatened us for a long time.

Such a long time.

"Momma?"

"Yes?"

"I'm sorry about this afternoon."

"Its alright. Just don't do it again. Did you finish the dishes?"

"Yes, Maam. Did you like the spaghetti, Momma?"

She gazes towards the stars, trying not to look at me. I lean my head against her chest. A power bosom, it is. She hugs me awkwardly.

"*Ms. Ida* said I wouldn't even have to go anywhere to learn the piano. She has a keyboard. And she told me if I wanted to, she'd come over here everyday if you--"

"So *that's* what it was," she says, jerking me away from her. "That's why you've been purrin' and rubbin' against me all afternoon."

"That's not why. You know I always hug you. But Momma--"

A heavy, anguished pause...

"Momma, I need to learn. I want to play so bad that it *hurts*."

No answer.

"I need it, Momma. Today, when I was walking home--"

"What did I tell you the last time?"

"But you didn't say anything to me last time, Momma. You just told Ms. Ida that you'd let her know. Remember?"

"I'm letting you know right now..."

"Momma please...please..."

"No."

The word chills my bones.

My soul.

"But Momma I don't know what I'll do if I can't play." I gaze up at her, rubbing her face softly. She takes my hand gently…

And squeezes it.

It makes me draw a sharp breath, and I lean over a little. Her grip is incredible.

"I said…no."

This second "no" dispatches heat. My Italian blood simmers in me, and I wrench my hand free, shocking her with newfound bravery.

"One day I'm leaving you here and I'm *never* coming back!"

Boldly I march into the house, slamming the screen door behind me, then my bedroom door as well.

While I sit pouting in my comfortable chair, I don't let myself imagine her standing motionless. Peering through the walls of the house at me.

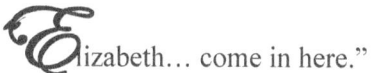izabeth… come in here."

"I *won't!*"

"You don't want me to come in there."

"I don't care. I don't care what you do, you can't make me not want to play!"

"That's what I'd like to talk to you about," she says, voice nearly trembling. "But I'd like to tell you out here. I need for you to come sit with me."

"Are you going to let me play?"

"Come in here first," she says. "And then we can discuss it. Like women."

When I open the door, she is on the couch, hands folded in her lap. A picture of repression. She lowers her eyes. I go to the couch and sit down, noticing her strange, defeated expression.

"Well?" I ask defiantly.

"I…"

A pause…

"I'm going to have to whip the blood out of you."

It is a different kind of fear. The kind that spreads slowly into every part of the body. I stare into her gray eyes, into her expression, which has begun to change.

Oh, does it change.

"But I…"

"Go to your bedroom and wait for me. And close that door."

I do it gladly, stumbling once as I walk over to my bed. I have been whipped before. And they are always painful, which is bad enough…

But she has never spoken those words before.

I can only sit anxiously, trying not to be angry at my music teacher for causing all of this. But the anger is easily done away with. Ms. Ida is not to blame.

But the *fear*—

Nervously, I listen to her walk into her bedroom. I would love to run after her and throw my arms around her, begging for forgiveness. But instead I sit in dumbness, trembling inside while her black shoes clump towards my door, freezing me again when she opens it.

"Momma, I won't do it again. I promise to God and Jesus I won't."

"Come here to me."

"Momma…"

"I said… come *here* to me."

*I*t is the worst whipping I have ever gotten. Afterwards, she had thrown me to the floor and stormed out of the room, while I sat there in tears and disbelief, sobbing and coughing like I was going to die. Even so, Mother had come back a few minutes later, wearing only her bra and half slip. Her huge bosom was the last thing I saw through clear vision, as she had grabbed me without another word, whipping me again, with the same violent energy as before.

The pain was like fire on my skin, I suppose.

I languish in my comfortable chair now. Listening to my classical station—looking at mountains in a picture book. How I wish we had a television so I could have something else to do. I can easily hear Mother in the bathroom.

On my arms is the evidence of promises kept. The red welts are hard and thick, and they itch. Tiny, bloody specks are on some of them.

I hate myself.

Why do I keep making her angry?

My Chinese checkers lie hidden under my bed, calling to me. I slide it out, gathering the marbles from inside. Marbles I love to play with. Colors that I need. Bright, pure red or blue, yellow or green, white or the blackest black. I climb on the bed to play with them, still noticing the itching and burning on my arms and legs. My rag doll, games and toy animal farm lie neglected in the closet.

The walls of my little room are pale yellow. A mirror rests on the back of the dark brown three drawer dresser, upon which are no photographs, or decorations of any kind. Only my notebooks and pencils are there. But the window view is pristine, showing part of the barren field, with the woods bordering a good distance away. The yellowed shade is rolled to the top of the window, like always, between light blue curtains matching the bedspread. I sit with bare feet apart, tablecloth dress over the new leg scars. Arranging the colors as I see fit.

What is this?

A calling!

When I glance back at the marbles, every color fades to gray. Then fluidly, the blues glow brighter as the orchestral appears… smooth, clear, and perfect. When I touch them, they give the energy of their key, expanding in my mind. I can *feel* the little piano concerto again, flowing from the essence of blue. Every marble is gray, except for each of the ten which share this color…

And when the piano's voice emerges, a green light glows, popping as brilliantly as ever! The notes play on, as the greens flicker brightly and dimly, in keeping with my mind's music, borne from my soul's piano. The blues are in unison, as the green lights dance…shimmering like summer earth stars in my vision.

This world is so intensely vivid, so inescapably a part of me that I cannot hear the angry pounding of bare feet, thumping in bitterness towards me from the other side of Creation.

I can see the world through your gray eyes.

I can see the way they longed for you, when you made your first appearance as a widow among them. The painful jealously in their faces, the repression, the resentment flowing. Their tongues bound, shaking their heads, knowing that the child in your arms is fatherless. Believing you have somehow reaped the reward for your sin.

The men who chauffer you in the taxi. The ladies in the grocery store, or the department stores, or in the little boutiques you love to browse in. The men and women in the little Baptist church you drift to, carrying me bundled safely in contempt. They all look at the beauty witch with suspicion, and gaze upon the devil child with unspoken disgust.

The preacher and his wife, whoever they may have been on the day you walked in. I know your discomfort, Mother, your self-consciousness as you sit quietly in the back row, trying not to excite lust in the preacher with your youth and sex, praying to God that your beauty will not light a green fire in his wife. The church is your last hope, isn't it? The cushioned Baptist benches. The smell of pine and gentility. The look of the burgundy carpet at your tired feet.

This is the bosom of community. Your last chance at redemption.

Mr. Shirley has allowed you to stay in your home. The flock gives so many eggs for you. There are too many in the flock. You are overwhelmed. You sit in church, holding the quiet thing, feeling it breathe in your arms, too afraid to despise it today. I rest asleep, unaware of your grief, the misery, and the terror you feel. Are you afraid of their staring? The spirits of sexual envy that flow from the pulpit and the pews, drifting to where we rest helpless in the back of the country church? But this is the place where the Divine lives. You need to be here, Mother. Without this place, your life can have no meaning. No purpose.

Here, you don't despise your baby as much.

Every now and then, your eyes will wander, and you see one of the fine ladies on the Board of Mothers, staring at you with flaming hot coals. You tuck your sensuous lips, lowering your eyes in respect, watching the child rest in your lap fast asleep. Almost, there is a vague longing, a faint, distant echo of warmth in your icy bosom. Briefly, I am yours to love if you choose. To have as your child and companion.

Their feeble worship has ended. Their prayers have gone unheard, unanswered for another Sunday. Quickly, you gather your black overcoat, your mourning cloak, but you cannot escape. They have gathered around you, like honeybees to the brightest flower. Humbly, you accept their oos and ahhs, nervously allowing the girls and ladies to take me into their arms. Your face, your smile, your eyes...your humility is more than many of them can bear. They have never seen a story book fantasy in life, a Beauty Witch made flesh and blood, and they are afraid. From magazines and picture shows, even from their most forbidden dreams, there you stand before unbelieving eyes, while your child pricks unresisting hearts.

One of the ladies has mercy on your nervousness, and they pry me away, placing me back in your arms. With a bright smile and a pleasant goodbye, you refuse every offer for a ride. Holding me tight, you attempt escape. But they usher you into one of their chariots, and they whisk you down the eidolic road, across the miles that will haunt us for a score of years.

We are alone.

9

As rest in morning sleep, my dreams are of Mrs. Brooks... Ms. Ida. I wonder if she awakes with a start on this Saturday morning after my twilight? Sunlight drifts through the blinds in her bedroom window. Cool, early morning rays of future's hope, and past winter's warmest dream. I see Mrs. Hirschman-Brooks sliding out of bed, in the same heavy guilt she feels every Saturday morning. Her head swirls and aches with something like a hangover as she shuffles to the bathroom, not caring at all that this is the Sabbath.

She thinks of me. Carmen Coletti.

She looks at her curly black hair and weakened expression in the mirror. Studying her attractive middle aged face. Staring at the prominent nose she hates but her husband finds sexy. The so-called laugh lines around her eyes aren't funny anymore, and she wrinkles her mouth in disgust, and washes her hands.

She decides to go back to bed, more than thankful that another one of those ridiculous school years has come and gone. Those little tone deaf imps, she thinks, though having no real resentment towards any one of them. After all, it is not their fault, that the heavenly language is not given to them to understand.

Ida slips back into bed. Drowned in anguish, not caused this time by her resentment of days long gone, years of orthodoxy, and pressured expectations of greatness on the black and white keys. Maybe her mother won't mention the fact that she is only a music teacher this time. Or that her husband is not "one of them." She dreads the visit to her parents' New Jersey home in Sewell again, just like she does every season. Ida lays still and quiet in her bed, staring up at whatever fan or light fixture there is above her.

The little girl is on the edge of a life of misery with that woman, she thinks. The mother is kind, with a sweet disposition. But somehow, Ida is afraid of her. For another instant, she ponders the amazing truth, that Barbara Coletti had actually struck a spark of *fear* in her soul. There is something in those pale gray eyes. An epic something.

Something.

10

*T*he Bantam's voice is like a wet lash across Mother's back this morning. The blood gathers at the veins in her head, and pumps sharply through. Only two hours after slumber has given mercy, her eyes are open again. There are eggs to gather, a breakfast that needs cooking. Not for herself, because she is not the least bit hungry. But there is another mouth to feed.

Barbara shifts her powerfully voluptuous body to the side, then onto her back. Breathing the longest, deepest breath. Sighing the deepest sigh.

Sometimes, her body still aches for him. A burning desire. A seething, boiling lust of memory. She rubs her temples, ignoring what she wants to do to her body. Hands above the covers, her own mother had said. One lustful thought, one careless brush of the hand can lead to temptation.

No religious fanatics here. Not in this room. But holy apples tend to rest near the Righteous Tree. Her beautiful, black hair is far too long, as are all of her dreary skirts and dresses. And she knows it, but cannot bring a pair of scissors to those silky raven strands, nor to the gray, navy, and black hemlines in her closet. Somewhere inside, in the deepest part of memory, it will always be a sin for her to cut her hair, or to show the bare skin too far above her ankles.

This Saturday has no more sleep to give. But she is too tired to get up. The lighted hands on her little white electric clock tell her it is an ungodly hour to still be in bed. Dawn has already lit the white shades, and the pale blue walls of her sanctuary just enough.

The girl will wake up in a minute...she'll get the eggs...

Mother bites her thumbnail, and rolls over on her side to face the wall. This wall of guilt forms again before her eyes, forcing her to look at what she had done yesterday. Starting with that hideous slapping, which had seemed to come from nowhere. From Destiny's Flame it had emerged like some lost demon. Possessing her. Controlling her will so completely that she marveled at its power.

And the force of it had carried forward into the evening, waiting for her daughter's quiet rage and disrespect. But even after the second whipping, she had simmered in the same deep pit of rage, until she had to storm back into my room, yank me off the bed in a shower of marbles, and wail the tar out of me a third time.

It had been building, threatening for years. Even from those days when the child began to nurse the life out of her. She had felt her own hatred, buried deep inside her, many times desiring to see it choke. Sometimes, that hatred had gotten the best of her, and she would spank the infant hard, or lay on it, feeling it squirm and scream underneath her body, trying to force herself to cover its face with her skin. Today, guilt cut and hurt her deeply, frustrating her, when she considered that her daughter was truly lucky to be alive.

I am lucky to be alive.

"Barbara Jean! Barbara Jean Daniels!"

Her own mother's loud, strong voice. The grandmother I never knew. Calling her from the past, to send waves of phantom misery through her-- then intense, nearly ethereal satisfaction, because it is only an echo of a bygone reality. She is an adult, with a child of her own, over a decade free from her lonely childhood. But still a captive of the pain of memories, old scars, and wounds that run too deep to heal.

Mother ignores the lateness of the farmer's hour, pulling her other pillow close to her body. She closes her gray eyes, and drifts into a deep, mourning sleep.

11

A new dawn drifts from the darkest nighttime, awakening me from one consciousness to another, as if from a spirit's world of sound and color. Sunlight shines dimly around the edges of the window shade. Sleepy eyes blink into full alertness. The old clock radio shows that I have overslept a little.

The eggs...

In nervous haste, I throw the covers back, sliding quickly out of bed, paying little attention to the burning that still itches every part of my skin. A quick rub to my arm shocks me, because the skin feels very rough. It is a scab, crusted over a brutal scrape. It lights the tiniest flame of sorrow, as I ponder the evil that Mother has done.

I didn't deserve it.

Did I?

I submit to the pouting, as I slip out of my summer nightgown. I have not seen the blood yet. A tiny spot of blood at the bottom, collected from a welt last night. Just like every morning, I hang the little white cotton gown in the corner closet. My faded denim Saturday dress awaits, already worn when Mother had pulled it unashamedly from the church donation box. The frayed thing hangs loosely over my thin body, displaying country poverty with spiteful misery and neglect.

There might be four dozen eggs this morning. Apprehensively, I drift through my house of fears, through the morning day, aware that the melody I hum is my mind's own, visited from the long, restful night's sleep. Sleep is often a refuge…my only place of rest.

The glow of the new sun permeates the warm air high above. Pale orange is fading into the blue of day. A growing humidity holds the early morning coolness in check, making the air stale, and hard to breathe. The sky looks hazy.

The lonely, dusty scent of rain. Strangely, the smell reminds me of winter, which is still another world away.

The flock is calm—clucking, strutting and scratching about. The strange colored, feathered things hold small fascination for me anymore. Except for the white rooster, which is my favorite. The sturdy wire fence gate swings easily open. I step through their morning placidness, into the back of the unpainted, wooden chicken coop, carefully gathering each white and brown egg, one from each of the fifty or so nests . In all the years, I have hardly broken a single egg.

Would I like to crack one over Mother's head? Fear perishes the thought.

My pink lip is still pushed forward in a pout, if not in bitterness, at least in disappointment. But truthfully, no more than an egg's worth of pain can I wish for even a wicked witch. The coop was cleaned just yesterday, but while gathering the Hen's Labour, I notice the ammonia smell is already strong again.

The wicker basket is heavy. I hold it carefully by both handles as I leave the chicken yard, shooing them away from the gate before opening it. As I walk towards the house, I finally allow myself to wonder whether I truly deserved to have been whipped three times, or even if I deserved to have been punished at all. The itching is mercifully light, but something new has formed from this whole incident, something powerful in its vagueness, that holds me captive with feelings I can neither resist nor understand.

Stepping unawares back through the kitchen door, I cannot comprehend my own emotions, which have crossed a boundary from yesterday, from childhood apprehensions to preadolescent fears. From this comes the seed of disappointment, which may become nurtured, threatening to grow into mild despair. I battle this new sorrow, feeling it creeping up to me in form, having the power to engulf me in depression more severe than what I have ever known. But I will fight it valiantly, even while putting the eggs in the gray paper cartons in the refrigerator. The feelings inside are replete with the loneliness of ages, the iciness of death itself. But in childhood ignorance, submission to it is no option. So I choose my weapon, and guird my armour against the enemy.

I must prepare this little shoulder, for the weight of the cold it will have to bear, towards the beautiful woman who sleeps soundly in the blue bedroom.

12

Shall we leave behind unloving arms
To return to our Mother's loving arms—

    The music teacher has a husband, and two teenage sons. They are a good family. But she's done with having children. Sometimes she cringes at the thought of having to go back to school again, and listen to screeching little voices.

Breakfast is over. Her husband is away on some errand or another. He really does like to spend time with her. Really. He just has to keep busy. He'll be trapped in the car with them again soon enough anyway, driving north.

Ida puts the last plate in her dishwasher, and switches it on. The humming has its way, soothing her nerves. Berlioz's symphony has already drifted from her mind, though it still sings its melodie fantastique, softly from the stereo in the other room. She marvels at the composer's good judgment, at having decorated his masterpiece with the inspired ball dance. Perhaps, that alone is truly fantastic.

The dreary landscape of longwinded romanticism. A sea of abstrusion. Discursiveness, masquerading as lyricism. Unbeautiful.

It is a strange and wonderful morning, one of leisure, and thoughts of long, restful days ahead. Her sons' voices pierce the humid air outside. From the back door, she can see them tossing the football back and forth, noticing how much better her younger son is at throwing and catching it. He is like his father.

Ida wonders how it is that neither of her children seem to care the least bit about music.

Music.

Why has this child captured her emotions? Why does her image still haunt her waking thoughts? Is it the nonsense of having no daughter of her own? Is it the foolishness of her pretty little face and hair, or that prodigious little talent? What is the fullness of it?

From the first day Carmen Coletti walked into her classroom, she has felt it. From the lightning spark at the piano, even unto this day poised at the edge of another long hot summer. In this little girl, she feels a sorrow, an unearthly soul of hoping. Power drifts from winds of memory, warming

37

her heart every time she thinks of the girl with the dark eyes, the smooth, fair skin and the long, silken black hair. In her expression, Ida Brooks sees that distant longing. That profound, indefinable sadness.

Carmen Elizabeth.

Carmen...

She finds herself whispering these words in the dusk evening, and in the dawn of so many mornings. This girl, whose image haunts her mind, and whose spirit drifts into her soul. Sometimes when she thinks of her, a tear will fall, and she wipes it in frustration, chastising herself for her silliness—for shedding tears over a child she barely even knows, and whose life seems to be just fine and dandy.

And then, she will think of the Lovely. Hair pitched in ravenwood. Eyes—bewitching—as the gray of an approaching whirlwind.

A shiver trembles Ida's nerves. She shakes her head, trying to clear her mind of those two.

13

My desire to play the piano has risen up again. I cannot control my little attitude. While we prepare the supper table, she knows I am angry. She draws satisfaction from watching my little face twist into a frown, and listening to my sharp little tone of voice.

I am a prisoner of fear. But I am still a child.

"You may as well forget about that piano foolishness," she says. "I don't know what made you think you can learn to play anyway."

How ignorant she is! As I sit down to dinner, I even laugh a little.

Her look changes slightly. A twitch of jealousy, over the secret power I share with an outsider. I giggle again, satisfied, because I see her become self-conscious as a Virginia farm girl, thrust in the company of intelligence, artistic interest, and breeding.

Within my smugness, my complacency, I feel sharp tug on my hair, so hard that it burns my scalp. She escorts me to my bedroom and flings me towards my bed, though I am already more regretful than she can imagine.

The few little bites of dinner are all that I have eaten.

"You had *better* not leave this room again, unless I call you."

"Yes maam."

She stands there. Tall in front of me. Towering, staring, studying me for insolence or bravery. She wrinkles her beautiful mouth in severe contempt, then whirls elegantly out of my room, closing the door rather gently.

As always, I retreat to my place of melody and song, only the slightest bit hungry, but very fearful inside. Is she going to return tonight, and stripe the blood out of me?

This the first time since I was a baby that you have taken a meal from me. I will sleep in hunger—too young, too naïve to know that in the morrow, and to the dinner hour of the one after that, you will not allow me outside my room, and I will soon come to know the truth about hunger.

14

From the mists of an unrestful sleep, Barbara thinks she hears a knock at the door. In her mind, she calls *Elizabeth* in forced politeness for her to answer it. It wouldn't do to let Mr. Shirley hear unpleasantness. She pulls herself from sleep, listening to the Carmen Dove, cooing to the round waisted, forty something year old man with the gentle voice. He is always on the edge of a laugh. A friendly, kind man, whose company she very nearly enjoys.

But not today.

"I don't think Momma's feeling too good this morning..."

Smart little thing… taking care of me. Such a good little girl…

She listens to the middle aged man with the big, smiling face and the big tummy attempt small talk with the twelve year old, whose brain hardly gives her the ability to string two sentences together without stammering. Barbara listens to him ask how many they laid for her this time, and she hears him in the kitchen, taking over for her little black-eyed dove bird, pulling out the big, grey paper cartons himself.

Easy money.

"They were busy this time, weren't they Lizbeth…"

She perks up, to see if the girl will say another word.

She doesn't.

Ike Shirley clumps heavily through the house, chattering in full southern drawl about how sorry he is that her Momma isn't feeling well, and how he hopes to see her on Monday morning. Barbara listens to his boots thump down the front steps, and she hears him slam his truck bed closed, imagining his disappointment at not being able to get a look at her this morning. She knows these visits are the highlights of his little farming life. She has always known. Its as though she is kept for him to see. To enjoy.

But she does not want to feel his eyes on her today. She doesn't have the strength to give him his country pleasure. Her big, courteous smile, the velvet voice, the blinking, pleading eyes of eternal gratitude, as an adopted daughter, the lover of his most distant, unimaginable hopes and dreams.

Not today.

Does he know? Does he know that I rest at the edge of a pit? A chasm of suffering?

42

The truck struggles to life, rattling slowly away. Little footsteps move slowly, carefully towards the outside of Mother's bedroom door. Then they move lightly, fearfully towards another room.

Another place.

15

he child has survived its premature birth, growing stronger each day. Slowly it nurses the hope, sucking the bravery from your spirit, taking your happiness in gulps, nourishing its body to greater life. One day you look at it and take a deep breath of revelation... you cannot do this alone. With a trembling hand, you send a letter to the woman who bore you in blood, who bore the blood from your body with the wood of trees, and with leather from creatures of the field. Your back bears the memory of her love. Fair skin tells of it. Her love is Wrath. Her wrath is Beauty.

There is no waiting for a response that will never come. You had left her in defiance, in the sin of lust and love. But fear and despair have won. There must be a return to the chilly mountain farmlands. The mountain farmlands are calling. It is the winter season.

Poor Mr. Shirley. Allowing you to see your foolish plans through. He will hold the land through the cold winter, praying to himself that you will return. A man who has a strange desire, both romantic and paternal, not knowing himself which dominates his spirit the most when he thinks of you. You should be in school, he thinks. Not running all over winter's creation with a suckling child, and the burden of a widow's heart.

The bus trip is blessedly long. You savour the passing of winter evergreens, even the patches of snow covered country. Clutching tighter the child, sometimes looking into its face, feeling tenderness and appreciation, neither of which can breathe a loving spirit into thee. Your heart is kind and humble, but replete with terror…and bitterness.

As the motor lulls you to sleep, you remember Evelyn. The woman who taught you a hundred ways to cry for mercy, and to beg for her forgiveness. And Hugh Daniels, the man who stood by, a willing servant of the perverted violence that has scarred you from your shoulders to your ankles.

Mountain Pentecostalism. The promise of spiritual perfection through self sacrifice and denial. You close your legs further, gripping me tighter as you remember the Bible being taught from Genesis to Revelation, taken literally, received as law, and as the infallible Word of God. Remembering how it was possible for even a young girl to lose her fear of snakes, as you watched them handle the sleepy rattlers in the theater of secret lust in sweat, remembering the blazing hot summer days in the rickety church, at the edge of the darkened woods. The frantic, hopeless screams of condemned flesh, burning, burdened with desire, and cursed with inability to satisfy it.

They are whipped into a frenzy of demonic repression. Lustful craving to feel every inch of their flesh on fire with erotic torment. They are striped bloody with rage of unrequited passions, impossible instincts to repress. They scream with praises masking pain, agony erupting from the pit of their own tormented flesh and blood. They shriek with primal fervor, jumping around the church in tribal fury, pledging with wild eyes the eternal struggle against abomination, swearing with worshipping mouths to remain pure of thought, relishing the poison of temptation's claw.

They desire happiness. A life without daily struggle for the impossible. The striving for perfection in the eyes of God—the perpetual sorrow of disappointment at their inevitable failing to please Him. You see Evelyn's sour expression, you can feel the strength of her resistance to evil's soothing manner, even as her husband, your father, speaks with frightening tongues of men and of angels, spitting fires of Heaven's prophecy at Hell's legion. The snakes call in warning rattles, having bitten them many times, and many times they have shaken them off in the haze of hypnotic faith, feeling no ill effects from the toxin, bruising the snake's condemned head with the souls of their shouting feet. Theirs is a life of exquisite mayhem and misery, an existence without smiles of happiness, or even the hope of simple joy and laughter.

Your skin itches, as you remember your heavenly correction, the days and nights of extreme discipline, as they endeavored to beat both your body and soul out of Hell. You begin to ask yourself, "How can I return to the mouth of torment, to be clawed and devoured again in the misery of years past? Will they allow you back into their arms of safety? What will you endure from them, before you can even hope to be forgiven for your prodigal sin?

Evelyn Louise Daniels. The strong, stalwart, fiery Christian, the prayer warrior from Old School, believer in witches, and corruption of the body through thoughts alone. You were a girl of seventeen when you left home, after the worst of your tortures had only just begun. You try not to remember the barn, and the way the summer twilight breeze hardened your exposed nipples. You try not to remember the fear when you were hogtied, bound backwards over the little wooden bench, the wood twisting agony into your lower back. You try not to remember the birch as it cut your naked breasts, while your father read bible verses aloud, hardly watching his wife coldly strip your rebellious blood from the front of your body. The blood runs in streams.

You were warned, Mother. You were warned not to see that boy, the boy who delivers the feed grain, ever again. An orphan, a loner, hiding his heritage under the name Cole, who had seen you in the field, and at the market, and on stolen trips to your country church, sniffing like a dog at your feet.

Evelyn knew. She smelled it on you. And she was prepared to stop the sin before it even got started. Your beatings, your whippings, Mother, became too severe for you to endure. Her perversion surfaced like a shark fin in ire, stalking these waters of discontent, and she locked the two of you in private, and she made you understand the nature of God and shadows, and you learned that you only thought you understood what it means to suffer.

Did she make you remove your clothing? Did she disrobe before you in regal power? Did you marvel at the mountainous bosoms exposed, above the curved, fleshy waist, and the fullness of womanhood in broad-hipped splendor? Were you bewildered when she laid you on the bed bare, and climbed on top of you, holding your hands behind your back underneath you? Could you breathe while she whispered threats of unthinkable torture into your ear? Did you scream while she held you tight, bending your fingers so severely that you thought she had broken them? Did you promise through your tears, to honor and obey her for the rest of your miserable life?

16

My future blossoms from the seed. I have spent the night without supper. Not since I was an infant, have you denied me a meal.

A knock!

There is always so much to fear, from a fateful knock at the door.

The whole house takes a breath. The knock comes again, and I hear the voice of my dear Ms. Ida. And now comes the soft, determined sound of Mother's shoes, stalking quietly into the living room. I walk towards the door, thinking she is going to let our visitor inside. I so desperately need to hear Ms. Ida's voice. I want her to use her intelligence, her education, to wear my mother down to nothing while I listen. I imagine that Mother will come to my room and beg my apology for her ignorance, and give me her blessing to spend many summer days at Ms. Ida's house. Laughing, enjoying the happiness in her home, learning to play the piano.

Mother bursts into my room, her face both fearful and frustrated, quickly closing the door, standing there like a demon is trying to get in. I have never seen her look so vulnerable. I pity her, but I am afraid. She hurries over to my window, lowering the shade, quickly returning to the door, nearly running in the effort. She is like a beautiful creature hiding from a predator.

But when I open my mouth to speak, the predator's instinct arises from within her. I am the prey. She nearly leaps to my side, clamping her hand around my mouth, dragging me to the bed then sitting down, holding me close. I can hear my breath in my nose.

"Don't you make a *sound.*"

She hisses it, like a human serpent, sleek and beautiful. It fills me with a longing for escape, and I beg God in my heart to please not allow me to be punished for speaking. But my prayer is answered with truth rather than hope, when Mother wraps her legs around me and pulls me back onto the bed. It is the scene of a full grown, lovely woman, with her long skirt wrapped around half of a helpless little waif girl's body, her arm around the girl's waist, and her hand around the little girl's mouth.

I lay there immobile. Weak from lack of food and water, heart beating fast. Mother's soft hand smells like soap and lotion. Like always. Her grip is strong. Even if I tried, I couldn't escape. While the knocking continues, her fear subsides. Our hearts beat in rapid unison. I feel her power increasing, drawing strength from my helplessness. Her breathing is slower. Deeper.

The knocking ceases. The intrusion has gone away. The music teacher has left disappointed, unaware of what her visit has triggered in my life. The knocking has died, but Mother's fire has not.

Her legs are tight, locked around me. I feel her heart pounding against me. I remember this day, in my twelfth year, when the truth is born from a single knock at the door.

For a long time, she holds me there. Even re-adjusting, getting comfortable, squeezing and pressing hard against me. Ms. Ida's car…where is the sound of it? It must be parked on the paved road. I cannot hear the starfire of her departure. I only hear the sound of my voice screaming into my Mother's hand, while she pinches me on my thigh, hard enough to make me squirm to get away.

I can only imagine what my pitiful screams, and the feel of my soft, helpless little squirming body does to her. She hisses in my ear for me to shut up, while she continues to twist the skin on my inner thigh with all her might, grinding her fist against the cloth of my underwear. Of this sensation in my body, I do not know. Eventually, I stop squirming, and work harder to shut my useless sniveling.

She rolls over onto me heavily, onto my back, looking closely at my face. Watching my tears fall onto the blue bedspread.

17

I languish in a new place. One that I have always feared, praying it is a place I would never be. An ice world, frozen by the soul of her bitterness. But I am not even aware that I am beyond the gate, that like a dark prophecy, her own suffering has reached out to me, and begun to wrap me up, preparing me for my burial. As I sit on my comfortable cushioned armchair, I am unaware of the pain of futures, of the torment that has been made a part of me by birth, and by predestination.

I remember her on top of me. Her strong arms and legs like chains around my body. Locking my twelve year old form to hers. Pressing down, squeezing, whispering dreadful threats into my ear, until I was too afraid to scream. I wanted to tell her that I couldn't breathe. I remember that I could hardly draw a breath.

But I do not even know the extent of my pitifulness. My pathetic, clinging little personality. Extreme trials reveal the heart of a person, and mine is a heart of gentleness and fear, filtered and made pure by the extreme love I have for my Mother. What she did to me has not caused my spirit to darken with anger. I think that what little wrath I had has already been beaten from me. All that is left is an emptiness. A spirit replete with that distant longing. I hold fast to a dim, fleeting hope, that each passing hour will bring us closer to removing the barrier that divides us. I want her to come in tomorrow morning, to talk to me lovingly about how disrespectful little girls deserve punishment, and then I'll throw my little arms around her and kiss her, agreeing with her as she cries, telling her that everything is alright.

I stand at the door, listening to her shuffle around quietly, humming beautifully, as she is often inclined to do. I think she loves music more than she ever lets on. Sometimes I will drift to the window, trying to enjoy my view of the empty grass field, wishing that my mother and I were there. Walking together, talking of joyful days. I love her in my young heart, even as my dream begins to fade with the daylight, and my sorrow arrives upon the evening, and despair drifts in upon the twilight.

Through my window, I watch the shadows draw strength from the approaching nighttime. The long day surrenders to darkness, and my hope fades under cloak of night. The day is past, and my mother has given me no food to eat, nor water to drink, nor a word of greeting to nourish my spirit.

Tonight, I am visited by the Spirits of Melody, who breathe the first full expression my mind hath wrought. A tiny, three movement sonata for piano in C major. A model of childlike simplicity, which I will commit to memory.

Everywhere apart from the gates of Hell, mercy abounds. If we are alive, we have hope.

Mother let me out of the room this morning for breakfast. I had hugged her pitifully, pulling her face down to mine, even giving her rosy cheek a gentle kiss. I know that I can never again mention Mrs. Brooks, and I have internalized my craving for music. I will let it live deep inside me, where it will blaze an inferno, lighting my mind on fire with color. Many of the prettiest melodies I will ever know will come to me in childhood dreams.

I don't really know Ms. Ida. But I think about her often. I know that she is married, with two sons. Many times, I fantasize about becoming part of her little family. Being the daughter that she never had. I wonder where she is today? Has she abandoned me? Will she ever tell her mother about me? How will she tell her dear Jewish mother, that she is going to abandon the Law, to worship at the foot of the Cross?

"You remember that wicked stepmother from Snow White, Momma?"

A curious glance from her mother, from whatever has her attention. Dishes, dinner, a checkbook. Do such things matter? I suppose she is at the kitchen sink. I do not know.

"That pinned up, black hair," Ida muses. "Those big, beautiful eyes. That fair skin."

"What is it, Ida?"

"She's living back in Martin County, North Carolina. And she's raising the most beautiful little girl I have ever seen. And I can *not* stop thinking about her."

Her mother smiles. She is short. Thick waisted, with short, brown hair. Motherly, but very attractive. Her manner is strong, but pleasant, I imagine.

"Is she one of your students?"

"Yes."

"Well, what's so special about her, besides her pretty little face?"

It is the kind of question that makes a person feel sorry for the asker.

"You're right," Ida says. "But she does have a face to see, though. They both do. You'd have to see it yourself to believe it."

Mrs. Hirschman can perceive her daughter's concern.

"If you're worried about her, then say a prayer for her, Ida."

A prayer. To God.

Which God?

"Momma?"

"Hmm?"

Ida watches her, as she dries the supper dishes, putting them away.

"Momma, what would you say if I told you that…that I'm Jewish by blood, but not…"

I imagine that the plate or cup in Mrs. Elaina Hirshman's grip clanged against the other dishes in the cabinet. Do daughters live to torment their mothers?

"I hope. I *pray,* that you never let your father hear you say that. To hear that you even *thought* it. He would be in the hospital with another heart attack. Do you hear me talking to you?"

She doesn't pronounce it *"tawk-ing."* More like *"towa-king."* New Jersey.

"I used to joke with your father about you being the death of me. You're not the same person I raised, Ida. It's the south, right? Its where you live that's done this to you. They don't call it the Bible Belt for nothing, do they?"

She returns to her chores, biting her tongue. Biding her time.

"I'm serious, Momma."

Elaina straightens her back, braving the fear. Breathlessly, she creeps over to the table to sit down.

"Its only because you have not prayed enough, and you've spent too much time in that church. What did I tell you about churches? What did I tell you would happen? Ida Hirschman you swore to me that you would never do this."

"Do what, Momma?"

57

"It is a false religion! A trick of Satan. Its only a test Ida. Another hindrance for you to overcome."

Ida glances down, at the gold wedding ring on her finger.

"Have you done it yet?" she asks. "Please tell me you haven't allowed this in your mind, because once it gets a hold of you…"

"No. I haven't."

"Good. Then there's nothing to fear. You're here with us now. We're going to service this Saturday, and the rabbi will be glad to see you there. That, I can *promise* you."

I can see Mrs. Hirshman, in mature shapeliness, hugging her spaghetti thin daughter tight, whispering about how tricky religion can be, and how easy it is to overcome with meditation and fasting. Will Mrs. Hirshman want to slap some sense into her daughter? Will she want to cry?

I think that Ida is afraid, when she thinks of her mother's anger. How hurt and furious she is going be, when she tells that her mind is already made up, and that she will soon lay her future on Calvary's Hill.

19

*F*ate is often inclined to mercy, igniting the tiniest flame of joy in me. Something I can draw strength from. Something to help me remember that I am loved at least by Him. I will have to look to it often as my only light, guiding me through the gray, among the dark'ned silhouette.

I am fortunate that Mother is away at her little job, while I rest in my room, immersed in melody and song. Reading the hymns in back of the white hardcover bible we own. I have not yet seen my thirteenth birthday, yet the seeds of my salvation are already growing, as I have begun to understand what these black lines, and curious black dots above the lyrics mean. I am using the key I was given, the key to another reality. Often, when I focus, the music plays in my head from velvet string or piano tones, corresponding

to the notes and chords on the paper.

But this music is not my joy. It is my sanity. The release of emotions that have already begun to build up inside me. It is my shelter and fortress. My fire of life in the arctic winter. From inside this flame, I hear the soft, nearly timid knocking at the front door. Fate will often knock softly, so as not to cause a fright. In my world of color, unbeknownst to me, I hear the angel of joy knocking at the door.

But I am still unnerved, because Mother has told me to never answer the door without her permission, and never when she is away. Her reclusiveness is becoming a part of me, and my natural shyness is being magnified, intensified by her reactions, whenever there is a knock. I have no intentions of answering it.

But yes. Destiny flows independently. Inside this clamour of knocking, I hear a voice reach out to me, pricking, drawing me through the house, floating, until I am at the front door, opening it gladly. Ms. Ida stands there in smiling thinness, her brown eyes twinkling with joy, her anguish released from her shoulders like a burden lifted.

"Well hello, Carmen."

"Hey, Ms. Ida."

I stand at the screen door, too nervous to unlock it. But she boldly tells me to do so, and my hand reaches up and obeys her, and she steps inside my mother's home. Her beige pants and white blouse seem lovely to me. She hugs me enthusiastically.

"Where's your Momma, honey?"

"She's still working. But she won't be home until 4:30."

"Its just as well. I don't think she'd be too happy to see me."

The truth of it shames me into lowering my head. She gracefully ignores it.

"Well, I can't stay, sweetie. I'm getting ready for a trip to my mother's. But I knew I couldn't leave before I gave you this."

From her black purse, she lifts a green silken cloth, holding it in the palm of her hand. She opens it, and inside is an Italian crystal figurine, molded in the shape of a rose. My heart flutters, and my breath draws in of its own accord.

"But Momma won't…"

"I know."

There is an assurance in her voice. As though she understands.

"I was going to buy you one later this summer, and give it to you when you came back to school. But last night, I dreamt I was coming here to see you, and there were white roses growing on a bush in the yard. They were so pretty that it looked like they didn't belong there."

Her brown eyes betray her anguish. She does not wipe her tears away.

"I think this might be the only crystal rose in this whole town. But I want, no, I *need* for you to have this."

"But Momma won't let me have it Ms. Ida. You know she won't let me."

"Then it'll have to be our little secret. You hide this in a safe place, now. It'll help you to be happy."

I can hardly breathe. My own tears have gathered. Ms. Ida sniffs, wiping her eyes. Her face shows a somber, elegic manner, prompting me to straighten up and give her my full attention.

"You read Psalm number 37. You might not understand it all, but I want you to read it. Whenever you feel like you're not going to be alright, turn there. There are some things there that might make you feel better. And pay special attention to verse 4. Now what did I tell you to read?"

"Psalm 37."

"Which verse?"

"Verse 4." I have a cooing little voice.

"That's right. That's your special Bible verse. Okay?"

"Okay."

"I can hardly wait until this fall. We'll figure something out, so I can teach you the keyboard during school hours."

I want to tell her my ability is more profound than she realizes. I want to tell her that the keyboard is the least of my troubles. That the trees whisper melodies to me.

"Take *good* care of yourself, Carmen."

She hugs me once more. A long, lingering hug. An heartbroken embrace.

As she walks across the yard, down the dirt road to her car, I hold on to my silken cloth, my crystal point of happiness, and I cherish the memory of her curly brown hair, smiling face, and her caring, compassionate tone.

With a knife, I make the tiniest sliver at the head of my old mattress, under the bottom. Inside, I hide the beautiful cloth, and my rose crystal. Safe from the crushing hands of my time.

20

"Carmen Spaghetti! Carmen Spaghetti!"

Why does my poison take the form of children? Why does Sarah Brown head my legion of discontent? I do not know what shore she will drift to. Whether or not it is a happy one, my mind can never fathom. I believe it is a happy one.

Sarah came to my world when I was ten. I was a grade behind all the other children. She was nine, but so much bigger than me, in body and spirit. She was new then, and made friends so quickly. Whispering, talking, laughing from underneath a head of flaxen, with the face of Heaven's prettiest cherub, that fantasy angel of man's twisted reckoning. Why did the girl allow the woman's sin into her so completely? That demon, affecting women's bodies even before they begin to blossom. Devil eyed jealousy, which threatened her deep, somewhere beyond her ability to know.

Why was she threatened by me?

"You're poor, aren't you? What's your name?"

"C...C..."

"Ha! Ha ha ha ha! Kim, what's her name?"

"Her name's Carmen Coletti."

"That's a maid's name. Country Carmen. Country Carmen Coletti. Country Carmen Spaghetti. *Carmen Spaghetti!* Kim, come on and sing it with me..."

Kimberly please, don't

"Look how ugly her clothes are. And she stinks..."

It hurts when you hit my head with your knuckle, Sarah. Don't tease me anymore.

Have mercy for me.

How unlucky can a child be? There are other buses in the school yard. So many other buses. Why then, must you ride this one? This was my sunshine chariot, safely whisking me away from the stormy sea, the school prison house and yard. The other children were not as unkind before you came to me.

The boys were simply being what they were. They pulled my hair, but not too hard. They threw spitballs at me, but I wasn't the only one. The girls sometimes gathered around me, and spoke of beauty, as though it applied to my face and hair. I think that I would have had many friends, had I not been so dreadfully afraid to speak.

But you, dear Sarah. For two years you were the catalyst, the agitator, their galvanizing force. Mobilizing them, stirring up all the strife that flowed beneath their young civility. The evils were taken into the air above me, where they coalesced into clouds of storm, which blackened, sounding doom, looming gail breezes from a hurricane of future sorrows, resting misery at my young feet. You, my dearest Sarah, were the first whirlwind which blew into me, devastating any chance I may have had at becoming normal.

I will not be afraid.

I will not.

I...

I will.

I wanted to be your friend. More than anything on this earth, I wanted to be your friend. You were pretty. You were strong. So much stronger than the other girls. I wanted you to take me under your angel wing, and protect me from the others. I wanted you to lead me through the darkened maze, the haze of forest trees that was my time in school. I wanted to serve you in obedience, in exchange for your protection from those who sought to bring harm to me. I sought your blessing, I needed your teaching, your guidance through that strange world I was in.

Why are you going to beat me up after school? What did I do to deserve it? What crime did I commit against you? What sin?

You want the other girls to hold me down on my back, while you put my legs in a wrestling hold your brother taught you, until I can't breathe from the pain? You want one of them to bring her knee down into my stomach while you have my legs locked in torture? Why ? Was I too mousy? Were you sickened by my passivity? Did my friendliness disgust you? If I agree to do this, will you allow me to be your friend?

Help me, Sarah. Help me not to be afraid of the world. Teach me your strength, your perseverance against the wall of eyes that stare.

Have mercy for me.

21

My crystal fashions a new desire, and Sarah Brown is pushed from my memory. I want to look at it, but Mother might

walk in the door. I would rather never see it again, than to risk her knowing that I have it.

She'll be home soon.

Every rose sings its own melody. Even a crystal rose. I rest here, in my little room, reclining in my comfortable armchair, listening to the radio. But the music is a distraction. I have to turn it down, so I can hear the music of the crystal…

Oh, my…

What is this?

The room has darkened. A crystalline shape appears, floating bodily into the room. A large diamond crystal. If I am dreaming, then why am I still awake? But it is not mine to touch. If I move, it will vanish away.

It is dividing...no...replicating itself into three. Three very large, diamond crystals. The first crystal begins to speak its voice to me. It is the voice of a *harp*. The crystal shimmers a golden light, to correspond to the playful pizzicato. Does the tessitura call for an upper part? It does not. This melody does not call for a violin. No. The crystal melody is alone. I hear every plucking of the invisible strings. A melody that would work so well on the piano key.

Do-re-mi...fa...fa... F...no, something else, but I don't know what...I don't know that it is F minor. Too simple, and too advanced.

The first crystal goes silent. The second flows into the same golden glow. I can remember every note of the first part. How can this be, that crystals sing with voices of color? It is not fantasy. Is it science?

The third crystal sings its golden rondo without restraint. The melodies are so pure and clear, nearly operatic. Only seven minutes have passed, and the crystals have quieted their voices. They stand silent in my darkened chamber. Am I afraid?

I am not.

Daylight, like the morning dawn, returns light to my sanity. The crystals are fading... I see the world around me. I can feel my chair again. My dresser and the pallid walls and wood floor, with my oval rug. The rug is a travesty. A tragicomedy of atonality and non-committal. It is not the azure of my curtains, nor my bed covers.

I... I am a composer.

It will be my first recorded piece. Crudely, I attempt to write down the notes in my school notebook. Checking them, making sure I can refer to them again. I don't know what I'm doing. How can I write music? But this begs me to learn. I begin now.

"A song for a harp," I write. A Sonata in F minor for Solo Harp, it is. Another melody for me to whisper.

A Crystal Sonata.

22

*Y*ou are glad for the ladies, aren't you? Our Ladies of the Cloth, who savor every moment of each Tuesday, Thursday and Friday. The days when you are among them. Riding in their chariot to the harvest loom, where the cloth is spun in every color. They admire your beauty and grace, watching you inspect the cloth like a Lady of the Castle, looking over the silken fabric of her newest evening gown.

I see you resting quietly, attentively in the front seat, while they chatterbox themselves into a small town frenzy about their husbands and boyfriends, with love disguised in good natured resentment. You listen, so glad they have accepted your reticence, your refusal to share and gossip. Perhaps they carry on about a Christian co-worker of theirs, who divulged an unmentionable about herself (that God makes love to her because she has no husband). Somewhere deep, you understand that kind of lustful insanity, though you pity her delusion, knowing that your God cannot be tempted with sin, nor doth He tempt any man.

You listen more closely now, when she speaks of her teenage girl. It reminds you that your twelve year old has a future that must be. She will not be twelve forever. In the cold autumn rain of this very year, your daughter will be thirteen.

The blue Cavalier moves along the country back roads, carrying three united in community. But among them is a fourth, a quiet Lady of Yore. She watches the trees and houses become more familiar, as the carriage approaches her provincial kingdom. A realm of uneasy calm, and stormy anticipation.

The chariot crosses into the eastern town. Rolling casually past the lonely dwellings. Moving unconcerned past the shops and busy marketplaces. You stop in front of a small, rickety matchbox of a house, and you wave a friendly goodbye to the first lady, the oldest who, like you, has lived a lifetime without learning to drive. You can hardly watch her walk across the half dead grass in her sneakers and socks and long denim skirt. You pity her uselessness, don't you Mother? You smile, and wave nicely to her.

The talkative younger one is still in the back seat alone. A teenager, I suppose. Already condemned to a life of mediocrity. Her husband is away too much, she says. He goes to be with his friends as soon as he gets home. Why is that? Why won't he sit at home with her? Gladly, you say goodbye to her, when the Cavalier leaves the parking lot of her little apartment house.

There is only you and the driver. She is close to your age. Blonde, rather pretty, with a slant toward sophistication in her pretty blue jeans, shirts and sweaters, possessing the sweet, accommodating personality you require. The less attractive version of you, only without the flower of bitterness growing. A divorced woman drawn to your beauty, inviting you to places, having grown accustomed to your polite refusals, understanding your reluctance to open yourself to people. Valerie Kirkland has been sent to you, Mother. You know that she will do anything for you.

The two of you are more comfortable when you're alone. She is thankful for the miles of road that lie between here and your country home, somewhere south of the city limits. She lives in the country too, not so far away from you, but not close enough to be nearby. A divorcee, lonely. Craving your company.

And now, this last mile of your journey from labor's bosom. I suppose that you talk comfortably with one another. Her asking aloud why her husband decided he had grown tired of her. You wondering aloud why your husband died on these highways, along the path of best laid plans. She enjoys your sensible, level conversation. Considering it a privilege, relishing her time with the Southern Beauty Witch, the Signora Coletti. She is still amazed that you are not Italian.

Does she know how old your daughter is?

Does she care?

Her chattering lulls you into placidness. You think that you might like to spend time with Valerie away from work. But she has accepted your friendly lonerism. Your pleasant, but standoffish self. By now, perhaps she is something close to a friend.

Gray skies loom above you, as you course the windswept back roads. Across the fields, above the southern forest trees, your mind is drawn upward. You feel yourself drifting forward in time, at one with breezes of warning. Sliding, gliding downward, swirling around the young girl—who stands near the edge of these atramental woods—lost in the first, the origin, the genesis of her own deepest sorrow.

You draw a breath, when Valerie shocks you from the dreaming of Eve, from your gloaming of gray. Politely, she asks you where in the world your mind was, and you smile. Apologizing, telling her you were thinking about your landlord, wondering if he had come by today while you were at work. Wondering how many eggs were broken at the gathering.

How old is your daughter, Barbara?

Twelve.

I'll bet she's the sweetest thing. I don't get to see my daughter much anymore. Not since her father remarried and moved up north...

Do you feel sorry for her, Mother? Do you pity her longing for her daughter?

You do not.

Here is the turn off the main road, deeper into our beloved country. The trees live in greater congregation here. The fields are adorned with life and color. The country breathes with melody and earth song. Rows of green corn and tobacco rush by the window of your chariot, hurrying by unaware, unconcerned with the Divorce Maiden, and the Raven Widow.

There...there is the fine farmer's brick castle, past which is the smallest part of his tiny tobacco kingdom. Somewhere past this field is the dirt road, the place where Fear and Despair shall rule.

The blue car rolls, drifting slowly down the little dirt road, until it comes to rest near the shadow house. The Raven opens the door, fearfully listening to the Maiden's fleeting decree that they must get together soon. You agree with her, but in silent prayer that it will not be today.

The blonde watches after you. She watches your shape, moving briskly across the little yard, gliding towards the house to whatever awaits you inside. But she cannot see the ghosts that walk with you, whispering things in your ear, infecting your spirit, injecting your body with grieving. She cannot feel the torment of your soul, squeezed, crushed by a prophecy breathed from a generation ago.

Just a few minutes before you arrived, I had been shocked awake from the edges of another musical slumber, visited to me at the edge of the woods. I had gone there, drawn, pulled, called to the isolation of the forest wood. I had felt your eyes upon me when I was there. Your arctic breath had touched my skin. I had fled to the house immediately.

I can hear you at the door...

Coming for me.

23

"Hey, Momma."

The little voice is like a blast wave, devastating the Mother's warm heart with a chill. She watches the pale, spindly thing walking, suppressing a run, smiling its ghoulish, girlish grin. It arrives, clamping spindly arms around her as tightly as it can. It latches onto what is left of her, and begins to leech the warmth of life from her. The woman feels it drawing freedom and health from her body. A cold pain, flowing down her back, and out through her empty womb. Like a river.

"Hey," she says. She pats her daughter's back. Gently. "Did you get the eggs?"

"Yes, Maam."

Her daughter's clinging and staring are too much for her…

"Alright, that's enough." She peels her daughter's arms away. Carmen feels the icy blow. The sting of it. "I'm going to rest for a while. I'll cook later."

"Are we having potatoes?"

"Is that what you want?" Barbara steps toward her bedroom. Carmen follows.

"Smoked sausage and potatoes. I know how to cook the sausage. Do you want me to peel--"

The door closes unceremoniously, separating them. Carmen listens to her mother shuffle around in her bedroom.

"Do you want me to peel the potatoes, Momma?" She does not perceive the frustrated sigh, or the roll of her mother's eyes.

"Go ahead if you want to." *just leave me alone you clawing little bitch do whatever the Hell you want just stay the Hell way from me*

"Do you think you can cook the potatoes?" she asks.

"I think so."

"Just slice 'em up, and put 'em in the pan with onions and a little shortening. Keep 'em covered until they get soft. Then uncover 'em and brown 'em. And you've got to watch 'em so they won't burn. Did you hear me?"

"Yes."

"Alright then."

The Mother listens to the little waif going to the kitchen.

she'll ruin the dinner…

if she ruins the dinner, so help me God--

Wake up! Wake up, Beautiful Mother! The smell of this country feast shall tempt you awake. The soft sounds of gentle knocking. The tapping of little feet. What is that you feel? It is the cool, soothing touch of an angel, rubbing her hands gently over your

brow. Your skin is damp from the humidity of sleep. The sweat of anguish rests upon your lovely forehead.

Wake up! Wake up, Beautiful Mother!

Come with me. I will stand here as you rise to your feet. I will endure the contempt in your eyes, the puffy, defeated expression upon your sleepy face. Take my hand, come with me to the country feast I have prepared. It is my first fully prepared dinner. Did you think me not capable of it? Was your confidence in me a cruel trick? You expected a house full of smoke, a den of culinary iniquity. But here we are at our supper table. Our dining hall.

I was a fish in water. A Carmen Fish.

You cannot believe your eyes. The table is set as beautifully as a twelve year old can accomplish. Our plates match today. The two prettiest plates, white ceramic with the requisite little blue flowers. I have always loved these plates. These forks don't look familiar to you, I suppose. I found them at the bottom of the others. They are smaller, shinier, with floral moldings in the silver handles. Do not mind the head of the Daffodil in the tiny vase on the counter, my loving Mother. They grow wild in the field, away from our Enchanted Cottage.

Your mood softens. Sit with me, dear Mother. Let us partake of this country feast I have prepared.

I am afraid for you to taste…

You taste…

Your brow wrinkles when you taste the onions and fried potatoes…

From where, Carmen? Where did you receive this gift? At the age of twelve, performing a genie's magic in the kitchen?

Your Father…your Father whom you have killed, Daughter. He was a magician upon the stove. You have your Father's beautiful disposition. The same gentle, hypnotic stare. You look something like me, and perhaps even his mother I would imagine, but you have

his kindness, his meekness, his gentleness…

His cooking.

At Twelve, you are ready to cook for me. To tend to my approaching sickness. To care for me in these coming years. You are ready, my Daughter, to take your place among the dead. In this sepulchre, you will rest with the buried Queen, waiting upon her for all time. As I taste the succulent meat you have made, I know from whence you have come, and for what purpose you were given to me.

"Its good enough," she says. "At least you didn't burn it."

Ah, there it is! The cruelty! But I know our feast is sumptuous, Mother. I know that I have pleased you.

24

There is no one to greet you in the mountain twilight. Darkness falls, and there are so many miles to go. Pity is in great measure at the station. The beautiful widow and her baby. Miss Barbara Jean Daniels.

Mrs. Barbara Coletti.

They don't know Hugh and Evelyn. But the car is waiting to carry you there. The address you know well. All roads lead through these Blue Ridge Mountains of Virginia.

Snake handlers...

Hugh and Evelyn have read the letter. Were they together in bed? Did they discuss what they were going to do to you?

They wait for you, Mother. The prodigal, returning from her land of wickedness and sin. The trees look familiar now. The taxi man is quiet. But he knows the address. These mountain Pentecostals. Backwoods dwellers.

Your baby hardly ever cries. You have pinched it in frustration before, because it dares to be so quiet. So peaceful.

You know this back road, don't you? The route number. The distant neighbor's houses. The fences on their property. It was only a year ago, that you dreamed of wandering these same roads, holding your lover's hand. You can get to the church from here, can't you? You sit forward in anticipation, as the pretty new taxi gets closer to the little white farm house.

There it is. Nestled in a clearing in this snowy mountain forest. The big field is covered in patches of snow. A cold light glows in the window. The car rolls to the front of the house. Your heart flutters wildly. If you hurry, your things will be out of the trunk soon. When you beg the driver to hurry away, he looks at you strangely, speaking the price of the trip to you. So much lower than it should be. The poor widow. The poor widow and her baby.

Two silhouettes open the front door. Your beautiful smile flashes for the driver in pretend happiness, as you hand him your money. He is as out of place as a preacher at a party. As a sinner at Communion. He can feel the silhouettes. Issues are too heavy. The air is too thin and cold. As quickly as he can, he retreats, with no offer to help with your bags. You look nervously after him as he drives away.

The masculine silhouette shakes its head, drifting away. The other silhouette stands there alone. She is alone. The door opens, allowing this phantom to move in shock down the steps, and out into the dusk where you stand.

What did she say to you, Mother? What did grandmother say to you? Is she the same portrait in gray that we are? She is beautiful, isn't she--tall, strong, heavy bosomed. What is she like, the blood that bore us? What is the flesh of our flesh, the spirit that breathed us accursed into this world?

Grandmother is a tower of strength and unadorned prettiness, with large, perfect eyes framed by premature wrinkles, and a somber, brooding look. Her thin lips are tight. Her black hair is pinned in the tightest bun. There is no nonsense in her. She is hardened. Her compassion is calloused.

She approaches. You smile anxiously, and coo hopefully… "This is your grandbaby, Momma."

"Seven," she says, without hesitation. "I'm gon' whip you every night for seven days."

The blood drains from your face, as she takes your baby. A little gypsy-witch, it is. She tells you to go to the cold barn. You are not yet worthy to live in the house. The baby will drink formula, or it will not survive. You will not nurse it again. If it lives, it will soon curse the life of another.

The barn is ice cold. There is your breath in fog. But you're a mountain girl. Already, your skin is used to the icy air.

Your skin…

You have been beaten before. This is simply the life you have known.

They took your baby…

You will endure.

But they took your baby…

25

*C*an you feel the powers at work here, Mother? The isolation calls us to fore. Pulling us. Clawing at us. Mr. Shirley is in the living room right now, speaking my destruction for next year. His voice is hushed with secret longing. Your submissiveness to him is admirable.

"I can't tell you how much I've enjoyed you and little 'Lizbeth bein' here."

"I've always loved it out here, Isaac. I don't know what I would have done if you hadn't let me stay." A knowing smile from you. A naughty twinkle in your gray eye.

"You satisfied with what they're payin' you out at Eastern?"

"Well, it won't get me in Brandmere Estates, but we'll manage."

"Reason I asked is 'cause I wanna start sellin' fresh produce. You know things like watermelons, tomatoes, squash, green beans. There's a demand for 'em, but I ain't got the time or the strength, with these tobacco fields and all…"

Poor little Chickens! Held captive, forced to serve in little comfort, with not a single kind word of gratitude upon your dismissal!

"…its too late to worry 'bout it this year, but I'd like to see it happen next spring. I'm tellin' you now so you'll have plenty a time to think it over. If you decide to do it let me know, and I'll pay you enough so you can quit work and run a little vegetable farm for me. Prob'ly just tomatoes and watermelons. Somethin' you and Lizbeth can take care of by yourselves."

"Next spring's a good ways off isn't it?"

"I know, but, well, the real reason I'm telling you now is 'cause…well, if you want, Barbara, you can quit work any time 'tween now and then, and I'll pay you a workin' wage, minus the rent of course, but I'll pay you enough so you won't miss it."

Tomatoes. Watermelons. How apt. You are his ripe, juicy tomato. And what succulent sweetness does your bosom remind him of? He is not quite old enough to be your father, is he? You are a whisper away from being a kept woman. You will be well cared for.

When I listen from my bedroom, I see. I see the charm, your demure grace and power, emanating from burning chastity. Perhaps the two of you are lucky. You have that rarest gem, that most precious feeling between you. It is not quite love, nor is it friendship or lust. With him it is protectiveness, a sense that he owns your loyalty and affection, which you give so willingly, and so convincingly. From you, it is eternal gratitude and appreciation, knowing that you could have been cast from Eden a decade ago, or even propositioned for another kind of loyalty. You were so young and afraid then.

But he respected you. Allowing you to feel his worship from afar, and he did not threaten you with it. You were a flower, brightening his little farmhouse—your smile, your radiance has healed every aching in his soul. But his life's love is his own wife, and he is Southern Church, born to love monogamy, bred to fear the consequences of its betrayal. Or perhaps he cared for you so much that he would have died before violating your trust in him. You must continue to feel safe with him. Protected.

You and Ike Shirley. Lost souls in this little country house. Isolated— somewhere between affection and gratitude. Somewhere between Father and Benefactor, Daughter and Mistress.

Somewhere.

26

Approving voices echo in my mind. I still feel normal, even a little pretty when I look in the mirror. Like Mother, but different. My skin is less pale than hers. My eyes are not as catlike. They are as black as Christmas Night.

Sometimes I look at her, wondering if I am adopted. Found on the doorstep, in the garden, or at the edge of the morning woods. Is that why she has contempt for me? I think not. She is strong, I am weak. The strong have pity, and then contempt for the weak.

Who do I come from? Whose blood burns the hottest in my veins? Is it that of my mother, which boils with suppressed anger, surging with a decade of repressed desire and memory? Is it the blood of my father, which ran as cool as a mountain stream, ebbing and flowing smoothly over life's roughest path? I feel a blood in me that does not come from them. One which makes me prone to fear and nervousness, given to bouts of melancholy. Trapping me in a continuous dread of the world itself, a terror of not pleasing others, with trepidation for noises and shadow silhouettes.

This blood flows from Mediterranean shores. Was she like me? Married to a young ne'er do well, with a fiendish gift for performing strings, and an equal gift for wandering, bohemian vagabondism? Was her skin the color of crème, her hair the black of a country midnight? Was her voice as sweet as warm milk and honey?

My father's mother. I wonder if Alicia Coletti had beauty. Or if she was afraid like me. When Grandfather Coletti died so young, why did she die so soon after? I think she died from fear and grief. Here, so far away from the Pesaresian Land, in this strange, evil place all alone. Alicia Coletti's blood is my capacity for Love and Sorrow, and my predilection for Fear and Dread. I have my Italian Grandfather's music, and my Italian Grandmother's deathly fright.

You are not Italian, Mother…

And you are not afraid.

You do not fear the Serpentine, the minion of pitch, curled upon itself in waiting. Your warrior's blood does not burn in me when I approach the nest to look for eggs, and see the living black rope which sleeps with black eyes open. My hand jerks back from its smiling face as if I have been burned, and my coward's blood runs cold as I run back to the house on feet of ice.

I know you are not afraid as I begin to stutter, stammering, eventually hissing the demon serpent's name, pulling you outside into the cool morning air. I see no fear in your gray eyes, only mild irritation when you look upon the black snake, knowing already that it has no venom inside its condemned body.

I tremble with revelation, while I watch bravery's hand take hold of the thick, five foot long devil, pulling it out of the poor hen's nest, its body lazy with sleep and cold, drunk upon its beloved egg wine, the craving of its final day. In a haze I see your mouth move, but I cannot tell from whence you speak, until you approach me and grab my arm, shaking me, pushing me towards the house. I stumble to the kitchen, emerging with the razor cutting knife, watching the snake's body writhe underneath your foot, wrapping around your bare ankle while you hold its head skillfully in your white hand.

In shock, I watch you snatch the knife from my hands, pulling the rope thing's neck tight, holding its head steady. I watch its tail whip desperately at your leg while you slice its head from its body, tossing it bloody into the grass nearby. You unwrap the living, dying body from around your leg and throw it disgustedly to the ground, admonishing me to finish my egg gathering, walking unconcerned back into the house.

Rat snake! Serpentine! Dreadful Serpent, desiring my body and soul! With no commission from Above, thy wicked hands are bound. Thy evil image puts laughter in my veins! Thou art powerless, with fruitless devastation. Fearful creature, Prince of Darkness, condemned Pawn of Fate—

Defeated enemy of mine.

27

*I*was Twelve, when the spirit came to me.

I am twelve, when the Spirit has come.

It wakes me up on this warm July night. My mother is fast asleep, and the moonlight shines brightly through the window pane. I wonder if I am immersed in a dream, but I am not, even though I can distinguish shadows on the floor. It is so warm, so hot, that I am compelled to go to the kitchen for a cool drink of water. My gown is as white as the Lilies of the Field. My long hair is as black as this dark'ned night.

Strangely, I am compelled to open the back door, in the middle of the night, stepping onto the porch. A warm, gentle night breeze whispers past my hair and my gown. The hens are silent, but the crickets are loud in Creation. The stars are all so bright, so brilliant that I cannot fathom. I think there are a thousand melodies in them.

I am twelve, when the Spirit has come to me.

Yes, there are some who do drift alone in the Open Field to pray. I go down the back steps, gliding in wistfulness, helplessly across the night field, still gazing into the starry sky, where the bright moon rests high above in rounded splendor. I know I must do this. I know it must be done. Am I the only one? Are there others who have perceived this Power? I believe there are many who have.

And now, above the rolling black hills of forest silhouette, I look beyond the sky, to where it is that Heaven rises. In my mind, in my heart, I ask the Spirit to come into me. I ask the Spirit in his Name, to give salvation to my soul. I beseech thee, I pray for this gift, that You will make me whole, make me worthy to stand before Thee, make my heart as white as snow.

I am Twelve, when the Spirit has come to me.

My vision begins to blur the stars. Star light shimmers in earthly vision. The stars do twinkle in crying eyes. Why do I cry? What are the need for these tears, pouring down my face? Do I really understand what I have done? Have I been liberated, or imprisoned?

As I turn away from the nighttime, stumbling back toward the darkened house, I know that from ages before the world was formed, this night was forged into my soul. Now future's truth is come to light, in my soul's prosperity.

I am Twelve, when the Spirit has come to me.

"Well, hello Mrs. Coletti."

Ms. Ida stands hopefully at the locked screen door. My mother's eyes gaze from the kitchen doorway, across the living room at her. I know if I open my bedroom door to see, if I make a sound, it will be the Death of me. The desire to see her is piercing, like a knife in my heart.

"Do you mind if I come in?"

"Not at all. Please..."

Mother unlocks and opens the door for her. Beaming falsely, buoyantly roseate. She is taller than Ms. Ida. Stronger.

"I thought I'd come see if you and Elizabeth are ready for the sixth grade. I know how shy she is, Ms. Coletti, and I'd like to help by having her meet her new teachers. You know, so she'll have an easier time of it. I don't know what it is, Barbara...may I call you Barbara? But that little angel of yours has got a hold on me that I..."

Mother stands there, hiding her growing displeasure. Is it displeasure? In pleasantness she smiles kindly, suppressing the pangs of jealousy and envy. A whirlwind of feelings threaten to remove her friendliness, as she watches the skinny, plain pretty woman with her cute little imperfect smile and laugh lines chatter on about the walking dead named Carmen Coletti.

Carmen.

As if inspired, an idea looms now at the tip of my mother's tongue. One so hideous, one so sinister, so terrible that she dare not allow it to be born.

But there is no will, no purpose formed outside of Predestiny. From a seed, a purpose is grown, blossoming to its fullest intention.

"…and of course I wouldn't have to take her today, but believe me I'll be glad to do it whenever you say I can. And I'd be honored if you could come with us. They won't believe it when they finally get a look at the mother of that child. If you don't mind me saying so, Ms. Coletti, you might be the prettiest woman I've seen in these parts, and every bit of it's on your daughter's little face."

Brilliant, Ms. Ida.

But futile.

"What a lovely thing to say. Thank you."

"Well its true. Nobody believes me when I tell 'em. But they'll know it when they see it. I tell them all the time that you look like an Opera Diva."

Are you blushing, Mother? Are your cheeks the colour of roses? Your lips are tucked in, and your demurity is breathtaking.

"You've been kind, Mrs. Brooks. I can't thank you enough for how nice you've been. And that's why what I have to tell you is so hard. I can hardly find the words."

"Is something wrong?"

"No, but…well, Elizab… *Carmen* doesn't live here anymore."

I feel the floor beneath my feet lose substance. The cold seeps into my blood, between the cells of my body, threatening to disperse them. By strength of determination I do not faint, or cry out.

"B…but wh…"

"Things have been tough for me here. I only work part time, and I don't know if I'm going to stay past the fall. I thought it might be better for us both if she had a more stable place to live. So, I sent her to my parents in Virginia. She'll be starting school there next month."

They stand breathless, the two of them. As if in a room without air and sound.

"I…I don't know what to say."

"I know it's a shock Mrs. Brooks, but trust me, you don't have to worry about her anymore. *Ever again.* She'll be well taken care of. Oh, and one more thing, I have something here she wanted you to have."

"Oh, well…alright…"

Ms. Ida waits, while the witch glides regally across the floor to her bedroom. She emerges, eyes on fire with ice, holding the world's terror, Earth's destruction in green, silken cloth.

"She begged me in tears," says Mother, "for me to give this to you. She wanted you to know that she'll miss you, and she'll never forget you."

I imagine Ms. Ida's trembling hand, reaching for her little rose. A secret in crystal, pulled unmercifully from the shadows of warmth, thrust into the cold light of day. She does not ask what county, what school, what far off place I have been sent to. As she turns, opening the screen in near fainting, she does not ask if I will be back, or upon what southern wind I will drift, landing again in this provincial town.

I am resting on my bed in tears. Glad that I am still not languished upon the dark floor of my closet, listening for mice in the walls, crying for her to have mercy. I am glad that my hunger will be satisfied tonight, and that my thirst lies quenched. I curse my tendency toward isolation, wishing I had been on the front porch instead of closed up in my room when she came. How different would the day have gone? How different would my life have been?

Mother stands in power, watching the thin, pitiful woman stumble defeatedly down the dirt road to where her car awaits. Mother's lips are parted, amazed by her own prowess, her lioness nerve, unmoved by the fear that has settled upon her house. It flows through her like a water spirit, whirling above the country floor. The Spirit of Fear moves through my door, to take control of me.

My legs, my back, my arms bear the signs of interrogation. I could not endure another beating. I am only twelve, and I have been slapped to the floor as an abused woman. But even after I showed her what I was doing at the head of my bed, I was beaten again, and dragged by my hair and thrown into the darkened closet to recover. A week's worth of time seemed to drag around me, though it was but two days and nights. On the third morning, she released me from the grave, and I did not ask about my crystal rose, believing it to be crushed to powder, its ashes scattered in the field beyond knowing eyes, its silken cloth cut to ribbons, and washed into the Saliferine Sea.

My poor Ms. Ida! I can feel the weight of her tears! The burden of her sobbing despair, the pain of loss that wrenches her body as she drives away. And I must bid forever goodbye. Farewell, my angel of mercy! Your smiling face, your kind and caring soul will always be mine. I carry in my heart the sweetness in your voice, and the compassion in your gentle touch. The Psalm carries me aloft, to a place of hope, and my heart is lifted upon the Rose, the flower of my darkest day. Even in the gloomy mist, the clouds will send the brightest rain, enlightened by the crystal, the hope that your heart hath shown to me.

In this hour of my darkest season

The brightest rain falls in power

When there is no reason to travel onward

Blessings loom from stormy skies

And the voice of Heaven cries my Redemption

As I am nigh to a lonely grave

I brave these troubled times of strife

In a life renewed in my darkest day

Having prayed for blessed reprieve from bondage
My answer hearkens from the Evening Day
When the brightest rain falls in hope and power
Devouring my every sorrow away

Thunder rumbles the sky, like drums of eternity. Lightning flashes in the clouds. Mother is in the house, guarding the gate. No melodies will come. I stand at the window, watching the first tears of this storm begin to fall.

I think I will love the storm.

"Elizabeth!"

The cry of the blackbird. Here I am at the door of my room. I cannot touch the doorknob.

"Elizabeth!"

"Yes, Momma?"

"Come out here a minute."

Fearfully, I open the door, seeing the tall lady at the screen door. She watches the first drops of rain fall, as I sit on the couch. The house smells of rain dust. I won't be whipped today. I have done nothing wrong.

Turn to look at me, Mother.

"Yes, Momma?"

A sharp flash of lightning, followed by loud treble thunder, making me jump nearly out of my skin. Mother stands still, resting comfortably in the storm. The raindrop spatters lightly upon our tin roof, growing by untold hundreds, thousands, until my mind cannot count them anymore. The wind begins to whish through the bushes and trees, bending them to the storm's mighty will, sending the rain blowing sideways up the road, across the yard, onto the porch, and through the screen at my mother's black shoed feet. Low heeled, laced shoes made for comfort and walking. Her dark blue dress is long, covering her legs halfway down her shins. I see tiny dark flowers in the midnight fabric. Her white skin is not covered by her sheer black stockings today. Mother's legs are creamy, but replete with faint, tell-tale marks from a former life.

"Momma?"

She turns her head slightly, just enough to acknowledge that I called her. Her black hair is pinned tightly, stylishly to her head.

"You didn't have to tell Ms. Ida that I moved. I told you I won't keep secrets from you anymore. And I won't ask about the piano again. When I see her in school, I'll tell her that I don't want to learn anymore, and its true."

Mother closes out the rain and turns to me, coming over to our little sofa. She sits down beside me. So tall and strong. Yes, I am afraid.

But why?

"I told her that you were gone, because I don't want her snooping around here again. And she most certainly would have when she saw that you weren't in school next month."

Sometimes, a comment will not register on the brain. We hear it, but do not grasp its meaning. It is as though the speaker has lapsed into foreign tongues. Confounding our understanding. I blink up at her, unaware of what she has just said to me.

"I'll get to school alright, Momma. She'll see me, but I won't let her teach me the piano, and I'll tell her to never come here."

The house is quiet, despite the clamour of rain. The look on Mother's face is one of unstable calmness, uneasy patience, brief mercy for my sluggish young mind.

"True to form," she says, matter of factly. "You never do listen, do you? What did I say?"

"You said that Ms. Ida might come back if she didn't see me in school. But I won't be able to hide from her. She'll come looking for me. But I'm ready to tell her not to bother us anymore."

"I meant what I said. And you know it. You're just being stubborn."

"What?"

"What did I say?" she asks.

"You said that—"

Suddenly, I cannot think. But my mind has mercy, giving me her bloody answer. Preparing me.

She will not see me… will not see me… oh God she will not see me…oh God…

"I've decided its too much trouble, and too much expense. You know how to read and write, and that's all you'll ever need."

Slowly, my body releases the fear into my bloodstream. In small, safe doses, so as not to shock my heart into failure. Do children have heart attacks from fear? Has anyone known the Depth of Fear, on this side of Blessed Sanity?

"You won't have to worry about going to school anymore."

I see her lips move, as if in slow motion. Her lips move, but disconnected from the words coming out of them. The rain falls steadily around us. Above the sound of my own heartbeat, I speak…

I stutter.

"I w…want to go, M…Momma. I can s…still go if I w…want to go c…can't I?"

A deep breath, an icy look…

"No."

Yes, the thunder does announce this day, this first day. The true beginning.

"B…but why?"

"I told you why. You're nothing but a farm girl, Elizabeth. That's all you're ever going to be. You don't need to go traipsing—"

"I'll run away. I won't stay if you take me out of school."

"Elizabeth, just listen to me. It'll be alright. My Momma took me out of school, too."

A lie. You quit school so you could elope. You're a mountain girl to the soul, Mother.

"I don't care, Momma. I'm not gonna stay."

"Oh really? And just where is it you think you'll go?"

"I'll find her," I say. "I'll find Ms. Ida and I'll beg her to let me stay with her."

What courage. What bravery! How is it that I am able to look into the eyes of the blackbird without fear? Even as she stands, my blood boils in this new cold, and I am prepared for my whipping.

"You're not going to stay with me?" she asks.

I am quiet. Prepared for the strap. I will release my anger through screams of pain. Mother walks calmly to the door and opens it. The rain cascades noisily, sliding off the roof and downward, falling around us in a shower of tiny streams.

Why is she looking out into the storm?

What does she see?

"Come here."

Boldly, I go. Still expecting the pain of blows. Her hand leaps to my arm, gripping it calmly, sending a spark of cold through me as she opens the screen door, and I feel myself floating slowly, inevitably onto the porch. She closes the screen door, and there I stand in my old denim house dress and long black hair, sleeveless, staring at her through the screen. The rain is noisy. Lightning sparks across the sky, and thunder crackles as the wind whistles cold water onto my bare arms.

I remember the strength of Mother's hand.

"When I understand that you're sorry for your disrespect, your impudence, I'll let you back into my house. Now…

"Get off my porch."

I turn to look at the howling summer rainstorm, wondering what foolishness I have done. Understanding how much blood she wants to cut from me, knowing that this is mercy. I creep slowly towards the rain, cold, frightened. When I look back, mother stares quietly through the screen. Not having to speak again. Waiting.

"I'm sorry, Momma. I won't s-say anything else ab-about s…school."

Silence.

"M-Momma. Momm--"

Lightning strikes overhead. Loud, screaming thunder crashes around me. I run to the screen, ready to end my foolish game. Wherefore doth the sparrow embattle the Krowraven?

"Get off of my porch."

Her face. Her eyes. The serpentine, resisting its natural strike. Drawing power from repressed instinct. Do I dare beg? I do not.

My courage to accept the lash is gone. I creep back towards the steps, towards the driving wind and rain. It stings my face with cold from high in the sky. The rain falls from Satan's Domain, to torment the earth below.

I take the first step off the porch. The heavy, driving rainfall coats everything in a mist. My little black shoes with my socks are wet. My hair and dress are already soaked. When I look back, I see the Blackbird standing in power, pushing me forward with her eyes. I take the second step. The third. The fourth puts me upon the wet ground. The rain is so cold. Intrusive. It violates me. My skin cannot adapt.

"Momma? Momma?"

Her response is to move away, and to close the door behind her. What shall I do? I go back to the porch, but the door opens, and I know to immediately go back into the rain. The house is wired for my destruction.

Disobedience. Insolence. They shall not rule here. The skies shriek, mocking me, crying approval of your ruling. The trees bow to the wind. Beasts of water roar and lunge at me. I run. I flee to the back of the house. The back porch will be…

The raven! She is at the back screen door. Watching me. Peering through eyes the color of the storm. The wind whips the rain in my eyes. My black hair sticks to my face. But I know I am safe in the storm. It protects me from true wrath—the deluge. She closes the door.

The tiny feed shed. My shelter from the rain. The trees sway and swish in this stormy wind. The rain sweeps across the open field as I approach the shed. The cold rain has soaked my dress. My wet hair clings to my skin.

The wooden shed smells of chicken feed. It is dry in here. The rain is loud, imprisoning me in a box of sound. My clothes are dripping wet, and my hair smells of dirty wetness. I rest easy now. Looking at the axe in the corner. The feed pail rests beside the big sack of grain. There is mouse poison around the edges of it, and around the edges of this tiny box of a shed. It is bigger here than in my little closet.

From the distance, I hear the train bells ringing. Singing of my approaching death… it has come for me. I can hear the chiming of the whistle train, whose song is like the voice of pain itself. Mourning the agony of souls…

The solace of my soul's domain.

29

The wind and thunder are my teachers. I hear them calling to me, trying to speak of my future. But I cannot tell what they say, their language is yet unknown. The warnings are yet unclear; they are hidden in the voice of this storm. I cannot hear it say to me that she has the soul of a Warrior Queen, and has taken up the wicked sword against me.

What do you think now, Mother? Are you afraid for me? Do you rest on the sofa in anguish? Your maternity is not dead. You tremble inside, fearful for what you have done. You worry for my safety, because I am not a dog to be tossed out into the violent storm. I am your daughter.

Go on…bite your pretty nails! Fiddle with your dress buttons, and your hair, stylishly pinned! Pace the floor, flinching at the loudness of this barrage of thunder. Where is your beloved Daughter? Where is the flower, born from your garden? Where has the Rain Flower gone to rest?

You drift into the kitchen. Moving the curtain from the door window, looking for me. There is the coop and the shed. Maybe the flower grows in the coop. Are you guilty? Is there a soul underneath your beauty? Does your heart beat with compassion?

You cook and eat your dinner alone, testing your nerve, hardly looking towards the back kitchen door, wondering where in the world it is that your daughter could have gone. I see you, Mother, trying not to care, swallowing your meal alone, wishing that I had prepared it for you. You know all too well that misery will invite a blessed sleep. You hope, you pray, you know that somewhere I am safe and dry, kept safe in a beloved sleep.

Dinner is over. The dishes are clean. You take no pride in your heartlessness, as the thunder claps, killing the lights. The lightning strikes, the thunder claps again. The house is pitch black in the stormy evening. It is dark outside. Where, Mother? Where in the world can it possibly be that your daughter could have gone?

A tapping…

A quiet rapping…

Silence.

You do not hear it again. You rise from your sofa, walking to your bedroom , carrying the lamp. Nothing. Why do you close the door to your room? Why won't you go to look for her?

Compelled, you go to my room, staring at the window. Nothing. Or is that something that you see? Does a face look at you from the Cloak of

Night, drowning in the darkened rain? The window shows only your dark reflection, holding the flaming lamp, creeping towards you, undeterred by anxiety. The lightning strikes! Lighting the world! The demon is at the window. A tiny, wide eyed devil, a drowned rat with white skin and black hair draped over big, black eyes of fear. The sight is a sight causing such a dreadful fright, and you try with all your woman's might to breathe, holding your heart, praying that the demon at the window will not climb in through the glass without breaking it to get you. Punishing your audacity, your nerve to not go look for where it is your daughter could have gone.

What is this demon that you see?

The demon is me.

You approach the window, amazed by my appearance. I stand there dumbfounded, putting my hand hopefully against the glass now. The house is black inside. There is only a tall, dark figure, carrying a lamp flame.

"*eld mit ow!*"

I do not understand…

"Get in this house!"

I thank you. I praise you while I splash through the soaked grass to the back porch. There you are with the door open. Waiting for me. Water pours from my clothes to the floor. The lamp is on the kitchen table.

"Go to the bathroom and dry yourself. You can have a slice of bread for supper. And then I want you to go straight to bed. Did you hear me?"

"Yes, Momma."

"Why were you punished tonight?"

"Because I was a smart mouth."

"What exactly did you say that made me punish you?"

"Because I said I was gonna run away?"

"Now you listen to me…"

She bends down in the flickering dark. Her breath smells of sweet onion. Her face glows in the darkness.

"You will *not* be going back to school. Why? Because I said so. That is all."

"Yes, Momma."

She studies my eyes. She can see that I am not broken. It gives her pleasure. The fight pleases her.

"Now go dry yourself."

"Yes, Momma."

I stumble through the darkened house, water pouring off me, more frightened than I was in the shed, my back sore from blessed sleep. Still aching in my soul, aching because of what I know, that you would not have come to see, where it could be that your beloved daughter could have gone.

I am dry now, and warm in my bed.

30

You survived the first night in the barn, but this one approaches. Cold waiting, for the entire day. Your body itches under the cold, then betrays with phantom pain. Have you eaten, Mother? She fed you a good, hot breakfast. You will need your strength. Did she allow you into the house, to warm your lovely bones?

In your father's eyes, there is anger. The hurt you caused him when you left. But in your mother's face, within her exhausted beauty, there is only bitterness. The kind that comes when one truly endeavors to please God in this life.

Sorrow.

And now, the Evening...

Descending fear. You have not asked Evelyn for mercy--hoping that compliance would evoke her pity. But as the twilight approaches, so too does the fear you have known from the beginning.

All day, you allowed the memories to come back, and have their way. You remember the day you became a thirteen year old woman. The day Evelyn humiliated you into low self-esteem, by calling you accursed. She made you stand in the middle of the bathtub, holding up your dress, feeling the warm blood run down your leg. She made you watch the blood gather at your feet, painting the white porcelain red from your toes down to the drain.

There was no whipping that day, was there? She didn't put the lash across your young back, while you stood in Hell's Humility. While you were being made to understand that to be born is to be cursed, and to live is to suffer. What came to your mind, while the hot blood tickled your thighs? While the warm life trickled to your ankle?

Days of innocence. Imagination carried you away from the bathroom, to the school classroom, and to the teacher, and your little friends. You wanted to go to your room, and read a storybook. You needed your mother to reach in, and pull you back from the drowning blood, and clean you, and whisper about how special you were, and how much she loved you.

The sound...

The calling of your execution.

Hugh and Evelyn Daniels have arrived back from their sudden errand. Twilight has fallen. You know that it may happen in the dark. By lamplight.

But they come straight to the barn from the truck. There is the length of thin, new rope in his hand, and she carries a black horse whip, or perhaps a cane. A whip.

They will bind you, Mother. They will extract the screams that have built up inside, striping the blood from deep under your skin, from your back, to your fleshy young hips, to the bottom of your white legs. Evelyn will marvel at your swollen breasts, watching the milk and blood drip from them.

The blood will trickle in the cold.

Accursed woman.

31

*T*his is the last of Summer Vacation. Mother has not quit her job. Mr. Shirley's plan will have to wait for the next planting season. He came by a few days ago, and took almost every little chicken away. We won't have to gather eggs for him anymore. My hen house cleaning is easier. There are only twelve chickens left, and no rooster to bother them. Their yard seems much bigger now. Even our own house seems emptier.

Why does this seem like the last day of my life? Is it because the chickens are gone? Am I just lonely, because mother is at work? I stroll through the field at the noon hour, wanting to control my little destiny, knowing full well that I cannot. For the first time ever, I have a longing to go to school. I wander towards the edge of the thick woods, facing the approaching days with fear.

If I had been going to my sixth grade year proper, my apprehensions would be about Sarah Brown.

The edge of the woods. I remember the body of the black rat snake, and it makes me turn around and go back towards the house. Sarah's memory still affects my nerves, even though I may never see her again. I wonder how much bigger she is than me this year? How much prettier? But I wouldn't have to worry, because if I go back to school, Ms. Ida will learn about her and the boys who trip me on the playground.

But I think I've been lucky so far. Luck has kept her from cornering me in the schoolyard, far away from the teacher's sight, and punching me in the stomach while the other girls hold my arms. How many times has she pinched me or smacked my forehead, and then laughed as though it were all in good fun? How many times has she touched the tip of my nose and pushed it until it hurt?

Once, on a rainy day when we were in the gym before school, Sarah rested her forehead to mine and said, "you think your hair smells good, don't you?" And then she left to go play tag. Somewhere deep down, I think she liked me. Maybe she was good for me. She would have toughened me up a bit.

Somewhere, in an unknown future, a future that will never be, you are my dearest friend, Sarah. I am your refuge, your fortress in times of turmoil. The shoulder for you to cry on, the listening ear for you to tell every trouble and heartache to. I know things about you that your dear mother cannot imagine, and would never want to. The two of us will walk the halls together. The two of us—disguised in humility...

One with Raven locks of coal, the other with hair in Shimmering Gold. We are inseparable. The talkative blonde who is in every club and activity known, extremely popular. And that quiet brunette, the Italian Girl who writes classical music, striking desire in the hearts of the bravest souls. A hypnotic stare, and a Nova-curved waist, with very big bosoms and perfectly fashioned hips. A face and body to kill and die for, they say. But I do not care. I make my perfect grades in quiet, unapproachable, accessible only to the most privileged among them. But only you, Sarah, only you are my equal. Together, we will walk the Ivy Path. The two of us… disguised in Humility.

But alas! This can never be! I walk this Apprehension Field, frightened by what I see. Endless days of imprisonment. Many nights plagued by stygian dreams. I cannot know the height, the breadth of what has been prepared. The suffering she hath prepared for me. I will drink from this bitter cup, and learn through tears and blood, to surrender to the Rule of Suffering.

"Hey, Momma."

"Hey."

Despair. A mild depression, clouding your features. I rush over to you, hugging you desparately. There, I have you trapped. You cannot move now, without being cruel. The guilt you feel from the storm weighs heavy.

"My Beautiful Mother…"

Our phrase of worship, slipping out on its own. I feel her hand touching my back.

Gently.

"I know I can't go to school tomorrow. Right Momma?"

"That's right."

"I'm glad. I'll be able to stay home and keep the house for you, and learn how to cook for you."

"That's...that's my good girl. Let Momma go to her room now."

"Not 'til you give me a kiss."

Grudgingly, she bends down and lets me kiss her on the lips. She pulls away, gliding in tallness towards her room. Her black skirt is long. Her white blouse is simple and elegant.

"I think Sarah's gonna miss me a lot."

"Who's Sarah?"

"She was my best friend."

"You never mentioned her before."

Silence. I've been caught in a lie.

"You'll get along fine without her," she says. "You don't need friends outside your own family. You have your mother for company."

My friend. My companion.

My gatekeeper.

32

How many whippings will you suffer, dear lady? Two? Three? How many nights will you lay in the cold barn, shivering from cold and pain? Praying for sleep?

Did you steal me away after the second morning? The third, even while your body still burned with hot whip lashes?

Your wrists are sore. Your shoulders ache, from being pulled off the ground.

They stripped you naked again last night, and tied your ankles together. Hugh watched his wife tie your wrists completely, staring blankly as she put your wrists over the metal hook in the air. Your breasts are still cut from the first night. Every inch of your body is laced with crusted red sores.

Your mother watched you strain against the scream, because the pain in your shoulder was unbearable already. Your father was behind you, reading your condemnation from the Bible:

"The book of Ecclesiastes, chapter seven and verse twenty six...And I find more bitter than death the woman, whose heart is snares and nets, and her hands as bands: whoso pleaseth God shall escape from her; but the sinner shall be taken by her..."

The word of God hath confirmed your accursedness. Your womanhood. What other verses in the Bible did he read to you? Did your tears fall while he read them? Did your mother's eyes burn with desire?

Five minutes. Ten. Fifteen minutes of the Bible. Enthusiasm trembles his voice. Your mother stands still, not the least disinterested in your nakedness. Your toes can barely touch the ground. Your shoulder is in agony.

His voice goes silent. A silence that cries your destruction from one side of creation to the other. You watch the whip uncurl in her hands, and your voice begins to moan pitifully on its own. It is so cold. So cold, Mother. How will you endure the hot whip on your cold skin?

The first scream is ripped from your body. Did you scream to God and Jesus, the way I will someday? How will you endure slavery's lash on your white skin, the bondage to a God you cannot please, whose love for you flourisheth in the midst of suffering? Do you pray for Divine intervention? Are you screaming to be released from the torture of the flesh?

The cold is insignificant, now. The whip snaps pain into the air, which hits you firm across your buttocks and thighs, stroking fire into you, pulling deep screams from you, even as the blood has already boiled over, and trickles down the backs of your legs. You bleed easily, Mother. Your fair skin bleeds so easily.

Do not cry for deliverance, Mother! As the spit falls from your mouth, cry for the strength to endure the pain of your birthright.

After the whipping. She now stands before you, twisting and pulling your sensitive nipples until you no longer remember your name. The pain reignites your body. It is different from the whip lashes. It is like being stung continuously by a poisoned wasp. Your father watches. His daughter is being chastised by the Lord. The Lord chastises them that he loves.

She picks up the cane. She stripes your massive breasts until you cannot remember how to speak. Until they are networked with bloody red marks. You can barely breathe enough to scream. Your screams struggle to escape from the Hell fire in your body. You hang there like a piece of animal flesh, cured in the flame of this punishment. Your soul will be made clean.

Why were you not blindfolded?

So that Evelyn can see the life, dying in your eyes. Upon this death she feeds her lust to inflict sadistic pain, until she has drank her fill. She does not know where this need arises. She only knows that it must be fed. You must be devoured, Mother. She wants to break your leg. She wants to break your leg with a sledge hammer.

Did she tell you she was going to break your leg after the last whipping? She didn't say that, did she Mother?

33

*U*nderneath gloomy autumn skies, I stroll the barren field of plenty, moving towards the forest trees. The woods are so far away from the house. This November Day is not too cold for me. The trees have all shown their true colors, and now the leaves have begun to fall to the grass beneath my feet.

This is the doorway to my thirteenth year, where I have crossed just a few days ago. I'm trying to see whether or not thirteen is different. Yes. I do feel older. Quieter. Already, I have accepted that I may never see the schoolyard again, and part of me is so very thankful, that I did not have to fear the other children this year.

These forest woods are not as fearful in Autumn. I imagine that in winter, when the leaves have fallen, I can walk among the tree skeletons unafraid, because the dark leaf canopy will have fallen away. I creep along slowly at the edge of the woods, trying not to think of the serpentine, which lies curled in power, waiting for me to enter in.

I step into the barren forest, listening to my feet crackle the dead leaf carpet. The sound carries through the air. I know that the woods are deep, and all I can think of is getting lost. I'll stay at the edge of the woods, keeping the house in sight. I gaze deep into this gray world, at the tall sticks of autumn trees, wishing I could climb to the top of the highest branch, and see the other side of the forest. The bark on this tree is pale and smooth, like death. These are autumn trees, not yet cursed with winter grieving, not yet spring trees in waiting.

Someday soon, I suppose I will gather the twine, and tie it to this tree, my White Tree, and I will unwind the white string deep into the forest. Then, I can explore without fear. I will get to know the living and dead trees, I will learn the many paths to the lost places. I will love to get lost, as long as I have the twine, to find my way back to the light of day.

But Autumn Days are shorter, and I can feel the coming night chill. I'll have to go inside and wait for Mother. But wait… I hear a bird…a Bird in the Woods, coming to me upon the flute, in the company of the quiet harp! I have learned that I cannot yet conjure melodies on my own. From where they appear I do not know, nor can I force them. But they are more frequent now…and *stronger*. The shapes I see are often complex, and the colors more vivid. But this instant, I only hear the notes and chords in the air around me. I have to look about, swearing that the sounds are real. But they are not.

I am at the edge of the Forest. Listening to the Bird in the Woods. I cannot see mother at the chicken yard, looking across the field at me. Is she standing still, hands on her hips, afraid to call me, fearing that I might not answer? She has no wrath to give today, and she turns disinterestedly, and goes back into the house.

When I get to the house, I am frightened to see she is already home. I stayed away too long. My stupidity knows no bounds. Did she call me? If she did, then I know what will happen, because I didn't answer. I knock on her door, flinching when I hear the bitter *"what?"* snapped out at me.

"I…d-did…"

"What do you want?"

"N-nothing. Um…do y-you want me to c-cook?"

I can't even string a sentence of words without stammering. I hurry to the kitchen, uncertain, but remembering the way the dinner had impressed her that time before. I know that she likes for me to cook. There are sweet potatoes in the cabinet; I know how long to leave them in the oven. And, yes, I think I know how to pan fry the ham. I think I do. I want to cook fresh greens, but I know better than to try.

Depression is a spirit, Mother. Flying from your room, moving quickly to where I stand at the sink. In our house's silence, I feel you thinking of your husband. I know you are lost in thought, imagining the life you would have had. A life stolen from you by me; a life of love and leisure…and luxury.

Coletti Farms. An egg empire it would have been. Father was enterprising with the dear chickens, wasn't he? The flock was so large then. Mr. Shirley collected many eggs before father died. There was a blessing with Michael Coletti. But you…

When a blessing meets a curse, which shall be the victor? You should have prayed, Mother. You should have prayed for your life's curse to be taken away. Perhaps then, it would not have reached out to your husband and choked the roots of his blessing. Had he never met you, he would not have died. He would have been a rich man. But you...you are not going to be rich. You will writhe in poverty.

You will not have an Angel Estate, with a gate protecting you from the world below. There is no limousine for you, gliding away from fancy stores in the far city, whirling you across the countryside in lonely wealth and affluence. Rolling you smoothly through your open gate, past the Great Lawn, tree shrubs and statues, perhaps even the requisite fountain. The glissadic sliding, up to your grand southern palace of brick, a cold mansion of illustrious dreams and high, glorious living.

Look! There is no winding staircase to a palatial hall, with plush carpet guiding you to your Queen's Chambers! No handsome husband to greet you in the twilight. No silken evening gowns draping your fair skin, or diamond necklasses enhancing your mountainous bosoms just so. Nor dinners in fine restaurants, or nights at the opera, or dancing in exclusive club party gatherings. No nights in satin sheets, enraptured by pleasures too painful to bear, too violent to contain your screaming voice.

No, Mother.

There is only you...and your Southern House of Poverty.

The thing awaits you in the kitchen. It lives to remind you of the life you cannot have. Sleep, dear lady. Let the thing in the kitchen be for now. Let it take care of you. Give lust and craving its briefest rest.

Sleep, Mother.

34

I am only thirteen, but the music has started to flare, blazing white hot, inspiring me to the notion that the creative fires burn brightest after midnight. When I am awakened by a melody in the night, it is incredible. No matter how long or complex, the piece forms finished in my mind, allowing me to study it. I suppose I am the most thankful for my memory, for once I have committed the colors to my mind's archive, I do not easily forget them.

Only from church hymnals have I learned a single thing about notation, which I partially ignore anyway, and sometimes I wonder if Mother has suspected why I sit in a trance, dumbfounded by the music pages for two hours every Sunday. I stare with dim-bulb understanding, knowing nothing of rhythm, hearing the notes in my head fully chorded, sometimes with embellishments that I tend to ignore. In mensural notation, what is the relationship between the *long* and the *breve?* I do not care. My *mode* is my own.

But these crude markings I make in my school notebooks have grown in number, and threaten to mold me into a creature of habit. I find that every day, by the noon hour, the compulsion to read or write music has built up inside me until I have to obey it. Inevitably, the notes have shifted in the bar to positions that are most comfortable to me, so that the music I read in church is correct, and the scribbling I read in my notebook is mine. Anyone who saw it would surely dismiss it as chicken pecking. Someday, I may learn to write correctly. My laziness is certainly a product of my mind's facility, but perhaps the fault is not my own. I have no music book, nor understanding teacher to guide me.

Do I understand how my mind balances the separate functions? How does the accompaniment support and display the melody? Is melisma important to sustaining it over a duration?

I do not care. I only know that it is beautiful.

At this moment, my mind is enraptured. Something pure and simple, which is usual. Another sound, yes, an engine. I wonder if every car engine sings a different tune to the trained ear? I hear the song of the Valerie Car. I quickly put my notebook in my top drawer underneath my clothes, not understanding that Mother could never believe those dots and lines could be worth a chick pea. I hear the raven coming up onto the porch, but what else do I hear. A voice? Voices?

A stranger's voice. Another woman's voice. A maiden, to accompany the raven into the house!

Foolishly, I step into the living room to greet my mother, who has stepped in first, embarrassed by her poverty. Immediately behind her steps the late thirtyish lady, short dark blonde hair and tiny, tasteful earrings matching her sweater. Jeans. Light makeup. She has a pretty look about her. She is comfortable with people. Worldly. Quietly lustful, I think. I know she craves my mother's "company." I know it already.

Why did I let her see me? I lower my head stupidly, horrified. Then, I duck away like a whipped dog, cowering from its brutal master.

But she has seen me!

She is cooing already. I hear her. Heavenly Father, please do not pull me into public scorn. Please don't let her see me again. I think I am trembling. But why? What harm can she do?

"Is that your little girl?"

"Yes."

"Barbara, you *have* to bring her out here. Right this second."

"She's the scarediest thing in Williamston, Valerie. Trust me, you don't want to be bothered…"

"If I don't see her right now it'll kill me. I swear to God I'll die right here in front of you."

"Well, alright. But…"

I rush to my chair and grab my Bible, skittishly biting my fingernails, listening to the footsteps come to the door. My heart flutters wildly. The doorknob rattles and opens, and mother peeps inside, as though she is unfamiliar with both the room and its little prisoner. Her lips are as fearfully tucked in as mine, and the look of total humility on her face is fascinatingly beautiful.

"Elizabeth," she calls gently. "Come here a minute, sweetie."

The comfortable chair pities me as I get up, stumbling through shock to the door. Staring as my beautiful mother reaches out for my hand and guides me through my fear, to usher me into the living room. My shiny black hair is long and straight, silken, with body and healthy substance to spare.

"Oh my *God,*" she says, alarming me, covering her mouth as though she has seen a ghost. "Oh, my God," she repeats, softer, moving towards me. Why am I so scared? I shouldn't be.

"Elizabeth," she whispers. "Can y…can your aunt Valerie have a hug?"

Dulled, dim with fear, I stare right at my mother.

Waiting.

"Go ahead, Honey," she smiles. "Its alright."

Valerie Kirkland reaches down and pulls me into a firm embrace. Her arms are weak and spindly. She smells of strange lotions and perfumes, faraway people and places. She smells of freedom. But I do not know her, nor do I wish to. I wish to escape from her.

"Would you look at that," she says. "Look at this girl's face." Her voice is filled with awe. She glances at Mother. "Her little brows are arched just like yours Barbara. She's got woman's eyes already." She laughs as if tickled, stroking my eyebrow with her thumb.

"You'd better go finish your homework, now sweetie," says Mother.

Homework? But I'm not in school. Should I open my mouth and say it?

"Okay, Momma. Its nice to meet you Miss Valerie."

When I get back to my room, I stand by the door, amazed by the strangeness of this day. In all the years, my mother has never before had company. I notice that she is different around other people. She is different when Ms. Valerie is here.

These are strange goings on. To be sure.

"I've never seen…" her voice chokes.

"Valerie, what's the matter? Come sit down and tell me. You've been so sad here lately."

Mother's voice is as sweet as honey. Dripping with empathy and compassion. I can hear you comforting her. Is it genuine? Do you really care? The two of you have a chemistry. She is the talkative, unstable butterfly, and you are the Great Flowering Tree. A place for her to hide in the storm.

"I didn't want to burden you with this, Barbara. I shouldn't even be crying. But when I saw your daughter, I—"

I hear quiet sobs.

Are they genuine?

"She's got the prettiest little face I've ever seen. And she looks so sad and afraid. Is she alright?"

"Oh, she's just shy. I told you about that, remember? Now what's really bothering you, Valerie? Talk to me."

"Well, Gail's not, I mean… my daughter's not coming home this Thanksgiving. She said she doesn't know when she's coming to see me."

Her sobbing is muffled. I imagine that she is comforted by Mother's Bosom. Those big, soft cushions. People show more sympathy to friends and strangers than to their own families.

"Every since she turned fifteen," says Valerie, "she hardly ever wants to talk when I call, and she goes on and on about her stepmother. I don't think she knows she killing me, Barbara."

"Why don't you just go visit?"

"New York is just too far. And she's got half brothers and sisters. They've built their own little family…and when I saw Elizabeth I…"

The mournful wailing. It is the sound of pain. The poor woman, I almost feel sorry for her. But the moan of her full, woman's voice, groaning deeply with hurt is too exhilarating. I am chilled by it.

Give her the comfort she needs, Mother. The crying shoulder.

"I can't believe I'm doing this," Valerie says. "I swore I wasn't going to bother you with this."

"I knew something was wrong," says Mother. "To tell you the truth, I thought you were mad at me."

"Now why in the world would anyone be mad with you?"

I can almost see Mother's humble smile, deflecting the compliment. Deflecting the guilt.

"I'm going to my parents' for Thanksgiving, in Fayetteville. I'm almost afraid to ask you to come with me."

"Well, I'd like to Valerie, but…well, my daughter."

"Hmm?"

"She just so—"

"Shy? She'll be fine, Honey. We're not cooking *her* for dinner."

A hushed, whispered voice.

"I just don't want to go alone, Barbara. Please say you'll come with me."

A pause. Mother pulls a deep breath.

"I know you don't need my problems," says Valerie. "You've got your own daughter to worry about. But you have a strength, Barbara. Do you know that? Its very powerful. The truth is I *have* been kind of upset with you, because I needed you to open up to me, but I was afraid to say anything. I didn't want you to think I was comin' on to you or something."

Nervous laughter.

"If I had, what in the world would you have thought of me?"

What questions cease the flow of time?

What answers make it go again?

35

The dawn of the third day. They will beat you into insanity, or death. But somehow, you know it is not your destiny to be whipped until you die, and be buried deep underneath the waiting soil, with your child.

Death.

Unrighteous indignation fuels their hatred. Sadistic lust, which had lain dormant in their bodies, awakened when you returned. Their desire for one another's sin has died, while their desire for sin itself lives and breathes. They crave every inch of your submission. Every bloody inch of your repentance. They long to see you broken like a slobbering animal, stripped of your faculties and your dignity, and perhaps your life.

Do they love you?

Your hell child will be sold. And they will imprison you, and teach you the meaning of life. If... if you survive their absolution.

You don't know how you'll do it. But you know that you must get away. You must get into the house, and get your baby, and walk the miles of country road, until you reach civilization.

Mountain country. These are an isolated people. Do you risk being seen? Neighbors might not help you escape. Can you risk asking them to help you, if they see you on the road? They'll come looking for you, Mother. But if you wait until the twilight, you will be bound, and punished again.

Fate decides over reason. Destiny overrides indecision.

You will stay until dark.

You will be whipped again.

*T*he Christmas Season has come and gone for another year. Peace is lifted from the Earth, and in its place falls the blanket of winter white.

It's too cold in the chicken house. My skin burns from the whipping, and I can still remember the metallic taste of blood. I brought this upon myself. I was warned not to ask again.

But I wanted to go outside…

And the snow was so beautiful.

Does Ms. Valerie know that I don't go to school? Why didn't she come today? If she had, this might not have happened. Mother keeps me in the house all the time now. I can't go outside without her permission, even when she is not at home. Sometimes, she goes to Ms. Valerie's house, and she will stay until well after dark. I always cook for her now.

My mind has written a symphony in the field of snow. The first of many, I suppose, conceived from intense concentration, born without effort. With a stick from inside the winter woods, I have drawn a bar in the snow, and even dotted the first measure in the white ground. The gigantic clef is perfect, I think, as is the tiny melody it oversees. An A Major symphony has come complete in twenty minutes, and I shall remember it, for it has kept me in this cold place. I know now, why the spirit whispers to me. I understand, why I must hear the voice of nature's song. It is my salvation. My comfort. The truest solace bestowed upon me.

But I am only flesh and blood. I need warmth. I am starved for food and company. My little snow girl, a hopeless mound of snow with no eyes, stands lifeless at the back of the house. She can give me nothing. I suppose the chickens are comforted by the snow girl. The snow does not bother the chickens. I think they like it. But now, my melodies are gone. There is no solace out here. I stumble clumsily, crunching through the snow field in the tracks I made before, back towards the lonely house. Above me is the gloaming of winter gray. The tree skeletons near the house are like shadows. My feet and hands are icy cold.

Mother whipped me when I asked to play in the snow. And then she dressed me warmly, marched me through the kitchen and threw me off the porch into the yard. My lip was bloodied somewhere in the midst of it all. She had been engrossed in one of her romance books.

"Let not your heart be troubled" ...

Verses come, trying to comfort me. But there is no warmth in words. Words cannot heal the broken heart. Only time. But this is not my time to heal. I stand trembling, broken at my Mother's Door. The kitchen door is locked. I would like to knock, but do I dare put my cold knuckles against the door? How can I resist it? But I don't want to hold the poor chickens anymore. Holding them tight, to keep my hands from freezing. So many hours have passed, and I am cold and hungry. And it is getting dark.

"Knock, and it shall be opened unto you..."

Fearfully, I knock.

No answer. But I have to continue. No matter what will happen, it will be better if she opens the door for me. There is her silhouette through the kitchen curtain. The shadow turns off the kitchen light and disappears to another part of the house. Even so, I am compelled to knock. I hurry through the twilight snow to the living room window. I will torment her by knocking. On its own, my voice comes out, calling "Momma, please Momma!" I don't know how long I will knock until she comes. But I cannot stop. I am hopeful when I open the screen door, but not surprised when the front door is still locked.

"Momma. Momma let me in!"

My fear of the winter night is greater that the fear of another beating. Perhaps an hour has passed since the first knock, because the world has turned to black. But I am protected. Somehow, I know I am protected from death.

Will I die tonight?

At long last, I have true courage. The kind that comes from fear itself. The kind that makes a person run through a flame to escape the burning house. Fear claws at me, the night snow shines blue at me, until I am brave enough to go to the light at my mother's window, and I pound on the glass so hard that I might break it.

"Momma! Momma I promise to God and Jesus I won't ask to go out again. Please, Momma, please!"

The window shade moves up slowly, and Mother is there. Tall and dark, staring at her cold nestling, shivering in the snow. She goes slowly toward the back door instead of the front, so I will have to walk further to get inside. The doorknob turns. The blessed doorknob! I step into my beloved house of safety, every part of me numb or burning from the cold. My hands and feet are lifeless, bitten by the arctic air. The wood stove is aflame, the house is warm. So vividly, irrepressibly warm as I hurry to the living room, so the heat can tingle my white skin. I love my mother's house. This is my castle. My refuge.

Mother! Where are you? Where have you gone? I don't care if you scold me. I will go to wherever you are in the house, and I will shower you with love. I will drown you in affection.

"Momma? Momma?"

My lips can hardly form the words as I stumble stupidly, simple-mindedly through the warm living room, turning left into my mother's quarters. I reach out to where she stands at the window, gazing plaintively into the new fallen snow. I grab her from the air, pulling her down to my lowly self, clinging to her life like a vine to a tree.

"Th...thank you, M...Momma. Th...thank you."

What creatures make tracks through the night snow unawares, not caring who the woman in the window is, unconcerned with what she has done to the child in her arms? What lonely backcountry mouse, or lost kitten of the woods? Does the wood devil, the screech owl, care that the cold nearly burned pieces of my body away? We stand still together, both Mother and Daughter by the window. There is no one to witness, to see the tormentor and captive, to look upon the misery we both share. In the window light, the woman holds her daughter close to her body, grateful for the passing of this latest cruelty, fearful of what further evil she has left to give.

What further evil.

Weep not, dear Mother! It is the vile blood coursing through you that shall make it happen! It is the seed planted by Evelyn Daniels. This is not a fight against flesh and blood. How can one fight the principalities? Rulers of the Darkness of this World? One cannot resist the powers that shall be. Perhaps, you are not to blame for what you must do to me today. Anxiously you come to my room, seeing me watch my marbles on the bed. You are afraid for what you have to do, but the ire you have is rekindled when you see me sitting there like a dummy. I am a witless, whimpering girl puppy. A stubborn, willful little bitch.

"Put those away."

"Yes, Maam."

Rest, Mother. Sit comfortably on my bed while I put my colors away, embarrassed. With my lips tucked in, I walk obediently to where you sit.

"Why did you disobey me yesterday?"

"I…I won't do it again. I won't ask to go outside again."

The snow covered country glows white outside the window. Instinct tells me to walk over and lower the shade, but I know that such pitiful, pleading desperation is unwarranted. Unavailing.

"There is something I want you to learn about punishment," she said. "Sometimes it comes in parts, with or without warning. And it has to be this way, Elizabeth, until you learn not to disobey me. To *never* disobey me."

An eternal pause, with me trembling in its wake…

"I told you not to ask again, didn't I?"

"Y-Yes m…m…"

I think that the types of fear are many, and are uniquely distinguished. The terror that plagues me is not the fear of death or dismemberment. It is as though premonition has enveloped me, and suddenly, I am fearful of having my breath taken away.

"Go into the kitchen, and bring me two dishtowels."

I feel a haze of relief. I can endure a good leg or back striping with a towel. But why two? Compliantly, I bring her both of them. Without a word, she takes them and slowly makes me understand what fear really is, tying my wrists tightly behind my back. Then she binds my ankles together with the other.

My wrists…my ankles…my heart…I cannot breathe, as I am pulled onto the bed…I cannot see, as she wraps my body tightly in the linen…now I feel the weight of her strong body looming, moving above me. I cry…begging her to believe that I will obey. And now, the weight of her body, pressing full upon me like a lioness upon a cub. My arms are underneath me, behind my back. I cannot kick my legs…I can hardly move a muscle…I can't draw a single breath…

I can see you, Mother. Watching your daughter's face push against the thin bed cover. Watching the mouth open under the fabric, feeling the tearful, breathless screams. The face makes an impression in the cloth. Here, in isolation, beyond the seeing eyes of community, you nourish the seeds of wickedness grown. A forest grove of sadism, bursting free from the snow, to be cared for in private, until it will flourish into a paradise of violence, blood and perversion.

Let me breathe, Mother. Please, let me breathe. Let me look upon your face, so that my eyes can tell of the repentance that my screaming voice cannot. The light through the covers is growing purple. My mind swirls into a fog. The pain and fear is too great, my body will collapse. But suddenly, panic strikes, and I can feel myself shrieking hysterically, trying with the last ounce of strength to move. But I cannot.

I cannot breathe, Mother. Please let me breathe...

I can...

I perceive a sudden lightness. I am drifting, tumbling into daylight. The air is cooler now, I think. I can feel it inside me. Is that you at the edge of my bed? I think you are undoing the bonds from my feet. I hear you speaking, something about obeying... punish ...I can't think. Don't call for my attention, for I cannot think. There is no fear or sorrow, only the memory of pain. My chest is on fire with pain, my head is sore. And now, I see a Lady Ghost in darkened cloth, floating away.

Can either of us claim sanity? Are you sane, Mother, as you sit in your room and cry?

Don't cry, Mother. Please don't cry.

I love you.

37

"I've even thought about leaving that place," says Valerie. "I'm sick to death of it."

"Its not so bad, is it?"

"You're only there part time. Sometimes I'm there fifty some odd hours a week."

"Well, what would you rather be doing?" Mother asks.

I hear them in the kitchen. Hardly a day goes by now that they aren't together. Sometimes they go in Mother's room, so they can whisper about things. They know I'm always in my room. Listening.

"I was thinking about going back to teaching." Valerie says.

"What?"

"I told you, I won't be trapped in that zipper factory forever."

"But teaching?"

"I was a substitute teacher when Gail was little. I told you that when we first met, remember? I'll bet you'd make a good teacher. All you'd have to do is look at 'em, and they'd hush up right then."

I hear spoons and cups clinking softly. They drink so much coffee when they're together. I keeps them from eating, I suppose. Sometimes, they sit in the living room and watch the little color TV that Aunt Valerie gave us for Christmas. I think Mother is glad for her gift. It is good company for her. But she won't let me watch TV. I know that I'll never ask again, nor shall I ever touch it. The blood will run, if I touch it. Crimson on my white socks, drying into the color of rust.

The blood will run, if I touch it.

"But you've got potential you don't even realize, Barbara. I know you're smart, and that *face.* You're too beautiful to live out here like this. Hiding from the world. You don't even look like a farm girl."

"Thanks."

"I just mean you're so darn pretty you seem out of place here. You should be doing more with your life. Maybe you really *could* be a teacher. Listen at me, I sound like your mother or something."

You would teach them good, wouldn't you? You would love to teach them their lessons, with your pretty hands across their backsides, or at their little throats, while twisting the skin on their tummies until they couldn't breathe.

"Well, why not?" asked Valerie, in forced, high pitched ignorance.

"I didn't even finish high school."

"I know its just talk," she says. "But you could get your GED, and go from there. Wouldn't it be something if you and I were teaching together at Hayes in a few years?"

"If only," says Mother. "But not likely. I might not look it to you, but I *am* just a dumb country girl, Val. That's all I've ever been."

"Don't talk morbid," she says. "And I don't think you're dumb in the least... *Eve.* "

"What's that?" Mother gasps.

"Eve."

Honey.

Sweet milk.

Mother's words, the sound of her voice, dear Valerie. What does the mellow smoothness of her silky voice do to your body? How does my Mother's face cool the burning of desire? As the mountain view nourishes the poet's lonely soul, as the pine forests rise and fall with the peaks and valleys near and far--the warm glow of Signora Coletti's fair skin feeds your soul, the contour of her mouth, the shape of her perfect nose, the piercing, angelic stare in her bewitching gray eyes. The pale gray of winter skies' alluring calls you, beckoning you to tell her of what longing she creates, and such craving she inspires. Talk to her, dear Valerie. Speak softly of the need which has blazed an inferno inside of you.

Why do you run from her? Claiming to need rest for the morning? You don't bother to tell me goodbye anymore. But why should you? You'll be back tomorrow.

Savor this! Close your eyes and feel the mountainous peaks, the valley curves of her waist and hips against you. Let the Nova Curve work its magic inside your body. Let it cause your spirit to flare with the energy of a million suns, and feel it radiate power to your womanhood tonight, dear Ms. Valerie Kirkland! My Aunt Valerie! Taste the sugar upon your mouth, imagining that you could drink deeply from her lips. Writhe in the torment of want, squirm your hips with desire. Hug her, and breathe the sweet bouquet which is her hair, tremble your departure upon a whisper in her ear. Upon the morrow, Dear Lady. Rest well tonight. Farewell, until your splendid tomorrow comes.

Lust? Love? How are they distinguished? How are they extinguished from thee? Shall they leave your flesh bye and bye? Goodbye, Ms. Valerie.

Until tomorrow.

The piano is the key. It dominates my early composition. I am a child of melody. A Daughter of Harmony. Simple, clear little essays in neoclassical structure, sound and form; all in requisite exposition, with very little development, if it can be called that at all. Tiny earth stones and trinkets, treasures to me, each more precious than the last.

I search the ground. I search the air. I search high and low for the rocks of color, painted every purest color in the rainbow. Earth stone more precious than silver and gold. More precious than diamonds. More rare than every treasure in the mighty deep. Fairer than every pearl of the

Dark'ned Sea. I search the ground, having *found* the earth rocks of color, having value to not a single soul but me.

I would exchange these precious stones, for the chance to know my destiny. A thing more rare than treasures of the deep…

Fairer than pearls of the Dark'ned Sea.

I regret that my little piano concerto is alone in its mighty inspiration, and I have not the skill to manufacture phrases at such a level. It was my mind's first composition, though incomplete, but only now am I trying to record it. My *Summer Concerto*, given to me in the twilight, on the last day of my fifth grade year. The last day of my education. How do I determine what instruments make the harmonies? My mind separates the chords for me, and I can hear each note, and somehow I know when flutes or horns are hidden among the winds, as opposed to bassoons or oboes. *Horn* color is the most beautiful, like Haydn and early Mozart. And Coletti.

How shall I notate the orchestral parts? This, I do not know. But it will be done. I will sit here like a dummy, with my little tongue parting my lips, lost in the idiot's hopeless concentration. Would that I had a teacher! Notation is elementary, my dear Carmen! But my summer concerto sparkles with like ingenuity as the *Crystal Sonata*, and I have to write it now. But often, inspiration requires prodding, aided by conscious effort. My craving for the piano is satisfied by my crude composition.

What would I do, were it not for this avocation? Colors breathed upon me in Muse, abilities rained upon me by appointment? Every part of Nature emanates color and melody. These that I hear are not for the world, for had they been, surely I would not be a prisoner! I would be in the second half of my sixth grade year, learning scales in secret, staccato and legato, even a song or two, striving to impress my dear Ms. Ida, eventually having the courage to tell her that this new melody or that is come into the world by me. Would I have played the concert halls at seventeen? Twenty one, perhaps? Unremarkable. The Italian Concerto #1 for Piano and Orchestra in F, by Carmen Angelina Coletti? Slightly less unremarkable. A modern concerto, powered by modern orchestration, but seasoned by late Bel Canto, uncontaminated by chromaticism. Mozart, Beethoven, Grieg, Hummel, Field, Tchaikovsky, swirled into a Rossinian whirlwind, thundering through the Great Music Hall, above the countryside, high into the mountains, down through the valleys and across the open plains.

If only.

Upon this Holy day, the Lord's Day, I sit in back of the country church with my Mother, engrossed in the bars of the Hymnals, hardly able to hear the droning of the Baptist sermon over the piano in my head. I find that I am able to see the keys in my mind's eye. Sometimes, I will sit and stare at the real world, at the church piano for the entire two hours at a time, seeing an imaginary woman sitting there. A very thin, unassuming sort in a skirt and white blouse, playing the music I desire to hear. She appears only in church, and never in my dreams or secular visions. I expect that her playing is heaven sent, and could hardly be duplicated except with extreme preparation, motivation, inspiration and ability.

Who is the angel I see? A projection of my desire for a teacher? She plays a Golden Key, in diamond melody and crystal harmony. Mother sits beside me, bolt upright, beautifully ignorant. She cannot take my muse away. It is mine to have, to protect my fragile sanity.

What protects you, Mother? What barricades your mind from Insanity's Wave? Is it grief? No. Grief is the salty sea, eroding your sound-minded shore.

The fine southern ladies sit up front. The same four sit in the same place every Sunday. Their hats are proud, as are their colorful dresses. Why do they strut in their fine feathered hats like the peacock? Every so often, I hear them talking here at the back of the church near the door. They compare dresses and hats, bragging boldly about how easily they made their outfits, or about what city they drove to acquire it. Sometimes, they say "Hey Barbara Jean," and Mother will say "you always look so pretty Ms. Wise." Mother's dull clothes do not aspire to prettiness. Neither do mine.

It is cold outside today. The remnants of a snow are left outside in the grass. We rest inside the warm church building, cozy in community's bosom, both in our plain dresses. Mother's is the color of blue midnight, and mine is off white, with tiny little faded flowers. The dress was never new, and the cloth looks dingy to me. I think Mother gets me clothes only because I outgrow the ones I already have. I think, I feel, that she wishes to wear black, but she satisfies this impulse with her black stockings on

Sundays, and long black coats for every season. I have not been spared, having received my first long coat in this same winter.

I know the other Ladies are glad Mother does not care for fashion. Their husbands have trouble enough, trying to keep their eyes away from her. And though she wears no makeup, the women who meet her almost always stare at her face like one stares at a red macaw in a bird cage, trying not to seem impressed, but still always asking her anyway whether or not she is wearing it. Truthfully, her complexion is as smooth as a porcelain doll's. A true natural beauty, which is very rare.

And whenever they mention her daughter's face, her body cringes. A deep, powerful jealousy, churning, burning the pit of her soul with fire. Just this morning before church, she held my face in her hand, staring, coming to terms with the womanhood about to grow into my features:

"That's a shame," she said. "If only…if only your face weren't as ugly as it is. I swear you've got the ugliest little face this side of creation. Your eyes are so big it makes you look like a fish."

I don't know if I can describe what I felt. I think it was terror. I know now that when people tell me I'm pretty, they're just being kind. Mother said I'm a "cute head"—so ugly that I'm actually kind of cute.

"Go in your room and wait", she said. "so I don't have to look at your face anymore." Then she stepped into the bathroom, to check her beauty.

I sit in church oblivious though, immersed in music, not remembering the hurt. I had choked the tears back the best I could, crying only a little, careful to pretend I was fine. The walk to church this morning was quick and cold. It froze the reservoir of tears inside me. Mother loves to walk. She accepts no ride to or from church. If it is raining, then we wear our hooded rain cloaks, and we splash onward. If it is hot, then our fair skin bakes in the sun. If it is cold, we turn into walking icicles. The three miles are her kingdom. Our Land.

Are there any others here like us? What family secrets abound? What is the depth of their wickedness?

I cannot say this is not a sanctuary. It is a refuge, a place of comfort for the lonely. A spirit of calm resides, a force of quietness. The brick building is simply designed, with its requisite steeple in place at the top. All manner of powders, perfumes and colognes and sweet chewing gum aromas are in the air, all dominated by the scent of fresh, new carpet. The stained glass windows are very colorful, if primitive, and they hold no melodies for me, no matter how long I stare at them. The stained glass windows are dead. The people are dead to misery. Their sorrow is suppressed behind smiles of cultured civility.

I do like to run my fingers over the smoothly finished pinewood benches. The carpet underneath our feet is burgundy, like the cloth on the money table. Their lust for money is not restrained. The deacons look very happy as they collect the money from us. And every Sunday, I stand and watch the robed choir march in from the back of the church in pride, feeling sorry for the lot of them, hoping they can be released from their bondage someday. Piety is their shackle. They are chained by ceremony.

Mrs. Fischer's husband looks at Mother and me all the time. So does Mr. Askew. And Mr. Louis. And Mr. Rucker. And Mr. Small. And Mr. Rosenbaugh and Mr. Coley and Mr. Black...

They don't look at their wives the way they look at Mother. Their eyes don't haze over with longing when they look at their wives. I don't know if its Mother's appeal or if its just the way of men to have wandering eyes. I think that a wife's beauty cannot prevent the Roving Eye. If the witch whore was unpleasant to the other women, they would descend on her like a flock of crows on a corn wagon, and then peck out her pretty eyes. But Mother has developed her public humility face to perfection, which is probably very genuine anyway. Smartly keeping us a good yelling distance from everyone whenever possible.

What secrets abound?

The service nears benediction. Mother makes me put on my coat and black scarf and gloves. We are two dark figures, stygian, united in mourning for this life, in longing for the life after. When the service ends on the D chord, the A-men chorus, the others begin to mumble and mill around, smiling, shaking hands, laughing, lusting, suffering. But Mother and Me head through the white doors, grinning a last wave at whoever is there to stare after us, usually a deacon that has sneaked out into the cold to have a smoke. No one calls after us anymore. They do not signal for our company. They know not to bother the Coletti woman and her daughter.

Do they like them? The widow and her 13 year old, floating down the icy steps, their breath freezing in the late winter air? Two ghosts, ready to brave the frigid miles, moving quickly past the Dead Tree Forest, the Sleeping Woods? The trees are a congregation of gray skeletons, leering coldly at them as they go by. Knowing of the sins that cover them in black and grief, feeling no compassion for their pain.

Gray winter skies loom above them as they travel the back country road. The two of them—in the snow flurry, their own world of thought, their own places of warmth. Two—together in the Eidolic Plain, lost in the wilderness of their birth. A mother and her only daughter, who had both longed for a time of joy, but who now trudge through life in perpetual want, the need for love, and the craving for affection and laughter. These two, on the road to freedom, winding through a valley of tears, into an icy tomb, and to the shores of Azurean Sand.

We walk quietly together, me right behind her, confident that I've done nothing to deserve punishment today, thinking of what I might do to please her when I get home.

Secrets…

"Are you telling me you walked to church in this weather?"

"Why not?"

"Mountain Girl," Valerie says disapprovingly. "You're crazy."

Mother doesn't answer. Their coffee is strong in the air. I am glad they didn't leave me here alone today. My door is open, so that my room will not freeze me. But I am careful to stay out of sight. Mother told me to stay out of sight when Aunt Valerie comes over. I saw Mother's eyes light up like stars when Valerie's car pulled beside the frozen yard.

"They're talking about layoffs again," says Valerie.

"Who said?"

"Diane called me last night. She heard 'em talkin' about it yesterday. I was there too but I didn't hear anything."

"Who'd she hear it from?"

"Tammy."

"Oh."

"I don't think you need to worry about it," Valerie says. "And you know you can't believe half of what Diane says, anyway.

"But she heard it from Tammy," says Mother.

"Well I tried to warn you. I told you to get on full time with me, didn't I?"

"I'm too lazy to work full time now. I couldn't give up the days off after all these years."

"You don't like it much anyway, do you Babe," says Valerie, her voice softening.

"I'm not sure."

"Gettin' tired of me already?"

I hear Mother laugh such a perfect laugh. A sweet, docile, accommodating giggle, powerfully submissive. Begging. Reassuring.

"We should go somewhere," says Valerie, brilliantly nonchalant. "Just you, me and Elizabeth."

"Where?"

"Maybe we could take a long drive this summer."

"You don't mean to New York, do you?"

"I mean just the opposite. Somewhere out west. Yellowstone or the Grand Canyon."

"I've always wanted to see the Grand Canyon."

"Careful," says Valerie. "You're gonna make me think you actually want to go somewhere."

"Well, maybe I do."

Mother, what lies do you tell? The ditch is your Grand Canyon, country girl! You are isolated in this curse with me! You are a vortex, spinning hopelessness into you, like a black hole of despair. You suck the life out of everything around you. Flee, Ms. Kirkland! Flee the Spider's Web, while you still have life, and strength left in your woman's blood!

"I still haven't figured you out yet," says Valerie. "You're religious alright, but I think there's something underneath."

I imagine the look they exchanged over their coffee cups could have lit up a darkened room. What sparks fly, that threaten to light this fire?

39

I have heard the rumblings of change. They talk often about their job, and the possibility of Mother's departure. I would like to ask Mother about it, but I dare not let her know I listen to them talk. Yes, I hear them whisper quietly. Their goodbye kiss is very loud. Valerie moans her goodbye kisses.

In this spring of my 13th year, melodies resound the Great Music Hall of my imagination. Winter's chill has lifted from the Earth, and the tree blossoms have fallen into the wind. The young leaves flutter in the warming breeze, dreaming of infinity, having no knowledge of their rapid life, nor of their colorful death in the Indian summer.

My craving to learn, my desire for knowledge is satisfied by the chords. The loneliness, the isolation is held at bay by the synesthesian visions of color and sound. Every noise in nature, every sound carries a tone inside it. A breeze, the clucking of the hens, footsteps, speech itself, all correspond to a particular key. A plate crashing on the floor is rich with chords.

It seems that more than ever, my mind is ablaze with *melody* and *harmony*, arranged and colored as I see fit. As always, from where these melodies appear I do not know, nor can I force them. But if it is one I like, I will begin to hum it softly, and commit it to memory. Often, Mother will touch me or call to me, and I will come to my senses disoriented, as if awakened from a vivid, powerful dream. I cannot relate how many times she has yanked my hair, or hit me on the head to get my attention, and the towering structures in my head have come crashing to earth, reassembling at a later time. In a fog of confusion, I will hear a woman's voice telling me that I'm too stupid to be in school anyway, asking me sharply if I'm "retarded or something." Maybe I am.

My retarded brain and me are in the spring field, receiving the message from Nowhere's Land. A message comes forth upon the high C, in the purest song for the violin to sing. I am amazed, here inside a golden hall, and I see a view above a lush green river valley, fed by a sparkling waterfall. Here inside the hall is an orchestra of players, expounding the melody to perfection. A full blown concerto for Violin and Orchestra in C major, colored with the sound of spring, tinted with harmonies of life and renewal.

I return from this vision in tears, remembering the brightest spark my feeble brain has yet produced. As I stumble across the field toward the house, I see Mother come out to take in the laundry. She didn't go to work today, and did not tell me why.

But I know why.

"I still can't believe it," says Mother. "I still can *not* believe it."

Valerie's presence here has never been so comforting. Their silence is heavy. Mother's vulnerability is epic.

"Eve, what are you gonna do? You don't want another factory job, do you?"

"I don't know."

"What about your landlord's offer?"

"I don't want to farm," she snaps. "That's why I left it behind to start with. I grew up with my fingers in the dirt."

"You know I'll give you what I can, don't you?" Valerie says.

"I can't ask you to do that."

"You can't ask me not to, either. Consider your rent paid until you find another job."

Mother sweetly allows her to think she needs her rent charity, knowing Ike Shirley wouldn't charge her a penny for a dime until she found work again.

"You've been too good, Valerie."

"No I haven't."

"You give me rides, take me out to dinner, and I've never paid for a single one. We go shopping, and you're always such good company.

Maybe I *was* lonely before I met you, I don't know. But I don't know how I'm going to thank you."

I hear the voices of sweetness, bathing the women in cream. Tempting their tongues with forbidden fruit. The blonde pretty, and the brunette beauty. Do I hear the smacking, the loud appreciation kiss? It lingers, it feels ripe with purpose. Let the softness of it wash over you, Valerie. Let her soft lips tempt your flesh.

"What would I do without you?" Mother says softly.

"You'd die without me."

Laughter. A part of me wants to open the door, and pretend to go into the bathroom. So I can see what it looks like, the intimacy between pretty woman. That's why you're best friends isn't it? You're attracted to each other, like hummingbirds to a red honeysuckle.

Your libido, Mother. Your sensuality. It calls to her—hypnotically. A woman who had never considered such a thing before. Valerie hasn't made it obvious yet, has she? How much longer will you tease her? Tormenting her with pretend ignorance? Take her into your arms, and make her beg, Mother. Dry her tears with your warm, tender kisses.

40

The fertile ground is dark, rich with possibility. Mr. Shirley has tilled the soil. This season brings the planting seeds. The vines will grow, yielding the juicy tomato and the wet, sweet watermelon. Your benefactor is in his private heaven now, even when Mrs. Shirley herself walks the grounds, to see what it is that her husband has done. She is matronly in her glasses, but very kind. Her mind cannot fathom such a thing as you. Your beauty blinds her to the truth, and you make her giddy. She is floored and swept away by the daughter she wishes her own had been. I am a grandbaby for her to coo over.

My imprisonment is easy to hide. Everyone thinks I am doing well in school. I don't see the outside of the house during school hours anymore. You hardly let me out of the room itself during the school hour. This is the late spring, the beginning of our new path. Our isolation is destined, so the word can be fulfilled in us. We will suffer, you and I, as accursed women. We are meant for suffering.

Valerie has no more use for the cloth factory. Without Mother, what need does she have for the Harvest Loom? She quit the job only a month after Mother was laid off, and quickly became a substitute teacher. The two of them are quite a pair. Laughing, whispering, coming in after dark with bags of new things. I think that happiness has crept its way into the both of them. They are at once like sisters, best friends, a connection formed in loneliness, kept hot by a molten river of desire.

Saturday is their time. Sometimes, she's here the whole day. She loves to walk with Mother among the tilled rows of the field. The field is plowed only halfway to the woods, so that beyond is still enough of the grassy plain for me to drift in. I can hardly wait until the little seedlings grow. Gladly, I will work in the garden, weeding the harmful roots from the fruited soil.

Fate shall weed this garden. That which grows amiss in Destiny's Field shall be cut off, and taken up by the roots.

"Mommaa! Momma help me, please!!"

My squealing voice carries through the house on the warm Sunday morning. I imagine that Mother sits bolt upright in the dawn, too startled to curse her accursed spawn, and hurries in country blue lace to my room. There I sit with my bloody white summer nightgown pulled up, gazing in terror at the blood covering my little white hands.

"Momma I'm bleedin' to death! I got a disease, Momma!"

Mother flings the covers from my feet, staring calmly at the rosy red stain on the sheet between my legs. Her response is to wrinkle her beautiful mouth, and breathe a deep sigh through her nose. But from where cometh compassion? It flows from the Raven's mouth! I know now that I shall not die. She tells me to go to the bathroom, and to accept the Curse of Womanhood with neither gladness, nor sorrow, nor fear.

I am in the bathroom in shock, obeying her voice, which tells me to stop whimpering and to run a tub of water. I feel the blood flowing down my thigh like warm water, and I cannot grasp the spirit of calm that has come over my mother. The bathtub is soon full, and when I am inside, the water quickly turns pink, as though it is has been colored with rose petals.

Bathe. Wash the blood from your white skin…

Accursed Woman.

"You'll never guess what happened today…" Mother whispers.

A screaming, gleeful laughter. Mocking.

"I'm *bleeeeedin'* to death, Momma. I got a *diseeeease,* Momma."

More laughter.

"Call her in here."

"I shouldn't."

"Call her in, Eve. Please?"

"Well, alright... Elizabeth!"

I heard you already. Valerie calls you Eve now. You wish to drag me out from hiding, so I can be ridiculed.

"Elizabeth, come out here!"

I don't want to. But fear opens the door, and drags my frightened, humiliated feet into the kitchen, where the Raven and the Maiden sit at the table with their Iced Tea, which I despise. There they sit, waiting for me. Valerie crosses her arms, then bites her thumbnail. Her eyes sparkle at me.

"You can come in honey," she says. We won't bite you."

Her eyes are bright with laughter. I glance at mother, who cannot look me in the eye while she hides her mouth with her hand. Valerie reaches behind my head, pulling me down, kissing my forehead.

"You're not my little girl anymore, are you?"

What is she talking about? And Mother still can't even look at me.

"I can already see the woman in you. Give me a hug, baby. If I don't hurry up and get a picture of you, it'll be too late."

Mother's eyes watch me, while Ms. Valerie hugs me tight. Eyes of repressed, jealous rage.

"You'll grow into a beautiful young woman someday."

Someday.

41

*T*he heat of summer looms over our country paradise again. Southern breezes blow over the dusty roads, whirling dust devils into the air.

It hardly even bothers me that I am not in school. Its only been one year, but it seems like a lifetime ago. I take a quick break from my sweeping chores, sitting down at the kitchen table. The blue scarf over my black hair matches my dress, which is the color of a tropical ocean, with the tiniest white flowers all about. I can see my toes in my brown sandals, another present from my Aunt Valerie.

My radio sings with two voices, one violin and one piano. Lyricism is dull without melody. I have to focus on the play between the violin and my instrument. My mind has never given me this combination. I wonder when it will happen? The clock radio sits on the kitchen table, lulled to sleep, perceiving the composer's struggle, and concluding that his efforts have been in vain.

The world laments for the death of melody. Even in these tender years, even with my little listening repertoire, I know that melody is a dying art. The modern strivings, the atonal clunkings are dead to me.

Melody is the air I breathe. My youthful desperation. I have searched the radio wilderness, the length and breadth of it, for the full bloom of Mozart in another composer. True Mozartian flair, filtered through other forms. Other styles. Mendelssohn's magic made me wonder, for a while. I have wondered too about Schubert. Chopin…

And Beethoven.

But I can hear his eternal struggle, screaming from every phrase. There is labour in his inspiration, disguised by an Olympian genius for theory. They all aspire to Mozart's flair—a necromantic skill for conjuring melodies from the air. Music bristling with life, as if *found*, not composed. Precious few compositions are born this way. Beneath the Music Sea, is an ocean of manufactured scribblings of intelligent music making. From Bach to Offenbach, an infinity of bankbook and notebook inspired talent.

Where is the Crown Prince's genius? Structure and form, be cursed! Imagination is better than knowledge! Melodies of extreme inspiration… ingenious bursts of great beauty and power!

The sleepy sonata ends after a brief eternity. What? The composer is famous! I cannot believe it. No spark… no inspiration…

The cheerful radio man prattles on about this or that. Things which seem a million miles away. And now, silence…

An explosion of harmony, bursting forth like lightning! The opening chords of inspiration, exploding from the little speaker. I stare alertly, with understanding, listening to Divine Madness spring from the radio.

I've never heard this music. The color of it shivers my body. A Cerulean Symphony—breathed from Meditteranean shores, flowing from the speakers like *water* before my eyes. I can see it, but I am too afraid to touch it. Is it Mozart? Then why haven't I heard it before? Spontaneity. Purity. Undiluted joy breathes from the sounds I see…

…*"one of the most famous overtures of all time, from the opera The Barber of Seville, music by Gioachino Rossini, a legendary performance by…"*

Dear Mozart! You did not die! Your spirit flowed from your body in death, drifting to and fro, coming to rest upon this Italian! A new *Prince of Melody*, writing with the divine spark. It has struck a fire in me.

The daytime shadows are less fearful now. I finish my sweeping chores, then put the broom away, in the corner by the kitchen door. What does it feel like, when the broom is struck against my body? I think I just had a flash of premonition about the broom.

The skies are crystal splendor today. I gaze upward, while hope drifts in on this summer wind. Harmony will write these symphonies for me. Six little opera symphonies, *overtures,* for string orchestra, flown from the Meditteranean Shore.

Melodies call from a distant place
Harmonies from beyond the sea
Phrases of such sublime beauty
As never before were wrought before me

Voices of instruments
Colors of wood and string
Brass tones
Winds of purest velvet

Ingenuity breathed from Jublilee
Old voices of originality
Lifting my soul aloft...

Drifting on clouds of every season

42

The twilight has come and gone. Night has fallen.

You did not have enough strength in your body to eat the supper they prepared you. You lie shivering on the barn floor, breathing the scent of the cold, wishing that you had died tonight. You remember her compassionate voice in your ears after the whipping...

"This too, shall pass. He chastiseth them that he loves. You are an accursed woman, Barbara Jean. You must take up your cross, and endure the life of suffering he has prepared for you. You will not be rewarded in this life. But you will learn to rejoice in your suffering. We will pray for you in church tonight..."

Those words. Those last three words, echoing through your exhausted mind. Your gray eyes twitch with life. They are going to church. You will be left alone.

They have locked you in the barn again. But tonight, you gaze longingly toward the large window, crisscrossed with tiny panes of glass and wood. You see the rays of the full moon, floating towards you.

There is an axe in the barn.

Fate has mercy on your bleeding soul, when you hear the truck driving away. But you wait breathlessly, making sure they have gone. Do they care if you die tonight? You know they will be gone for many hours. They will lose themselves in the frenzy of worship. They will spill their sin onto the wooden church floor, where it will ignite, burning with a dark flame.

I can see you, Mother. Your black hair glistens, long and unkempt. Your gray eyes are full of pain. You are broken. You are beautiful.

The axe. Claw your way to the axe. It feels heavy in your hands. The walk back towards the big window is long. Swing the axe, mother. Swing with the wrath of fury.

The glass shatters loudly. The wood splits. You continue, until you have broken a jagged hole in the glass and wood. You climb over the equipment shelf, and you fall out of the window into the cold, mountain air. Falling, tumbling through space, until you hit the icy ground. Awakened. Have you died? You have not.

Your strength returns just enough. You can sense the impending freedom. The trees are a black mountain silhouette.

There is the house.

Your baby is in the house…

43

*L*ittle Ms. Teacher! You look at me, raving so much that Mother's disgust is palpable when I walk in the room. Why do you sit up so quickly on the couch, buttoning your blouse when I open my door? I pretend not to notice as I creep across the floor to the bathroom. But I see it. You were in Mother's arms. You jumped like you had been stuck with a hot needle.

What are you doing with my mother?

Where is your daughter?

But Mother is better for your being nearby. Perhaps I am too. Our days are nearly happy, even though I am still a prisoner. You know about me being out of school, don't you? But these country days are too pristine. You can never challenge Mother about it.

Eve.

"I don't want to pry, Eve but...well, I went over to Edwards today."

Fear...

"They said she didn't enroll the entire year."

Silence.

"Its not permanent, is it?"

"I don't know," says Mother. Pitifully.

"Well, can you tell me why, Babe?"

I imagine Mother, pink lips tucked in, being unable look Aunt Valerie in the eye.

"Of course," said Valerie, "its really none of my business."

"Its only temporary," Mother said. "I just needed to get my mind--"

"Eve, Elizabeth is *your* daughter. And she's not the only farm girl around here who's not in the classroom."

"Are you going to tell anyone, Valerie?"

"What do you think?"

"I don't know."

"Best friends don't betray each other. I'd die before I'd do something like that. But you do want her to have an education, don't you?"

"I suppose so."

"Trust me, she's gonna need it more than you can imagine. Even you made it to high school."

"Did me a lot of good, didn't it?" Mother says.

"But at least you had the opportunity. I'm not challenging you, Eve. But I'm here to *help* you now. And I do know that Elizabeth should be in school."

A pause...

"We'll do it together, Babe."

This storm has passed, and thoughts of school have faded into brief history. Today, they're concerned only with dinner, cooking on the barbecue grill. The smell of the charcoal calls one to leisure, and expectations of a tasty meal. I am in the small watermelon patch, fascinated by the ripening melons, which seem to appear out of nowhere. They are vegetables, disguised as Fruit for the Gods. When I look toward the house, I see the wind ruffle your dress while you and mother are at the grill. Your blonde hair flutters in the breeze while you watch her tend to dinner. You wear dresses more often now, like Mother. Your golden hair is longer.

But winter is coming, Ms. Kirkland. You do not belong in this Garden-- where pain is planted, and despair grows unabated. When the wheat is taken, the chaff must be cast out. Joy cannot be harvested in this field.

I hear the voice of doom, speaking a riddle of discontent. This, when summer's leaves have turned to color, after they die and drift to Earth. In the Holiday season, I hear doom's voice, telling that your daughter does not want to see you again, and that it is because you were unfaithful when you were married. Is that true? You say your ex-husband lies to your daughter, poisoning her against you. We can give you no comfort. Barbara Coletti and her daughter have reminded you of what you cannot have.

In the Tears of December, you hold on to my mother for dear life, whispering, crying. A mournful wail, a woman's sorrow. And voices breathe your destruction, our devastation, as you say to Mother…

"I need to be by myself for a while, okay, Babe? I'll be alright. I'll come back sometime before Christmas. We'll spend the whole Holiday together. I love you, Eve. Tell Elizabeth that I love her."

Peace descends to you, sometime near this Christmas season, this season of my fourteenth year. The newspaper claims that a local schoolteacher is found dead in her home on December 22nd. Mother cannot believe it. She cannot accept it. But there is the name. The name of her only friend.

Don't cry for the women you left behind, Ms. Valerie! Do not weep for the Daughters of Misery.

Rest, Valerie Kirkland.

BEAUTY

44

*W*e are alone.

For two years, we have drifted alone, lonely in our own Field of Dreams, as so many others have and often do. Mother's face has turned to sorrow, but no less beautiful, as we brave every planting season. Watering and fertilizing our garden, watching the tomato buds appear small and green. They grow large and bitter, dreadfully sour when unripe. Impatiently, I watch the green fruit phase into orange, turning bright red in their harvest season.

Much of what I had that resembled hope, seems to have been buried under the years. I still look to the sky often, beyond my place and time, knowing that this grieving land is an impermanent place. I still hear the melodies call, they protect my sanity from harm, even as my body and spirit lies broken and bleeding under the lash.

Hitting. Pinching. Twisted wrists and arms. Hairpulling...

I am a country girl. Surely tough enough to endure the incessant strappings, and the beatings with the punishment stick. I can do nothing right. I feel as though I can do nothing right. She tells me that I'm so stupid, it's a wonder I don't forget to breathe.

If I bump into her, she hits me. If she finds an egg that I did not gather, she whips me. If she calls my name, and I am in one of my musical trances, she whips me. She rarely speaks to me anymore. She buys and reads untold dozens of romantic novels, and she is engrossed by her soap operas every day. Her face carries a perpetual frown, and there are no kind words for me, except at the Christmas season. The kindness, the pleasantness in her public demeanor is growing colder, and she has few smiles for the church onlookers, and fewer words of friendliness.

When she goes shopping, she will tell me to go to my room, and to not come out until she gets home. I learned that this is what she meant, when she came home in the taxi cab the first time, back when I was fourteen. Like a fool, I ran happily from the back of the house to the cab, as if it were my beloved father back from the grave. When the groceries were in the house, mother calmly asked me...

"What did I tell you when I left?"

I stuttered, stammering my way to a non answer about the chickens. Mother went outside to the shed, where she gathered the axe. With it, she chopped the broom handle to a satisfactory length, and she beat me until I couldn't breathe. The punishment stick crushed my bones to powder, smashing my muscles to a mass of bloody flesh under battered skin. The bruises covered my body, from my shoulders to my ankles. The stick was raised in the calm of controlled fury, and lowered in the heat of unfathomable rage. I squealed in disbelief, as much I screamed in pure pain.

I am afraid. Each day, I live in fear of the Raven. Her beak, her blackened claws seek to devour me, cutting my skin to streaming blood.

What is abuse? It is only the life I have been bequeathed. The life that I own. It is mine to live with, and to learn with.

I have felt the approaching hurricane. Within it churns pain I have not yet known, blood and bruises I have not yet seen. Perversions I have not yet imagined. In my mother's eyes, in her expression spins the whirlwind, the vortex of lust and violence.

These are the warmest days of my sixteenth year. I stand in our backyard, which overlooks our tomato and watermelon field. Each article of clothing, each dress, each piece of linen is my pleasure to hang across the line. A southern breeze whispers to me, blowing my dress firm to my body, swirling my long, black hair up behind me. I watch the white linen blow up into the new summer wind, waving its life of perpetual surrender to the birds of the air. The clouds are fluffy and white in my Azure Sea, above the green forest leaf canopy.

I feel the woman in my blood, moaning, speaking softly to me. I am no longer a child. My bosom is heavy from its inheritance, above a waist very small and curved. My hips are wide and rounded, shapely beyond the

Reason of Man. In this breeze, upon this Song of Summer I am lifted, drifting to my days of joy, and my hour of peace.

But suddenly, I am pulled from the bosom of hope, when I feel the hard slap on my face, and hear *"stop your daydreamin' and get your fat-ugly behind in that house you stupid cow"*

Somewhere, underneath the calmness, is a cavern of sorrow. I feel it churning, burning deep in the core of my body. I chide my stupidity, wishing I had not closed my eyes, and breathed the breath of nature's beauty into my lungs. I did not see the Lust Witch, standing at the kitchen door, staring at the younger version of herself, the young woman who embodies the desire of men and women, who is told by some that she is a beautiful creature.

I did not hear the screen door flung open, followed by the heavy feet of jealousy, clumping across the porch, marching down the steps into the yard. I did not feel the ghost, the spirit of hopelessness come to me with a raised, open hand, to smack me hard across the face and make me stumble backward, causing me to look at her with pain and bewildered fire. As I stumble into the house, somewhere from beneath the sorrow comes resentment, the fires of which are quickly put out, when I look back at the only woman I have ever known, and I go over to her and hug her, telling her that I am sorry for daydreaming, and that I still love her just the same.

This habit I have developed, hoping it will calm her nerves. Sometimes, she will simply move my hand from her waist, and tell me to stop my "rubbing and purring" on her. I have gotten used to that—at least it is not an insult. But today, this hour, this minute of my sixteenth year comes with the words I prayed would not be spoken again...

"What'd I tell you about daydreamin'?

Stuttering...

"Answer me you sniddlin' little... I said what'd I tell you about daydreamin'?

Stammering...

"Too stupid to open your mouth and put two words together. What am I gon' do with you? *Answer* me before I stripe the blood out of you, I said what am I going do with you?"

"I...I d-don't kn-kn..."

Yes. I am that sniveling mouse. That pathetic, weak woman that other women despise. I coo and whisper like a dove, shivering words into the air like an ice phantom. I have never even ridden a bike. I know nothing of high school and days on the beach, and there are no well spoken, confident friends to comfort me, and teach me not to be afraid. None except the walls of my little bedroom, and the lines and black markings on the paper—rain fallen from that strange world of sound and color.

"You're too dumb to do anything except disobey me, aren't you? You answer me before I slap the spit out of your mouth. I said you're too dumb to do anything but disobey me!"

"Yes, M-Momma."

She gazes at my hair, around the edges of my face.

"What am I gonna do with you," she whispers. Rhetorically.

You are my daughter. My greatest desire is to love you...
But I cannot.

You are my deepest longing. Your existence has power, and I am afraid of you.

You are my daughter. My greatest desire is to love you...

But I cannot.

When you look at me, Mother, your heart is contempt.

Your greatest desire is to love me...

But you cannot.

What is the new look in her eyes? The new emotion? Sometimes, I see her look away when I glance at her.

But I can see behind the pleasant gaze—a flame burning low, kept alive by a new energy. I see the first signs of her deepest psychology, the most impossible part of our history. A bounty has grown, a harvest planted when Evelyn made her strip in the Dark of Isolation, and beat her with her bare hands, then pressed her body on top of her until she understood. Because of that Italian boy, Mother, remember? It happened because who did you think you were, to deserve the goodness of love, and the pleasures of happiness with a husband?

Sensual jealousy....

Morphing slowly. Threatening to change into...no.

It has already changed.

"How does it feel to be sixteen, girl?"

"Its fine."

Laughter.

"You better learn how to talk without whisperin' and stammerin.' Nobody likes a weak, sniveling little bitch Elizabeth. And those *betties* are gonna split your bra, you eat so much. Why are you eating again, anyway? If you keep it up you'll be as fat as hog. Maybe you'd have a chance if it wasn't for that face of yours... I really do feel sorry for you."

Her pity is genuine. As is her laughter.

I am ugly.

For hours after, I go back and forth from the mirror to nowhere, looking at my face, remembering every twisted part of it. My skin, my nose, my eyes, my lips, my cheeks, my chin, every part is now an individual piece of ugliness. But the concerto on the radio, a harmony from my beloved Mozart brings me a bit of comfort. I'm lucky, I suppose. It takes me to my great music hall, and I can see the violinist and the Orchestra in glorious sound.

It ends, and I am in my usual euphoria, my entrancement. The winds that closed the heavenly concerto still echo in my body. Then, among the wind harmony, a voice that does not belong. Eve's call. A gentle, echoing sound, having no anger, but laced with quiet malice.

She calls me to her room, and I see her putting one of her beloved paperback romances away. Aside from her little color TV, what else is there for a repressed recluse to do? What other diversions do we have but music, and the occasional book?

"What did I tell you about that radio?"

I can only stand there. Pleading silently.

"You think just because you're sixteen I won't give you what for, Elizabeth? Hmm? Stop starin' at me like a milk cow, I told you about that damned radio bein' too loud, didn't I?"

"Yes, Maam."

"I already dreamed this. I dreamed you were getting rebellious. You've been lazy and stupid your whole life, and now you're going to add stubbornness to it. I've told you a thousand times about that radio being too loud, haven't I?"

"Yes."

As I stare at the floor, I can feel her gaze. Frustration, born of perpetual resentment, which has grown into a mild, continuous anger.

"Get undressed."

"Maam?"

"I said, get undressed."

I may as well be in the middle of a parking lot at rush hour, fumbling nervously at my dress button. But I know better than to act as if its not going to happen. So I quickly undo the top buttons on my country thrift store dress, and let it fall to the floor.

I can hardly stand to imagine my body under my clothes, even in my underwear. I am certain that my face is bright red, while she sits at the edge of her bed, staring unashamedly at my over-developed breasts, stuffed in a plain white bra that was too small a year ago. Somewhere in my brain, I think I hear her tell me that I'm "not too dumb to eat, that's for sure," and that she will be glad to "burn the fat from my stubborn hips."

She snaps at me, telling me to pick my dress up from the floor, fold it neatly and place it on the dresser. Then without reservation, she tells me to lay across her lap. I have never been disciplined in my underwear. I think I am more afraid of the insults than I am of being spanked to bruises. I know the sadistic delight is there, I can feel it. But it does not appear on her face. Her expression is stern, and matter of fact.

Mother whacks me once, extremely hard. A single, deliberate, resounding blow, right in the middle of my white cotton undies. My fear instantly turns to shock, while her hand rests there, sliding off slowly, then whacking me hard once again. She orders me to relax my "fat backside," and then she takes a firm hold of my hair, hard enough to remind me of what *could* happen. I lay there, enduring the humiliation, braving the slow, hard slapping on my buttocks.

Am I a child, to be punished this way? Am I a dumb animal, with no feelings? Every blow shakes my insides. The blows are so slow and deliberate, that I wonder if it will continue. But it does, for the better part of a half hour, slowly up and down even the backs of my thighs. Sometimes, pinching my flesh firmly, continuing to spank me with enough force to keep fear on notice, and pain at her beckon call.

But I know she doesn't require my voice today. The voice of pain, she does not need. My head is sore from the hair pulling, and my skin is on fire from the blows, and yes, Mother, my sniffling is from the River of Tears, and the crying you have beaten slowly from inside of me.

45

*W*henever I leave the yard for church or town, it disturbs the fortress around me. Forces protecting my nerves are shattered. Today, while we gather our groceries from the taxi, and take them inside, Mother smiles pleasantly to the driver, and I am comfortable that all is well.

Mother returns to the living room to peer out of the curtain, as if the cab driver is lurking around, even though he is long gone. In the kitchen, I begin one of my favorite odysseys, the journey through each bag, which is a pleasure to me as I pull out each item in rediscovery, remembering where everything was in the store. I suppose for a reclusive country girl, it is sheer delight putting the groceries away. My mind always remembers exactly how many items we bought, and mother tolerates my ease at keeping track of the cost. I never seem to forget. Numbers play in my head like children. I pull the big, glass container with my favorite, sweet orange nectar, staring at it with rapt attention, when I feel a sudden sharp tug on my hair. Mother grabs my face with the other hand, slamming my head against the refrigerator. My precious orange juice is among the shattered glass, in a large puddle on the floor.

"You were teasin' 'im, weren't you?"

"Who, Momma?"

"Answer me!"

"I don't know who you're talkin' about, Momma!"

"That boy in the drug store who was starin' at those bloated tits of yours. You were lookin' at 'im weren't you?"

I cannot answer, because I don't know what she is talking about. Surely, she knows I didn't look. Surely, she knows.

"If you think you're gonna add bein' a slut to everything else that's wrong with you…"

"Momma I didn't look. I didn't M—"

My voice is suddenly muffled, from her hand over my mouth.

"Because I swear to God and Holy Jesus I'll hang you by your feet and whip you until the blood drips off your hair…"

"mm dn't lmm" Her hand slips away. "I didn't look. I swear I didn't. I don't even remember what he looks like. I didn't even see his face. You know I can't look people in the face. You know that."

"All I know is what I see. And I see you stickin' your chest out and fiddlin' with your hair everytime we pass a man or a boy, and they can't stop starin' at your whorish, ugly face."

"I fiddle with my hair because I get nervous when they come around. I can't help it. I'm scared to death of 'em Momma, I can't even look at 'em."

"You get nervous because you're full of lust, you slut."

If I move the "s" from "slut", two spaces forward in the word…

"I get nervous because I hear 'em laughin' at me. Boys laugh at me every time. Why do they always laugh at me?"

"They're laughin' at you 'cause you're ugly and you've got hair like a pile of weeds, that's why. They're laughin' because they would love to get their hands on an ugly big tittied somethin' like you. They'd have you raped and murdered before you could spell your name backwards."

H…T…E…raped…B…A…Z…murdered…

"I wasn't lookin' Momma. I swear it."

"Shut up and listen to me. You damned right you weren't. 'Cause if I thought for one second you were makin' eyes at somebody I'd gouge 'em right out of your fat face. Do you understand me?"

Yes, Momma. Yes. Momma. Please don't push your thumbs into my eyes, Momma.

"I'm gonna take a hot knife and gouge out your eyes right now, you rebellious little…"

"Momma, I didn't look! I didn't look at 'im!"

She succeeds again. My voice comes out in wailing.

Like a siren.

What is the truth about sin?

He who is preoccupied with sin is a prisoner of it. I suppose. But what child understands the source of their parents' wrath? Why is she so angry with me? Surely, she is not jealous of somebody like me. A farm thing. A country Carmen.

While I tend to our tomato garden, I remember the path we almost took. How our life's design nearly grew into something other than this lonely sculpture. Poor Aunt Valerie. I miss the affection between her and Mother. The comfort she brought to our aching spirit. Is it irony that she craved the very thing we have, and that craving caused her to look for peace in the Land of the Dead? And though we have what she once desired, it is pain for me, and suffering for Mother. How far into the abyss shall we go?

Ms. Ida! Where have you gone! The muse sings to me now. The F-A-C-E of melody brings me joy. But they are written in code. Which note does the infinity sign show! I think it would be impossible for even you to decipher. I would be too afraid to even whistle them to another. Sometimes I draw only the top, middle and bottom lines, and my notes are often incorrectly shaped, with odd spacing and curious markings. Only I can read them. My papers are gathered and hidden as I complete a piece, or even an inspired fragment, and I hide them in plastic, underneath the house below my bedroom floor. Someday, I might even bury them in a box, deep in the forest wood.

My back is sore. I am done in the garden. Gladly, I go inside, out of the hot sunlight. The kitchen fan is very cool on my skin. I blows my hair. On the kitchen table, I notice the packs of seed that have come in the mail. Immediately I take the red, white and pink rose seeds to my room, cradling them as if I have found a treasure.

Mother is a farm girl. She wouldn't mind if I had a rose garden, would she? If it were maybe on the far end of the field, away from the house? Or maybe a tiny rose bush, near the corner of the front porch? She is on the porch now, in her leisure chair. Surely, there is still room in her heart for a flower garden.

"I don't care what you do with those things, Elizabeth. They're gonna die on you anyway."

"I can plant flowers here in the yard?"

"I said I didn't care, didn't I? Go make some lemonade. I'm thirsty."

"Okay."

"And don't you take all day, either. Elizabeth, did you hear me?"

The taste of a lemon is shrill, like the unbridled voice of the *flautino;* the piccolo, which must be sweetened with skill and care, so it will sing like the nightingale at dawn over the Tuscan Wood.

I would like to sit on the porch with her, and talk about things. I want to ask her about Ms. Valerie. She hasn't mentioned her since she died. What does it do to a person, when the pain of grief goes undealt with for three years? Mother has no other friends to talk to. I'm sure she felt a whirl of every emotion when it happened, betrayal not being the least among them.

On the porch, I give her the lemonade, along with a firm kiss on the forehead. I have learned not to dwell on it with looks and waiting. I know how she feels about me. But today, I don't rush away. I am compelled to turn and gaze into the mid summer sky. The air is clear and light, but very warm without a breeze. Every part of the sky I can see is blue.

Does she sense my growing confidence as a young woman? A part of me is settled, resigned to inner strength. I think these fiery melodies have settled my nerves. They burn complacency inside me. There are even times when I refuse to give place to fear. Times when I choose not to follow my best judgment.

"How's your lemonade?"

The ice clinking her glass is the only answer I can expect.

I step down into the yard, looking at the tops of the new forest leaves. Soon I am at the edge of the porch, sitting down in front of her, my feet dangling just above the ground.

"Sometimes I think about about Ms. Valerie," I say. "Maybe we should go and visit her grave."

I turn to look at her.

"Do you ever think ab—"

My words are choked off in ice cold liquid. I cannot breathe or see. Revelation falls from my face, running down onto my dress.

"If you ever mention her name again—"

"I won't Momma. I won't."

"Get your behind in that house before I skin you alive…"

I run onto the porch like a pig running from a farmer's knife. Inside, I am confused, not knowing whether to go to the bathroom or the bedroom to hide. Why did I open my big mouth?

The screen door creaks open behind me, and instinct pushes me to the bathroom to dry myself. I suppose I will wash my hair tonight. The shampoo smells like strawberries. As I look at my wet face, eyes still burning from the lemonade, I hear her in the kitchen, pouring herself another glass. She marches back through the living room, and onto the porch.

I will never think of Valerie Kirkland again. Let the dead bury their dead. Let the ground have her lovely bones, if it may.

At the very least, Mother likes my lemonade.

46

*W*hy do these men persist? Why do they insist upon trying to get her attention? The women in this church are seething with something beyond jealousy. I suppose its unavoidable, because my mother's face and figure are something beyond extraordinary. Sometimes, when I look in the mirror, I see her in my features. Sometimes.

I languish in these last days of innocence, afraid to look people in the eye. Terrified to open my mouth and speak. I don't think a single week has passed in over a year, that I have not been whipped with my mother's belt. Her whipping belt, she calls it, one she bought specifically for me. Soft, flexible leather, just right for raising huge, blood specked welts, but not really cutting my skin. That privilege is reserved for the tree switch. The tree cane. I was in the store when she bought the belt. I wonder if they thought she was buying it for her husband?

How can such a woman not be married, the church people wonder. Is it the thing that follows her, clinging to her every step, bumping into her like a blind maiden? A dunce, mute, like some creature girl in a ghost tale? Does that thing hold her mother's womanhood captive, drawing the strength from her sexuality, requiring so much care and attention that her poor Momma has none left for any man?

No.

Her love for me is only instinctive, like a bitch to her one remaining puppy dog. She feeds it, she protects it, then forgets what it looks like when it is not around. I suspect that someday, her instinct will fade, and the scent of me will sicken her. I dread the coming of that day.

No.

It is not me, Mr. Hollis, that keeps her from smiling at you when you chase her down after church, asking can you drive her home. You must be new here, sir. You lack understanding. Can't you feel the arctic winds, Mister, freezing your skin? Her lust burns for a memory of the dead, her cravings are woven into perversions you cannot fathom. Your good-looking face and inviting smile have made you overconfident, but you can do nothing for this Ice Queen, who has buried her desire deep. It is frozen under years, untold layers of permanent frost. She would die before you, or any of the others, would cause it to even begin to melt. Her libido is contained, and channeled through her imagination into twisted fantasy, reading her romance books, watching her stories on TV, remembering her dead husband and best friend, while punishing the living dead with scourges and whippings.

Who are you, Mr. Hollis? You stare at her face, your gaze slips downward to her neck, and what is bound tightly underneath her dark gray dress. You cannot believe your eyes, can you? Are they really that massive? You cannot tell. Soon, you will be forced to find another outlet for your needs, lest desire consume your body into ashes.

Mother! He needs your body! He lies in bed at night, thinking about you. He wishes he were me, so he could see beyond the sky, into the heavens. Paradise, which would only be a glimpse of you in your bra, bent over, removing your black leg stocking. Visions of a country bosom, a mountainous cleavage will torment the poor man forever.

I am glad. I hope he suffers, thinking he is worthy to speak to you. To even look you in the eye.

Ike Shirley still carries your heart though, doesn't he? A part of you still owes him. But you don't smile at him as much as you used to. You compensate with hugs and firm kisses to his chubby cheeks. You two have settled into the father-daughter dynamic. I am his dream granddaughter.

Ike Shirley. He allows you to call him Isaac.

From the far end of the tomato garden, I see Isaac come smiling from around the house. His eyes light up when he sees us in the garden. I feel the gloom lift, and lightness comes over your face. You stand up like a happy farm momma, hands on your hips, bosoms stretching your button down blouse to near breaking, though you don't realize it. Why do you hug him so pleasantly, escorting him willingly down the rows to see the tomatoes, and yet if I ask you a simple question, I risk having my lips pinched, or my forehead slapped, or being scolded to within an inch of my life?

But I like him, too. I like him because of the way he makes you feel. He asks how I'm doing, and even stutters a fearful question about me and school. Gladly, you tell him that school wasn't for me, that I'm too simple for it. Even a little slow. Yes, my mind's alright, you tell him, but I'm too scared to open my mouth to anybody except you. That is the beauty of it. The whole truth. Truth is beauty.

I look at you two, walking the small field, picking at the vine leaves and ripening fruit. He can't comment about how big the tomatoes are, can he? Not with yours shoved right in his face. It would be too vulgar. But I know you are talking about more than the price of organic tomatoes and seedless watermelons. Do you speak of his aging wife, and how his children have disappointed him again about this or that?

Loneliness returns heavy when he leaves. There is only you and me left, and our little tomato farm. My mind often follows him into his big pickup truck, dark blue, but faded from the years. His heart is as devoid of life as the empty back roads. He drives onward in mild despair, drowning in the exhaustion from a lifetime of treadmill labour. A small time tobacco farmer, quite well off from the skilled use of land, and the careful management of money. He has struggled into a place of modest financial security, comfortable enough to not need this little house, and the small plot of land he once worked with his own two hands. Still eternally grateful that he never sold it away, though many have admired its isolation, its serenity, and have offered to buy it from him.

He does not understand the power. The force of nature driving his feeling for the widow and her daughter. Something as intense as love itself, though not intruding upon the wholesomeness of friendship. Thankfully, his longsuffering wife has been made aware of his need to care for us from afar, so that she feels no threat, and cannot interfere.

Genuine beauty is as rare as an earth jewel among rocks and sand. Mr. Shirley often remembers the day his jewel came, the day that the humble, friendly couple came to his home in the raggedy old truck. A woman and her farmer husband born to the dirt, from his blue denim shirt down to his brown boots. He remembers the day he learned the truth, when he looked into Michael Coletti's truck at his young wife. Sixteen years separates Isaac Shirley from that day, but he thinks of it often, as though it were sixteen days ago.

Is predestiny a force, a power that cannot be denied? He wonders why had he not sold the tiny farmland already, before the Coletti truck arrived. Why no one had wanted to rent the house without a buying option. It was as if this place were in waiting for the Woman and her husband. Mr. Shirley had felt the spark, when she gazed with those gray eyes, smiling that lovely, disarming smile.

He gladly took my father's money, giving him the key to this Paradise. Keeping his mind only on the young farmer and his drive to build the fragile empire. The Egg Kingdom. Isaac still remembers the fear in the widow's eyes, when he came to the house after the burial. The relief that flooded over Mother's face when he told her she could stay. And his heart still grieves from the minutes she spent in his arms, sobbing, thanking him, asking him why did God take her husband from her, even as the girl infant lay still and quiet in the other room.

Our landlord drives onward, in something close to fearfulness about us. He worries about the woman and her daughter, knowing that someday the tide will change, and that we cannot escape the Winds of Time.

47

*here is the phantom ghost. The spirit of that lovely young girl
tending the fields, who saw her mother walking casually towards her with
the punishment stick. You asked "what did I do Momma? Please tell me
what did I do?" You watch the spirit of the young girl in glowing winter
wisp, as she is beaten and broken before the mountain pines, without ever
being told exactly why.*

*When you get to the old white house, you break the little glass pane,
unlocking the back door, creeping into the blackness. The rooms, the
smells are as familiar as they were in the days of your departure. You
smell leather among the scent of cooked food. You can feel the oppressive*

spirits, those demons of lust and violence, and religious fanaticism. The ghost of your past is here. It is inside these walls, drifting helplessly in eternal pain, and infinite misery. You were born in sin here, and shapen in iniquity.

There. Your ghost is here, among the dust and old wood. This is a place of isolation. A house replete with loneliness.

There are only two places your baby can be. But instinctively, you know it is too unholy to be in their room. So you creep through the darkened house, towards the place where you slept through many nights of agony. The place where you learned to cope. Such a beautiful, statuesque young woman. Born to suffer.

There is your baby. Kicking and cooing in the dark, fully awake in the cold house, comforted by the unseen. A wave of fierce protectiveness floods your spirit, and you quickly pick it up, and for the first time, you are its mother.

You are my Mother.

Breezes kissed by winter's warning

Ghosts of what they once were

Children of nature's unkindness

Alive in their death season

Leaves—

Blowing over the grass

A wasteland of forgotten memories

Dancing in the autumn morning

Swirlings of brown and yellow,
Echoes of their life of green
Tossed in eternal sleep—on winds of uncaring cold
Seeking a new place to go

Somewhere, every leaf breathes with purpose—
Having direction—
Predestiny
Appearing as chance to them who do not see

Who cannot see the leaves when they gather
Moving with thought—
Walking, running in fear
Talking with fervor, having anger

In groups, contemplating their course,
Deciding to go another way
Leaves...
Blowing over the grass, the wasteland

Devoid of the life that cannot see
Filled with the afterlife of green
Hiding, jumping into autumn breezes...
Flying to where they wish to be

49

$\mathcal{A}$s Autumn drifts from the north region, I sit in our holy temple today, listening to the preacher drone beneath the voice of my mind's piano. Remembering that we are them who he warns about. Daughters of sin. Ghosts of suffering...

Whether or not the Spirit of Fear comes from above, I do not know. I only know that it is here, and is a part of me.

It plagues my mother as well, taking her peace of mind, binding her tighter to the gospels, and the need for church. It seems that some are the accursed fruit of their mother's tree, and the religious bondage that gripped her parents has reached out to her in part, making her afraid that her own private evil will rise up, and take her corrupted soul into Hell.

We do not engage the crowd of well wishers and true believers, nor the hypocrites and fanatics. After every service, we quickly slide into our long black coats, which are hardly as black as our hair, giving contrast to our fair skin. We walk out of the brick sanctuary into the cold autumn day, grateful that we carry our black umbrellas with our Bibles and purses. The clouds give little rain as we stroll the miles of country road. They are as gray as our bleak future.

We cross the yard in the same dreary silence as always. Comfortable with one another. I have grown accustomed to being afraid, and she has adjusted to her soul of bitterness. It has transformed her, removing the traces of the smile that once made her impossibly beautiful. Her dresses bear no pretense to fashion. Gone are the sheer stockings and pretty flowered cloth. No more skirts and blouses to reveal the shape she was given. Her legs are now hidden underneath jet black stockings, opaque all the way up to her thighs. Her dresses are every shade of gray, even the occasional black cloth, with only one navy blue, for the tiniest variety. Buttons adorn many of them, from the top all the way to the bottom, and I wonder how her fingers can endure the monumental task of undoing them all.

And what is that walking behind her? What does it attempt to be?

A young female. White faced, with large black eyes, wide open and alert, but filled with tragic naiveté. Arched eyebrows, raised in a permanent expression of wonder and lack of understanding. Shiny hair, jet black, draped down the length of her scarred back. Hair grown in the shadows of Pentecost, though she is fortunate enough to be a generation removed from it, enjoying the peacefulness of Baptist comfort every Sunday. A girl who has seen the passing of her eighteenth birthday, a farewell to days of youthful hope and childhood freedom of expectation. A heart filled with scripture and song, a mind ablaze with melody and harmony. A baroque woman, who causes whispers, stares and laughter wherever she goes, who can see nothing good upon herself, nor can she feel it in her soul.

She is nothing.

Deprived of tenderness and affection these 18 years. Having never felt the gentle touch, except when it is a prelude to the roughness of the belt, or the punishment stick, or the palm of a mother's brutal hand. She would like to tell her mother how she feels.

But she cannot.

Why can I not tell her how I feel?

She is my life force. The brightest star in my heaven. She is the very air in my lungs, the blood coursing through my veins. Though she takes the skin from my back, though she draws her portion of blood from me, she is the light of my very existence, my reason for being, my purpose for living in this life. I want to tell her. The desire to tell her burns a hole in me. A place I have filled with song and meditation. I cannot know the face of happiness. Joy has hidden its face from me.

Why can I not tell her how I feel?

Because her rejection would kill me where I stand…

And I am afraid to die.

I drift beyond this melancholy shore, upon the River of Sorrow, past the place where roses should have been. My mind draws upon its colorful repertoire, which are hundreds of melodies, among them being many of dreamlike inspiration. I hear my shoes clunk softly up the front steps and across the porch behind Mother, who holds the door open out of habit rather than courtesy. We go into the dark'ned house without words, and I can feel the pain inside her as she goes to her bedroom. I whisper no

lohIa

questions at her today. The house smells of the bacon breakfast I cooked for her so many hours ago. If she were hungry, she would tell me so.

My room is in the same place it was 18 years ago. The few dresses I wore as a child were taken from me, my denim and checkerboard poverty dresses. They were taken, even as I pleaded with her to let me keep them. She snatched them out of my clutching fingers and glowered at me, until I knew not to challenge her. I saw her take them in a trash bag to the curb at the end of the road. Why didn't I sneak out that night, and rescue the souvenirs of my time? The essence of who I was, hauled away as garbage.

I try not to think of this as I remove my coat, and hang it up in the closet. Mother allows me the pleasure of one pretty sky blue dress, which I wear to church every so often, but not today. Today, I am comfortable in my charcoal dress and black leg stockings, like her. But I have to change, because if I don't she will give me a whipping. Quickly, I remove the dress from my figure, which has grown and curved the way of its predecessor. I am used to my heavy bosoms, and the flesh on my hips arouses no curiosity in me. I cover my large chest in my dark green cotton blouse, which is the color of grass after sunset. My long, pleated peasant skirt drapes over my hips, covering the shapely sinfulness from my eyes, and my skin from the touch of my corrupted hands.

I will be glad to rest in my comfortable chair, letting these cold hours drift away. In my mind's reserve are untold scores of compositions, great and small. But I have not written down a note for many days, as I await the arrival of the colossus. Among my newest melodies are pieces of increasing sadness and lyricism, the continued chipping away at the edges of formal structure; classical beauty, touched with modern romanticism, orchestrated heavily, though still transparent in texture. I think that perhaps today, the first period of my composing has ended, blown away by this wind of change. A mature work---for piano and orchestra in a higher key, a melody of Olympian Beauty, colored by the sorrow I feel in my mind and body. My creative energy is stored, having wasted none on trifling scratches for solo or chamber. I have been too easily persuaded by my mind's inspirations. Too accepting of ideas as they come to me, not allowing them to rest, and fully develop. I feel that today, I can begin writing the parts of this concerto.

The allegro is restless—anxious but reassuring, bristling with controlled energy. The andante is heavy with double basses, slow and dreamy, rich with more wind color than I have ever seen in my own writing. And the finale is quieter than the opening, with less pretense towards happiness, marked by a solo flute among the orchestra, the haunting, but playful voice of my little Bird in the Tuscan Woods. All of this is shaded with a distant Longing—a profound, indefinable sadness—and the memory of a lonely child I once knew.

I know what churns beneath civility.

She does her best to hold the pretense—that the massages, the lengthy hair washings and hair brushings, dress unbuttonings and bra unlatchings are simply these, and nothing more. But I think, I feel, that this façade will soon wither of its own volition, and fall expediently away. Depression and bitterness have both taken root, and she has long ago ceased to treat me with any real courtesy. So when I hear her call me in this evening, in the dusk of this bygone Sunday, though her voice is laced with kindness and beauty, I think that I may be as unnerved as ever.

As I step timidly into her bedroom, I see her standing in front of the mirror, wearing only her plain white bra and underwear. My mother's body is as curved as an hourglass. Her breasts are as big as the melons we grow, and the flesh spills over the top of her tight bra. I don't know whether to glance away or look directly at her, and I'm sure that in my characteristic way, I appear as awkward as ever. She meets my nervous gaze with hers, those piercing winter eyes, those bewitching eyes, which can slice fear through me like a sharp blade. But she speaks gently, assuring me that I have done nothing to warrant the tree switch, or the punishment stick. I have been beaten more times in my life than I can remember.

"It's my shoulder," she says. "I need you to help me. *Close the door.*"

Has any woman ever really needed help removing her bra? But I obey her quickly, keeping my cynical thoughts out of my expression. I approach the beautiful woman behind closed doors, but she tells me not to remove it just yet, but to take a moment, to massage her sore shoulder.

I can feel the strength in her body, as I gently rub her upper arms, her shoulders and her neck. Her skin is very fair, almost pale, and except for the raised scars on parts of her back, is otherwise smooth and unblemished. These are the scars that heal, which betray the presence of those that do not, the ones that lay bare the soul and spirit. One cannot know the form of darkness, until it has descended. I do not know why, but I think her pain has begun to erode the fortress she has spent a lifetime building around her emotions—her mind's protection against whatever storm rages beneath her prim, proper exterior.

I am saddened by the mere thought of the Faith that I love, which watches over me, but which will allow these sepulchral spirits, these caliginous beings, to invade our lives. How long shall I be haunted by them? Ghosts of what is unspeakable? As I continue to rub her shoulders, I listen to the first sounds of madness, this new melody, flowing from the deepest sighs and moans, which seem to come from the depths of her very soul.

"*Unhook my bra.*"

The white strap is very wide and strong, pulled tight by the weight of its burden. I undo each clasp, but not too quickly, knowing I am not supposed to make haste. Why do I know this? I can feel it, even as I slide the straps from her shoulders for her. What pleasure does this create inside her? I have never seen her unclothed bosom, and I am curious. But she puts her hand across the front of her bra in false modesty, and tells me to return to my room.

I don't know if she felt guilt, embarrassment or satisfaction as I left her room. But I obeyed without the slightest requirement of explanation, as I am well trained to do, and I am quietly back in my music room, at my little radio. Content, at least, that she has found a way to draw pleasure from me without whipping me.

For the rest of this day, and for many days, I drift in a fog of new apprehension, worried that I might speak the wrong word, or cast the wrong glance. But maybe, I shouldn't worry, because her demeanor is as nonchalant as ever, even without shame, and I dare say that her behavior is suddenly more agreeable. These massages, the unlatchings, have become standard, a private part of who we are, signaled by the rising and falling cry of "*Liz-beth...*"

But whatever new pleasantness this may have born has now died, and there is no longer a voice of gentility. Hostility rules her voice once again, except in the twilight, when she calls me to soothe her pain. Deviance is the end result of painful resistance, and one must yield, or learn to endure the suffering. I think that when we go to church, she is ashamed that she can no longer fight the evil tormenting her, imagining that every mind in the building dwells upon what she does in private. But I feel no humiliation. I am not a part of this holy collective, sitting in judgment of one another. Of this alone, I am unguilty.

But as the weeks pass, I can see her quiet bashfulness fading, and these new habits have become as much a part of her as anything has ever been. And sometimes, her demeanor when I rub her back and shoulders is quite boisterous and breathy, and unequivocally unreserved. Our sessions have moved to the bed, and I straddle her across her hips, giving firm and gentle therapy to the aching muscles of her mind and spirit.

51

We make it to the highway in the winter dark. But you are so weak. You can hardly walk anymore. You collapse into a darkened heap on the side of the road. You want to get up, but you cannot. Now, you must go to sleep. Your baby is asleep, protected from this torment by a profound, unnatural slumber.

And now, you sleep.

A compassionate driver sees the widow on the side of the road. The driver and his wife are glad to take the baby from your arms, and place your lifeless body into their car. Soon, you will wake up in the hospital. The doctors won't know who you are. There will be no one to call.

The doctors and nurses see that your skin has been whipped from your back. They see the lashes across your buttocks and down your legs to your ankles. You are malnourished. They ask you who did this, but you do not tell them. You will never tell. You are the Widow Coletti from down south, and you need to get to the bus station, so that you can go back home. Even the social worker can get nothing from you. You have committed no crime. You will not name your violators. They cannot force you to speak of it.

The days there are restful. But they cannot hold you. They release you and your healthy little baby. The two of you are taken to the bus station. Your ticket is a blessed thing.

When the Virginia farming country disappears for the last time, there is no crying for lost love, because your Momma had never given you any. Your Poppa was a servant of her evil.

Your scars run deep, Mother. The truth will cut deep, and leave scars.

You have a baby to tend.

52

*M*other enjoys preparing the Thanksgiving Feast herself. A turkey, dripping with flavor, along with dressing for a king's table, a taste exquisite enough to defy description. One spark of a positive thing, passed through my Mother's ancestry.

Thanksgiving.

"Elizabeth...*Elizabeth!*"

Oh, no.

O-my-god I had forgotten about the—

"Elizabeth Coletti, get in here!"

Quickly, I abandon my scriptures, my comfort, shuffling into the kitchen, wondering how it is possible that I could be so absent minded.

"Where are the eggs?"

"I…"

"I said where are the rest of these eggs! There should be a half dozen eggs in here!"

"I…"

"Answer me!"

"I broke 'em."

"You… why didn't you tell me when I went to the store yesterday there was only one egg in this carton. How am I supposed to cook stuffing with one egg?"

"Did you check the henhouse?"

"Didn't you check the henhouse this morning, stupid?"

"Yes."

"Then you know they didn't lay any today. You broke almost a half dozen eggs yesterday, didn't you. Didn't you?"

"Yes, Maam."

"Why didn't you tell me we needed eggs Elizabeth?"

Her pale face turns rosy pink with genuine rage, and suddenly I see a flash of light, as she smashes the egg onto the middle of my forehead. The thick slime is cold on my face. I can only open one eye. It hurts my whole head.

I think that fear makes me stupid. It makes me forget things.

Why did the chickens betray me?

"Why didn't you *tell* me?"

"I was going to but I forgot."

"You don't have the brains that God gave a plow mule, Elizabeth. How am I supposed to COOK!"

Mother shoves me hard in the face, and storms angrily to her room, yelling something about having to call a cab and go into town. She can't understand that one egg would have been fine just this once. Rage clouds a person's judgment, I think. It makes them think illogically. The stuffing will do fine with one egg.

"Wipe that stupid look off your face and go clean that *shit* off your head!"

A profane!

In all the years, a profanity! This is new, Mother. The uneasy stability we had has been shaken. Your great and powerful righteousness, that tree of holiness has fallen! I hear the bare footsteps of undiluted fury, storming towards the bathroom where I stand, wiping the egg off my face. She yanks me out like an empty hatbox, and pushes me hard back towards the kitchen.

"I didn't mean to break 'em Momma!" (it comes out "*I din meando breag em, mobba!*")

"Shut up! Shut the f…"

She draws a deep breath.

"Bring me that tree switch."

"But Momma, I…"

She grabs my hair with both hands, gritting her teeth, shaking my head while pushing me into the kitchen. Already, my voice has started the loud whining. The kitchen smells of Thanksgiving turkey.

"Raise up the back of your skirt."

"Huh?"

"I said pull up your skirt or I'll tear your clothes off and cut your skin to pieces!"

I slide the pleated skirt-thing up to my waist, my 1910 style peasant cloth, revealing to her two healthy fair-skinned thighs and white underpants, with a set of the widest hips this side of Creation, made for childbearing to be sure. Without another word, she lifts the tree switch from its corner by the doorway, and takes me by the front of my hair. In the next instant, the hot sting from the tree cane cuts into the back of my legs. They buckle forward, but she holds me upright by the hair. Through screams, I beg her, but knowing not to move again.

"I didn't mean to break 'em, Momma…"

"Shut up and stand still…stand up straight or I'll lock you in that bedroom until after Christmas!"

The pain slices into me again. I wonder how many people know the pain of being cut with a branch from a tree? A switch, it is called. It cuts my skin to blood, as I hold onto my skirt for dear life. The lotion on her hand smells of flowers as she covers my mouth and stings the daylights out of me. Her hand is the barrier for my voice; it gives me permission to scream as hard as I can while the tears wet my face.

I am a young woman, Mother. I am a woman, at the end of my eighteenth year. I give thanks, at the door of my nineteenth.

I feel a tug, a hard yank on my hair, pulling and then pushing me hollering out of the kitchen, a pitiful fool. The pain makes me cough. It hurts so badly that I don't even remember to lower my skirt. There I am, the kitten, crying again from the witch cat's cane. I hurry into my room and close the door, nearly slamming it, angry, hurt and afraid. Letting it all out through my voice as I am accustomed. I am a deep, loud screamer. Sometimes, I think the screams are what she craves.

But not today.

Laying across the bed, I cry loudly into my pillow, my scarred legs still partly exposed. I am an adult now, aren't I? Can't I just run away? Only a minute before, I was resting comfortably in a state of thanksgiving, reading my scriptures. My 37th Psalm. Its words are forever burned into my memory.

I scream one last, loud voice of frustration into the pillow. But I am not a brat. My voice is quiet now.

What is she doing to me? What is happening?

The birchwood sting is burrowing into my legs like fire worms. From my burning legs, it goes inward, infecting my anger with something more.

Something.

53

My spirit bears both Love and Sorrow
Misery grieves a heart with pain
Haunted flesh endures a distant longing
Indefinable sadness burdens a weary soul

From whence shall thy salvation breathe?
Upon what wind drifts the Day of Peace?
Fate hath shackled me to a mountain
Long months hath drifted into waiting years

This flame consumes me night and day
Ambitions spring forth as a fountain
Through inadequacy I push forward in fear
Crumbling underneath desire

No confirmation falls from above
Through a wilderness I travel alone
Only Heaven's Light guides me in darkness
Shining in this Promised Land

54

What are you afraid of?

Is it Death? Is it Hell? Have you to taken to heart the religious cloak, while draping it over yourself? Is your soul really among the converted, or do you sleep in Hypocrisy's Tomb? A sepulchre of corruption; loving the Divine, but still unable to end your perversion? Has it built up inside you, threatening to devastate your façade? And what of your sanity—how much of it still remains? Since the Thanksgiving Autumn, and through the winter's passing, I have watched your descent into asperity, and have felt fear and distemper take root inside you.

215

The temple is still your place to hide. To hide from the devils that torture you. But this place is not our salvation, nor our deliverance.

I think that it will be the death of me.

Our new pastor is very friendly and handsome, is he not?

And what of his wife?

Mrs. Davis mistreats us with her eyes. Ire gazes at us from underneath yellow blonded hair and thick makeup. A city woman, blown on southern winds from her Northern throne—to be the big lady fish in the little country pond. But when she looks at the woman in black, who sits in back of the church with her grown daughter, jealously bores into her like a parasite. For months now, she has been quietly civil, even as new whispers have begun to fly, that Barbara Jean Coletti and her daughter practice *witchcraft*.

Compassion had touched Mrs. Askew's heart, and she was nice enough to tell Mother this foolishness a month ago, so that we could brave the icy looks. I saw the fear and hurt in Mother's eyes when she heard it. Even our beloved church, our sanctuary, is not the refuge it used to be.

"Ms. Coletti, may I see you in my office?"

"Well, I really do have to be going."

"It'll only take a moment, and it is rather important."

"Well, alright…"

Although her smiles have long since departed, Mother's public demeanor remains absolutely demure. Her humbleness and courtesy are in full bloom as we are escorted through the after church crowd, through the mysterious door to the unseen back way, down the hall, and into the small office near the pastor's study.

"I'd like to speak to you alone, if I could."

I am not smart enough, or brave enough to take the hint. Mother has to tell me to wait outside, and I stand out in the hall, watching Mrs. Davis glare at me without subtlety while she closes the door.

"You've been a member here for a long time," she says. "One of the longest memberships here, I see."

Superiority churns in her voice. Her irritation is evident.

"Where is your husband?"

"My husband passed before my daughter was born."

"I see. Are you Italian?"

"My husband was. Um…what did you want to see me about?"

Mother's voice is sweet. Gentle.

"May I speak frankly, Mrs. Coletti?"

"Yes, Maam."

"I've been watching you from the beginning…"

Mrs. Davis' voice takes on a sudden harshness. I imagine that Mother is as shocked as I am.

"…I've watched you since the day I first laid eyes on you. You seem to have some kind of a power over these men."

"I…Mrs. Davis I can assure you that—"

"That what, Mrs. Coletti? That when my husband touches me like an animal every Sunday evening its not you he's thinking about?"

"Mrs. Davis…"

"I'm speaking, Mrs. Coletti."

Mother's tone is one of quiet amazement. Months of pent up anger threaten to tremble Mrs. Davis' voice.

"You don't speak. You hardly make eye contact with anyone. And if you'll pardon me for saying so, you both dress like you're in mourning. Some of the wives think you've got spells over half the husbands in this church. The way they parade back and forth to that bathroom every Sunday is shameful. They do it so they can get a good look at you. Even my own *son.*"

"I...I only have feelings for my late husband. Mrs. Davis, if I have done anything to attract anyone, I swear to you it was unintentional. I know they look at me, but I would rather die than disrespect myself, or my husband's memory."

An epic pause...

"My daughter and I love this church. We've always enjoyed being here, especially since you and Pastor Davis took over. We would consider it an honor, if we could be allowed to stay."

I don't hear anything. Has the honey worked its magic? Why won't they speak?

"If I have done anything, *anything* at all to displease you, Mrs. Davis, I ask for your forgiveness."

Mother's voice trembles now under the weight of lies. Of idols, and unspoken human nature.

"Perh...perhaps my concerns were misplaced. You and your daughter are...there's nothing to forgive, Mrs. Coletti."

The office window is hazy. I can't look inside to see if what I imagine is true. That Mother's power has ignited a flame in the pastor's wife. A raging, roiling sea of feelings she cannot even understand. I imagine that mother hugs her tight, pressing her body full against her, whispering warm thank you's deep into the Davis mind, so that her spirit will torment her from here until the end of time.

"Good day, Mrs. Coletti. Elizabeth. I'll see you next Sunday."

Mother walks before me, leading me away from this dungeon. An Enchantress, working magic in our southern world. I can feel the smirk, the satisfaction, knowing that she has tuned this poor woman like a Stradivarius, and played her like a string on Easter Morning... smooth, and with feeling.

I think that now, Mrs. Davis is afraid.

Like me.

"*C*an wisdom be found in the carcass of a white horse?"

When she asks me that, my body freezes in the summer sun. Incredibly, her expression is sane. A breeze ruffles her hair.

"Did you hear me?"

"Maam?"

"I said, can wisdom be found in the carcass of *A WHITE HORSE!!*"

She raises her hand at me, as if I have done something wrong. While I cower stupidly, I make the mistake of answering...

"I don't know!"

I see the rage come over her face, like pain and frustration, and she slaps me hard over my eye, and in the next minute I feel her pounding me on top of my head with her fist. I am glad our life is hidden.

"What did I do? What did I do, Momma?"

"You were born, that's what you did. And you're too goddammed stupid to breathe. You dumb *bitch!*"

"I don't know, Momma! I don't know why the horses—"

"Shut up! Just shut your stupid mouth before I break your neck."

Frustrated, she leaves the harvest field, and goes into the house for a short while. Probably to the bathroom. The tomatoes are ripe for harvesting.

Why did I fade to cold, when Mother asked me about the white horses? Like the sailor who knows the storm is over the horizon, I could feel the breeze in that fearful question.

These storms will blow over our lives. Until *sanity* is devastated by them.

56

No wisdom can be found
In the carcass of a white horse
Cease the vain examinations
And seek the truth where Gospels be

From out of the Giant Tree Forest
A monster sings its hungry voice
Forcing us the flee to the plains
Where the mountain hill rises into view

Atop the snow capped mountain peak
A whirlwind appears in violence
Spinning snow into its funnel
Sending frozen rocks into the clouds

High above our plain of safety
Giant rocks fall from the sky
Seeking to destroy each one of us
Individually

*S*he has bided her time through the summer harvest. I sense a powerful restraint, preventing her from the fullness of what she desires for me.

I can no longer tell when she is in a bad mood. Her face is always sullen, her expression often sour. Today, misfortune has me in front of her as we walk in from the field. I am pushing the wheelbarrow, which is filled with round, dark green watermelons. Seedless, and perfectly sweet.

Why am I so clumsy?

I am the clumsiest cow on God's Earth, she says lividly, while I stare at the two watermelons broken on the ground. *Do I know how much time and money I just threw away,* she says. She calls me a clumsy good for nothing while she pulls me by the hair all the way from the field to the house.

It is a warm summer's day.

With my hair in one hand, she pulls me along skillfully, with me stumbling up the back porch steps and falling like a sack of potatoes. My clumsiness is remarkable even to me, and if she wasn't angry before, she is fuming by the time we get into the house. Pointlessly, I start the requisite pleading, but she will have none of it, laying into me with her patented tongue lashing about how precious every single watermelon and tomato is, and about how many I burst open every year, and about how many times she has warned me to be careful.

I want us to be happy.

She acts as though she's at her wits end with me. In her mind, none of my discipline is from a manufactured cause, though sometimes she is not the least bit angry when it happens. But this day brings a definite rage from deep within her, and she is the righteous disciplinarian, while I am the wayward, inept, disobedient child.

She grabs me painfully by the arm, marching me to her bedroom, screaming at me to strip my skirt and blouse off. I don't know if I'm afraid or relieved, because the spankings are indeed the most tolerable of the things she does to me.

But her expression is different this time. Full of irritation and disgust, with none of the sneaky, self satisfied complacency. She stands with her hands on her hips, studying me. Looking for defiance as I pull my blouse off, and begin to slide my skirt away from my hips. Her contemptuousness is growing right before my eyes. She looks as though the sight of me is making her ill.

She closes the door when I am sufficiently undressed, and goes to her nightstand, taking out her biggest hairbrush, the one made of burnished wood.

"Momma…"

She doesn't speak, nor does she return my look. She only sits on her bed, crossing her legs at the ankles. She lays the brush beside her while I stand there in my big, white underwear, calling her gently, asking for her to "please give me one more chance." She pierces into me with those gray eyes, and I begin to approach her as if I were made of snow and she were a hot stove.

The walls of Mother's bedroom are pale blue, like the clear sky on a cold day in autumn. The rays of golden light shine through the window, but lend no warmth to the cold, nor to the dispossessed.

She grabs my arm assuredly, pulling me across her lap, wrapping her legs around mine without effort. In the next instant, I can feel her pulling my underpants down to just below my buttocks, and she proceeds to spank me with her hand as hard as she ever has. I flinch and strain, but I cannot cry out, because truly, I am accustomed to this humiliation. But after only a minute or so she stops, pulling my underwear up.

The next thing I feel sends a knife blade of razor acid through my skin. I draw in a breath and try to look back, even trying to cover my hips with my hand. She gladly whacks my knuckle hard, forcing me to grab her leg and the bedspread. Another hard whack with the brush sends lightning through my body, out of my mouth and into the pale blue walls of her bedroom. Only five times she needs to hit me with it, until I am reduced to begging her in the name of God and Jesus to have mercy. I have never felt such pain.

In my screams, I hear a warning. In this summer, on a new autumn breeze comes my last days.

I need to hear a Melody. But none will come to caress my sadness away. To give voice to the sorrow I feel.

No melodies will come.

But I do hear the Winds of Time...

Calling me.

The pale, violet glow of dawn.

The rooster's voice is too loud. She might serve it for dinner tonight.

It's time for her to fix breakfast for her husband. It's time for her to press her lips against his, moaning softly until he opens his eyes. Its time for the long hug, and the deep, gentle kiss.

They'll eat breakfast together. Then he'll do the chores, and she'll watch him in secret. Just like always.

She'll watch the clock in horror, as it get's closer to two in the afternoon. As it gets closer to the time he has to leave. To commute to the next town, to earn extra money for the baby. For the child.

For this thing...

For the thing in her stomach, that makes her sick, weak and tired. That keeps her husband from devouring her body the way she craves.

Michael isn't here.

There is only that big ball pushing her stomach out. Making it hard for her to breathe. And there is something else here with her now...the sound she's been dreading all night long...

Heavy, authoritative footsteps, clunking up the front steps onto the porch.

The footsteps have stopped.

Knocking...

This is when the troopers come. When their visit is unwelcome.

"Are you Mrs. Michael Coletti? Maam, I'm as sorry as I can be to have to tell you this, but..."

Briefly, a numbness. A feeling that a part of herself is vanishing away. And now the thing in her stomach begins to move. It begins to claw at her from the inside. It wants to get out now—to begin the days of Hell, mocking her forever, reminding her what she has lost. The thing bends her over in pain, to make her sorry she was ever born. Now she is thankful for the troopers.

It claws its way out of her early. A pale, screaming, writhing little monster. In sorrow, she gives it the name he had chosen for it. In misery, she takes it home with her...

Carmen Angelina Elizabeth *Coletti.*

She is beautiful.

Virtuous. Devout. An upstanding woman of the highest Christian standard. A lovely woman with a pleasant but serious expression—underneath a head of shiny black hair that is always pinned up. Always. And hardly a Sunday goes by that she's not sitting in the church. Sitting in the very back, beside a younger version of herself.

Today, she is thinking about her husband.

The love she feels for him is painful. A young, good looking Italian boy in Virginia—with a kind, humble soul. Her own quiet, unassuming nature, all sweetness and demurity, appeals to him. She even bears the look of an Italian Beauty. But she is a Virginia farm girl, with two stern parents who have never spared the Bible or the rod of discipline.

When he looks at her, she is helpless against it. The love hits her hard, like the thunderbolt. Both her mother and father warn her, though, to stay away from that chicken farm boy—"that Italian boy"—and she will endure more than one severe whipping because of it. Her mother will nearly break her fingers because of it. Her mother tells her that she is accursed like the whore, and that her face is filled with sin. She tells her that if it takes years, she will beat the devil from her soul.

They elope.

They are in deep, passionate, obsessive love. Quickly, her innermost feelings, the deepest, most unspoken part of her humanity comes to the surface, and she begs him to dominate her *violently*—to treat her sadistically, and make her his slave however he sees fit. But this kind of violence is hardly a part of him, though he does his best to accommodate her. It seems that the more pain he gives her, the more she likes it.

To each his own.

Six months into the marriage, she is seven months pregnant.

"But you don't have to take that job, Michael. We'll get by. I don't want you to leave me here every day."

A factory job, in a town thirty minutes away. A real job, with real wages. But it means he will be gone ten hours a day. What is she going to do if he isn't here on the farm with her all day, every day? She can't breathe when he isn't around. She can't think.

But he takes the job and commutes to the factory. And she always waits for him at night. Waiting to have his child, hopefully a son, that will grow up to be just like his father. A perfect little boy angel.

But he would like a little girl, and seems to believe that it will be. His little doll to show off, to dress up, and to hear her laugh when he tickles her and makes funny faces and tells funny stories. He dreams of hearing her run through the farm house when he comes in, screaming "daddy" in her little voice. He will then pick her up and spin her around as she giggles and squeals in delight. A sweet little version of her mother that he can nurture in joy and love.

But ah, there's what is planned—

One night, her husband doesn't come home.

In the heart of memory, Spring breezes swirl around her daughter, blowing her hair and her dress. The white blossoms fly down at her from the forest wood.

The young woman pulls the last item from the washtub. One of her mother's dresses. A midnight blue dress. A dress she wears every so often.

She loves her beautiful mother.

Through tears and blood…

She loves her.

We leave church early.

A long, quiet walk. Filled with tension, simmering rage, and fear.

She holds on to my wrists, pulling me along, digging her nails into my skin. In her silence is the clamour of sadistic anger, a cry that has already begun with a firm, painful pinch on the waist.

"Momma? Momma, please tell me what's wrong. Momm…"

"Shut up."

Not another word is spoken.

She has turned every mistake, every shortcoming, every flaw into an excuse to make me suffer. I live in fear of every moment. Flinching at the sound of her footsteps, always expecting to feel an open hand, a shoe, or a stick across some part of my body. The life has made me very clumsy, awkward and fearful, causing me to make more mistakes. Always breaking eggs and dishes, always forgetting small details that Mother gives me.

But I have to search my mind, even as far back as yesterday, trying to remember what I did to make her so angry. But I know better than to ask again. The last time I did, some of my hair got yanked out by the roots.

It doesn't matter anyway. They all amount to the same reason.

She hates me.

She *despises* me.

As we walk the miles of back country road, I draw small comfort from the blue sky, and the fluffy cotton clouds floating by. The Indian summer breeze whooshes dangerously through the woods, stealing the leaves, swirling and whistling of its season of death, and of the coming of the cold, north wind. The Autumn leaves fall to the earth in every color, like natural confetti, appearing their most beautiful as they drift towards their final resting places.

I listen to the trickling sound of the stream while we march quickly over the little bridge. The tiny stream is sometimes an angry, monstrous flood splashing loudly below, threatening to drown any careless thing that happens to fall in. The water seems to emanate from a forbidden source, deep within the forest—a dark realm of purple and gray silhouette. And as always, when I focus my mind, even the tiniest bit, every sight and sound had its own note or chord, which is transformed into phrases of Mozartian and Rossinian brilliance—melodies and harmonies of such beauty that I sometimes wince in amazement.

Suddenly, the colors of sound turn gray, when Mother snatches me forward so hard that I stumble, dropping my Bible and purse on the ground. As I pick them up, she towers over me, solid and strong, glaring down at me in silent, bitter impatience and a growing, contemptuous displeasure.

But she isn't just angry with me.

She is just *angry*.

Years of suppression and self denial. Beneath the surface of her prim, chaste demeanor is a boiling ocean, filled with two decades of repressed lust. And her thoughts, desires and fantasies are *perverted...*

Her time is spent in quiet jealousy and envy, at the very thought of other young women in love. Young beautiful women who enjoy those forbidden, secret acts. Young, pretty women, cinching themselves up, poking their little chests and hips out, smearing their faces with make up and jiggling and giggling like pissy little Christian whores...

Hiding their lust behind a white mask of false modesty and phony innocence. Fooling some poor man into thinking he's the only one she's ever thought of loving. Getting him to marry her, biting and clawing at him, working herself into a trembling, weeping frenzy of pain and ecstasy. And then lying exhausted, enjoying the painful tingling on her skin, remembering the way her husband had attacked her, and given her the pain and pleasure she needs.

Sometimes, Mother has a twisted fantasy about making one of these little priss pretties suffer.

Barbara Jean Coletti hates her daughter.

She *despises* her.

The familiar odor from the chicken yard is strong now. When we finally get to the edge of the lawn, I feel a sudden, familiar rush of fear and dread. At the very least, it isn't cold today. It always hurts worse when its cold.

We march fervently across the yard, *Wrath* and *Terror*, and go inside our little country house.

"Go put your things away," Mother says, "then go into the kitchen."

I hurry into my tiny bedroom, hanging up my coat, placing my Bible and my purse on the little nightstand. My room is very clean, and in perfect order. But there is barely any color. No telephone. No flowers. No pictures. All of the color in my life is in my imagination, and the secret pile of papers that I still keep well hidden from her.

These papers are full of lines—and little black markings.

The walk back to the kitchen is a nervous one. When I get there, she stares directly at me. A cold, calm expression.

Leaning in the corner is the *punishment stick.*

Has she held me, and beaten me with this thing, hundreds of times over the last decade or so?

Perhaps.

"I saw you. And don't act like you don't know what I'm talking about."

"I didn't look at him Momma I *swear* I didn't. I was looking at the hymn book, remember? And when I looked up, I saw him. I swear to *God* that's what it was. I swear to *God* and *Jesus* Momma."

"And now you're going to stand here and swear *lies* to me?"

"I'm not lyin'. I *swear* I'm not. I saw him when I looked up, but I didn't look at him."

One of the few lies I have ever told. I did look, but found him as a jewel in Ennui's Crown.

"I should've let you go to God when you were born," she says. "You've caused me nothing but grief since the day I brought your filthy carcass into this world."

Her voice is calm, but full of venom. She sounds like she wants to cry.

"You're nothing but a *curse,*" she hisses, "and you've cursed everything around you. My Momma called you an ugly, corrupted little gypsy bitch when I tried to go home. And she was right. You've made my life a living Hell."

She glowers at me with piercing, gray eyes.

"Every day you look more and more like a slut. You sit in church every Sunday like you're such a good girl, but I can see the little gypsy whore in you. I can *smell* it. I can hear you begging me for it every day. And I want you to hear me bitch, I will *never* get tired of punishing you…

"Look at me when I'm talking to you!"

I jump, and look her dead in the eyes. My expression only angers her, and my tears are making her sick. She would like to lick every tear off my face, and spit them back into my eyes.

Slowly, she steps over to me. I don't dare look away. She brings her face very close, until I can smell her sweet, chewing gum breath, and feel it on my skin. Mother has a cold, fearful gaze—an icy stare, radiating from her tortured spirit.

"You think you're beautiful, don't you?"

She slaps me hard across the face. A loud, monstrous slap, which stings my cheek, making me stumble to the side.

"You will *answer* me when I ask you a question! Do you think you're beautiful?"

"I know I'm not pretty! I know everybody laughs at me because of how ugly I am."

She watches the tears stream down my face. She smiles, shaking her head.

I think she feels sorry for me.

"So the whore is a woman now... and she thinks she's beautiful."

She throws her head back in a hearty laugh, spinning around and walking away. She stops near her punishment stick, stroking it once. Lovingly.

"So you want that boy to lick and slobber all over you, while you scratch and moan like a cat in heat? Is that it?"

"*No*," I say, in shock. "Absolutely no."

Mother suddenly rushes back over to me, grabbing my wrists, pinning my arms to mysides.

"I know *exactly* what you want," she hisses. "You want to invite him over here, and let him start touching you all over, kissin' and bitin' you on the neck, until he gets his hands in the right places...

238

"And then, you're gonna let him put it in you. And I *know* you. You're gonna wiggle and scream like he's killing you. And you're gonna do it over and over again until you get pregnant. And then you'll sneak off and get married so you can lick and suck on it. So you can learn how to slide it deep into your mouth and choke and spit on it. I *know* that's what you want. I can see it all over that *disgusting* face of yours."

Mother stands up straight, taking deep breaths, heaving that huge bosom up and down. The massive things taunt me, reminding me who is in charge. A non-issue, because she is so much taller than me—and infinitely stronger. I am too frightened to move. My face stings and itches from the slap and the tears.

"And after you and your little boyfriend get married, you'll move into a nice, big beautiful house in Brandmere Estates, and you'll live happily ever after. The boy, the whore, and all of their little *bastard* children. That's what you want isn't it? *Isn't it!*"

She raises her hand again, making me recoil.

"No Maam," I whine. "I wanna stay here with you. I want you to help me not to make you angry, so I can take care of you."

"You'll never be able to take care of anything," she says. "If I don't take care of you, you'll starve and die. And if a man ever gets his hands on you, he'll beat the Hell out of you every day until he kills you. Do you want to stay here?"

"Yes, Maam."

"Do you want me to throw you out, so people can get their hands on you?"

"I wanna stay with you, Momma."

"Then you'll learn to *obey* me."

"Yes, Momma."

"What'd I tell you about lookin'?"

"You told me never to look at 'em, and I swear I never will again, for the rest of my life. I'm sorry I disobeyed you, Momma."

"You're always sorry, aren't you? And yet you keep doing clumsy, stupid, willfull little things just to make me angry."

Now, the venom…

"What if I get my razor, and cut the skin from your ugly face? Then would you think you were beautiful?"

"Momma, I'm too *ugly* for that. You're beautiful, not me."

I take a chance, gently touching her face. But the look in her gray eyes goes well beyond misdirected anger and frustration.

"Do you understand that you were disobedient?"

"Yes, Momma."

"Then go to my bedroom and wait for me."

"Yes, Momma."

I imagine that she closes her eyes, and breathes a deep, trembling breath while I walk away. Then she locks the front and back door…

And closes every curtain.

*I*nside the blue bedroom, I listen to her fumble noisily about. Is she getting the stick? Or the big spoon? Is she looking for the other switches?

I would like to tell her that I didn't do anything wrong. I would like to stand up to her. But I don't know how.

Once, the broomstick hit me on one of my fingers. The result was a sprain that swelled up so much I couldn't move it for three days.

There she is…

She steps boldly into the bedroom, closing the door behind her.

"Take off your clothes."

She stands and watches me, as I slip out of the pretty blue Sunday dress, and place it on the bed. After folding my dress, I make the mistake of tossing my hair out of my face.

She rushes over to me and *slaps* me as hard as she can. I grunt deeply from the shock, and stumble backward.

"*Get* your ass over here," she hisses. "Who the *Hell* do you think you are? What gives you the right to think you deserve anything good in your miserable life? You make me *sick.* You're so useless and pathetic that you make me want to *vomit!*"

Every word drips with poison and hatred. I wonder if she is going to strangle me on the spot. She grabs the back of my hair, marching me over to the mirror.

"Look at yourself", she says, jerking my head. "Look at that matted bird's nest that you call hair. And your face is so ugly that that I can hardly stand to look at you. You've got big, fish eyes and disgusting, bloody looking lips. Your nose looks like a bird's beak and your skin is pale and pasty. And you stink. Half the time you smell like you belong in a barnyard, shoving those bloated bags of yours into a pig's mouth. I should lock you up in the shed anyway because you're too *filthy* to live in the house! Is that what you want, to live outside like the fat, stupid, lazy sow pig that you are?"

"No! I'll act right, I promise!" My head throbs, and my face is contorted with shame and sorrow.

Already, I am crying—

And my punishment has not yet begun.

People never punish righteously. They do it because of sadistic or vengeful urges. An inherent need to make other people suffer.

Discipline, thy name is *Pain*.

"Put your hair up," she snaps. Now, turn around and look at me. You think you've been punished before, don't you? Well today, you'll learn what discipline *is*, sweetie."

I stand in my underwear, hair pinned up, with my arms crossed in front like I am cold.

I *am* cold.

"Now let's see if you can get this right. Go to my closet, and get the belt hanging in the back, against the wall."

I obey, and bring the hard, black leather belt to her. It is a belt I have never seen before.

"Take off your bra."

She peers at me sternly, and without embarrassment. But my humiliation is complete, as she watches me jiggle out of my big bra, knowing every inch of my bosom is inherited straight from hers.

"You look like you can nurse a cow," she says.

In that instant, she whacks the front of one of my breasts with her hand. Very hard. I scream and recoil, as if stung by an angry red wasp.

"Come back here!" she yells. "Stand still and put your arms down or I'll hit 'em with this belt."

She quickly hits the other one, sending the same stinging pain through my body. But this time I don't recoil much. I just shake and scream, as if I've been stuck with a needle.

"That's it", she says. "That's the sound you want to make with the boys, isn't it?"

"No!" I sob breathlessly. "I swear I don't!"

She tosses the belt on the bed, and begins to unbutton her gray dress. She is calm.

In her face, I see *'you're finally going to get what you deserve.'* From her manner, I hear *'and I swear I'm going to enjoy every second. Every blessed minute of it.'*

Mother removes her dress, revealing a long, white slip underneath. The slip hugs a shape that is clearly the origin of my own. The mature version, with gigantic breasts, and hips much fuller and wider. She slides off her stockings and then her slip. How can a bra hold so much flesh without bursting?

I am in awe of her.

"Momma? Momma please have mercy. I promise I won't disobey you, ever again."

She picks up the belt, and moves slowly over to me. Her full hips are beautiful. A mother's hips. The buckle tinkles loudly.

"You would like it to be this easy, wouldn't you?" she hisses.

A chill moves through me while I watch her place the belt on the dresser, and return to the closet. In beauty, she emerges with the leather whip.

I would like to speak. To breathe. To beg.

But I cannot.

With one of her stockings, she ties my wrists tightly together in front, shackling me to the bedpost in silk. The black fabric contrasts with my fair skin.

"One for every year I've been alone," she says, anguished. "And two for every year of your miserable life."

She pushes me, making me stand up straight. The small, black whip hangs unfolded in her hand, as she draws her arm back as far as she can, bringing the first of over *sixty* lashes across my naked back. The hard leather shocks me, causing me to cry a short scream and bend at the knee.

"*Momma*! Momma I won't be disobedient anymore! In the name of God and Jesus, forgive me! Please forgive me and have mercy!..."

She continues to hit me across my back, my buttocks and my legs. The serpentine wraps itself around me in cutting. Slowly, deliberately she hits me, hearing the music of her rhythm, the song of the whip, slicing big, red marks into my skin. Every lash raises a large welt. A few of them are already bleeding.

"Momma please! *Momma please!"*

Sometimes, she has to grab my arm, and pull me back into position. She enjoys every squeal and scream, every twitch, every shudder, and every jiggle of my flesh. She directs the blows onto my buttocks and my back, which she always hits the hardest, through grunts and clenched teeth. Twice, she hits me with the ebony handle. I bend over and grip the tall bedpost, shaking, slobbering. Bellowing. Trying not to lose myself. My sanity.

In bitterness, envy, and for every broken dream…

She whips me.

The last welt is created on top of the first one…

Shut your mouth, she orders, slightly out of breath, voice trembling. Her chest heaves. In her lovely hands, the serpentine begins to curl in upon itself. She unties me from the bedwood. She tells me to take the belt back to the closet and hang it *exactly* as I found it. If I find it hanging differently, she says, I'll beat you again.

I sob in weakness, stumbling over to the closet. My body is on *fire*— throbbing and itching like nothing I have ever felt. I know that my skin is cut and red down to the backs of my knees. I can feel the network of angry red welts, some of which have bleeding sores where skin had been. My back is in so much pain that I cry out loud. I intend to cry until Mother tells me to…

"Shut up!"

Immediately I close my mouth, dealing bravely with the burning on my skin. I endure it…

As I am accustomed to.

She enjoys the look of my bloody skin. But what she savours is the look in my eyes. The light of hope has already grown dimmer. The loneliness and regret for living that has plagued her is beginning to take firm, complete hold of me.

This is what she had always wanted for me. To teach me. To make me understand that to be born is to be cursed…

And to live is to suffer.

In easy power of her command, she gracefully tosses the serpentine whip to the bed, telling me to put my arms to my sides. Modesty has no place here. I can never hide from her. In weakness I lean forward and try to kiss her.

But she pulls away.

Go to my nightstand, and open the top drawer, she says.

I do as I am told. I do only as I am told.

"Bring it here."

I pick up the big, wooden hairbrush and take it to her. I hand it to her crying, shaking my head no.

Oh yes, she says.

"Please don't, Momma."

"Take your panties off, and turn around."

The fear and hopelessness have taken form in my body, and begun to flow out through my voice.

"I'm going to tear the skin off your backside. And if you move, I'll make you wish you were dead."

She kneels down, and with my own bra, ties my ankles together. Then she takes hold of me, standing close against me. But before she begins, she studies the pain in my face.

It is beautiful.

She holds my waist tightly, and with quick, hard motions, swats the big wooden brush onto my bare skin. The hard wood cuts and burns my flesh, making me wail the name of God and Christ to the top of my lungs. Mother watches me closely, watching me abandon hope, watching me learn that there is no deliverance from suffering. She hits me as hard as she can with the brush, going well past a hundred blows. Admonishing me not to faint, lest I be beaten again.

She concentrates the scores of remaining blows on one side, slamming the brush into my bloody skin, in the same spot, until she raises a lump—even hitting my back twice, thrilled at the struggle that ensues. She continues, listening to my screams grow very rough and hoarse.

She is breaking me down to nothing.

Misery will be served. It will have its company.

It will be satisfied.

Mercifully, the hard beating is soon ended.

Look in this mirror, she says. I want you to see how disgusting you look.

She unties my wrists and my legs and stands close behind my nude body, pressing hard against the broken skin. I suck my breath through my teeth, while Mother's bra scrapes against my bloody back. I feel her soft curves, squeezing tightly against the back of me.

"P-Please f-forg-give me," I whimper, with no strength left. "Please forgive me. I didn't m-mean to curse you, Momma. I didn't mean to...."

She watches me closely. Watching my spirit darken.

Then, she takes my hair down, and lets it spill over my shoulder.

Look in that mirror, she says.

I gaze forward, at a wet, ugly, red faced, fish eyed, pasty, beak nosed, wild haired baba-yaga of a thing, with a waist too freakishly curved, and hips too wide and breasts too big and fat. She moves my long, silken black hair to the side, looking down at the welts, noticing that streaks of blood have stained the front of her bra. She presses hard against my bruised buttocks, making them hurt worse. The dresser creaks against the pressure of her pushing against my body. She wraps the prickly brush with my bra.

The room seems darker.

Colder.

She feels the perversion, flowing from every part of her, gathering in the center of her flesh. Making her understand that there is one more thing she must do. With one hand, she gently takes me by the throat. She begins to massage my stomach and my arms.

Then I feel her hand, fumbling with her bra.

Soon after, the cool, fleshy mass of Mother's left breast spills out against my skin. She fumbles with the other side, until they are both mashed together like two huge flesh pillows against my bloody back. My only thought is that they are cool and soft against my wounds. Almost comfortable.

Mother takes my breasts into her hands, and begins to squeeze them, massaging them fully. Slowly. Deliberately.

I am *hers.* To be dominated. Humiliated. Chastened. Degraded. Debased.

Crushed.

I will *never* be allowed to know whether or not I have beauty. All that I have, even what beauty there may be—my tears, my pain and suffering—all of it is hers to control. She will make me afraid to breathe. Terrified to speak. Terrified of life. Of death.

Of shadows.

You are nothing, she whispers.

Two sharp, stabbing pains run through the front of my breasts. Mother holds them, twisting them while I scream and try to push back against her.

Be still! she yells. Then she finds my ear with her teeth.

"I'll be still, I promise, I prom…"

My words are cut off by my own shrieking. I can only sob. Begging with the tearful, wailing *"please,"* for her to have mercy.

But there is no mercy. Not for several, agonizing minutes. Then finally, she releases them in a hard, biting pull. She lets go of my ear, and takes a firm hold of my throat again. Twenty years of repressed, pathological hatred, contempt, obsession, blame and perversion…

I feel Mother begin to squeeze against me again. Repeatedly.

In the mirror, I can see her face. Her eyes are closed. She has an intensely anguished, frustrated expression. I can feel her movements becoming more determined. And her hand is still clamped firmly around my throat. The hairbrush holds—tight between her legs—to keep her hands free. Her fingers are memorizing my body, lubricated by blood, then the hairbrush wood slides painfully in the back of me, in the manner of those in the Valley of Siddim, in the judgment city of Sodom. The blue fire in my bowel is tinted black.

I am innocent. Ignorant.

But I am not stupid.

I close my eyes. In my imagination, I leave the room as far behind as I can. I disconnect myself, and soon I am outside, walking down the dirt road beside our house.

The evil grabs hold of Mother's flesh. My bra cloth wraps the prickly brush, to protect her inner thigh, which clamps it immobile between her legs. Her movements become involuntary thrusts, and she suddenly feels the exhilaration of the forbidden. Unbearable sensations.

Her hearing goes dull. There is a purplish haze where her vision has been. She loses awareness of her body's movements, and her eyes close again on their own. She shakes her head in denial—and steadies herself against the flood, which she can feel approaching, gathering extreme force and momentum...

And suddenly, with more power than she could have imagined, two decades of repressed energy *explode* into her body.

I try not to, but from my imaginary walk, I hear her begin to wail. A wail that grows louder and louder, until it turns into a pitiful, hopeless scream. A scream for the ages. A scream for mercy.

A cry of the damned.

I am pulled back into the room, forced to watch and listen. I am amazed, as I feel Mother convulse and jerk against my sore body, like she is being tormented from the inside. She screams very loudly once more, then not as loud, many times after. It is like a siren. It causes my ears to ring.

I watch and listen as Mother whimpers and moans, trembling, quivering as though she barely has the strength to stand up. She sighs and moans all over my shoulders, neck, and the side of my face. She breathes in the scent of my hair. With her hands, she gently absorbs every inch of me. The blue and black fire burns me from the inside out. The wood handle has split me in two. It wears my blood for a veil.

I belong to her now. My thoughts. My feelings. My hopes. My innocence. She has taken them all. She has taken everything from me.

I am hers forever.

You are an *accursed woman,* she whispers, her voice soft, high pitched, quivering. You deserve nothing in life but scourges, and beatings, and the severest punishments and abuses. You deserve to be tortured, until your body dies. You don't deserve to be loved, but only hated, and then forgotten.

She pauses.

I am the only person in the world who could ever *consider* giving you love, she says softly. But if I ever see defiance in your eyes, if I *ever* hear it in your voice…

I am going to kill you.

A long pause, with her breathing loudly in my ear.

A *list*, she whispers. I will make a list. I will write down the things I will do to you, if I ever sense defiance in your body. If I ever feel it in your soul.

My eyes are wide open, staring into hers. She looks deep into my eyes, at every inch of my expression, studying every small, insignificant corner of it. I notice the tears in her eyes. Her look is calm.

Do you want forgiveness?

"Y-Yes, Mother."

Do you want me to love you?

"Yes, m-my—" The words are choked. "...*My Beautiful Mother*, I ask for your mercy and your forgiveness."

If you mean it, then I will forgive you.

"I do mean it. I do."

She pauses...

I need your *kiss*, she says. I can tell from your kiss if you've repented.

I move my head closer, kissing her nervously on the lips. The tears are streaming down my face.

Put your tongue in my mouth, she whispers.

Clumsily, I push my tongue into her mouth. Warmly she sucks my tongue, gently, slowly, up and down the length of it. Sucking the life. Sucking the life from her daughter's spirit.

All of my confidence. All of my remaining joy and self esteem is vanished into a vapour of hopelessness.

I will retreat. Whole heartedly, into a private world of darkness. Where there is only prayer.

And color.

64

*W*hisper to me, dear Mother.

Whisper your warm breath into my ears...

In my sleep, I hear the voice of profound weeping. The sound carries through my dreams, into my mind, until it pulls me from the walk at the edge of the night woods, looking for the widow weeping. I awaken suddenly, hearing her sob to the Heavens, begging Providence to forgive her for letting it happen.

My body aches more than ever. I think my gown has stuck to the healing wounds on my back. Though I can hardly move, I am compelled to get up, and drag my bruised body through the darkened house to my Mother's room. But when I arrive at the door, I have no courage to knock. I can only turn around in sudden fear, hurrying through pain back to my resting bed. Her sorrow is too great. I can provide her no comfort.

When spring hath renewed its promise, I shall give her a flower. When the White Rose is in bloom...

Her love for me will blossom.

LORY

Listen to me dear Daughter. Hearken unto me.

I am your Mistress.

You will learn how to suffer. How to beg, and ask properly for forgiveness. You will learn how to accept pain for my pleasure. Do you understand? Do you understand, dear Daughter? You will learn what needs I require, whether it be your strength, or your weakness, your dry eyes, or your tears. I am your brightest day. The light that rules your darkest night. Without me, you cannot breathe. Without me, you cannot survive. You will suffer to give me life, and in turn I will allow you to live.

Do you wish to suffer for me?

That's a good girl. You cannot resist pain. That's it, let it out of your voice. Let the pain flow through your body and out of your voice. Your voice is the outlet for the pain. Yes. Let it flow. Breathe with it. Move with it. Never resist it. The more you resist, the more pain you will feel. Now, put your lips to mine. I need to feel your suffering.

There is the electric trembling, Mother. The energy passing through your body. Your muscles tense on their own. You shake into convulsions…your voice screams into my mouth, going down my throat, trying to corrupt me. Drink…drink deeply. Let it quench your deviance. And now, lick the tears from my face. Wet every inch of it with your tongue, and dry it with your soft lips. Rest easy, now…rest easy after Violence. Let my tears nourish you back to sanity. My spirit is no longer my own.

I am your child.

The Indian Summer bathes our country landscape with hopeful memories. The house is warm as I prepare for twilight. Our dinner is eaten. I rest comfortably in my bedroom before my bath, writing a pristine melody or two. Does she wonder how it is that I can stay in my room for so many hours undisturbed, even when she does not lock me inside?

All day, she has been kind. A special day. Gentle kisses on the cheek. Soft caresses on my shoulder. When we did the laundry, she did not order me to hold the wet linen carefully as we hung it across the line. She only admonished me gently, with a high pitched voice of pure honey. *"Oops, careful now, don't let it touch the ground..."* She was patient with me at the store, as a mother should be. Telling me they weren't concerned with my face, and it didn't matter if they stared, or even if they laughed. But we are safe out here again. In my world apart, my Land of Freedom. I rest in my cottage by the sea, immersed in melody and evening song.

I hear a pulse…a beat…

A knocking.

Ms. Sweetness comes in through the door. I hide my melody page in my Bible, which I only pretend to read, still hearing the Quartet for Indian Summer playing in my mind. It still plays, even as she comes to me, and asks me to approach her. We stand in the middle of my room. She is close to me. Caressing my hair.

"Did you enjoy our little trip today?"

"Y…yes."

She laughs a little.

"But you'd rather stay out here wouldn't you?"

Why am I afraid to answer? Her eyes are gentle. Her bosom is pressed firm against mine.

"I can feel your heart," she says.

Mother laughs again. With her finger, she follows the shape and contour of my face, my eyebrows, my nose, my cheeks, my lips. She paints my lips with her finger.

Slowly, she undoes the buttons on my dress. Breaking the flower pattern more with each button. Her soft look hardens enough to banish my modesty. She makes no error in her message, with her intention, as she undoes my button dress to the waist, and pulls it down off my shoulders.

Her freedom is as the wind. Liberation, as she unbuttons her navy dress. The shade to my room is up, but she feels no shame. Do you, Mother?

She slides my dress all the way over my shoulders, downward, until it falls to the floor at my feet. She waits for me to kick it away, but I cannot move. With her feet, she pulls my dress away, pushing it to the side.

I know I cannot hide from you. You need not go any further—

She unbuttons her own dress, and slides it off, never taking her eyes from mine. Then she peels her slip off over her head. Her bra is bursting with flesh. She steps back to me, pushing them into mine. It is the collision of worlds. Of generations. It is the soft cataclysm. I can only stare at her wide-eyed, hopelessly dim, recording the Indian Summer quartet in my mind. The lonely cello is her voice. Her tortured spirit, crying from the grave.

She leans to my face, and kisses me full on the mouth. A lover's kiss, opening and closing her mouth upon mine, sucking my lips a little. She whispers for me to open my mouth, and I do so benignly, and she unleashes her kiss upon me, caressing my mouth with her tongue. With natural skill, she seems to coax my tongue away from hiding, and I have joined her in the kiss, glad that she is tender to me, knowing this is better than the pain she could have easily done to me.

I feel her tongue licking broad, warm stokes across my neck, down over my shoulder, then slowly to my neck again. She sucks a final, deep, wet kiss from my mouth, moaning her approval. Mother has a power, a command for this that may not be given to many. Without further pretense, she undoes my bra, and pulls it off, and slides my underwear away.

In front of me, she reaches back, and undoes her own bra. Her white underwear are gone quickly after, and I see every inch of her body exposed. An artist's dream it would be, sculpted by nature's muse, born and grown in perfect voluptuousness. She steps back over to me, resting her skin against mine, reestablishing our connection. I am so embarrassed and afraid. Does she know?

I am not worthy of love.

I listen to her breathe. I watch her look change. Her expression carries the anguish of extreme desire.

Without warning she lowers her head close to me, and I feel the wet softness of her lips and tongue, pulling my nipple deep into her mouth. I draw a breath of pure shock, nearly trembling as the sensation travels to the rest of my body.

Mother! You repay the cruelty I inflicted as an infant! Hungrily, you devour my life—my self-esteem flows into your mouth!

Roughly, with gentle roughness she turns me around, pressing her body against my back, which still bears the gentle scars from the Evening. Rocking me slowly, whispering yes's. Telling me that I am her good girl.

You have condemned us, dear woman.

Accursed woman.

67

I didn't want it to happen this way, she says, breathing deeply, with loud whimpering. Why did you force this onto me? You did this to me. You pulled this out of my body. Because you're a witch. You've got Satan's power. I can feel you right now. Pulling it out of me. Can you...can you feel what you're doing to me? Can you feel it in my body...my bod—

Whisper to me Mother.

Whisper Perversion's Blame. Let your witch's voice pitch high and low with the power of sin, as you hold me underneath you, grinding your hips. My arms are pinned, I cannot move...your body has absorbed the energy from mine. Whisper, as the force builds in the center of your desire. Spit your blame lovingly onto my tongue. Let your blame fall upon my tongue while your energy builds. I can offer you no solace, I am no protection against the wave that is coming for you. It looms above you, over your pervertedness, your deviance, your corruption.

Whisper deeply to me.

Whisper into my mouth the blame for this! Whisper about your guilt, the unbearable pleasure, the deep despair that this wave will crash in you...you cannot whisper, your power of speech has been taken by the wave...you cannot breathe as it washes over you. It blinds you, you cannot open your eyes to see the truth as you stop writhing, your mouth hanging open, as you wait for it to claim your body yet again. With all of your heart, you do not want to scream, but you know that you will scream...

The wave has passed, and you can breathe again. Now whisper to me, dear Mother, whisper the blame of your perversion. Whisper your warm breath into my ears.

Whisper to me.

*W*hat does a dream communicate to me, when I see her wearing that which pertaineth to a man? The dream is clear, not one of hazy intent.

It is as though she projects her spirit to me as I sleep. In my sleep, she sits me gently on the edge of my own bed. She walks to my dresser in nudity, and takes the member from the top drawer, even though it is something I have never seen!

She steps into the harness of straps, sliding it upward around her hips. In front of me she tightens it, while the member hangs from the front of her, looking as natural and as real as it can. The sight of it flares terror in me, and she speaks, saying *There are things that I need to do, Elizabeth, but you don't have to be afraid when they happen.* She moves close to me without shame, holding it in her hand, and she rubs it across my breasts with knowledge and skill, even tapping it against the front of them.

I want you to slide it deep in your mouth, she says, *and I want you to choke on it until the spit is dripping from it...*

The dream is a signpost for me. I need not be afraid.

Am I afraid when it happens?

I am.

*T*he fire in my bosom is melody. It burns me with a fever too white hot to endure, until I feel that I will burst into a flame. It allows me to see the depth of desire, even if hers is one I do not comprehend.

There are times when her manner is vaguely apologetic as she kisses and undresses me. Through pity, I know that I can never show my displeasure, being that I would rather die than make her feel humiliated. I will help her undress me, always careful to show interest at what level she requires. She will usher me to the bed, as I lay down willingly, looking at her as she removes her underwear. I admit that my fascination for her body is not diminished, as it is curved to infinity. This is one of her greatest pleasures, to disrobe in front of me, especially the removing of her bra. Sometimes, I see the look on her face touched with regret and shame, but knowing that just as the alcoholic must take his drink, she must take her part of the forbidden. At these times, she will tuck her lips and refuse to make eye contact, as she climbs on me, and her expression takes on a demurity that is painfully beautiful to behold.

I am glad for the closeness, as she slides her bosom across my skin. The breath she breathes is the harmony of strings, the feel of her erect nipple is the violin solo among them. When she is done with this, our first movement is past. She will approach my lips with her bosom above me, and I know to receive it in my mouth and nurse every drop of its nourishment, while the glimpse of her expression reveals anguished, determined endurance. After many long turns of the color wheel, the marching and whirling of time, marked by the basses in every register they know in this andante, I release it, and she resists a shudder, while she quickly gives herself over to what she must do. She puts her mouth to my nipple, which causes me to relax in her version of what is kindness, and even love. I can taste the aggression in her lips and tongue, that which comes when her hunger is too great for her to feign cruelty or control. Her expression is deeply, intensely distressed in an unknown pain, as her head bobs up and down upon my breasts as though the sucking is feeding her starvation. In this, she is pitiful; a slave to something that may plague many or few—this I do not know. She is an addict to this, the substance of desire, and of what pleasure my body can provide. In a look that seeks to betray hidden tears, she sucks my nipples to their full erection, even while their rhythm dances this Fantasy for Violin and Strings. She builds it up, storing energy with each hungry pull, until the crescendo can go no higher in her body, and begs to be restored to a state of rest. She puts her flower to mine, which admonishes my legs to their missionary position. Her breasts hang and jiggle as white cloud mountains inverted, pointing their blame at me. Guilty! I am guilty of this! I am the fault of her need, the origin of this unholy desire. I watch her demurity, her tucked in lips, her skin of ivory cream, her eyes as bewitching as the winter whirlwind, highlighted by the midnight brows arched to natural perfection. She glances at me in a quiet pleading for understanding, for me to not be afraid, nor to curse her in my heart for what she must do.

With my legs open and back, she begins to slide herself into position as the female dominant, reaching down with her hand and opening her petals, exposing the long bud within. I watch it, I feel it slide onto my own, and we are locked in this that she must do. I let the sensation have my body, while I raise the barrier to my soul. But my heart is open to thee, Dear Mother, for you to take part in this that you must need! You are raised up on your hands above me, in the skill of ages, eyes closed now, to have your privacy from me. I study the concentration on your face while your hips push your phantom member in and out of me, while you siphon still more of my life from me. I watch your hips jiggle, the impossible girth of them, flowing from the waist even as small as my own. I see the skin above your bosom begin to redden, as you feel the new pain begin to build, this pain that drives your craving, the terror that you must endure. You are confident enough to open your eyes to me now, as I have closed mine in courtesy. But as if I am called, I open my eyes suddenly, and we meet in this that is done, as I take my place as caregiver for this sickness, while you suffer the healing that must needs be.

Close your eyes, Dear Mother! Take your rest in this secret thing! In this favorite thing of what softness we share! This, our missionary—your prized position, made perfect by your strong arms holding you erect above me. Enjoy the feel as your breasts obey the laws that govern their motion. Love the wiggle of your hip flesh as you thrust, savor the electric tingle of the clitoral, and their erection and exposure to one another. Feel the rising of our skin, the full flowering of this fervent desire! Look at me, Mother, with what power your thrusts do to my bosom. See them bounce their rhythm to thee! Pray as their harmonies sing, that their music shall not die to thee! Now close thine eyes, Mother. Prepare thyself for your burial, for thine entombment beneath what must be! As the rose begins to blossom from your lovely neck to your mountainous beauty, I see it growing, I feel what pain must overtake thee!

My hands are suddenly raised on their own, guided by the song in this key, and my fingers grip your nipples in knowing—while your thrusting is no longer of thy volition. The look of your beauty is transformed, on the edge of this agony, to the look of unearthly and painful sensuality—your lips part in their way, so that breath can escape, so that the sweet breath from thy body can move over thy voice, to give life to the sound of the trumpets, a fanfare for this collision, for this conquering of the night's perversion. Your mouth opens upon the nipple pinching, sending a signal to your door to open, to release the flood onto the valley floor, so that nature is renewed in splendor unknown, and the rapturous coming of new life.

The sound of your torture is loud in our isolation, Dear Mother! The pleading for relief rains upon my grief and knowing. I massage your bosom in mercy while the suffering flows from the center of your body, past your Velvet Call, and into the air above and around me. Rest, Mother! Let me kiss the tears from thy face. Tears from your body's relief, the rare cry from Climax alone. Tears born not of sorrow, but only from the overflow, from the waters crashed into the valley. Feel my tongue caress your neck in warmth to soothe your soul back to peace—your mind back to blessed sanity. Breathe, Mother. Allow the life in your body again, so that you may rest my soul to thee.

Dear Mother, Rest thy soul to me.

he winter has come and gone. The spring trees are no longer in waiting. Wisdom has planted every seed, promising to grow. The leaf canopy is full—green in the way of its calling.

I am no longer a stranger to the sight of my reflection in my own mirror, unclothed, with her unclothed behind me. Holding her preferred weapon of the moment—carved in ice and steel. No small knife will suffice, and poor me, so dumb, so fearful, that I cannot understand that if she were really going to cut my throat, the razor paring knife would do. If there is any joy she feels, it is when she remembers the time in front of my mirror, in this summer of my 20th year, months after the day joy died forever in me.

We are naked together. In the heat of a late summer's afternoon. The setting sun paints the air around us in a color that has no name. I am standing here trembling, nude, while she is nude behind me, pressed tight, her hand at my throat, saying *I'm going to watch you bleed today, Dear. If you want to live, Darling, then don't move. But flinch, or squirm my Sweet, or try to get away while I cut you, and you will die before the sunset.* At this moment, I think I hear genuine pity in her endearing charms.

I hear nothing of malice in her voice. No false emotion, but only the soft spoken Word of Truth, making me zero at the bone. I stand obedient for as long as I am able, but every time the cold, razor steel touches my neck, I cry out and flinch—no—I scream, and shake bloody murder against her skin. Her patience is terrifying, and I can feel her nipples harden against my back, and the pulse of her heartbeat is in lightning rhythm with my own.

For several minutes she stands even tempered, forbearing. Refusing to engage me unless I stand still and cease the useless whimpering, to dry my tears from the inside out. She says, *if the sun sets before you bleed, I'll bury you in the field by Moonlight. I swear it on your father's grave...* the sound of which freezes me into quivering obedience. I stand still, looking at the girl who lives inside the mirror, in the fading light of day. Eyes wide, still trembling. Waiting for the cold steel to mix with my hot blood, to run in warm streams down my exposed breast, to my stomach, past the flower to my white thigh, to my knee, then to my ankle and my foot.

I am prepared, though I cannot close my eyes without difficulty, as she has ordered me to do. When I believe I have lost my nerve, she whispers of the Sun Over the Western Gate, and I close my eyes, and prepare for the feel of the blood pain, even while I tremble and whimper, and my face is drowned with tears. Mother grips me tight, our nude bodies hot together, and she whispers, *I need to see the blood run...* she touches the knife to my throat and slides it across—the girl in the mirror opens her eyes in terror beyond the grave, and screams as from the Lake Fires of Gehenna.

In my haze of shrieking, in her domination dream, I know that the blade has sliced my neck just enough to make the blood run, and mother clutches me still tighter, pressing the knife harder until I am choked. Then somewhere from inside her, from the soul of her, I feel a trembling, which makes its way up through her body to her mouth, and I hear the distinct, fervent sound of *depravity*—the purest, most undiluted, pristine blade of a gutteral scream, as if from pain, punctuated by the motion of her involuntary rhythm, all of it leaping out of her on its own. When it passes, she takes the knife away from my throat, then I realize in humiliation, in the clinking of it on my dresser, that she has only touched the *back* of the blade to my skin!

Blood Sister! I shall not see thee today!

71

*T*his, you do to me, with purpose and determination! On the eve when my Sister screams from inside the mirror! Hungrily you devour <u>all</u> the milk of my life, my esteem flows continuous through my nipple, into thy mouth again! I breathe the breath of lust into my lungs, of relief that the knife is away, feeling the dampness grow in me.

The pleasure is unbearable when she pulls my breast out of her mouth with a loud kissing, and takes the other one in. My body shakes again, this time not from fear, arousing her a second time. I know it, because she grabs me and holds me tight. I think that I am moaning. This, I cannot tell.

Roughly, with the same gentle roughness you turn me around, pressing your body again against my back. For the first time in my life, I am fully aroused. Is it relief. Is it fear? What would I do, if you were to abandon me? I would scream for you to kiss me, My Beautiful Mother! To put your tongue so deep into my mouth as to choke me. What have you done to me?

When her hand caresses the front of me, I draw a breath and make a sound. I wish to pull away, but her grip is unbreakable. The sensation is electric, I cannot bear it. *Hold on to me,* she orders, and I know that I must obey. She tends my Garden properly, too well, as I feel each stroke building a tension in my body, pulling it tighter, beyond what I thought possible...I cannot bear it, my mouth hangs open. Already, the energy wave climbs to the skies above. I cannot breathe...

And I hear something in the room around me, a voice, *my* voice in a wailing, a pitiful howling. I am reaching back, to hold on for dear life, knowing that the wave is going to drown me, and cause a scream, and then drown the breath from me for the last time...

Then the tension in my body breaks, releasing a life of energy stored. The wave above me crashes down over my quivering, taking the breath out of my scream. She rubs me harder, pushing me further into shrieking, holding me tight, showing me no mercy, whispering blessings and curses as lightning to my brain.

But she has mercy, so as not to lose her moment completely. She holds her hand still, watching me catch my breath, feeling my heartbeat return to slow rapidness. She remembers the way I clung to her. The way I clawed her skin like a clawless cat, trying to find hold in a drowning hour. I suppose she relishes the pain of my hands, when they furiously pinch the flesh on her thighs. My body, my convulsions are meat for her appetite. My voice is wine for her thirst.

When she rubs me again, gently, I have to shake, in the aftershock of the quaking. Tingling, tickling me into leaning back against her, and holding on for dear life again. *Hold on to me tight—don't you move a muscle*, she says, *just let it out through your voice…*

She tends my Garden again in its proper place, its improper place, and my body vibrates as I breathe and strain. *Relax,* she says, *and let it flow out through your voice.* And I bellow deeply like an animal, enduring the pain, the tingling of electric needles in my groin. She rubs and caresses, until the tingling has passed, and my body has adjusted to its cruelest pleasure. I feel the breath in her quicken a second time. In the light that rests beyond the setting sun, before the glow of night, her thrusting emerges, this time voluntary, in struggle and effort, which rattles every inch of my body to its foundation, the slapping of wet flesh, with the strength of powers none but her possess, and I hear the high pitched calling to the Almighty, followed by uncompromising loudness in my ear, while my arms are pressed to the side of my body. She pushes with a solemn grind, to feel the deepness of the invisible member she hath placed inside of me!

She holds her daughter tight now. With both hands, absorbing her essence. Engorging herself on the force of life remaining. Rocking, whispering breathlessly about her good girl, tasting the sweat from her daughter's face. There remains no more sacrifice for her sin, there is only that fearful looking back, awaiting the hand of the Unseen.

We are condemned, dear woman!

Accursed woman!

72

What is a sexual sadist?

Mother—

What magic are you privy to? How are you able to bring yourself to fullness, simply by laying upon me, pinning my arms underneath me, and bending my fingers until I have to scream and beg for mercy? I can always feel the waves of energy going through your body. Sometimes, you barely move a muscle, and it will still happen. By what spirit? You have even made me a willing victim, because I am too afraid to fight, and I need for you to love me. Does this give me security? Am I a masochist?

Often, I will lay very still, feeling her pound her hips into me like a piston. Her head thrown back, eyes closed, bellowing deeply like a wild animal. I watch in disbelief, amazed at how completely the act can consume a person, possessing her, laying waste to her dignity. She is like one controlled by a force too powerful to resist, pleasures so unfathomable as to be nearly painful. Feelings so intense that rational thought and self control are no longer possible. The shaking, the screams that pour from her body, the look of pain on her face shows the agony of her unbearable ecstasy. Deep, darkly impossible sensations that I doubt few have ever known.

I often marvel at the power of her thrusting. Underneath her full, soft curves is a body of powerful muscles, the strength of which I am well acquainted with. Many times, when she is behind me, either standing up or on all fours, she will pound into me with enough force to rattle my brain. Always in rhythm, either fast or slow. There are times when I wonder whether or not she is receiving any pleasure at all, and is only doing it to drive fear deeper inside of me.

But often, when she seems the least enthusiastic, not gripping me but merely standing or leaning full against me, seemingly out of nowhere I will feel her body tremble, and then literally quake from the energy of premature pleasure. Rarely is she able to restrain herself from allowing it to escape her voice. I think that sometimes she has no control over when and how it is going to happen to her, and she is capable of bringing her body to pleasure many times before she is done.

I have seen what churns beneath cultured civility.

Sometimes, I wonder if she is not truly possessed with a power. Something evil and otherworldly, that has condemned her. If not her soul in the next life, surely, her body in this one. I want to help her. But I know that I can do nothing, but provide her an outlet for this perversion.

On rare occasions, after my bath is done, I will go back to my room in my towel, where Mother has placed candles around the darkened room. The room smells of burning candles, and clean linen. She removes my towel, and tells me to lie still on my back. Slowly, I watch her remove her clothes, and she is drawn to the unshaded window, as if she sees someone looking in. It is her own reflection, looking back at her.

She takes her hair down very sensuously, standing in front of me, caressing her hips and thighs for the longest time. I would not look away, even if compelled, because I know it is an incredible thing she is about to do. Hardly opening her eyes at all, she climbs onto the bed with feline smoothness, and straddles me with serpentine ability. Her movements are slow, and deliberate.

She begins to massage her own breasts fully, squeezing them slowly and firmly, and gently pulling her nipples as far outward as they will go. After several minutes of this, she lifts one of her own breasts with one hand, taking hold of the front of it with her lips, and gives it a deep sucking and pulling with her mouth. Her body moans its approval through her voice, which seems to come out independent of her own will. She is an exotic beauty in the candlelight.

I have already learned quickly, that when she does this, she has no desire to be touched, or for me to move a muscle. The first time she did this, I made the mistake of caressing her while she was entranced, and she punched me in the stomach so hard that I nearly lost my breath. Another time, a cough escaped me, accompanied by a hard slap and an icy look.

She sits still, breathing slowly and deeply, feeling the shape of things around her, becoming one with the room, the house, and the darkness. She sits astraddle, well past the half hour, and I watch the creamy skin on her neck and chest grow rosy with desire. I watch her massive breasts swell, and listen to her breathing grow deeper. Her head begins to sway slowly back and forth, like a lady musician upon the piano, lost in the adagio, the lyrical andante, patiently awaiting the approaching finale. In amazement, I watch her slip into another realm of consciousness, where there is only pleasure of such intensity as to defy description. Unendurable, agonizing sensations of physical ecstasy, though the full measure of it is still yet to come.

I watch in awe as her ruby, sensuous lips begin to part, and she seems to hold her breath, as if breathing might cause the spirit to leave her unfulfilled. Her face reflects the growing tension in her body, as if she is nearing a painful plateau. In her voice is the pre-cry, the breathy, high pitched moan of extreme longing to be released from agony. And then, before my eyes, after several more minutes of gentle swaying, I see her face contort into a sudden expression of pure helplessness and regret, as if she has gone too deeply into the well. Her breath begins to flow silently from her open mouth, accompanied by the wailing, which continues until it is a full blown, involuntary scream of pain and pleasure. Every muscle in her tenses, until her body is tight and curved, except for the gigantic bosoms, which quiver mightily upon the waves, flowing through her body like an electric current.

I do not feign ignorance about it. I will admit that I know she is in touch with the Spirit of Sensuality, whatever that may entail. The energy in the candle room is always powerful, and frightening, making me feel as if I could be lifted off the bed by it. This meditation leaves her in tears and begging, as though it has nearly done her body harm, and that she will never do it again.

An extremely powerful orgasm through meditation, achieved with little or no apparent stimulus, appearing as if by magic.

A Witch's Crown.

73

*T*his day brings a newness in what we know, in the midst of our journey through perversion. Pretense falls as blossoms of Spring. Swirled up into purpose, and carried away by what wind is preordained. The sunlight through the kitchen window rests warmly on the opposite wall, to reflect the window panes through the open curtains, divided in shadow by the shape of the Cross.

Our latest breakfast having been prepared and eaten, mother is in good spirits this early summer's day. In 20 year old vigor, I lean over the table, washing it in more soap and foam than it needs, unaware of the many looks she has glanced, or the many more she has suppressed, until the pressure builds into something she cannot endure. In the ignorance of farmhouse vanity, I wear my latest thrift shop dress, in love with the newness of the off-white cloth in tiny rose flower pattern, and the feel of it over my body. Mother notices the unfamiliar way it hugs and twists with my shape as I lean over our breakfast table, working the foam into a lather too grand for its destination.

Hey, she says, calling me by one of my many names. I turn to look at her standing back at the sink, drying her hands from the drowning of our breakfast dishes in soap suds. She walks over to the young woman in the new used dress, and tells her to stand up. I do it, not knowing whether nerves are warranted. You can put the rag down, she says. The gray in her full length skirt is laced by the color purple, seeming to marry that which is faded from her tight blouse, which is the same color that has died. I stand ready in dull white cloth, as it clings to my body in tiny rose pattern.

She stares at me. Slowly moving her gaze from my long black hair to my eyes, to my nose and my lips, all of which I am ashamed of. I tuck my lips in—and she tells me *relax your lips. Stand up straight.* I do it, and her eyes are drawn downward to what the rose cloth hides underneath. I know better than to move or speak, or even to look away, or to allow even the echo of disinterest to show. *Move your hair back and stand up straight,* she says, a little sharper, and I flip my hair back off my shoulders and push them back in military attention. I am exposed beneath the cloth. *Relax a little,* she says—*undo those buttons.* I divide the dress in its proper place, releasing the tension, feeling the cool summer morning air on the top part of my breasts, which none other soul hath seen but she. In her face I see a surrender, reluctant. A coming to terms with what is destined in her daughter's body: that the bloodline flows to posterity. In the light of day, in the blinding glow of rational thought, she observes every inch of me in the cloth, while she hides whatever truth there may be in what she knows. I choose not to be humiliated by the stare, for I am hers to be looked at, or chastised, or ridiculed as she may see fit.

I want you to put your hand in your bra, over your right breast, she says. *Now take it out. Slowly. Not your hand, Stupid. I want you to take out your right breast. Slowly. That's it...*

The fabric tickles my skin a bit as I pull. In the next instant, I feel the weight of my naked right breast in the kitchen. I notice the deep breath in her, and the way her own bosom pushes the cloth of her faded purple blouse. *Now the other one,* she says. Her voice is low. Almost whispery. With more skill, I pull it out of my big bra, which is yet too small to contain their song in F major. In tragicomic decresendo, my left breast falls down to its place, to join the other in natural calling.

I stand open. Exposed. Feeling more vulnerable than if I were totally nude. From the back of me, there is long, black hair and a plain off white dress, while the front of me is a face framed by the hair, above the dress opened wide at the top, with two very large, low naked breasts hanging. I look down at them, to draw confidence as I can, and I stand up straighter, looking at her in veiled challenge, to see what pleasure or pain she dares to give.

Birds whistle the fading of the morning dew, to call mother to attention. She undoes the top buttons on her faded purple blouse. My heart races now more than ever, knowing that the undoing of even the first button is a lovely horn signal, echoed from a far off place, to announce the changing of the wind, and the new direction where it must blow. In beauty, she looks down as she unbuttons, then takes hold of the bottom of her bra. She holds it still while she pulls her left breast in measured, deliberate motion, one pull at a time, until the areola, then the big nipple pops into view.

I understand now that the journey itself is the destination. That the pleasure is in the removal of the breast from its cloth prison. She takes her time with each pull, until the phantom chord above G major spills over in massive, rounded splendor. She looks at me in triumph, as a teacher who has shown the wayward student the fullness of their unlearned condition. She holds on to her bra, and she pulls the other one, no less slowly, until the areola, then the big nipple pops into view, and the G major completes its forlorn exposition. She stands there. Queen of the Country. Ruler of the world we are in. From the back of her is the view of a statuesque female, a lifesized figurine, curved in full length purple-gray skirt and faded purple blouse—a long, beautiful neck and black hair pinned up. From the front are eyes as bewitching as a white funnel cloude, the blouse opened just enough, and two giant white breasts spilled out—hung low, big and rounded—exposed to her princess daughter in waiting.

I want you to suck your left breast, she says. *I want you to suck it as unto God. To suck the sin out of your body through your breast. Swallow the sin, so it can be taken, and so you can be cleansed...*

I take it up in my hands—as I have been taught to do—and I suck the unseen milk from it. Is it the milk of lust? Is it vanity or fear? This, I do not know. She tells me to hold it in my mouth, to move my hands, and hold the full weight of it with my mouth. It soon falls, flopping back into place. I pick it back up, glancing at her exposed nipples, which have hardened from the music of what they have seen. In loud smacking, kissing noises, I suck my left nipple. Raising it up again by mouth, shaking my head back and forth for her for many seconds before letting it fall again, which I know is fuel for the blue fire that burns. Of this, I do for a quarter of an hour, from one breast to the other, until my sin is absolved in her eyes. She steps full against me. Touching both of her nipples to my own.

Fully clothed, we stand as one. Our private obsession on stage for our world, which is only the birdsong, and the objects in our kitchen. She stands still, looking down at our skin touching, allowing me to see the pain of desire in her face, and hear it in her breathing. While we stand pressed together, she raises her arms to her hair, until the full beauty of it is down around her shoulders and the length of her back. Of this that she must do, she is sorry for it. She whirls me around and hugs me tight from behind, admonishing me in my ear that she is *going to have to [hump] me*, but in the vulgar slang, to which I heartily agree my yes' to.

I am pressed back against her while she holds both my breasts in her hands. Squeezing them unmercifully while I writhe, my tongue pushing deep into her mouth. Our duet begs to begin in perfect unison, sung upon our stage, and our curtain call in farming country. She bends me over the foaming table, and flips my dress up, and pulls my underwear down. I do not see her raise her skirt, and lower her underwear, I only feel it happen, and then I feel her warm self pressed against my backside. Then the pounding ensues, in the manner of her gift, of the phantom member she possesses. The waves of pleasure are transferred to me this time, quicker than I have known before, perhaps energized and pulled along the current caused by my bosoms in the foam on the table. She bangs into me without vanity, without pity, with the fever of her controlled madness—as one who runs hard through a pouring rain, when the relief of shelter is in sight.

She stops only once, to rub me closer to the edge, which causes me to raise up and lean back again for the kiss—in a voice more gruff and mature than I am accustomed to giving, taking her tongue as though I am starved for it. I lean back over the table, and the banging resumes again, in a more perfect place than before as I claw at the dying foam, and I hear the sound of my own voice in the haze, calling out on its own. In the midst of the final pounding I feel the familiar shaking of her behind me, and the pressing down on my back, and the cry of agony and distress from her beautiful voice in the air around me.

74

What is normal, behind closed doors? On what rhythm beats the heart of the truly perverse? Is it normal for some, to stand in the summer kitchen nude at the baking table, clad in waist aprons, breasts hanging huge and exposed for us to see? I wonder what sort of insanity this is, what gleeful abandon of reason this may be, while she directs me to break the eggs over my breasts. The egg is cool, but not too cold, when it slides down my breast into the big glass mixing bowl. She watches me with rapt attention, studying all four eggs as they die upon the mountain, and slide to their final resting place in the valley of glass below.

She tells me to put myself in the bowl—this, I cannot believe! But she tells me to lean my breasts into the bowl, and beat the eggs to another death! The moving noise is definite sloshing! The glass and the eggs are cool relief in the heat of summer. She tells me to slosh harder—to pick the bowl up and *slosh those eggs*. I do it, as if this were a cooking secret passed on through the ages, by an elite and chosen few. I put the bowl back to the table, so that my whole body shakes in time to the music of the sloshing. The rhythm of perversion is freedom.

After several minutes, I take the initiative, and I raise up. Looking down at what is left of the egg in the bowl and on my bosom. I take a part of the measured flour, and I sprinkle it over the egg on my skin, until they are white from the powder. I lower the mixing breasts back into the bowl, and slosh them all about, as though this is the road to baking perfection less traveled. I hear the voice whispering *oh yes* on its own, even the occasional quick moan of approval under her breath. Laced in the sound of her voice is the echo of disbelief, that I am able to feel and display so vividly her imagination.

When the eggs are embalmed in the flower dust, I raise up, and the thick, yellow paste covers both of my nipples and more. My areolas are hidden by the Golden Cream. Mother stands by helplessly, wondering what to do, or if I will know myself what to do, as we both know that they are somehow a work of art! I do not touch the pattern formed on my skin, letting the sunny yellow paste rest full. I reach into the bowl with my hands, and I place a glob on both breasts, watching it slide down the both of them, feeling again Mother's awestruck expression, as the liquid paste covers my sin and nakedness in the color of hope and wisdom.

Her fascination with my breasts is genuine, as she is so inclined; gone are the days of coy and shy looks—when I would turn and there she'd be, turning away, embarrassed at having been caught staring. She watches me now as sport and amusement, as one might view without self awareness a lady runner on the track, or an actress on the stage, engrossed in their every movement of being. It is something for her to do. To chase away Ennui's cat, the boredom and depression that haunts her like a ghost on a snowy mountain pass. Even on warm summer days, our legacy is the cold, and the land where pain presides above our death and burial.

Pain must seek the path of least resistance. Through the soul, into the mind, and finally through the body, where it can take its final form in a life. Appearing in public or private, as a force to make the world a better place, or to drag it down to immorality and perversion. Life is charged with the energy of broken dreams—we are all driven by one kind of pain or another. For her, for the woman who pushed me screaming into this horrible place—I know that her pain is that of lost love, and a childhood filled with that same energy, as were her days and nights of physical torture. From the little things she has said, I know that her own mother's discipline is what lights the fire inside, which burns her up night and day. I don't know if she fully realizes the twistedness of what she does, the epic taboo of her private avocation. All she understands is that the pain she feels must go somewhere—the pain of her own rapings by her mother from age 13 to 17 in the name of punishment and chastity. As I live and breathe, she suffers the heat inside, and her groin and bowels burn hot with blue and black fire. The torment of a young girl's twisted nipples, an older girl's breasts bitten to blood, and naked beatings with the buckle of her father's belt—the scars of this still burn—and the pain must go somewhere—even if only through self imposed exile, and a daughter taken out of school and isolated from the world. In her life, it forms into a youthful likeness of her, a living doll she hath created, to practice every means of forbidden pain and pleasure upon.

I flinch like a pinched housemaid at the clothesline, when I feel two strong hands grab and squeeze both of my breasts. I relax and try to turn around, but she says *keep going,* and I reach up to hang her lavender shirt upside down on the line. When I raise my arms, she squeezes very hard, which I would like to respond to with more than a fluttering eyelid and a deep trembling sigh. The strength in her hands is remarkable, to make me wonder sometimes if masculine strength would be any more or less. But my body's need is tuned to her touch alone, and the feel of her body, the smell of her hair and skin, and the deep whisper of her voice is enough to make me lose my mind. It is the spell she has cast, until I have to curl myself into a fetal position some nights when I am alone in my bed.

The squeezing is the foreplay of what we do. While I pretend to still hang the blouse on the line, part of me is thankful as I open the clothespin, suddenly remembering that it could very well be biting me at this moment. *Keep going*, I hear, but with more authority, so I try to focus on hanging out the rest of the clothes. I come to one of my dresses now, an ugly, faded flowered navy bluish thing from a thrift store, as I have never owned a new dress. I pinch the cloth onto the line, amazed that this massaging carries such a powerful new sensation under my shirt and bra. Maybe it is the forbidden nature of it out here, in the purity of nature itself—out here, under all of heaven exposed—watching me give place to desire forbidden. There are things I want to say in vulgarity to her that I keep locked away, so as not to kill our moment in the sun.

I bend down to pull another blouse, feeling her hands on my sides. I no longer care if it is wrong for me to wait, to wait for the feel of my mother's hands sliding back to my bosom when I stand up. She does this until the basket is empty, and I am finally leaning back against her, breathing in the scent of her hair and her skin. *Relax*, she whispers. *These are your Pain and your Pleasure. Every time I squeeze, it brings you closer to the end of yourself. I'll be there, to hear it in your voice, and to feel what it does to your body...*

What mother hath spoken such words to her daughter! What mother's hands hath brought her daughter to the edge of ecstasy with a touch! What fate awaits us in the perfect breeze, what warning does the wind breathe to my soul? Upon this wind, there is no judgment, no warning that I hear. For me there is only the burning of extreme pleasure, the pressure each squeezing builds up in the lower part of my body. *Lets go inside*, she says. I turn like a statue on a pivot in her hands, and she rolls me to the porch and into the kitchen, taking her place behind me again, to resume the buildup of pressure inside.

Through the mother line I travel, along the branch of our family tree. Back—backward through the far reaches of our time—to the little kitchen where my mother's 13 year old hands are tied behind her back for misbehavior perceived—genuine or false—of some benign childhood act unknown. There, young Barbara Jean Daniels stands with her dress unzipped and pulled down to where her young breasts are exposed, a song already in the key of C, even at such a young age, forshadowing the F key at 17, then to where the Redwood takes full height, where the key of J lives in a phantom twilight. I watch her plain but beautiful mother frown, and hold her daughter against the refrigerator by the arm, and proceed to bruise her nipples with the rounded cusp of the wooden spoon. All that Barbara Jean Daniels can do is what I have done, which is to wail the name of Jesus, to ask her mother to *please*…but please what? Stop? Have mercy? Can one ask a fire not to burn the flesh it consumes? Can the devil be beseeched for kindness? Barbara Jean Daniels accepts her heavenly correction, standing as still as she can, but screaming as loud as she can, as her own mother admonishes *"you better let it outta your voice girl, 'cause if you pass out I'm gon' beat you worse when you wake up…"*

What have you done, Barbara Jean, to deserve the pain she gives! What evil have you done? I see the red bruises of your youth, Mother, I hear the blue and black flames in your voice, and I understand, I concur, and I feel it coursing from my breasts to my groin. Yes! Open the buttons on my shirt! Prepare me for what needs I require! Expose my bra to the open air! Take my shirt down off my shoulders! Reach into my bra, and pull the first F-note into the kitchen breeze! The front of these notes are flat still, in their lack of understanding!

I am already breathing deeper, when she pulls the other breast free from my bra. She stands still behind me. I lean back not to move, not naïve enough to expect pleasure over pain, but sensing that she will relieve her own suffering today by undiluted pleasure to me, which is often pain itself. I lean back firm against her, exposed breasts heaving, naked for the kitchen cabinets to see. She takes hold, squeezing them very deeply, but not to pull or pinch the nipples. As the pain of her youth plays the theatre of my mind, I lay my head far back on her shoulder, not caring how such feeling can possibly find a release from my body. Then I feel her fingers circling the areolas, to call my nipples to fore. They only half respond, not being hardened to her satisfaction. She runs her fingers over one, and I have to turn my head and press my lips hard against the side of her face, even touching my teeth to her face in a calm, phantom bite.

I am her statue on a pivot again as she turns me around. The look in her eyes, the expression around her mouth is epic seriousness in the kitchen as she faces me, taking both of my breasts into her hands to study them. She squeezes softly, she shakes them, she bangs them together, holding them still again, staring expertly at them both. Then she pulls the nipples with her fingers. Her black skirt is long, her winter gray blouse is tight on her body. Her black hair is pinned loosely, in contrast to mine, which hangs the length of my back. She studies them as she leans over, in a deep knowledge of understanding, and she puts the first nipple in her mouth and sucks it gently. I watch her cheeks sink inward from the sucking motion, as she pulls memory from the timeline with precision. She does it again, in one direction, pulling from the nipple outward in a loud kissing noise. Doing it several times to both my nipples, until they are at rapt attention and sensitive to a breeze. This is her fellatio, our means to another end. Then she ceases the sucking to work them again with her hands, looking up at me. Then she pulls one deep into her mouth, sucking it up and down, in and out, her head slowly bobbing the motion of the Nun's Intercourse, the deepest feeling we have known in our chastity.

This, she does until I lose control of my breathing and begin to shake, and the hopeless kitchen reverberates loudly with the sound of my voice.

76

Sin will blossom, as the flower blooms. Sin doth blossom, like the rose in June. When experience has fulfilled its purpose, virtuosity beckons, waiting to be achieved. We are the virtuoso, she and I, to perform upon each other, a concert piece for only her and me. This melody is born of lust, which hath conceived, to bring forth the deepest perversion.

When this desire is born, there is nothing that grows it faster than my forceful aggression, which will have me take over as the superior. It comes as though inspired, causing me to use my strength against her just enough to keep her from raising up. From here, I am her mistress for a moment. To cause pleasure as I see fit, holding her down unafraid. Hearing her breath quicken. Her gigantic breasts slosh and wiggle in her last attempt to overtake me, and I grab one of them with one hand, sucking it in deep. She takes in a breath of surrender, holding it there, then releasing it in voice. A voice loud and womanly. An alarm, to call this part of Creation to notice. I suck deeply, in fellatio of the areola and nipple, moistening it with rough sucking, while she begins to squirm in something close to agony.

I press heavily on her, to dominate, to chasten, grabbing both in my hands like so much dough, to press and squeeze, to knead them into their submission. They are above the key of G, pitched upward to Heaven, to be a chord ripe with the most beauty I deem possible. I suck and squeeze their orchestra in full, until every string and wind has achieved their perfect balance, then I lay my tongue upon the G chord, to send voice through the walls of color. Licking both nipples together, sucking them simultaneously. Her body is my ensemble to direct, to play as I see fit. In the Satisfaction of Vengeance, this I must do.

From the last pull of her nipple in a loud kissing noise, to her pitiful trembling, her lost expression, to the biting of the skin on her stomach, to the licking and kissing of her naval, the memory of our lifeline. I slide my tongue back and forth across her stomach below the mountain rise, in the shadow of their majesty. Sucking the skin and flesh hard enough to cause pain and bruising, which has her babbling with a craving impossible to know. She is a double edged sword, adept to cut through either sadism, or the other. The bite upon her buttocks hath marked her skin to blood. She groans for me to bite her hard, which I do, leaving the imprint of it in her flesh, and in the walls of my bedroom.

The Rondo for Piano and Orchestra sings in beauty and power. It tells of things that must be, singing from her spirit in the orchestral, which answers from mine upon the keys. As I near the forbidden, the sweetness beckons my hand, and I obey, rubbing it to her chorus of *Oh, God. Oh, my God.* This is the last flame, burning white hot, for I know that soon I must fulfill her prophecy. She squirms so much, that I worry that she may jump up and either run away, or claw me to pieces. She is a woman possessed by an addiction, a hunger she had suppressed for 20 years, but which has erupted like the Judgment of Pompeii. Now, the fire spits in words *taste it, taste it for me,* and I answer, with inspired lack of fear, *beg me.* She looks bewildered, and I repeat it, *I want to hear you beg me.* Her lust is so complete that there can be no retaliation of aggression, and she breathes a heavy *please... please have mercy...*

In keeping with what I am, my attempt at punishment is colored by pathetic compassion, and I open the petals of this flower with my hands, and taste the sweetness with my lips and tongue, feeling her body twitch in a tiny convulsion. She begins to writhe and scream—as though she is being slowly, and painfully killed by me.

*O*ur orgasms seem miraculously timed, so that whenever I open my eyes at the precipice—I see her there as well, her face already twisted in passion. We so often fall in simultaneous flow—to our drowning deaths at the sea. But if I fall first—or perhaps she, the other is pulled rapidly along—plunging to the sea.

Above all things, we are tribadists, she and I. The crickets sing of this, as do the birds if it is early evening, chiming the Waltz of the Tribades, in keeping with the squeaking from the springs in my bed. As I sit on top, grinding her scissor style, about to explode, she takes hold of my hair, slapping my buttocks and saying *"look at me…I want to see the sin in your eyes… I want to see it on your face… this is how we make ourselves pure…*

this is how we cleanse ourselves in the eyes of God... " The intensity in her voice is enough to send me screaming over the edge, staring her directly in the eye as I fall to my death. She has found her ultimate justification; her conscious has seared through her moral sanity. For her, it has become a cleansing ritual, so that she may better serve Him when the lust is gone. For me, another part of myself has died, replaced by the music I hear. I know that soon the life of hope will be gone, and I will be a creature of pure melody.

My rondo has ended, replaced by *The Widow,* a symphony for women in mourning...

For two weeks, this has poured a crystal waterfall, to mark the Birth of Melody in sorrow. Restless chords of unearthly origin—a symphony unlike any the world has ever known.

In the minuet, there is a trio from the Great Music Hall. Above the River Valley of Nowhere's Land.

She possess a power that I do not understand. It runs from her life force into her physical body, resting behind her eyes when she looks at me, hovering around her as pure energy, invisible to every soul but me. I know the musician's touch, when she slows down as we enter the yard to our dreary house, placing the lovers arm around my waist. By the touch, the tone of it, I know whether I should flinch or not, though it always caresses the part of me she has awakened, tickling me with something close to fear.

Often on a Sunday afternoon, when our stroll from church is done, after the door to our home is closed, she will touch my hips and kiss me full on the mouth with hardly a passing thought, to remind me that I belong to her, and that my body is not my own. I consider myself fortunate if this happens, as opposed to the alternative, which is her anger. A nitpicking of a false step from anywhere in the timeline, which she will use as the reason to stand me nude at the kitchen table or the dresser, and cane or paddle my buttocks to sores and bleeding. The paddle burns me with black fire. The pain makes me scream to God and Christ.

But more often than not, I am lucky enough, that the fury is channeled though soft craving. When we have undressed in the afternoon, and gotten into her bed, she will press me down heavily underneath her, moving, kissing me in the mouth and on the neck, even by the ear, and upon my shoulders while she slides and moves her body as though we were connected. Playing my soul as a cello, with a smooth and steady hand, then she will raise up and look me squarely in the eyes until she has my attention. She does this repeatedly, until I am writhing underneath her and clawing at her like a cat in heat, pulling her buttocks down against me while I grind and jerk as if possessed. And then she raises up again when I am broken, and listens to me whimper and breathe as if I am holding back my loudest pleading voice, which I am.

She will say the vulgar of *do you want me back inside of you,* as though she has a member to use and grow. And I have to answer in pleading, sometimes on the edge of tears, a plateau of weeping and pleasures to bear. When I have begged and squirmed to her satisfaction, she rests on top of me, rejoining herself to me by mouth and birth, as one with me through this forbidden thing. She holds me down in an embrace, to make me feel every ounce of her weight and power, which I gladly accept, until my body is destroyed by her movement, and I deliver the muffled scream into her mouth. I am hypnotized into a craving so deep, a raging desire so violent that I am aggressive in my clutching, my pinching, even the occasional spanking of her buttocks to hold them to me, which I know sends a shiver through her perverted soul, and she responds in the deep mother's moan, kissing my mouth and tongue as though driven by a spirit. In this, there is no stopping, no raising up to torment me. We are locked in violence with one another by mouth and by birth, until the current runs through us both in the manner of the electric chord, even the chord that I have felt in whipping on my back so many times in our days and years.

Oh, how I long for Innocence! A place where the White Rose is in bloom!

Whether I have cried, I know not.

79

*W*e are the Endowed, she and I! This, the curse of our womanhood, through the Rose blood, grandmother's maiden name to fore! I refuse to obey their sensitivity, which calls me whenever I dress or undress, or especially when I bathe, when the warm water tickles the skin around them. My soul will not hear the allure—I resist to give myself their pleasure, even while the very air will often tingle every inch of them.

I have learned that hers are the center of her body's energy. The force around which turns her deepest need. They are blessed with greater feeling, which is part of her curse to bear. Through them, we have grown. Matured into the worship of them. While I feel no pleasure when I bind my own every morning—perhaps touching them only to rub an itch away—I know that the highlight of her day is when she latches her cloth, hefting them one at a time into their tight resting place. There, desire is captured. To have no outlet, so that power can build upon itself again. Each day of this only adds to hunger, becoming a pain of starvation for her spirit's craving. So often, they are the means to her satisfaction; even the focal point, and the inevitable end unto itself.

Mother has given in to what fires that burn. They consume the hypocrisy that once ruled in these walls, along with her Holy Dignity. When this lust hath conceived, it bringeth forth sin—a kind and duration known to an accursed few.

Sharply, she tells me to leave my underwear on. This, after a month of resistance, even refusing my requests to give her a massage. I know that when this new massage is come, it is the fullness thereof. While both of our bras are in place, we stand close together, still and quiet, facing one another. I feel her breath, warm on my face from across the Great Southern Valley, born from the mountains rising on either side! The pushing, the mashing displays her cleavage to mine, and she is a breast queen, her body in awe of its own creation. She closes her eyes and exhales, holding her head back in extreme beauty. What am I to her? I am the support for her to lean on, the bearing wall for her crashing, sounding sea…

Tonight, she has focused her body's desire to her bosom. When this is complete, she lets me go, and she slowly lowers each strap. In a smooth, dance-like motion, she lowers her cups until they are out, gigantic, smooth and white, the large dark areolas and nipples exposed. She slides her bra all the way to the floor without unlatching it, feeling the heavy weight of them pull towards the Earth. She returns to me, leaving her bottoms in place, touching the naked breast skin to my bra. I stiffen in a deep breath for her, pushing mine outward, in their own substantial girth and power. She puts her arms as far behind her own back as she can; it pushes her bosom out farther, making them seem higher and rounder. She shoves them hard against my bra. Pressing, brushing, slipping them back and forth over my bra in a slapping motion, hitting my covered bosom with force. It is a curious, oddly pleasant feeling, the hard bumping of her big bosom against mine. I know better than to move, to try and join the motion, fearful that I might cause her to lose what momentum she has gathered.

Take your bra off, she breathes.

This, I do unashamedly, watching her eyes stare at my nipples rising into view. When our nipples touch, I hear the breath leaving her in approval, in and out loudly. She attacks my new exposure with determined force and rhythm, the bumping now joined by the smacking of her naked breasts against mine. I put my arms behind my back, and steady myself for the pushing, the slapping and bouncing of her heredity to my own. I catch a glimpse of her face in the evening light, her mouth twisted into an anguished frown.

The breast bumping is interrupted suddenly, when she turns her back to me, fully aroused. *Milk them,* she says. *Milk them for me.* From where comes this carnal knowledge? It is passed through the blood! For I know to take them both in my hands with authority, squeezing every inch of their gigantic life, even twisting the nipples just enough to make them wet, pulling on them ever so slightly enough to cause pain. I massage, squeeze and shake them roughly while she snakes her hips back and forth against me. I take this cue, to press on her the domination she needs, speaking softly in her ear of the milking. She puts her head back towards me in gruff, loud groaning, and grabs my hips. I take her ear with my teeth, smelling the shampoo in her pinned up hair, while she squirms and moans her approval. This storm rages for a quarter of an hour, until my hands are dripping with her *milk*, and her breasts are as red as the juice of the sweet melons we grow.

80

*W*hat is Divine Negativity? Can deviance be a privilege, can suffering be a birthright to claim? What wrongdoing does He allow into a life, to provide the lonely a reprieve? When the mind's pain is too severe, there may be remedies unknown, to provide a cure from the agony, even by way of evils that must come. But woe unto them, except by his mercy, for He knows the imagination of our heart is wicked from our youth.

In us, it has grown and blossomed. To bear the fruit of a Great Flowering Tree and beyond—knowledge of such divine intensity as to boggle my mind when I remember, and even when I partake the sweet and bitter fruit it grows. This is sweetness to the taste, to satisfy the body's craving, and bitter poison to the spirit, when the body's satisfaction is known. We know this satisfaction, unaware that any others have understood, content that none would ever imagine what sins our lives have shown. This, we do gladly.

The months of it have burdened her breasts with the inevitable. It is the Revelation of Reward for Perseverance. Our daily ritual without fail, has been to engage one another's breast in deep sucking, either short or long—either rough or a gentle wave. She undresses me one piece at a time—my blouse—my skirt—my leg stockings—and then the gate is opened—my bra. Then she will often pull hers out until they flop over her bra in massive white glory. There is no key to play this music, there is no chord above G. Hers is an opera suite beyond G major (the key number in her bra is 36J), to push the limits of womanhood, and to show that there is a God. She is stared at, smiled at, and snickered at everywhere she goes, while people wonder how such a thing is possible.

If we are both standing, she leans over and takes one of mine in her hand, and sucks it so I'll know that my life is hers. My independence is daily removed in the sucking, and what was once pain is now a pleasure that my body craves. It is one of many. Skillfully, she pulls my nipple into her mouth deeply, with noisy hunger in a loud kissing sound, releasing them in a great sucking, popping noise intermittently. It is a sound we have both come to know and love, as it sends a signal to our mind, to stimulate every inch of our skin. She continues to suck my nipple and areola, holding the other breast in the other hand, squeezing it in unison with the sucking breast. I know instinctively when the last kissing, popping sound is made, to change the course in natural flow. If they are still bound, I reach into her bra and pull her bosoms out. Her J-cup breasts are gigantic—the true superior to most. Are they a gift from God—or is a curse? I do not know.

I get behind her and squeeze them like great pillows of soft dough, the bread and wine of my days. She lays her head back and breathes a deep sigh, to release every tension in her body. Afterward, I sit on the arm of the sofa in our living room by the summer breeze. Every window of the house open, both doors drawing the cool summer wind through our world. The screen door hides us from none of the grass and trees I see, nor from country spirits that stare. The wide open door, the bright sunlit day only enhances us, so that we are reminded that in darkness and in the light, we are fallen women.

As I hold her heavy breast with both hands, the nipple is flattened under my tender, noisy kisses. What she perceives as shyness is really pure nerves, from not knowing where this road will go. I stay with the kiss around the areola, over top of the flattened nipple, always glancing up, seeing her head back with her eyes closed, her expression somber and beautiful. I kiss in nervousness, beginning to lick over and around the nipple, hearing her breathe deeper. Soon, the tension draws her aerola in, and her nipple begins to rise higher, until I know to put my lips around it. I suck the nipple only, until it is as large as I have ever seen or felt it, to remind me of the country grapes on the far western edge of our yard.

I take her left breast into my mouth, and I hear her draw a breath that she cannot release. I look up while I hold and suck her breast, to glimpse the look on her face, her mouth half open, her brow wrinkled and determined in a grimace of pleasure beyond pain. I suck to the point of deep nursing, in fear and longing for the long road outside, which I can feel through the open door. No one in the world will know, no eyes will be lucky enough to see what miracles God hath wrought in what we do. I suck until I taste the sweetness from the fruit, and I swallow the white sweetness—taking my mouth away to squeeze her nipple with my fingers, to see the *milk* come through! Then I nurse it into my mouth until it is full, and I release the nipple slowly, letting her milk run down my chin onto her breast, and watch it drip white and sweet to the floor.

As I watch her take her other breast deep into her own mouth, I nurse with the same power as before, both of us taking mouths full of warm milk to drink from both of her breasts at once, and to wet completely each other's bosom, dripping in sweet and white to the floor.

81

When I stand in the middle of my bedroom floor waiting naked, with my wrists tied behind my back, I don't have the luxury of knowing which kind of pain it will be. Of what purpose can fear truly serve, except to war on the nerve—to cause the body more suffering? I have learned to control my fear through prayer and meditation on the bars of music—too many of my sonatas begin in trembling, to the chiming of a storm brewing nearby where I can hear. I know that this is her power and control, so much more even than the lust that trembles her body.

The piano is in time with the soft tapping of her feet through the house—the pulse of it activated upon each footstep, which I seem to feel in my spirit. Some would sing of the playful *tap...tap...tapping* of the Spring Tree Sonata, so blissfully unaware of the true source of the rhythm motivated by depression—inspired by fear. This is not the joyful dance of the snowflake, nor the happy hip-hopping of the bunny through the cold snow. It is the rhythm of the footsteps, the beating of a fleeting heart—the flow of a river of blood from my vagina to the floor. But today is not the curse of blood as I stand bare in the warm winter room—it is the curse of fear—that courses through every blue and crimson mile.

The tapping rhythm stops suddenly when the door is opened. I notice immediately that there is no belt or paddle or cane in her hand, which could mean that I am going to be beaten with her fists alone. But she only walks over to me, with the most serious look I have ever seen on this side of anger, and leans into me for a gentle kiss. I open my mouth readily, closing it gently in time to hers, until this kiss is done. In my soul, I know that I will not be beaten.

She connects with me through our vision until our eyes are locked. She looks down at her bra, taking a deep breath to watch the big cleavage rise and fall. She reaches inside the cup of her left breast and slowly pulls it out, doing the same to the right, until they both hang gigantically over her bra. She stands there for a moment, a country momma behind closed doors. Confident. Serious. Naively unaware that she could conquer the world in sin—to have the life of luxury she so desires. Barbara Jean Coletti, she would be.

She takes up one of her heavy breasts—huge, fleshy. She squeezes the nipple until the milk begins to flow freely. Then she takes the other one and does the same—even sucking the milk in a slurping, acknowledging in her mind a taste she has now acquired. Her attention turns to me, and she begins to squirt the milk to my big hanging breasts until they are coated and dripping. She does this until my own nipples drip as though they are lactating themselves.

In the next moment, I feel the electricity from the tongue as her mouth clamps around my nipple—sucking and pulling. Nursing. Her tongue slides up from my breasts to my neck, licking with sucking kisses, until I cannot hold my eyes open, nor can I breathe a steady rhythm. She returns to her own milk vessels—squeezing the milk onto my arms and my bound wrists. I feel it tickle my hips, until it trickles down my legs to the backs of my knees. Her tongue follows suit, licking both of my legs and thighs up to my big backside, where she sucks loud bruises onto both of my buttocks. I am hers to corrupt. Her perverseness is my own.

She stands up again and steps back in front of me, as the wind howls over the spring trees in waiting, while the winter blows hard against my bedroom window. She walks me to the bed and lays me on my back, my wrists still tightly bound—to indulge in what I know keeps her up nights in devastating want and need. She stands there looking, still serious, breasts hanging exposed, hips rounded out to infinity in her underwear. She admires me with small contempt, as though I am what she despises, but cannot live without. What Sapphic spirit there lives in this house is Queen. She climbs on the bed on all fours facing my feet, straddling my chest up to my chin. The room is noisy with her breath...

And what I feel next lights my body on fire—burning blue, tinted black. It is a flame struck by her tongue and lips, sucking and licking the center of where I live, until I writhe underneath her like a white she-tiger pinned on its back. Her body presses heavy on top of mine, her head is between my legs which are held far back and open, her head working fast back and forth. Her lips and tongue vibrate me to places I have known and wish I had never been, until my moans are turned to screams, and my screams transform into cries of mercy.

I cannot pretend that I don't understand the fire that burns her. Somewhere deep, the fire burns me as well, though I am not consumed as she. But I am her perfect outlet, having all the natural understanding I need to oblige. Gone are my looks of bewilderment and naiveté when I notice her staring at me while I cook. I glance at her and she looks away, and if I am so inclined, I might go over to the table and get behind her and rub her shoulders, to massage her morning or evening cares away. Because of the look she hides, I already know to undo the buttons on her blouse and slide it off her shoulders, and to squeeze the gigantic flesh inside her bra. I no longer pretend when I slide her bra down and expose her breasts, squeezing them hard. She will often put her head back and breathe the deepest sigh of appreciation. How many people are lucky enough to have such an help meet for them, with understanding so natural, without judgment, ignorance or pretense?

Gone is the bewilderment and naiveté, when I begin to pinch her nipples in the proper fashion. She lowers her head to look, as the first drops of white rain onto the table. I do this over and over, even lifting one up to suck briefly, and then I continue to squeeze the milk from her breasts to the table. What diversion this is, I do not care. It simply is, and that is all. I continue to do this thing; kneading, pinching, squeezing and pulling her nipples until we are both amused and fascinated, even boldly squirting a little up into her face. I am comfortable to take control of her, to exercise the power I have been given. We cease the frivolity, to work ourselves into our rhythm, to squeeze her like a milk maid on a mountain dairy farm. This is our uniqueness, the power of what sin that is bequeathed to our birth. She closes her eyes to feel it, to even hear it now—as the streams begin to make a large white puddle on the table—even while my breakfast is burning on the hot stove.

Gone are my looks of bewilderment and naiveté in her room, when I take up the scissors and cut a hole into her bra cups while she is wearing it, so careful not to scratch, pinch or cut her skin. It is part of what we do to pass so much of our leisure time behind closed doors, sharing in common with every other, who would not have their private moments made known. We wear a false face in public, to hide our faces of moral decay. We are unnatural, she and I—two extremes in God's creation. When we are in church or on my rare trip to the store, we are unnaturally chaste and quiet, our demeanor southern church and gothic. In private, I understand it when she takes her cut bra off and goes over to the window, and presses her breasts against the glass. In her mind, there is someone there to be devastated, to be traumatized or offended, to be thrilled or delighted by her nudity mashed flat against the window. It tells me that somewhere inside her, she is a flower meant to be seen. That she desires to walk boldly among women and men—to laugh, to smile, so share in their joy at her ridiculousness, that she is a tall white flower among weeds. To be noticed. To be made fun of. To be worshipped—or simply admired. But she is a widow, bound by an unnatural shyness and no self-esteem. Cursed with a daughter she despises, and a libido as big as the mountains of flesh she hides.

Unearned suffering is not always redemptive in this life. Perhaps there is only Fate, Destiny, and the Will of God.

83

$\mathcal{B}$y necessity, I have learned that what she requires most is my compliance, this often by my determined aggression. Her madness is becoming clearer to me, even a part of my body, and my own feeble psychology. I understand now, when we stand with our naked breasts pushed together, sliding, mashing flat and popping full again, my arms up around her neck like a slow dancing lover. I no longer feign ignorance of this ball dance, this private sway, this connection our eyes must make, or the deep wet kisses we must partake. I am privy, when she says *now give it to me,* and I lower my arms, our breast duel ensuing again. I allow her blood to join mine, to heat it up with pervertedness, and I bounce my breasts into hers in hard, determined fashion, until I have achieved a humping motion—a rhythm—letting myself enjoy the sensation of my nipples against her bare flesh. I still often cannot look her in the eye, though I compensate with increased intensity, wrinkling my brow appropriately, obeying her inner command. I give myself over to this breast battle, in the manner of the Virgin's Intercourse, this coitus of the mind, expressed through my bumping, grinding and writhing in full against her while she stands still, looking in quiet awe at me, that she is fortunate enough to see and feel her most twisted craving come to life before her eyes, and press itself repeatedly against her. She keeps her eyes open to watch me work myself into a frenzy of this breast intercourse, while I respond to her rough, low command, *I said give it to me…*

I do just that. Letting the frustration of it escape through my breathing, until she can only stop staring and close her eyes, joining me in the fray of wild hair pulled, vocal cries, and breasts bouncing against one another in burning. For her, this is often the ultimate act, the peak of our private session. When this happens, I feel the same hot agony in my body as she, as the rubbing together of the two proverbial sticks, both grieving to burst into flame. There are so many kinds of this violence for us, so many of them focused upon our breasts, none of which could ever be spoken aloud, except to the petals of this dear Rose, or through the weeping voice of my mind's Cello, and her beloved daughter Violin.

They don't know! Those at the church who profess to know Him—that profess the goodness of Him with their mouths—who deny the burning sin in their hearts—not knowing that they too are worthy of Hell's Flame! They don't know Depravity's Heart as we! Perversion's Fire, they have never felt! The Mind of Deviance, they have never known!

Which of the mothers has reached over to her daughter in the church, and squeezed the knee in knowing? Which of them have strolled the miles, past the Atramental Forest Wood, and taken their daughter's arm in knowing? Which of them have stepped quietly with their daughter through the empty farmhouse, burning in a lust too deep to know? Which of the daughters have allowed this to become a part of her, until she walks through the same Desire's Field, to take her place underneath the Kissing Tree? Under this tree, we stop our stroll, closing the door to sanity quickly, tossing our Bibles and purses to the meadow floor, kissing each other like starving she-wolves on a prey, hugging each other tight, slamming our groins together twice, three times, four times during the kiss, even before a stitch of clothing has been removed. Tongues probing deeply, drinking the moans from one another's mouths, tasting each other in full, swallowing each other's sex, undoing the myriad of buttons on dresses and blouses...

Before long, clothes are open and sliding to the floor, even while our mouths are still attached in wet, licking kisses, grabbing each other's head and hair, both of us on fire from Pandora's Poison, the kind that causes the deepest perversions to be born. Our shoes are soon kicked to the side while the rubbing and kissing continues, and we are locked again in passion, our white undergarment glowing our sin from behind closed doors, for no one but ourselves to see. Locked in the kiss, with our lower halves bumping hard against each other with violent, slow determination, both of us grunting our rough approval, knowing that this is understanding beyond knowledge, and wisdom beyond comprehension. Leaving underclothing on, to channel and direct the currents running through, she grabs me by the hips and lifts me up, and I know to wrap my legs around her, while our lips are still locked. She lowers me again to standing, and we resume our rhythmic bump and grind, releasing the kiss to look each other in the eye, and we keep time with the rhythm of the pendulum clock, her banging against me ever so skillfully, so carefully. Both of our voices singing a breathy chorus of two in four/four time—one...two...three...four...one ...two ...three... four...

This, to infinity, while the deep kisses begin again, until my own body is pushed beyond the cliff, and I cannot kiss any further, but can only sing the song of the Whistling Bird into the air in shrieks. This breaks mother's tempo into speed, though still in perfect four/four time, and she looks me in the eye while the climax comes out of her body in the same shrill, high pitched noises and trembling. We return quickly to kisses, with heavy breathing, supporting one another, holding one another up, bumping the slow rhythm again, in time to the Drowning Chorus we sing.

Everything she does in our chamber, she executes with passion. Every movement, every sound is with purpose of intention. It is as though a wellspring has been opened, and it erupts from her as regularly as the chiming of the noonday, or the stroke of the lonely midnight hour. When I think of the sweetness of this yellow fruit, so tantalizingly smooth and perfect, I cannot help but see it in its yellow skin, long and golden, as I sit on her lap on the edge of my bed. I am unclothed, as is she.

She has filed the rough edge of the fruit down to smoothness, so that I feel no scratching as my breasts are pressed together around it. She pushes it up and down rapidly between my breasts, watching it, telling me to allow my spit to fall down on it, asking me if I like it. I know what answer I must live, though I do not know what rests in my heart to give. My bosom jiggles and bounces while she pushes the long phallus between them, the inner part of them being wet from the spitting she requires so diligently. Every now and then, I see her brow wrinkle in her staring, and she succumbs to the sight of it, and she leans over and sucks my nipple hard and deep, pulling up my breast—releasing it in very loud sucking, popping sound, where it wiggles back to its place. At intervals along the seconds of her time, she does this several times more, until she can bear it no longer, and takes the fruit from between my bosom.

With me still on her sturdy lap, she gently but firmly and with meaning pushes the fruit in my mouth repeatedly, in and out, sometimes too deeply, until I have to cough and gag upon it. This she does again, with a devilish delight and awe in her eyes, and a deep tint to her voice; loving, rife with carnal understanding, admonishing me to let the spit come. She says, *don't swallow… let your mouth stay open when you gag…* Inevitably, I choke and cough clumsily, unable to resist the urge to swallow. But I learn quickly, until it is has moistened our goldenrod sufficiently, and is sliding down her closed hand in a foaming stream. Through watery eyes, I look at her, and I think I see a mother's patience in her features.

She ushers me to my back, placing the fruit sturdy between my thighs so that it sticks straight up, so that she can demonstrate the fullness thereof. She caresses it with a sure hand, with such tenderness and care that I begin to relax as if it is truly a part of me. I am in disbelief that these things are possible, even when she kisses it with as much softness as my own lips have known. She slides her tongue up and down the length of it, until it begins to grow in her imagination, followed by more of her kissing, sucking lips up and down, sliding down over the top of it now—then lower, lower until all of the inches of it are nearly devoured in her mouth. This she does again, but this time until she gags and coughs as I. This, I know sends a fevered chill through her entire body, for she repeats this, holding it in her throat beyond her endurance, until she gags so violently that I worry of what will be. But the vomiting is only streams of spitting, which she produces in such abundance that the entire fruit is dripping wet, and it runs down to the skin of my thighs. She takes hold of it slightly, working herself and her spit into a lather; stroking, choking upon it some more, until her face shows her suffering in tears streaming from her eyes. When she has endured the gagging, braved the coughing to satisfaction, she wipes her rose lips and climbs aboard this Deviance, straddling me over the groin, above where the fruit is raised in waiting. With both hands, I anchor it so that it will not fall free, exposing all the inches for her pleasure—and she slides herself down upon it. Letting it penetrate her as a sword tinted golden, to kill her pretense toward hypocrisy born, and the condescension of self-righteousness grown.

With the abandon of a woman condemned, vulgarities leap from her throat as she begins to slide up and down, up and down, clawing at her breasts until she works herself into a bouncing, screaming frenzy.

86

My training will often brush the edges of courtesy, which is only a warning whispered in my ear. Today, in the warm glow of winter's heart, she stands behind me, with her arms wrapped tightly around me. This, she does for several minutes until I am one with her, until I am relaxed enough to receive my discipline. Already, I am breathing deeply, my eyes closed, to prepare myself for what must be. She is soft against my back and my buttocks and my legs, sometimes bending me over, then raising me vertical again. Through the universe, in the first and second heaven, there is no power greater than she. She is the breath in my lungs. The life coursing through my veins.

Her nipples are as erasers against my skin. I am afraid that I might be beaten today, but I have to be ready in my heart. I have to endure it. But the fear is energized by a voice breathed loudly in my ears *I'm going to have to hurt you today. I'm going to spank you on places all over your body. I don't want you to move, or cry out unless you have to. Now, put your arms back and hold on to me...*

I believe that the telling of it, the telegraphing of it in my mind is part of her pleasure, knowing that I now wait fearfully for the first blow to my white skin. She places her hand on my thigh, this, not in front of any mirror, so that she is not distracted from my body's flinching, and from my effort to stop my trembling. Why am I still afraid of pain? Am I afraid that it will escalate into a beating, which might leave my face bruised and bloody and uglier when I gaze at my blood sister in the mirror?

She slaps my thigh very hard. I draw a breath, but remain very still. The fire in my skin is remarkable. It is the heat from the iron of her hand, tempered by a life of labour, lost love, and lamentation. She repeats it in the same spot, which increases the pain, while settling my nerves just the same. I hear her swallow, or rather, I *feel* it, and her own breath quickens slightly afterward. She whacks the same place on my right thigh a third time, which makes the red mark deepen to a place of permanence. When the fourth slap comes, then the fifth, then the sixth, my nerves begin to react, as I wonder how I will endure the agony of number 19, 20 and 21 without flinching. Already at number 10, a whimper escapes, and she wraps her left arm around me tighter, and breathes solace into my ear.

But she has had enough of my strength, my endurance, and is determined to feel my weakness anew—sliding her left hand slowly up to my right nipple, to give it the first of the continuum of slappings that will quickly reduce me to tears. When I cry, I know better than to beg her to stop. That would enrage her, and she would either beat me into wishing for my resting place, take my food away for a day or imprison me in my closet, or any two of the three thereof. I rest my head back against her, to endure the *fiftieth* slap of my burned thigh in flinching and loud yelping, still unaware of the fulness that awaits my bosom. My skin feels damaged and hot with agony. I reach my hand back and take hold of her head and kiss her cheek, quietly asking her to have mercy.

Coldly, she tells me to put my hands back to where they were, and she resumes. Each blow builds scream energy in my lungs, which I will need when my real torment begins. She takes both hands, and massages both of my breasts firmly, as if to relax me again. She lets me go and walks over to the mirror, to admire herself briefly. She raises her arms to her black silken hair, working a spell, causing it to flow down the length of her back. Her curviness is as a great waterfall or a snowy mountain peak. Born to inspire awe for an eternity.

It seems that the warmth from the kerosene heater is slowly dying. In the warm glow of winter's heart, I feel the cold reaching out to me again.

87

*W*inter has died twice since the Birth of Melody. A Spring day sings to me in birdsong. But I've not yet had the courage to give her a flower. I am 21 now. The girl I was is gone forever.

I am afraid of my own shadow.

I live in perpetual fear, as afraid of Barbara Jean Coletti as I would be of a hungry tiger. I have a pathological terror of her presence, which has settled upon me, working its way into my psychology. I literally flinch at shadows, which seem to move before my eyes, and every little sound will set my nerves on a razor's edge, causing me to nearly jump out of my skin. She pleases herself with me anytime now, and any way she sees fit, without pretense. I never know what form this will take, whether it will be gentle, or if it will involve pain and suffering.

She will often accuse me of being possessed. She tells me I have power over her, making her do perverted things. She says I like to go in the woods because I am a witch. A Witch of the Woods. She tells me stories of how a mother in her mountain community dealt with a daughter who put roots against her. The mother had locked her in a room for three days without a single drop to eat or drink, and they burned white candles at her door, and held prayer vigils that lasted for an hour at a time.

Mother tells me constantly how lucky I am to not be in her mountain church, where they would make me tarry for the spirit until I spoke in tongues. She tells me that when she turned sixteen, they took her to church the following Sunday afternoon, which had been prepared to receive her for prayer. They made her call upon the name of the Lord until her voice was gone. They took turns screaming at her to the top of their lungs for hours, until after sunset, and my mother told me she was caught up in the frenzy of it, smelling the stench of their breath and their bodies, until she started to feel sick to her stomach. She said she coughed until she couldn't breathe and her weak muscles shook, and every bit of her Sunday dinner came pouring out of her to the floor at the foot of the altar. The church then erupted into something like madness, shrieking about the devil having been cast out, and that she was no longer possessed with sin.

Mother says she was only possessed with dizziness, because they were sucking the air from around her, and she was getting nauseous long before she began to cry from fear and sorrow. She told me that her mother was genuinely affectionate with her that night, treating her like the good daughter, and for a while, she thought she was even her daddy's little girl. They believed she had been filled with the spirit. But they didn't know that

Mother's tongues had been inspired by pure fear, and the need to escape the deathly oppressiveness of that horrible evening. They didn't know she had been faking, mimicking the sounds she had been hearing for sixteen years. There had been no infilling of her.

She tells me that my time is coming. That she will not hold a prayer vigil for me, when my time has come.

She has worked on me since I was a little girl. Skillfully, systematically breaking me apart, then reassembling the pieces and shattering them again, until what is left is a trembling, broken mess. I have zero self-confidence, none whatsoever, not even enough to look at myself in the mirror without becoming fearfully disgusted at what I see. Since I turned 21, she has dropped the pretense of correction, making it clear that I will be beaten whenever she feels like it, whether I deserve it or not. I am afraid to cough, or even sneeze when she is in the house. And though I have not been hit for either one of those, I am always afraid that the very next time, I might.

Our house is often alive with screams, in the manner of which I have been taught, learning that dignity is the enemy of perseverance. I am nearly accustomed to my days in the middle of the living room floor on my hands and knees, while the belt comes down repeatedly, with enough force to make me cough. The floor underneath me often hazes to purple. When the pain reaches the unbearable, I am quick to open my mouth and let Creation know, I am here! I am she who lives in the farmhouse, who must learn to become one with Pain! My skin bears the marks from every type of stick and switch known, some which barely bruise, and others which leave my buttocks and thighs cut and bleeding. Mother has spent as long as 20 minutes binding me with rope until she is satisfied, then whacking my buttocks hard with hand or wood, sometimes continuously, until I either flinch or scream. Flinching, she cannot abide—though she tolerates any sound that I make in response to the tortures. She studies the marks that the wooden spoon makes, as opposed to the hairbrushes, or the thin metal rod, or the fiberglass cane, or the soft and hard leather belts and their respective buckles. As to which of these burns me with the hottest fire I do not know. When my breasts are tortured, often with clothespins, my genuine tears and pleading are to her liking. For this, there is no bravery, as the pain of my spanked or whipped breasts is enough to make me call the name of Jesus.

Am I surrendering to the Rule? What does it mean, that I am able to endure the humiliation of crawling through the house like a mule with her on my back, or the bowel pain of the enema water in our bathtub? Am I bold in Depravity's Heart now, that I am able to insert the tube inside her without shame, as she rubs herself to a moaning fit of bellowing, until the enema water sprays from her, even while her animal voice leaps from her throat? Do I dare face Perversion without fear, when it makes me insert all manner of things deep inside her with vigor, until she has to weep from the pleasure it brings? Why do I stare boldly at the eyes of Abomination, as she gives fellatio to the yellow fruit to gagging and tears, spitting coughs and choking? Is it weakness or strength, when I pin her arms by missionary, her legs thrown back, my hips hammering ourselves to repetition?

Am I learning how to suffer?

But there are times when I allow myself too much bravery. Am I trying to impress her, when I refuse to cry out? No. I believe it is defiance, which she can feel inside me like a banshee-demon feels human fear. Recompense had come quickly in the dead of this past winter, as I stood in the middle of the kitchen nude, while she was fully clothed. I stood weeping and wailing as she heated up a knife on the stove, in the manner of a prophecy to bear, telling me that she was going to put out one of my eyes as punishment for a rebellious heart. I am not even sure what crime I have committed, what sin, although I no longer understand what it is to be brave. When she takes the hot knife off the stove, I run to her unclothed in the cold house and get to my knees, wrapping my arms around her, screaming *"in the name of Jesus, have mercy Momma!"* I spend the next two days in a cold closet with no clothes, food or water, grateful for a single sheet given to me for comfort. As I drift to sleep on the second night, I have my first premonition of death, and I am convinced that I am going to die. My heart flutters, and my breath begins to give way, and I think that my spirit is going to leave my body, and go drifting into space. I have tasted Death. The Loneliness of it is greater than pain. The Fear of it is greater than suffering.

These last two years of severe, erratic punishments have kept me ill at ease in every waking hour, even when she is not at home. I have developed a fearfulness of being awake, and even falling asleep, sometimes waking up screaming in the middle of the night, convinced that she is going to gut me like a barn animal, and slice me into living pieces.

This is the fear I live under. It is the terror that I know.

The years of anger have not stolen her looks. But her lovely face does bear the mark of bitterness. I don't believe she has ever stopped being a widow, and the seed of contempt that had been planted in her womb was nurtured, and has grown into a something greater. Her regret for living often stands before her in white skin, big, black eyes, and long hair as black as a raven's feathers. We are *Wrath* and *Terror.* Coexisting.

She need only open the door of her bedroom—where she spends more and more time alone with her depression—and walk through the living room to send me into a fit of trembling. I never know when she is going to go to the bathroom, or into the kitchen to gather a punishment stick, and proceed to beat me across my shoulders and my back. Even this very season, I have awakened from a trance in the field, to the rhythm of the stick in my bones. Broom and mop handles, I think, will always remind me of my Mother.

This spring day finds me in the kitchen at the sink, cleaning a few of our delicate things. I listen as she emerges from the bedroom. But I feel no approaching evil this time, believing that she means me no harm, and I am happily immersed in one of my mind's creations. A short, happy concerto for that laughing wind, the clowning bassoon. The finale has just begun to form. So I am not really afraid, when I hear her shuffling from the bedroom. I do not tremble this time, as I hear the heavy, barefoot steps coming towards the kitchen. I am nearly relaxed, immersed in my gift.

Have I given place to pride? Allowed a haughty spirit to creep into me? Has complacency found root in me this day, because I know I have a gift for composition? Perhaps I think I am special, simply because melodies leap about in my brain like popping corn in a fire, and harmonies like happy gazelles across the plain? Am I special, because chords flash in my head like lightning, and rhythms like thunder?

I hear her creeping. Stalking through the living room. The one time I should be afraid, I am not. At least, not until she crosses the threshold into the kitchen, and the footsteps end at the doorway. Before I even turn around, the complex structures in my head begin to crumble, and I can hear nothing now but my own breathing, and my blood pumping through my ears.

"What's that you were whistling?"

"N-nothing."

"I heard you whistlin' in my sleep, girl. I asked you what..."

"Just something I heard on the radio. Mozart, I think."

Mother stands still, a good distance away from me. Waiting to see if I will allow stupidity to rule, and pretend she does not want my full attention. I pull my hands from the soapy water, drying them quickly, hiding my nervousness. Then, I turn to look upon the dread of my days and years.

She stands there, in her lovely blue housecoat, which is the color of sky, with every strand of her raven locks down about her shoulders and her back. I cannot imagine such a woman. Such exotic power. Her features are beginning to mature, becoming more sensual than ever. Her seasoned beauty, her drastic curves, and her bewitching gray eyes are nothing short of extraordinary. I think she is a force of nature.

My expression is already full of pleading, with as much humility as I can create, which is no effort for me. She looks at me with frustrated eyes of winter ice, even wrinkling her mouth at me in disinterest, which nearly sets my mind at ease. Maybe, her insults will be quiet this time, which I am accustomed to. But I know better than to raise an eyebrow, or twitch a finger, or even to act as though I am unprepared to serve her needs, whatever they may be.

Mother stands quietly, scanning me from the top of my head to my feet. I see how she feels about me today. A mixture of tolerance and passive dislike, colored by the need for my company. Slowly, inevitably, the first part of the fear that lies dormant in a person, begins to open like a flower in the pit of my stomach.

"Would you like me to fix you something to eat, Momma?"

She responds with a deep breath, at my audacity to have spoken. The tolerance has left her again, and her dislike is no longer passive. She resists

339

the urge to twist her face and mock me the way she has so many times. I very seldom have the courage to speak anymore. I drift through life silently. Like a ghost.

My lovely torment breathes another breath, and she unsnaps her pretty sky cloth in nearly a single motion, exposing her naked body to me. Her curved waist is cinched, from years of tight-waisted underwear. Her bosom plays a concerto upon the J-chord.

The house coat finds its way to the back of a kitchen chair. She steps over to me, staring boldly with a sly look, enjoying my discomfort, pushing me backward against the sink. I flail like a frightened animal, bumping my hand noisily against the glasses on the counter. She is pressed heavily against me. I can feel every inch of her soft flesh. I can smell her breath, which seems always sweet, because she loves to eat soft peppermint candy. Her kisses are always sweet.

There are two kinds of evil looks she gives me. One makes me wonder if she has developed her lust again. The other is a look of pure maliciousness, as though she wishes me great harm. This moment though, I cannot tell which, while her hands are on either side of me, my lower back pressed up against the counter. Her eyes have hypnotic power.

I don't even realize that my hand is trembling, until I touch her on the shoulder, and then her creamy smooth neck, and then to her face, which is now stern and uncompromising. There is no satisfaction there, only a look that lets me know I am even more at Fate's mercy than usual.

There it is now. The buzzing that powers my nerves, which makes my hands quiver more, like milk in a china bowl on a passenger train. I run my hands over her smooth skin, skin the color of crème, tanned slightly by the cruel rays of the farmer's sunlight. When I brush my thumb across my mother's natural ruby lips, she strikes like a snake! Wrapping her mouth around my thumb, gripping my entire body immobile with a single motion. I feel the sucking—her warm, wet tongue around my pitiful thumb. I watch the woman who gave me life begin to breathe just a little deeper, feeling her warm breath on my trapped hand. I watch her close her eyes, and make quick work of the soapy taste of my thumb, enjoying it, savoring every deliciously decadent drop of it.

And without warning, she clamps her teeth to my thumb. Gently, but firmly enough to make my heart race faster than it already is. I don't know what else to do, so I just lean forward, and kiss her on the cheek, but not pulling my thumb from her mouth, which she sucks gently and lovingly, as fellatio, before pulling it out on her own.

This is what I must do to live. It is my survival. Too many times before, her frustration in these moments has grown, until it manifests in violence, or a night of lengthy, illicit torture.

You can fix me something to eat, she says.

Slowly, deliberately she pulls away, unable to maintain the fire of whatever harm she had planned for me. She may have drug me to my bedroom by the hair, stripped me and held me underneath her, pummeling me in the ribs until I broke into tears. I am relieved, because I know I have probably avoided another beating.

What a heavy burden it is, that these Rose Diaries must bear for me.

"*Líz*-beth!"

My bassoon concerto has begun to sing in my head again. It goes silent. I leave my cooking chores and go quickly to her room. When I get there, she whispers the forbidden words in my ear, while she undresses me slowly. Her eyes are glazed with lust. She tries to excite me, being ever so skillful in the attempt, going as far as to place my own hand between my legs while she devours my bosom. She rarely touches me there with her hands, though she will often grind her groin against it hard enough to make me sore. The bud of her flower is not sacred. It grows the length of a finger. The taste of it shudders her soul to ruin.

"If you don't concentrate, I swear to God…"

"I will, Momma."

I do as I am told, moving, moaning, but my body will not give her what she needs. She suddenly becomes angry, hitting me on the shoulders and the head, until I am cowering like the whipped dog that I am. When it ends, she stands there, looking at me disgustedly.

"Put your arms down and look at me."

I oblige. I feel so stupid. It hurts my body to feel this way. I want to touch her reassuringly, but I know that if I move, she will slap a lightning bolt across my face. She steps powerfully against me, pressing her body full against mine. She leans towards me, and hisses directly into my ear.

"Frigid."

When she looks at me again, she smiles as though she wants to laugh. Her eyes are delighted. But vacant.

She goes to the bed and lies on her stomach, placing her hands underneath her. Her hips are very wide and shapely. Full—with soft, jiggly flesh. Faint, wonderful scars decorate her creamy skin from her shoulders to her ankles. I start to straddle her, to massage her while she pleasures herself, but she orders me to stand still and watch. I look on, fascinated, while she works her hips into a smooth, snakelike rhythm.

If I say it is beautiful, am I a partaker of her sin? Can I say that the waves of energy ripple her flesh like a gentle breeze over the surface of a meadow pond? Can I say that the wailing that flows from her throat does so with elegance? It is alright if I am in awe of her supple movement, and the way her flesh jiggles and twitches so completely, while her beautiful face bears the pained expression? Her movements are exotic, like those of a belly dancer laid horizontal on her stomach.

Her climax is quick, and full of force and power.

I know that later, when we eat our country dinner, she will be as comfortable as if it had never happened at all.

*T*he power of God is the power of Discipline. Whether or not Love is the key, I do not know. I only know that it is pain.

Today the flower folds, to turn in upon itself. Like petals that only bloom in the sun, when the eclipse passes overhead. Her need to punish me has reversed its course like an ocean current, transformed into the need to be punished herself, and be punished severely.

At present, the ropes that were meant for me are around her ankles and her thighs. Another length awaits her wrists, to be used in its appointed time. This, in the confined intimacy of the bathroom, though I have no idea why. Perhaps it is the coldness, the clinical hardness that invites her, to add to the discomfort she desires. With the door closed and locked to keep the spirits at bay, no one in the world could ever know that I stand in front of her with her big hips cupped in my hands, biting her nipple enough to make her sorry, then sucking the pain away in a loud smacking sound. This is the punishment she needs to bear; for absolution. For the sin she has brought into our lives, for having pulled her daughter into this corruption.

While I bite them in gentle violence, I listen to the pain in her voice and breath, no longer in awe that this is who she is, and that this is what we know. I pull the nipple with my teeth, releasing them in the last bite. I imagine that in this closed comfort, in the safety of isolation, my expression has taken on a boldness uncharacteristic. While I bind her wrists in the thin white rope, I glare at her in understanding that she is going to suffer.

In the same manner often meant for me, I stand close beside her, her wrists now bound in front. Her hair is pinned tightly to her head. Her white face bears the red mark of a brutal slap. She bears the look of a woman humiliated. A woman punished. Then with determination, I slap her buttocks with all my farm girl's might, repeatedly in the way of hard discipline—pulling my hand far back in long, broad strokes. Standing perfectly still, she takes a breath and lowers her head, releasing in a deep, loud grunting sound, as though this pain is the unleashing of some hidden, unknown repression.

Through her loud, deep screaming, I deliver the blows in kind from my bare hands to the wooden Hairbrush of Legend, until the three hundred of them have cooked her backside raw. The wood has given her the fiercest dark bruises with broken skin, and her weeping expression is wet with tears. I am exhilarated by this brokenness, this submission of her will to mine. As I untie the ropes from her wrists, she sobs the music of our rhythm, staring at her own defeated expression in the mirror. Her sorrow flows like a sea breeze, from her soul into my own.

The ropes are soon around her wrists again, this time in back of her. Without hesitation, I take the wooden spoon, and paddle her bosoms until they are striped with fire, holding her against the wall by her neck, even through her choked, childlike begging and pleading voice. When this is done, I take hold of her nipples, and turn the flesh in pinching, until she has to sob in wailing again. The tears flow with ease from deep inside her, from the waters of our meadow, and the river that runs through the place of our family tree.

When the pain has passed, when the screams and sobs have settled into the walls, I find the place where her flower grows, and I massage the bud of it in my hands until her weeping returns again, along with the shaking of her voluptuous body, and fervent cries for mercy.

But there can be no mercy for the wicked. Her wrists and ankles are bound. There is no mercy for the wicked. Where the Wrath of Woman is found.

In her crying, in her grief and mourning, I hear that her sorrow is epic…and greater than herself.

90

*H*er orgasms seem to come from another place, from a world far and deep within. It is beyond fascination to watch her, to feel her submerged in her gift, while she retreats from my world to the secret realm inside, where the spirits hold the energy of ecstasy she requires. She goes to this strange place to search among them. To commune with the spirits of her sublime gift, to partake of what force of power they may hold. She decides within herself, whether the light will be small, or to gather a large and heavy ball of light, to bring it back to the surface, to where her body waits breathless in the world we're in.

Anytime of the day, anywhere in the house, wherever it is the mood may strike, I will find myself a prisoner again of what offences must come. Those few souls who have ever looked upon our little wooden house have beheld a place of secrets untold, of depravities unknown and un-nurtured, a house bestowed with those things which the scriptures dare not mention, and of what the spirit of God has told are a shame for men and women to speak of. But to me, it is just the life that I have lived these twenty years, a year removed from what I know is my twilight, the day the sun went down over any chance I may have had at a normal life. What is abnormal, what is aberration is absolute for us; what is perverse is proper behind these walls, what is unnatural is natural under our rising sun.

This summer sun appears where I can see to our horizon—across the dirt road and the crop field abandoned, down to the distant trees that border our world. This is the Land of Renewal, these fervent lands East—above the distant trees where I remember the sun resting orange this very morning, having now climbed high and warm over our farm, to where I cannot see it through the window anymore. Mother is in her room today, where she has been through the hours since the eastern light—even forsaking the call of her blessed soap operas this time. It can only mean that she is in the bowels of depression, as condemned as the prophet in the belly of the whale, being carried not to where she wants to go, but where she is going to go regardless. She is carried up and down, high to the surface of the waters of sleep, then plunged far and way back beneath the surface again, where the slumbers are deepest and the dreams are most profound.

From this suffocation she finds herself trapped in a small room with me, then clawing her way up to where she can breathe—opening her eyes in the noonday, taking a deep breath of dusty, antique wood and faded linen, pressed so down and heavy by hopelessness itself, and the oddly bright glow of noonday sunlight in her room. Who she is, what time of the day it is, whether or not she has a daughter, whether or not her skinny pretty best friend Valerie Kirkland is really dead—of these things she is not yet sure. But as she lays her head back to her pillow, marveling at the smallness of the pale blue room she is in, her body begins to remember for her, causing her groin and bowels to ache, and every inch of her gargantuans to tingle. The sound of my name raises a ghostly echo in her spirit, causing her to close her eyes in tragic recall, that yes, this is just another day along the road of an unwanted life, and another time of expression to God; to obey the prompting in her soul, to escape the fear of Divine Retribution—and to do what it is she knows she has been called to do— which is to remind me that there is no hope for me in this life. This, on the noonday morning of her awakening, is the call of nature in her bowels, to press into her mind what she has only imagined but dared not entertain, to open another door along the corridor of our demise. She is bound and determined, I know, to relinquish our world of secrets and pretense, to release every pent up jealously and concern from herself into our living space, until every ghostly little painting on the wall is aware of us, and that we are what the scriptures hath hearkened to, of what is of unmentionable private life and shame. The pressing deep in her bowels, she has nurtured until this third day, until she knows it is an hour whose time has come.

I consider myself lucky when I hear the shuffling, warning footsteps flowing so loudly to my room, allowing me to pull myself from the waking dream of this happy clarinet and orchestra—given on such a spritely breath of wind, to voice a melody that I know must be the most beautiful ever heard by man on this instrument, supported, lifted, cloaked, carried and caressed by an orchestra of such deep basses and subtle winds—I am lucky to have heard the warning footsteps, which pull me running with outstretched arms from the bars of my notebook back into my room. The pencil lines mark the borders of my divine avocation—these pencil lines are the same to me as the perfectly parallel lines of ink are to the fortunate composer, who does not have to hide the colors of his life from grieving skies of gray. I quickly turn away from the dots and lines of my salvation to the poetic scribbling of some words or another I have dreamed or manufactured, pretending to write but only scribbling a bible verse *Blessed are the poor in spirit, for theirs is the kingdom of Heaven,* when she opens the door:

"Take off all your clothes, then come to the bathroom."

There is the familiar twinge inside me, that of fear and memory to my groin, so reminiscent of feelings I have known since before I first went to kindergarten, when I would have my private pinched as punishment for whatever I had done. Of that feeling that I felt then as a little girl, I can not tell. Of the bruises I suffered between my legs until I was twelve, I can never tell. I only know that the spirit of it rests and reigns in my body, and draws upon me deeply when she calls, to fill my entire body with desire and dread. Of the many spankings I endured to the front of myself, even when I was twelve, of this, I can never tell. Of the wooden spoon to my twelve year old nipples in the bathroom when Ms. Ida left me to die, of this, I cannot tell. Of the white water nozzle so deeply inside my bottom when I was eleven and twelve and thirteen, of this, I cannot tell. Of the heavy weight of her on my chest with me on my back, while I feel the pinching and spankings down and far away below, of this, I can never tell. I only know that my insides have begun to turn and thunder like the skies before the endtime, and my breasts have already begun to ache with fear.

She stands at her own door, prepared to greet me and take hold of me with her eyes when I leave the bedroom. She is already naked, body so pale and fully curved as few women have ever been, breasts played upon the unknown J chord, hung so mightily down and rounded outward, nipples so skillfully placed forward by nature to ensure their perfect likeness, both breasts hung so big and bulging, beckoned to stares of awe and disbelief, larger than any most would ever see upon a woman her size, at least ten pounds of it hanging big and bulbous before me. I stand naked on the other side of the room, her youthful counterpart—stupid, stiff, unashamed but unsure of what to do. Do I go to the bathroom as she said, and risk her wrath at moving without her permission? Or do I stand here like a dumb deer, to be screamed at and called a dumb bitch because I didn't move. In my mind, I here *you dumb bitch I told you to take your fat ass to that bathroom,* a thought which makes me take the risk, and go to the bathroom like she told me. But I somehow know to wait for her at the door, and I watch her walk nonchalantly over to where I am without ceremony, unbashful at her staring, looking at her amazing physique again, knowing that I am the younger version of the same. And though I have been told of my body's ugliness, I am still bold unclothed in her sight, strengthened by the likeness of myself in what I see on her, empowered by the size of my own breasts, in Olympian comparison to her own. We are truly Amazonian, the two of us nude, Our Lady of the Hips, we are—and our Lady of the Breasts, our waists unnaturally small and curved, above hips so wide, rounded and full.

Taller, bigger, stronger than me, arms and hands of goddess strength, she touches me on my back, waist and hips in full control, ushering me into the tiny space of our bathroom, closing the door behind us. But no. This is not the quiet kissing in the dark I knew when I was ten. This is not the French kiss of those days gone by, when my mother asked me did I know what a soap opera kiss was, when melodies burned my fourth grade mind in fire. Why are there so many who cannot fathom that the pretty, sophisticated woman hath known the taste of her daughter's tongue? But no. This is not our long kiss in the windowless bathroom in the daytime dark, the light creeping so casually under the door. The light is on— shining so bright above the mirror over the little sink. She stands in front of me. Looking at me, as if admiring my face and hair unwillingly, with frustration as if unable to resist the look and the stare. Defeated, she reaches over to the Olay cream in the jar, then watches me as she undoes the lid, dipping a generous portion to her strong hand, closing and replacing the jar. I can only stare and wait. Praying that I will not have to have my nipples twisted in repose.

Put your nipples to mine, she says, which I do with skill, until we are face to face standing still, breasts pressed together, our nipples locked, connected and covered by one another's flesh. *Put your arms around me*, she says, and I know to put them tightly around her waist, feeling the cold, creamy absolution, the smooth pressure which starts in the back of me, then worms up into my backside like a ghostly memory. She hugs not me, but my body—hugging it tight, staring at my devastation, my stupidity, my obliteration in my expression. *Kiss me* she says, rather she breathes, deeply through her voice. Of the feel of my mother's nipples to mine, of her tongue so deeply in my mouth, of the worm that flows rhythmically in the back of me—of this I cannot tell. And when it grows faster, I am forced to stop kissing her and stare at her, my face anguished, cheeks and neck flushed rose red from an energy along the timeline, passed from Evelyn Daniels down to me. I suddenly feel the worm pull out of my bottom, leaving a space of incompletion I feel. No, this is not only the kissing and the cream, of which I have known since I was 10, to when she pulled my twelve year old self out of school and promised herself not to engage upon me (a promise kept in every brutality throughout my teenage years, broken in cataclysm a year ago).

She moves around to the toilet seat and sits down, making herself comfortable, positioning me standing in front of her, gazing at the eyes of my breasts for answers. There are none. She pulls me close, hugging my body again while sitting down, breathing in deeply between my breasts, rubbing, mashing her face all around them, engaging my body as a plaything, as if there is no spirit inside it to be shamed by, as if it were a living, breathing nothing for her to use at her leisure. I am a standing, moving pillow for her to hug while she's upon the bathroom seat, reengaging the worm in its place, while pulling one of my hanging bottles into her mouth like a suckling pig. The grunt she makes is low and rutting indeed, pulling back away, causing the loud suction *pop* when my breast falls and flops away from her. There are now two spaces of energy loss I feel—when her tongue leaves my nipple and her finger leaves my bottom.

Please, O God, O blessed Queen of this noonday throne! Send this energy back through me! And Fate obliges one, when the worm is in permanence again! This is where the blue and black fire lives, manipulated by the cold cream—sending the strange waves to my craving spirit! And I hear her grunting voice again, and I feel her entire body stiffen and strain, then her voice is muffled again by my nipple sucked into her mouth, and I know that she is bound by the spirit of *defecation*, whose long awaited hour is come. Her burden is continued with stress and great travail, which I must close my eyes to, that I may better feel the power in her arms that grip me tight, the deep suckling at my nipple, and the cream worm pressed into my backside in grieving.

91

The earth trembles our sublime dysfunction. Or so it seems, when I lie on my stomach underneath her, my buttocks raised just enough to satisfy as the cushion for what she must achieve, raised up on her knees, on all fours like a great white horse with back legs bent, or a tiger white and beautiful in this same position. I cannot grow accustomed to this, what it is that mother must do. A deep and abiding lust—insatiable, unquenchable, flowing from an unending reservoir of regret and misery.

On my stomach in the deep twilight, with no light but what flows from the coming night, I can feel her push her new self into my bottom, feeling like the soft tip of a finger sliding in back of me. *Put your hands on yours* she says, while she grows accustomed to this new power, grown from inside herself from a place so deep as to have been undetectable before—as the ghostly misery passed down through the river of our mother line has haunted us, causing pain by which we neither saw nor heard any source for its arrival. She has learned of this enlarged female member her body has hidden for so long—a bundle of white nerves gathered as one, so sensitive as to have electrified her from her youth, which I feel now having expanded from her, pushing at least a double, a triple, a quadruple inch into my bottom. This is the first time she has been brave enough, the first time her body has burned hot enough to seer this barrier, to melt it in a fervent heat, so that in the darkness of the coming twilight, she pushes herself into her daughter's bowels. *Oh, Dear God…* she says in a deep, near sobbing tone as she rests it inside, not knowing that my grimace, the straining on my face is not from some pleasure she has ascribed to me, but from the pressure I feel inside my bottom, as she pushes her anomaly into its unrightful place. And I do feel the earth quake from our fervent resolve; or does it groan and ache from the grieving of the Almighty, at what evils he must lay witness to? Of what so many mothers do, and so many have done unspeakable, and under the cloak of secret? Inside her, I can perceive the weeping of revelation, I can perceive the crying from within, by the torment of what curse she was given: to channel the lust of the tornado through the wide and deep of the hurricane—and what world ending devastation it must cause. To be burdened by the fevered lust of the masculine, harnessed into the heavy breasted and round hipped feminine; it is the Curse of the Lady Titan she must bear, here in the dark of Twilight, resting it so deep inside me as to feel as solid as a serpent.

Yes, this is a woman's curves laid on me. Yes, it is a woman's voice that calls the name of God to help her endure her calling. Yes, those are heavy weights of womanhood I feel pressed down on my scarred back, big, warm Pillows of Perversion, their front, center and focus both as hard as erasers against my back. Do they perceive the damaged, scabbed flesh on my skin? Do they tell her of the fear, the terror I must endure from morning to night? Do they feed to her the melodies that burn inside me— the Solace of Roads, the house where I have built to hide myself—the blue and black fire bestowed from the River Valley, to protect me from what she must give and take? I feel the weight of them raise up again, the hanging baskets so large and low as to still be resting on my scarred back. Are they stained with the blood of my passion—the blood from the serpentine uncoiled? Who or what insignificant, one celled creature hidden upon this earth could have been healed by *my* stripes, by the shedding of *my* blood, uninnocent in its calling? Perhaps it is my future self—the woman I will become, the woman I must be, who will receive the blessing from this curse. Maybe, it is not the earth which quakes us here, in the darkness of the dying day. I feel the resurrection of every shadow, all which have lengthened to new life in the sunset, to cover the Earth in the dead of its approaching doom. In this gloom, I am awake, not as from so many of the dreams that have shocked me upright in the early morning hours, but the voice that calls the name of my Lord and Savior is *real,* and the quaking in my body is from the shaking woman who straddles my buttocks in the dark.

And from the rumbling of eschatological fever, from the quaking at the end of the world—the voice I hear in the dark above me is a breathless sorrow, from one who is born to Sorrow itself, who cannot understand the drug that plagues her now: that physical, honeymoon lust that aches, that has her held immobile in the straddle, her female member still inside me, in the return of the wailing I have known before, that has rattled the windows in my dreams, and that now rattles my ears with purpose of intention, burdened by the mixture of pain and pleasure, the sorrow of discovery, and the agonizing satisfaction of it. From her voice, I hear a pleading, which seeks to free her soul from the fear of Death and Hell, and her body from the fear of being racked by another wave of energies no human was truly meant to endure.

Yes, Mother, submit to the crying! Submit to the solemn tears you cry! Call on the name which is above every name, he who saves your soul, but shall not save your body from this flame! This fire of burning, dear Mother—it is your Destiny, your Fate—your predestined walk through this life! Accept your calling, woman! Behind closed doors, wield your instrument of diversion! Swing this electric fire through me! I know now that the crying you rest from is the third part of the truth, dear Mother! It is your realization, the message of the squirrels in the trees I see, who carry the demonic sting of poverty in their tails, who mock us that we have failed as people; that we are failures most epic in this life, and that your only hope to ease the suffering lies here, in the body of this pathetic strumpet you despise—the daughter of the loved one you buried—the granddaughter of the woman who gave you life, and taught you a hundred ways to cry for mercy in the dark. Cry. And shake the Earth again.

Accursed woman.

92

What is the power of God in a life? Can it encompass the unspeakable, the gifts that plague behind the walls of secret—when bodies burn in agony of what cannot be spoken or denied? Ours is the anointed sword of battle, where it is that this unholy calling lies in wait, which we can feel with or without pretense.

All day, we have worked the summer fields in denial, harvesting the fruit of our labor as it is too divinely appointed, the watermelons of our fervent need. Passing each other, pushing the clumsy wheelbarrows which break our backs as many times as they fall and break a melon or two. All day we pass each other, back and forth in the burning sun, trying not to feel the power in the spirits that torment us both now, where shyness has gone to its final resting place, and where between us there can be no shame. What would we do, the two of us, if the Lord himself were to walk the road in the cool of the evening, then approach us in the field to seek us out, to ask us from whenceforth cometh the thing that we must do? But even in the knowledge of the truth, in the knowledge of good and evil, we stand before our Lord and Savior unguilty, in isolation from the rest of the world, charged with these offences that must come, of the uncleanness that must be wrought in our bodies, of the deep agony of what is divinely depraved and sublimely forbidden.

Mother stands up from the weight of the melons we grow, and I see her stretch with her hands on her hips unbeknownst, pushing out with what she believes to be only the slightest stretching, then remembering that only the ghosts and spirits are in sight to laugh at and worship her figure, and she pushes them forward in a full stretch, which seems to make the buttons on her favorite old lavender blouse strain helplessly under the pressure. Though I am a twenty one year old woman, my lust is on fire as that which pertaineth to a man, and I feel every new beat of my heart, and every trembling new breath in my nostrils.

I do not avert my eyes from this rare sight under heaven, a woman with such a deep and abiding beauty about the eyes and mouth, with striking brunette hair, who carries breasts too heavy for any woman's frame, on a body whose waist is so naturally curved and small. She is a pioneer skirted woman, refusing to wear any of the modern skirts she once wore, with buttoned down shirts loosely tucked in, stretched tight over breasts that rest gigantic and low even in her bra. It is not a normal sight, Barbara Coletti's figure, but which I have been conditioned and adapted too, like the hermit nearby the forest of redwood and sequoia trees.

She does not see that I stare as I approach with the wheelbarrow, but feeling it nonetheless, meeting my eyes and telling me *we've hauled enough melons for one day,* long after our orange sun has disappeared, and the earth begins to dim the light for the coming evening veil. As I bend down to park the dirty, half rusted wheel barrow in its place for tomorrow, I feel that self same staring concentrated on the shirt that rests unbuttoned at the top, enough for her to see her daughter's cleavage when I bend over.

Go in the house, she says, approaching with neither hypocrisy nor pretension, as neither of us can bear the stench of them on this leg of our journey. Through her shirt I can see the burning blood, which has raised both her nipples already, as clearly as I think I have ever seen through her shirt and bra. She walks all the way up to me—tall, strong, her brunette hair pinned slick and tight, her nipples now vanished in the cloth of her shirt pressed against mine. I am the loyal slut hound, the uncompromising dog of her will and desire, staring her in the eyes like a fighter before giving himself to die in the ring. If she tells me to eat her shit, I will do it with hacks and vomiting. But what corruption this is comes of the spirit and the heart, the abundance of which moves her deep, feminine voice to breathe the words *go into the house. To your room. Unbutton your shirt but don't take it off. Take your breasts out of your bra, and press them against the window.* Without a word, I let the spirit of perversion turn me from her, and I walk toward the house with Divine Purpose, doing this new thing as unto God, as any who are called to suffer must do. But what suffering is this which races through my veins, and tickles every nerve, and rubs the front of me like a phantom as I walk?

I do not look back to see what manner of expression she makes, whether it is reverence or ridicule, whether it be passion or pity, whether she looks on with grieving or laughter. All that matters to me is to please her in this new thing, taking the back porch steps in bounding and fierce confidence, ignoring the song of the blue jays that scream my whorish name at me in mocking. I can hardly take the steps though the kitchen without running, beginning already to undo the buttons in my dark green blouse, (one of several I have owned, as she likes to see me in them the best). As I round the corner through the living room, the cool of the shadowed house touches the flesh of my tits still trapped in my bra, the coolness caressing the top of them which are folded over my hopeless bra which was too small for me a year ago. Through the haunted place which is my room, I walk through it as a ghost trapped in the past—as though I can already feel my future twenty years hence, and her suffering retreat into this heart of memory.

At the window of lost youth, I stand looking through to the other side of my life, which is across the dirt road to the open field of dreams, where I can see her fervent screams, calling in the wind. I think that I am still amazed by what I often feel within my own body, knowing that if I were to scrape the front of my bra against the window panes long enough, it would make the rest of my body tremble once from the pain of lightning washed through. Is this an inherited curse, their great sensitivity, or is it their learning and acquired trait, from the two years of torture, teasing and training they have received? Are these the echoes of scars formed and healed? Am I unique, that the feel of them in my mouth can relax my bladder to emptying, and my accursed bowels to slide free and clear? Am I unique, that they have been made the center of my universe, grown so big as to be as unnatural as hers? Even though they rest in the shadow of the Barbara Jean Mountains, they themselves have risen to magnificent heights of grandeur. I slide both of them out of my tight bra, both Mozart and Rossini, both Maria and Isabella, closing my eyes at the feel of the sisters emerging from the cloth, both nipples already big and hard in their calling. Gingerly, then with quick pressing, I touch both nipples to the cold glass, then slowly, obediently, I mash both against the window—both big enough to fill the two bottom panes, and then some.

I take a breath, and then another, preparing for the relaxation of waiting—not knowing how long it would be before she would come to where I am, or whether or not I will be beaten. Then somewhere, in the midst of paradise, in the midst of breaths which rise and fall, in the midst of vision that phases from dark to light, I open my eyes slowly, startled by the slow and determined appearance of my mother from around the back of the house, gliding as slow motion in my heightened awareness. What bravery I have is frightened away by the wicked gaze from her eyes as gray as winter, and an expression as cold as the snow. But what she sees at the window—another realization of her inner longing—relaxes her features enough so that I catch a glimpse of the awe, at the dark areolas big and rounded, smashed flat against the glass like two great eyes staring at her, daring her to move. Instinctively, I know to turn my head to one side, unworthy, unwilling to engage her while she takes an axe to what dignity I have left. Already, there is none. But from the glimpse of awe I saw in her cold expression, I have the confidence that it pleases her enough to maybe evoke a little mercy from my imminent undoing.

For five full minutes she stands frozen. Secretly enraptured, every so often glancing around as if someone might come by to stare and point an accusing finger, like Satan accusing the anointed, who are already protected from the Hellfire they deserve. She puts her finger to her lips, unknowing, unrealizing that I see and feel every pulse of rhythm in her body—biting her short nails now, unbelieving of the twisted, dark beauty of what she sees, and the sensations it awakens in her body. After this full five minutes is past, she turns on the current of grieving, and disappears from my sight somewhere in the late afternoon, to perhaps get lost in the shade of the early evening that approaches, to leave me standing dumb and stupid, a work of country art perverted to the unspeakable.

I stand there. Entranced now by the blue of evening bands, that stretch in the blue of dark gray as clouds over the forest horizon—across the road and truly so far from where I am. By now, I know to prepare myself for what must be, to take my refuge in Him, so that I can endure what passion that should come to me. And now, that passion swings the back door open in the high pitched creaking of neglect, which threatens to morph in my brain to the voice of a cello in high whining tone. I let this lonely cello be, to play whatever it will to comfort me inside—my brain cursed now more than ever to remember whatever it sings, and what accompanies it on my mind's piano. Her slow footsteps are somehow the rhythm of what I hear, in this song for the woman at the window, and what howling misfortune she must endure.

She takes that last and guilty step into my room, unguilty, undeterred, unsympathetic for her daughter at the evening window. She closes the door and without words, begins to disrobe quickly from top to bottom, which I am unable to turn away from, as I *must* see the hang of her breasts when she bends over to remove her tight underwear. The depressed and somber look of her expression is a comfort; it is so familiar to me as to provide solace that there need be no shame between us here, and that there is no need to hide what we are. The pain we have is expressed in blue and black fire—to burn with the energy of eschatology itself, and the coming end of the present age of man.

Fully nude, she walks over to where I am. Standing behind me, both of us looking out the window to nowhere, both on the edge of tears from we know not where or when. She pulls me back away from the window and takes both my breasts into her hands squeezing, breathing into my ear—*I need to hear it in your voice—all of the fear, all of the pain, all of the agony, I need to hear it from deep inside you, from where it is you try to hide— no...no... do not, do not try to hide the pain—move, breath with the pain, let it flow through your body and into this room*—and then the lightning strikes both my nipples, which has the opposite effect, causing me to suck my breath in and try to swallow the siren in my lungs—and she twists again until I have to cry out from the hot stabbing pain at my nipples, which seems to burn all the way through to my back—*yes...* she says, a tear on her cheek, *that's the sound, the sound of what we feel—the sound of the sacrifice we make to God for our wicked and sinful bodies—* then another twist, and a scream from me, followed by a sob at the edge of those same tears she cries. She backs off and has me take off my clothes, which I do, so careful not to show irritation in my face, or resistance in a single one of the trembling breaths I breathe.

When I am naked, I know to stand still in front of her, my expression bold but so respectful, unflinching as the tears roll down my face, which activate the small inches of the inner cock she wields. She turns me back to the window, both of us naked now, and takes my nipples back into her hands, causing me to moan to her to have mercy, but knowing full well that she cannot. The fire twisted into my breasts has to be released somewhere, and so I open my mouth and let the loud, deep, woman's screams fill the late afternoon darkness, where they will echo faintly into the evening.

Repeatedly, inevitably, involuntarily she twists to hear the genuine sound, the sound of a young woman in deep physical pain—screaming loudly enough to wake the *dead*, convulsing at the climax of acid burning my body from two points of origin, until suddenly she tells me to put my breasts back to the window… *put your legs together,* she says, and soon the soothing, rhythmic heat from the palms of her hands begin to scald the skin of my buttocks. The glass soothes the hot skin on my breasts, to counter the feverish and constant spanking to my bottom. The suffering in her face is deep now; her anguish is as complete as mine, watching the skin on my backside grow redder, then darken on one side to bruising. Oh, what bruising comes from calloused hands, pressed hot upon the skin of another! Hand spankings are as much a part of me as the ticking of a clock, a pain I have learned to incorporate as pleasure, having been walloped many times to unintentional shaking. Does she know this? Alas, I cannot tell. But things being as they are, I cannot divulge this secret in full, though she has surely noticed my kisses grow more fevered when her hand burns my backside at the same time. Though this pain is pleasure, I let it show itself as the mild whimpering, a whimpering that threatens to morph into sobs from again, I truly know not where.

She gets behind me at the window, positioning the fully erect part of herself against me hard enough so that I can feel it, like a small, hard knob pressing at me from behind, trying to get inside. Then she begins to move, trying to find herself, the right place along the timeline, the right door by which to enter. Then at last, holding on to the window, my breasts hard against the glass again, I feel the fervent and familiar pounding, feeling it deep in my bowels from behind: the pumping of masculine lust channeled through a woman's body, the woman enraptured by the bruise on my bottom, the memory of my voice in pain, and the memory of my areolas pressed hard and tight against the window. All of this swirls in her mind, in her spirit until she has to take my breasts in her hands again while she pounds me from behind, grabbing a handful of both at the nipples—to be the reins on the horse she rides…

And when the handful of breast is firmly, painfully locked in her grip, she is able to pound herself fully, and I hear her breath losing its rhythm, and somewhere in her final breathing I hear her beg God for mercy, and then the room fills with the depraved sound of a woman in sensual agony.

But as she stands behind me shaking, trembling, breathing in my ear, pulling me tight against her, I know that what energy lives in her lives on, and she is not satisfied.

The light from outside dims with each ticking of the giant earth clock, as it turns towards the shadow of the night, where I can see his Glory in the firmament of the second heaven. *I need you to cum for me*, she breathes, still pushing herself against me as if her lust had only just begun. *I'm going to have to do it again,* she says, *and I want you to cum for your momma. Can you do that for me*? I nod without speaking, though knowing that without my hand's passionate assistance, my climb to the top of this mountain is treacherous indeed—without a fervent rubbing, my climax is harder to come by. But it can, and does happen often.

She positions herself behind me again, the window beside us now rather than in front, to give side view to the spirits that watch and see. She begins the pounding again, with as much energy as before, but this time with my greater participation, my hand on the windowsill to anchor me, my other hand in hers, her slamming against me and bellowing like a she-bull in the effort—trying to achieve the impossible in my body, to heat it up by her selfsame magic; to begin the teaching again, that I may learn to shoot off like a rocket from merely a passing thought inside. I begin my concentration, imagining that she loves me, and that what she does is a symptom of that love and not the pain of hatred, venom and spite. In the love I feel for her is the activation of the heat in my groin, which grows as she gives the last of her energy in our early evening darkness, saying—*I need you to bounce back against me baby, do that for me until you cum— bounce back, yes, but no hands, don't use your hands... yes, pound back against your momma's thing, bounce against your momma's cock, baby, do it now... please... God wants you to do this—He needs you to do this for me—you want your momma to love you, huh? You want your momma to love you?* The yes's come out of me on their own, and I am lost now in the pounding backwards against her—feeling the love she has for me so fleeting, so carnal, born so completely from a craving in her body passed down—

I need to suck your tits Momma. I need to suck 'em...

And I turn around and take them both up in my hands, working myself into a frenzy while her hands are up behind her head in full pose, eyes closed while I drink the milk that drips free, letting it run back from my mouth, some down my throat, some down my chin to my own breasts— then she turns me back around, telling me to bang her, bang her good, which I do, this time able to feel the phantom member as though it were inside my bowels, feeling her with a handful of my breast flesh again pounding, until I feel as though I have fallen through a dimensional portal in the floor where I cannot breathe or see, and I work as if inside a dream—to draw a breath so that I can scream.

93

These are the last days. Our last days under this summer sun, where there still lives a dying echo of hope—not for freedom or escape from suffering, but for a time when we will come together as one heart, to brave the rising storm of misery. It approaches the two of us as an impending wave, seen far off shore, rising higher with each passing moment until our devastation has become apparent, and escape looms more impossible along the hour. My heart's desire can only be that we can stand in spiritual love, holding hands with one another as a mother and daughter in love and reconciliation. Resigned to what He hath bestowed, that unearned suffering is not always redemptive in this life, and that at least, we can declare love for one another before we die.

My mother's love is breast play. It burns her into heat, in some form or another almost every day now. Oh, what sights are these, of a woman such as she walking through the house in only her bra and underwear, or in her skirt and no top at all, walking boldly from the kitchen to her bedroom. Even after the years of solitary life and familiarity, I've noticed that her breasts renew themselves to me daily, and I am often still amazed that an average sized figure can produce and carry breasts so large and heavy. They are a glimpse into my future, I know, and from the pain of her own past, to those of Evelyn Daniels, whose were even more impossibly gargantuan, she has told. Breasts that she saw naked with her own eyes, held in her own thirteen year old hands, and nursed with her own thirteen year old mouth. Breasts that hung gigantic and bare, while Evelyn Daniels sucked my mother's own developing breasts until they were sore, throughout her teenage years until she left home. What evil is this passed down through the motherline, that corrupts our blood with breast obsession! What is it that can cause us to stand together in silence for so long, each holding our own breast in our hand, rubbing each other's nipple together with a fury that grows in her body until I hear it in her voice! What is the secret obsession, this devastatingly private progression, that has stopped the two of us in our tracks on Sunday morning before church, with her fumbling at my dress like a woman possessed, until one of my breasts is in her mouth as though she were a starving woman feeding her body! Her breasts and mine, my breasts and hers, it is deep—and achieved with spiritual reverence per session. It is not easily imagined, that some women are so deeply carnal behind closed doors, and are attacked by fetishisms so violent and complete. Even among those who claim such divine and spiritual reverence for God, they often burn hotter in sin than the heathen women do, and demonstrate in their private lives the necessity for Christ's Redemption, so that their perpetual sins are covered under the Blood. This is the Blood of Sacrifice, and not of my own, for the blood I have shed over the years can save no part of my immortal soul.

This obsession has hit her once again, tormenting hers which hang low and unbound inside her navy collar shirt. It is the burning that made her go without a bra today, which has her looking at my chest without the ability to stop. And though I try to tell myself otherwise, I know that the swallow I see her make is her mouth watering—from another kind of hunger. *I need to go to the woods*, she says, which frightens me enough to make me stop and stare from my cooking chores at the sink—holding a half peeled potato with the paring knife in my hand, too dumb and scared to realize that it could set me free, be it the skin at my own neck, or hers. *Did I do something wrong*, I say stupidly, regretting the question already—as she might hear enough insolence in it to run over to where I am and put her thumb to my windpipe again.

Dry your hands, she says. *Let's go.*

These forest walks remain the most fearful part of what we do. The energy ranges from that of a leisurely stroll, to that of a prisoner in chains walking the last mile. But always on the other end, at the far corner of our universe—awaits something for me in the summer or autumn woods, something that lays me open to the truth of who I am, of why I came into the world. I came into the world to suffer. To be that which God has made me to be—that human animal, that untouchable, that hidden, forbidden creature of the woods, who is cursed by God to know nothing of goodness, but only sorrow, hatred and fear. On the wings of these three, I am carried—over the soil of our days and ways, every stop more disturbing, more difficult than the last, as one who might be carried to where a large and angry grizzly bear awaits. The Hatred Fowl, the uncharitable wood hawk of venom; she lifts me up from where I was, from my house of melody, to escort me over the fields of green to the border of the summer woods. The hawk that carries me—it is in the company of two others: that of a Sadness I cannot dissuade, no matter how hard I try—and that of mortal Terror itself, which has each breath pulled in and out in a trembling. But the mercy of God is eternal, which blows across the fields in a warm, strong breath of renewal, which speaks to the three demons that would seek to have me. They circle again, then are carried away in this fervent wind, dropping me back onto the solid ground of our last days, these last days under the sun.

The white bark trees can tell me nothing of my fate. I imagine that when we get to our place in the small clearing we will begin as usual, with her standing behind me holding me tight, reminding me of our station in life as dominant and severe submissive; aggressively subordinate, boldly subservient in the face of fear. Oh, how much blood have I shed among these leaves, against the bark of the sycamore tree, where I have been tied to overnight so many times, and left to ponder Fate, Destiny and God. Her closeness to me, our magnetic energy grows upon our dreary walk this late summer afternoon—and I imagine that before long I will be told to strip naked in front of her while she does the same, here in the middle of the

Coletti Woods, where there are none to see our calling but the curious trees themselves. I imagine that in the cool of the green leaf canopy, I will soon feel her gigantic breasts and grape hard nipples against my scarred back, followed by her arms clasped behind my head in full wrestling hold, bending my body over, a body strengthened by the years of heavy, deep turmoil. Already, I can feel her strong arms bringing the pressure down on my neck, bending me over with no hope of escape, the dead leaves noisy under my clumsy, shuffling bare feet. Already, I can feel the weight of my own breasts dangling, hanging so far and heavily down, swinging with each toss and turn, the sound of our grunting and heavy breathing loudly echoing in the quiet space around us. What of the noisy jay bird watching us up a tree, when we are as naked as he, with me bent over in the pressure of her foreplay, as her body works itself up to a fervent heat, to melt away all pretense of hypocrisy and cold.

Her voice awakens me from this unintentional daydream, telling me to unbutton my old gray dress and take my breasts out, which I do. She stares as my fingers do their smooth handiwork, pulling these big white jugs out into the cool summer air, areolas already shrunken with desire. But it is that of my flesh only, that which my body requires, for my mind and spirit arise above the trees of life, to go where there is no need to fear the coming of Autumn's fervent night. I see her bottom lip relaxed unashamedly open, with as much lust as a teenage boy would have, watching me pull both tits to a heavy hanging outside my bra. We find our place at the fallen tree, which rises just high enough for a comfortable seat. She guides me to stand still directly in front of her, then she makes quick work of the buttons on her blouse, still staring at both my nipples as if she could read a message in them. Of this, their message to her is freedom—a brief reprieve from the pain of perverted addiction, caused by what was planted in her youth, and what was grown and nurtured by the bitterness of poverty and failure, and by the spectre of widowhood, and the profound sadness and agony of grief. She pulls both of her massive breasts free from the shirt, without burden of a bra to entangle their journey home. They hang big and free now, still too massive to be easily understood, of what would have to be seen to be believed.

Oh, what a sight these woodland spirits have born witness to! Of the beautiful woman fully clothed with only her enormous breasts laid bare, swinging free with every motion of the leather belt in her hand (her arm held back so high and so far, at the top of the pendulum swing), brought down hard upon her screaming daughter's naked body over and over again; or the rhythm of the punishment stick hard across the back of her daughter's bra and underwear, to elicit the deep and abiding scream from within her daughter's aching bones. Oh, what a sight these woodland spirits have seen, when the mother is fully unclothed with her belt wrapped in choking around the naked daughter's neck, pulling and swinging her dangerously about, until her daughter is flipped so hard and clumsily to the leaves on the hidden forest floor!

With her own breasts hanging free outside her shirt, she leans forward to mine, mashing her face to them, rubbing her face back and forth across them, preparing her heart to receive the medicine of its fervent desire, the medicine of its fervent need. When all resistance is futile, I see her mouth open on its own, her eyes closed, and I feel lightning twitch my groin, drawn up to where her mouth deeply nurses my breasts to tingling. But though I put my head back, to have to breathe deeply from the energy passing through, my mind seeks to stay on things above, somewhere outside my body, which is alive from the feeling of a beautiful woman sucking my breasts with perfect firm gentleness, and a gentle firmness that can only be a gift from God. I can only put my hands on my hips, in the same like manner as she, holding my head back, up and away from her privacy, listening to the loud pulling and popping sounds that have embarrassed us both in the past, but no longer. These are now the sounds of dinner plates clacking together when the table is set, to set both our mouths to watering. I stand still and strong, nursing my mother in the woods—feeding what hunger is passed from somewhere along the timeline, a hunger she herself does not understand. For the better part of a half hour I stand still, sometimes looking down, sometimes away— watching her lick and spit, suck and swallow this nourishment, until I must endure my own body's burning which I swear that today, I will hold in check. After this half hour, she lays her head against my chest, to rest and wonder and ponder what glorious past this hails from, and what future sorrow this would surely be, if she were to allow a man's seed into my body, to produce a girl child by which to cuddle and corrupt with our carnality.

She stands up and turns me towards the dead tree, sitting me down upon it, then laying me down on the trunk, both our breasts still wobbling free in the breeze. She leans over to take up arms again, back into the heat of battle, working on them again like a whore on a hundred dollar husband, which has me unsworn to my promise—where I now have to allow my body to do what it will. While she leans down, her own globes swinging so near my face, I have no choice but to caress it, then guide it closer to my mouth. She positions herself, so that she is still leaned over with my nipple pulled up in her mouth, and hers are hanging so nearby to mine. With the bravery of a woman diving into the ocean from her pleasure boat, I take her half-inverted nipple to my lips—not to drink the milk, but to drink the feel of her breasts in my mouth. What milk there is that must come, I give in and let every drop flow down my throat so as not to choke—soon feeling her hand grow stronger holding onto one of my breasts, then hearing her breathing lose its rhythm, then feeling her bent over body lurch forward on its own, with the power of a white horse twitched and trapped inside the bounds of a stable.

94

Milkmaids, I suppose we have become—but of a kind born in shame and nurtured in secret. But as to what shame there be, it is only in light of any other soul in Creation who should know of this, rather than just we ourselves, and the lonely spirits who inhabit our serenity. For us, our nursing is as any call of nature we partake, which we do without embarrassment or fear of Divine Retribution, but as a duty—as a calling we have no choice but to obey. But hilariously (or tragically), how are we any different from maidens on a dairy farm from a century ago, strolling casually to the family cow to squeeze nourishment and drink? Any who knew of this secret would surely snicker and snide the two of us into ruin, where we would melt as the wicked witches we are, splashed white by the pail of lifegiving milk we have pumped and drawn.

'We need to go the shed' will open the chords of this piece for cello and full orchestra, which during this summer I have heard daily—the summer of my twentieth year. She has taken to this discovery like a pioneer woman to a water strike on her desert property, having the both of us nurse fully from her breasts five times a day in the beginning, until the flow was heavy and established; and now I drink in full at least once a day, which my body has trained itself to love and crave. Whether it is the milk itself, the closeness, or the touch and feel of her naked breast—this, I do not know. I only know that the word "shed" has become as the chiming of the dinner bell to me, and I rise on the upsweep of this orchestra *en tutti,* gliding on the cello on a single G note, and my body flushes with desire as the full winds answer in a rapid and beautiful upswing.

As to this, our walk to the shed is curiously without fear, but is as a controlled march of purpose, where we both must resist the urge to run, I think, to where we must lock ourselves in, buried in perversion. Once, we were in the middle of what we must do here, and we heard the truck of our demise pull in from the outside world to ours, where we hid for 10 minutes while the landlord stupidly wandered and called and waited pathetically, both of us thanking God in Heaven that he thought nothing of checking inside this box of a shed. If he had pulled the door, it would have been locked from the inside, which surely would have given him pause and cause to wonder, and would have drained and diminished our power to less than nothing. But as it stands, he left disappointedly that day, with no view of my mother's nipples poking through her lavender blouse, and a bosom bestowed as a gift from God to man. From the sneaky eyes that pry, we hide and ride the summer wind to our tiny back yard shed. Milkmaids, are we, entrusted with this private diversity, given from a land beyond the sea.

They're full, are the two words I manage to speak from dumb lips, pressing against them, bound up tight in her dark green collar shirt, as dark as the color of grass after sunset. They are like two great balloons, pressed hard and round inside the cloth. *Are they sore*, I say, hearing the desperate answer from her—the quiet, whispered affirmative, touched by the testostrous ebbing which flows inside, colored by the deep and estrogenic energy in tow. She begins to undo her own buttons, so quickly and nonchalantly, without romance or pretense, as if merely changing clothes, or disrobing for a late morning summer bath. The bra underneath is simply bursting, straining mightily against what it entails, the white flesh spilling over the top and the sides, seeming to impede all pretenses toward any deep breath or two. This bra, I know all too well, for I think she loves the tight, bound up feeling it presses into her, and even though it is the tightest, worst fitting bra she owns, I know it is her favorite. But today, her breasts just seem out of this world big, as I watch her reach back to find the latch, still devastated by pure awe every time I see it.

She takes the big bra off at last, in a quick little voice of relief, and I notice that they are likely the biggest I have ever seen them, and likely among the biggest of any woman her size anywhere in the world. It is the unnaturalness of them that is their extraordinary beauty, as they hearken back to a time when women all enjoyed a queen's bosom, before the curse and the fall of man. Already, both of her flattened nipples are half erect in the air, a drop of milk appearing so casually on one of them. *Open your shirt,* she says, *take yours out but leave your bra on.* And as I begin to undo the buttons, it is her cue to take one of her own into her hands as casually as she would an udder, lifting it up towards her mouth and pulling the nipple in her lips with a genuine thirst, where I can hear the quiet gulping in her throat. After many breathless swallows, she pulls away from the nipple in a kissing pull, breathing deeply the words *its good*, words so deeply felt and expressed, returning to her fountain to drink, glancing unconcerned at my own milk bags hung so low and exposed, nipples gazing back at her from the front of them, the dark areolas in contrast to the globed and white rounded skin. She closes her beautiful eyes again, sucking, nursing her own breasts as if driven to empty them of every memory, of every painful recollection; pressing, squeezing them for dear life, wasting nary a drop of their fervent memory, the skin pulled so firmly and deeply into her mouth..

I stand quietly. In focused and deeply determined support, unafraid to touch the front of both my own, twisting them calmly, matter-of-factly as I watch the brunette woman service herself in the dimly lit feed shed, stopping every so often to hold her head back with her eyes closed. Taking a breath. Breathing a prayer of thanksgiving to her Heavenly Father, that he hath bestowed upon her such a potent diversion, such a profound and overpowering part of her soul to partake. So much of who we are, so much of what we do is to ease the pain of living. In admiration I watch this act, though not in pity, as she takes the other into her mouth to drink, to finish taking her fill of nourishment, the fervent elixir of medicine for whatever ails her.

As I finish this Song For a Milkmaid—the easy rondo for cello and orchestra— already, another piece hath come to fore, in lesser but more beautiful accompaniment than the first—this, for violin, cello and orchestra: the violin and cello playing call and answer twice in different keys, before being joined by a small but energetic string orchestra too heavy on the basses, as my orchestral pieces are usually so inclined. I am often taken aback by the strange and oddly inspired shadow pieces, often so unique and special—having no pretence toward greatness but still burdened by such beauty of expression that the colors strike me as impossible to look upon without bewilderment. Such a melancholy and pitiful call from the violin I hear, by such a soulful and somber cello response there is. As if in unison from this world to my own, I hear *come to the kitchen,* words spoken as if by the cello in my soul. From the energy of yesterday afternoon, from our moment in the shed, there has been a slow and steady build inside her, as the rising wind of an approaching deluge of rain.

I noticed that she kept her breasts to herself today, understandably, since her powerful self-service yesterday. *Wouldn't that be enough for a while*, I had imagined, so lost inside the bars of music, so glad that she leaves me alone to write what she thinks poetry, which she reads at times and does not despise, I think. She knows and understands that I pour my insanity into the pages of my notebooks in some form or another, while she pours hers into me likewise.

"Elizabeth," I hear, having taken too long to phase from the world of color to the real world. Still hearing the instruments sing the Calling of the Milk Maidens as I go into the kitchen—unsurprised to see the two silver mixing bowls on the kitchen table, but in shock at my mother standing at the table in the hour past the evening day, without a stitch of clothing on her magnificent body. I need you to get undressed, she says, nonchalantly walking back to the cabinets that were left open, closing them, bending over so slightly in the nude. As I quickly get undressed, I too understand that it does not matter that the door of our kitchen is open wide, and whatever hapless, lost traveler that should wander by would be treated or traumatized by the sight of what cannot be imagined, but only seen to be believed.

When I am undressed, I walk over to her in compliance but with only the slightest bewilderment, already knowing that the bowls on the table have something to do with the bowls on her chest. Has she finally lost her mind? Will she put the bowls against them as the breastplate of a Valkyrie, and stand in the middle of the kitchen floor singing hymns to God while I stand nearby with my breasts in my mouth? Will she then defecate in one bowl and urinate in the other? God forgive the fearful and vulgar thoughts that plague me!

She places the bowls on the floor, and gets to her knees, unclothed. Unashamed. *I need you to milk me. I need you to drain every drop from me... after you spank my ass and call me a filthy whoring cow.*

Mother! Grandmother! What demons hath plagued thee before I was born! This profane and vulgar thing I must perform, to ignite the blue and black fire in the room! And this, I do, until the white of her buttocks has gone red and speckled already from the heat. From the first whack, I saw her body respond, and the first drops of milk dropped into the bowl from both breasts, rapidly from one and slower from the other.

As I now massage her burning skin and the rest of her—her waist, her shoulders, her back—I here *milk me* sung in a deep and shameful, defeated whisper as she rests on all fours, her back so completely, so fairly scarred from top to bottom, as the raised, faint markings of a flower petal in bloom. This dark rose in bloom breathes a bellowing, animal sound in response to the milking, as I rest on my knees. Pulling and squeezing her elongated nipple as a cow in human form, able to suck it once well enough to bring the flow on as a steady trickle, which sprays magnificently when the huge breast is squeezed. And to the artificial light of our song, we do this dare, this calling of the milkmaids. The view from our backyard is the brightened kitchen and a giant breasted, beautiful woman of 37 years on her knees, having her breasts milked by a younger version of herself. Of what newness this is under the sun I do not know, as it lies under the hot face of the Desert Moon.

I pull and squeeze them both now—together, intermittently, aware of how much this woman needs me, even though beneath the craving for my company, she so unequivocally despises me. For her, I perform this calling. For her, this solemn duty is my own, until I know both her nipples are grieving from the pain, and the white life in each bowl would both fill a measuring cup to overflowing. Then as though responding to an inner command, I get up and squat to her back gently, until I am resting in full upon it. Laying down— forward enough to reach both breasts underneath her. Squeezing. Kneeding. Rolling. Pressing like so much bread dough wet from the pre-cooking, from the milk of their appointed time.

Then I am off her back to the side again, telling her to rest her breasts down in the milk—*put 'em in the bowls*, I say, both of us watching the milk fill up the bowls to almost overflowing around the breasts. *Raise up*, I say, which she does so obediently, the milk now dripping so forlornly, in quiet and desperate fashion downward. *Up and down*, I say—*soft splash*— which she knows so skillfully, so inherently how to do, her hanging breasts going up, down, up down into the milk, my lips at her ear—*splash your milk but don't you spill a drop*—and she begins to love the milk with her own breasts, baptizing them up and down, working herself to a plateau even she cannot so easily cross alone.

I hold her still now. Watching her suffer and breathe and tremble, taking my hand to back of her at last, to find the elongated female member, the clitoris grown to four times an inch where I cannot see. The mere touch of it makes her rise higher up on her hands and steady herself, returning her voice to the bellowing cow she has become. *When you cum*, I say, *don't you move. Let it come out through your voice—let it all come out through your voice,* the sound of this violin already stirring the heartstrings of this cello, as she relaxes her body and prays to God and Jesus, before I feel a powerful spray of liquid in my hand from her groin, then I see her body shake all over, as I hear her scream loud enough to wake the stars of Heaven.

95

Her orgasms have reached a new place in time, I suppose, as they now leave her devastated into relaxation; sometimes trembling for several minutes after. Every since the day and night of the Milkmaid's Chorus, I have noticed a more sublime and spiritual move of hers toward our deepest pleasure, and I wonder if Irony's Breeze blows at all, that the deeper we plunge into misery, the higher flights of Divine pleasures we fly. Is it science or superstition, raw rebellion or religion, that has her at times shaking on her feet like a tree in an earthquake and gushing water like a faucet turned too far gone? Whether or not she has pissed herself these times we truly do not know, as she claims it is a different feeling entirely, and often does not come in a steady stream but a single, rushing flood. But as to what we have done, as to what devilment we have achieved, is it the proverbial unwished for wish with which we have bewitched ourselves?

When she is on her back, legs up and nearly wrapped around me, I can clearly see the madness in her eyes now when she falls over the edge; I can clearly hear it in her voice, and I can feel it in wetness on the soaked sheets underneath where we lay, and can feel it in the long and profound trembling toward sanity she must endure. It is the Amazon's Curse, the Curse of the Tribade Women, that when they hath partook of such as we, when they have fallen so deep into the well of perversion, the pleasure is as unendurable as it is unavoidable, as irresistible an addiction as whatever drug of choice may take claim on an unsuspecting soul. Who should need such wildly embracing spasms throughout the body, evoking such screams as cannot be contained? Yes, there are times during the daylight hours, when I am compelled to put my hand over her mouth to contain the screaming, which emanates from a place so much deeper than lust, to where the origin of the Pain of Life begins. The screams and pleading, begging yelps I am privy to are from somewhere so deep in the past—so far and away from our little farm, across the forests and fields north, to the Blue Ridge Mountains of Virginia, where every perverted spirit known hath lived and flown, where Barbara Jean was born. Where the sadism, the masochism are part of the doors, the walls and windows, where Agony is the cause and effect of all discipline. It is the famed Domino Effect, which cannot be stopped as the bloodline flows from Eden to Gethsemane, and then on to Armageddon.

When I hold her wrists behind her back underneath her, what day in history doth her scream emanate from? As she writhes to be free from her missionary bond, what torture, what punishment from the giant breasted

Evelyn Daniels doth she feel? When she begins the long, hopeless wail of defeat and surrender, which voice from the Heart of Memory doth she emulate; is it the mountainous breasted woman who lays on top of the like breasted daughter, unashamedly, while the father sits in a dark livingroom with his eyes closed and his trousers open? Hearing the voices of pain and punishment flow at him, around him and through him in the dark of his epic witness to this truth? Evelyn does not know, nor can she ever, so that the pain she gives her daughter will be all natural and true. The two tall women of Appalachia, taller and fairer than he, women whose breasts exposed and mashed together he all but craves to see. Evelyn's bosom, the breasts of his wife so big and bound up, as the two of them would die screaming to the Lord before their marital Chastity can be broken again. When you hath screamed underneath me, dear Mother, is it the seventeen year old whose voice you bear? Or is it the thirty five year old likeness of yourself, so bitter mouthed, so unsweetened by time, lips burned into a frown that chars her beauty like a burn on a white fleece linen. Do your missionary screams tell this story, Dear Mother, of the moment when you felt the bones in your finger break behind your back underneath Evelyn Daniels? Do your screams reminisce the pitiful siren that rose from your Mother's open mouth, when the knowledge of your broken finger came at her in your death scream, and sent her soul to the edge of Pleasure's Heart, where all who enter must truly abandon hope therein? Is that moment burned inside you forever Mother, which grieves you to craving so long and so often, to be on your back in missionary style and helpless underneath me? For whom doth the Lord Jesus have mercy in your crying, Mother? For whose ghostly memory do you cry, *"Lord Jesus, help me?"* And from the look on your face I see, Mother, I know that thy pain is as genuine and as unbearable as the tragic pleasure you have grieved to feel.

In the wake of this memory, of missionary weeping from days gone by, I rest back against the head of my bed, sitting behind my mother who rests back against me. Perched atop pillows, I am tall enough to see over her shoulder from behind. So easily, when I lift her breast up, the nipple is where I can engage it, which only adds to her impending devastation on the heels of this relaxation. Her naked legs are open, with the bottom of her bare feet together. My hands caress and soothe the crown of her beautiful head, rubbing gently, smoothly her temples, forehead, cheek bones and chin—then the soft caress of her neck and shoulder, then down to only the nipple of those two globes, rubbing them, pinching, pulling and tweaking with both hands until they stand at rapt attention in the summer daytime dark in her shaded room. For this relaxation, she has pulled every shade and closed every curtain, so that she can rest against me on the edge of sleep, to leave every muscle in her body untensed, so that she may be carried upward by Aphrodite's Call. It is the call that begins unbearable at the nipples I drive, then continues with the hard but slow squeezing of them for so many long minutes, until her neck and chest redden ripe from the arousal.

My hands slide from her gigantic breasts down to her soft, curvy middle, where I stop to enjoy the squeeze of the flesh of her stomach, so perfectly formed and fit to grab, that super heroine hula girl waist, of an allure perhaps unique in Creation. From the landscape of this Nova Curve, my hands slide down to the white of her inner thighs, where the flesh is so far from thin, to draw my hands into the squeeze of promise, which makes her turn her head and groan in something less than relaxation, something less than comfort. And I allow the requisite *"shhh,"* the power of the shush to breathe solace to her lovely ear. And I wonder what pain this pleasure will be, as I move one hand towards the undying center of the heart of darkness, the apex of the unholy triangle pointed downward, the rise and fall of civilization, and the devastation of all mankind. The place where I came from in pain, and by pain I now return to.

The wetness shocks me like a bolt, which sees the quick jerking and twitching of her by this selfsame bolt, as she turns her head firmly toward mine, her eyes still closed, her breathing heavy laden with heat. My fingers melt with a fervent heat, that which burns in Australia, that place and purpose too apt to mention, its description so perfect for my feeble mind's rapt attention. My fingers swirl the purpose of incursion, as our inversion swims the depth of perversion. I feel my mother's warmth grow in my hand to such an alarming version of itself, which I can grab by my thumb and two fingers, and manipulate as that which pertaineth to a man. This I do for a time, then I return to the warmth of her completion, of her complete womanhood, still so drawn to the stiffness of what emanates from within.

Of how many spaces along our timeline hath passed, this, I do not know. Of what fears and fantasies, of what misery and memories she is plagued by, of which daemon this removes from her body, this I do not know. In this laying position, in the newness of this discovery rises the truth of her desperation, the rule of Testros and Estros in the bowels of her womanhood, which begs the call to itself again, but larger than I have ever known it to be, grown from hidden deep inside her to perhaps a fifth inch, which would cause unbearable shame if one were to know, that her clitoris is capable of such profound and anomalous growth, now risen up to its full self, partially covered in her pink skin, so vulnerable in its secret power.

At last! From over her shoulder, I am able to see the source of her power! The reservoir that feeds her breasts with the otherworldly sensitivity they possess! Look down Mother! Look down at the true freak of nature thou art! Gaze the raised flap of skin, see the white bundle of raw nerves poking out at the tip from within! There it is, Mother, the devil we didn't know! The furnace that heats this entire abode, the energy that fires this five inches of fury! Grown to the full firmness of function, by the power of witches brew! By the power of witches—it grew, Mother Dear, lay back and suffer what is overdue!

I take full and gentle hold if it, every muscle of her body relaxed save one! And I massage it with steady, firm and gentle rhythm, until that quiet and hopeless wailing comes out on its own. It is a quiet sobbing, the sobbing of defeat and profound inner suffering. I move my fingers upon it faster, unmerciful now, in craving to see what mountain spirit will flow screaming from her body. But this will be a spirit of weeping, born from the collected memory of who she is, and the full acceptance of what an epic tragedy she will forever be.

From deep within her relaxed body, she is powerless to stop the approach of this spirit, the ghost of the mountain woman, the heavy breasted woman of straw she knew. As she is powerless to flee, or to block the rising of this motherline wraith, who must pass through her in weeping as she relaxes her body, so as not to resist the flowing through. I hear the quiet and determined weeping from ages past, from the pioneer days of old, from the wooden cabins of early days in this New World, to the Blue

Ridge Mountain shacks of old and New Virginia, flowing in a sensual sobbing I have never heard before, as defeat begins to suddenly rise in a steady arc of water, that springs forth from inside her groin, and across the bed like a tiny crystal fountain.

96

Barbara Jean, O Barbara Jean
The mother with the biggest ding-a-ling
Who put it in her daughter when her daughter was twenty one—
And took her virginity like it was nothing but a thing

Barbara Jean, O Barbara Jean!
Listen to the cardinals and the bluebirds sing
In mourning for your daughter's chastity—
That died like a cut white rose in Spring

Barbara Jean—O Barbara Jean!
From whenceforth comes this accursed thing!
That flows through your blood from the mother-line—
To the lonely farmhouse where Perversion is king

97

The heat of our world is coalesced, to bring dark clouds of summer grieving, covering the earth in ashen gray regret. From these clouds fall tears of mourning, weeping for what they have heard from the voice of eschatology; from the booming, rumbling voice of doom that holds us prisoner, then blinds us with the lightning sparks in jagged rivers of light. The Wrath of God rumbles the very ground beneath our feet, wrath born from Divine suffering, and His grieving over having made mankind. Every tree swishes and swirls in the warning wind and rain—in desperation to flee the wrath to come, and the burning of blue and black fire.

Today, for the first time in as long as I can remember, Nadia's Theme did not come to rescue me from the doldrums of my farm girl's life, to cause me to imagine that it was as I could have written it, so that Mother and I might have a better life. I know that I can write music the way a Cheetah chases and captures his prey. Yet there is a barrier raised between me and the world, so that there can be no crossing over to even the pretense of discovery. As to what doors this talent, this blessing, this gift, this curse—as to what doors it could open for me, I do not know—nor can I say that I can really care. No. There is no Ida Brooks left in this cemetery, where I drift from room to room in my Death Chamber, my dusty mausoleum of glass and wood.

What loneliness I feel from every sunrise to every sunset is grown today, bigger and heavier than I can carry as I go from room to room, saving and discarding the melodies as they come. It flows like a mighty stream, from my inner being to my mind, where it rests in endless storage for me to gather as I see fit: it is a Divine Gift bestowed upon me by the Almighty, which I am beyond grateful for—for I don't think my feeble verses of word prose would be enough to protect my sanity from the Evil One. This same devil, who has no claim to my music, nor my immortal soul—but seeks to have what is left of my sound mind, and then my dead body rotting away beneath the earth. I know that every evil spirit in our midst wishes me dead, but not so easily as that—these are spirits of the profoundest sadism and savagery—wishing to see me bound up to where I cannot move, with my eyes covered and my mouth gagged full of cotton, so that each tiny breath through my nose is only a reminder that *no, I can't breathe* and no, *I will not live long enough to see another summer rose in bloom.* Of these gray spirits that roam—of their cold whispers and premonitions I am so dreadfully and inescapably familiar, yet this cannot ease the pain of their icy touch. Nor is it remedy for the dreadful fear they cause.

There is a layer of mist across these floors that I can see—flowing like a cloud of dry ice heavy with cold—pouring from my mother's room as an eternal wave of misery, flowing around and underneath the furniture, flowing from the living room to where I am in the kitchen at the open back door, causing me to wish I had the courage to flee into this downpour to the mud road and splash my way to freedom. But the hands of this mist are cold and true, to seek out victims by the force of Destiny, so that whom they might conquer has no chance of escape. So I stand here at the back screen, the kitchen screen door, where these self same spirits have just peered and leered through at what it is that my mother and me hath done. I stand here in the noise and smell of the dust and pouring rain, frozen still by the power of fear, which flashes bright as the noonday in a crack of lightning blast over the back woods, and as cold as snow from the icy hands wrapped around my legs and feet.

But from this living nightmare I quickly emerge, to the rabbit rhythm of my heartbeat, and the thunder rumbling and rolling heavy across the countryside like an earthquake knocking at the door. As I stare breathlessly through the screen door at the sheets of rain, hearing my mind scream the Rhythm of the Storm in E Flat, I come to terms with who I am inside: the scared, frightened nothing I am inside, and I understand that oh yes, Mister, there is so much more to fear than Fear itself, and there is *always* so much to fear from a fateful knocking at the door.

It is the buildup and release of an energy I felt when I woke up this morning, one new Sun away from the release of her crystal fountain complete. Of what this discovery, this unveiling of her now power has done to her, I can only imagine. But I do desire to be lifted far up and away from here, but not as an escape, but so that I can see how much of the Earth is truly covered with this storm, or whether it is as I suspect, that its flood and fire is more localized than would normally be possible, and that it is a sign of things to come. The spirit that torments me is, yes, it is the Spirit of Death, which calls me to accept the Truth as surely as it has called this storm over the forests and fields where we lay. As to what form, what structure, what articulation, what execution this death must take, I do not know. But what calling, what Divine Order, what Heavenly Commission is this terrible thing, that I must now learn to stand fast and tremble bravely at the approach of Death itself?

She has been alone and quiet in her room all day. Save for the occasional trip to the bathroom, to make water in its proper place and time, rather than across the linen on my bed. The memory of her release is burned inside my mind, and the power of it rages a blue flame that may never die. And as though to remind me that I am not in control, that yes I *will* suffer by the force and will of Destiny itself, I turn to the sound of another lightning blast of thunder, and see *Death* standing two feet in front of me in pale skin, black hair and gray eyes, and a mouth worn down to a somber grim pose and frown.

She does not move. Nor did she flinch a second ago when my own quick, high scream shattered the walls of silence in our house and tomb. She only stands there with eyes that glow in the daytime dark without pity, an expression that burns without compassion, and un unseen heart that beats without remorse.

What are you doing?

The words ring a chime to my brain, feeble such as it is, paralyzed with something beyond fear, begging me to speak in response, to save what little life it is I've got left. But my mouth will not move, only my eyes darting back and forth wide open, which her brain tells her is *defiance*. This sends a signal quickly to her right arm down to her hand, and the next flash of lightning I see is from the power of a heavy slap to my face in the summer storm. It knocks me to the side where my balance is pitched precariously, then righted and pulled up by Agony in my hair, which she has a handful of, pulling me up to her face to face, with her other hand held fast at the front of my throat.

I asked you what the Hell you were doing are her words, spoken from her in shock and disbelief, as though she cannot fathom that I have dared not answer a question she has asked.

"I…I…I'm…m—m—m…l—looking at the r—r—r— "

My stuttering serves its never ending purpose—to disgust her at the sight and smell of me, to ignite the fires of an unknown hatred and revulsion that fuels her life and calling. With the strength of the Amazon, the power of the Valkyrie, the brute force of a wicked Wonder Woman, she calls me a *dumb bitch* as I am turned and thrown by my hair and neck against the table, causing me to stumble hopelessly for balance toward the living room, slamming in a noisy heap flat on my face to the floor.

As I struggle so violently toward my feet (as if they were across the room from my legs), words attack my flesh like war metal from above…

clumsy piece of shit... get your ugly, fat ass out of my sight... which I do with every particle of speed I can create, which is considerable...

The floor of the kitchen, the floor of the living room, the pain in my hip, the fragments of my mother's voice burning my back—all blend with the rain clattering our tin roof and the lightning cracked thunder, to drive me towards the white doorknob on the brown door of my room. I fly through the door like a rabbit hiding from a hawk, slamming it too hard by mistake, standing still on the other side in dimness. Ear pressed to the door. Breathing. Listening.

Praying.

Barbara Jean engages the storm. Every particle of wind. Every drop of rain. At the back door of our world: the portal to life and freedom unused. Uncared for. A doorway to a life unimagined. She stands still. Engaging the gray, depressive spirits formed in the howling sheets of rain. Touching the screen door that cages her life. Unafraid.

Barbara Jean pushes the door to freedom ajar, then to the fullness thereof. Braving the strength of the wind that pounds her. Under the wooden back porch shelter, she flinches at the power of life and death in the clouds, sparking overhead. Crackling the sky in two. Then she holds on, to suffer the booming, crashing noise of eschatology, that slams the earth like a thousand cannons. Giving in to the devastation. Obeying the Call of the Storm. This calling she hears, as a cry of confirmation heard in her dream when she was awakened earlier by this same storm. The words *"obey thy calling,"* when she refused to believe what it was she has been commissioned to do. What she is called to do.

She watches the water witch form in the back yard, as it turns to whirl towards her already wet countenance. The already damp hair, face and lavender blouse concealed. Unable to do its own calling—to conceal the impossible bosom in the storm. Wind having pushed the blouse so tight. So tight against the body of the ages. The body that calls out to the end of the age. To the end of the world.

Yes, woman. Obey thy calling.

In the storm, spirits rise and fall. In the howling wind and rain, partially sheltered on the back porch, she begins to undo slowly every button between here and there. Between life and freedom. Between Truth and Delusion. Between what is planned, and what is meant to be. Unable to stop the motion, the rhythm of movement upon her blouse, which unbuttons it completely to expose her bra. Then her gray pioneer skirt is done away with, and then her underwear besides. And then she reaches back and unlatches the fabric, letting the straps slide off her shoulders— then the rough, scratchy fabric down and away. She takes the bravest steps, down from the porch and into the cold and driving rain, hair only partially unclipped, and now fully soaked to the skin.

She stands still, barefooted. The Mountain Girl, toughened by the youth of hot and cold. Drawn into the wind of the storm. Hoping to be carried away in the blowing mist of violence, to a land that flows with milk and honey. She walks so casually, unclothed in the driving rainstorm, toward the vast and empty watermelon field beyond the yard. Standing by the edge of the small sea of green, looking at the dark and deadly clouds over the trees in the distance. Hearing what her mind had not wanted her to hear. Listening to her soul in the storm. *"Obey thy calling"* rumbles from the sky again, after the high and hard line streaks boldly from Heaven to Earth in electric light and death. *"Obey thy calling"* is screamed by the water witches, who fly in outstretched hands formed from the rain itself, grabbing her by the heart and mind, taking hold of her neck and her groin, to infuse her with power. *"Take up thy breast, woman,"* she hears in time and space, *"nurse from the power therin."*

Oh, what things there be on Heaven and Earth, that the eyes of mankind have not seen! Those who might care, who might crave to see what is done in secret are not privy to this rare and special sight: of a nude, wasp-waisted, heavy hipped woman with watermelon sized breasts, holding one of them up to her lips, sucking. Nursing herself in the rain.

Inside the house, at my bedroom window, I am compelled to speak aloud—a prayer I have dared not speak, lest I anger Him, at not having the strength, the *Faith* to endure my calling. As the wind drives the rain harder into the windowpane at me, I must allow the words to flow from my immortal soul—*"Oh God. Please don't let me die."*

What prayers go unheard, falling in the wind? What fervent prayers are these, that go unanswered in the storm? It is the prayer that seeks to achieve that which is against God's Will, and that which is *not* meant to be. I take my place among the unfortunate, and I must endure the coldness, the infinite night which is Divine Refusal; that great cosmic *"No"*, that says in some form or another, yes... you *will* die.

Upon this heavy cloud passing, by the force of its devastation is the sound of the back screen door closing loudly, and bare footsteps I only imagine I hear. These are the footsteps of darkness, the footsteps of impending doom, the footsteps of Dire and Damnation. They step so softly. So assuredly. Yes. With such demonic determination—determinedly to where I am. And then these steps turn from the kitchen to the living room, to stop at my door upon the beat of a loud *slam* from the other side of it, which can only be the naked woman dripping wet, having released the rest of her anger, the surplus of power she feels by slamming her fists once, as hard as she can to the door. I jump and yip like the pinched puppy I am, trembling to the point of shaking as the white doorknob turns, and the door swings softly, assuredly, and so determinedly open.

The wet, naked woman only stares at the pathetic shell in the room. A face of mountain beauty. Baptized in Freedom and Truth. An expression that conceals the laughter of Divine Assurance, blended with the cry of Divine Suffering.

Insanity is the key. On the eve of eschatology.

She steps comfortably in the room, partially pinned hair dripping wet, closing the door behind her. I am struck by the smallness of her waist—unfed today, except for the swallow of power from her bosom—curved into hips that appear massively wide and rounded, beneath breasts heavy laden with milk. The hourglass figure is impossible to fathom; when married to her face, it is a figure of womanhood and beauty hardly seen since the Garden of Antiquity. She is the Daughter of Eve, not meant to be unclothed for others to see, lest it incite the heart to lust and sin. A woman of art, begged to be photographed for the world, but forbidden except for my eyes only. I think that the gigantic nature of her breasts, on a woman so beautiful and naturally curvy would ignite a storm of blue and black fire in the world, if it were to see her unclothed.

She walks slowly over to me, uncovered. Standing in front of me so that I must look up into her eyes. She stares down at me. Checking for the flash of defiance that will call to every warrior muscle in her body, to beat me until my eyes are blackened, and my lips are swollen to black and blue.

Take off your clothes, she says. Deeply.

After so many times over the years, why do my hands still tremble? The buttons on my rose pattern, thrift shop dress are soon undone in fear, and the dress slides down my body to the floor. She stays so close by, not moving at all, mouth relaxed to where her lips are parted, as she stares at every nervous move I make to get out of my clothes. Is it shame I feel, she wonders, or do I tremble from the fear and respect she craves? No matter, as she nearly trembles herself from the electric shock she feels from the accidental brushing of my hand across her erect nipple when I side my bra down and away. *Leave your underwear on,* she says. Turning, stepping away. She turns back toward me, marveling what she sees in contempt, with neither remorse nor pity. I wonder what it will be like to be beaten and choked to within a breath of dying? How long will it take? Will I fight back? Will I scream? Will God send an angel in from the storm clouds, and rescue me from the grave?

Turn around, she says. Staring at me from behind—the same tragically figure-eighted body as her own, the same freakishly curved waist and big bottom, with two white melons that complete our sideshow refrain. Can she refrain for much longer, from the Death of me that still remains? *Take off your underwear,* she says, *and come here to me,* which I do un-surreptitiously, in the aura of hopelessness and fear.

Turn around, she says. I feel her soon pressed hard against my back, her hands tight around my waist, pinning my arms to my sides. The smell of wet wolf-bitch is strong in my nostrils, and the damp skin of her human form presses hard against my naked body. She leans her head firm to my shoulder beside my ear, so that her spirit can flow more easily into my mind.

I'm going to have to fuck you.

Almost immediately, my heart beats faster in that unknown terror, and my breath quickens. So familiar to me and faster than usual, I feel the beginning of her lady member at my buttocks, which causes her to readjust herself against me. *I'm going to have to obey God,* she says, *and take your virginity.*

"No," I say, shaking my head. "Please don't. You said that—"

I don't want to. But what choice do I have?

"Momma you have a choice," I say, eyes fixed. Tears streaming. "Just beat me. Beat the devil out of me because I deserve it but don't stick nothin' there Momma, please…"

God gave me what I need so that I can carry out His will. He gave me that which pertaineth to a man, so that I can take this sin from your body.

"What sin, Momma? There's no sin."

There is only sin. And the forgiveness of God and Christ. It is only through Him that we obtain our salvation. If we love Him, we keep his commandments. He has commanded me to take the seed of lust from inside you. To break the wall if iniquity that separates you from purity. He told me it is the only way you can go to Heaven. The only way you can truly be saved is for us to become as one, for me to break the blood skin inside you.

"No, no," I say, wailing it. Brave enough now to step away from her gentle grip. "Momma, God wants me to be a virgin, I know he does."

God wants you to give your virginity to me. It is mine to have. Through this, the two of us will be saved. Saved by the Blood of Christ, and the blood of your chastity.

I begin to pull away from her. Whimpering, pleading. Praying.

"Why does he want you to do it, Momma?"

I told you. To cleanse us from our sins.

"But he already cleansed us from our sins Momma. The Bible says he did."

But this was a Divine Revelation, Elizabeth. He spoke directly to my mind. He told me to obey my calling. He told me to take your virginity and I have to do it.

"Momma you don't believe that do you? You don't really believe that…"

I don't want to believe it. I fought this for three days I swear to God. But the truth is I should have put a stick in you instead of my tongue when you were a little girl. Instead of biting you between your legs I should have *run a white stick...I should have put it in you to <u>blood</u> after your breasts came in. But I was disobedient because I didn't know any better. No... listen to me, Elizabeth... sometimes He tests us. He tells us to do things we don't understand and we have to obey or we'll be sent to Hell when we die. Do you want to go to Hell when you—*

"I...Momma..."

Answer me!

"N...no..."

Then I want you to come to your bed, and I want you to lie down on your back.

"Momma... Momma what can I say to make you stop?"

Nothing, Elizabeth. This is something we both have to do. A private and special obedience to God...

"Oh, God. Oh Lord Jesus help me," I say. Pitifully, as she ushers me to the bed, laying me there on my back. Burned into my mind is the image of her beauty as she had screamed at me a moment ago, while the tear ran so casually down her cheek.

The storm gives its tragic command, as Divine proclamation howls in the wind, and splits the sky in two over the forests and fields nearby. I lay down, obedient not to my mother's insanity, but to the fact that this evil is ordained by God himself, and I must obey the woman who gave me life, and who will now take it from me so abundantly.

Close your eyes whispers to me, which makes me stare more intently at my mother, but realizing that she said nothing. But my eyes remain stubbornly open, so that I may witness the lightning flashes in the summer daytime dark, illuminating the scene of her standing beside the bed in ritual, squeezing her mammoth breasts hard enough to push the milk out to dripping from underneath her fingers. I watch her pull her nipples outward, hands wet from milk and water. Pulling them out as far as they will go comfortably, which is considerable.

Beginning to settle in, relaxing, I hear the requisite release of breath she gives, as her brain feeds the perversion to every cell in her body. She walks closer to the bed now. My eyes are closed just enough to hide me, so I can gauge what she's doing. I can barely see, but I can sense her standing over me still and quiet, staring at every inch of my naked body in the storm. Her daughter's body. The Body of Chastity. The innocence it is her calling to kill. It is the last of me.

And as if in warning to me, I see the lightning flash as bright as the noon day, to show me her anomaly, the female member fully erect and protruding, longer and bigger than I have ever seen it! Is it the quintuple of an inch? This, I cannot tell! But I know now what has been willed by the Almighty God, as the bed dips down under the weight of her, and she climbs on top of me with the skill and stealth of sin and death.

I swallow the whimper, channeling it through the quiet tears I cry, feeling it trickle warm from my eye and tickle my ear. As I open my legs by her easy command, I notice that my sorrow flows a slow and steady steam, drawn up and to where she is like sea water into a white funnel cloud. Through a fleeting glimpse, I see her leaned over me, holding the thin member to full erection, looking down to where it must go, lurching forward on her knees, her face in deep, anguished concentration, to perform the new and deadly important task at hand.

When I feel the wet tip of it rub against mine, the shock pierces my soul, to match that felt from the cold droplet of water fallen to my breast from her hair. I reach up to try and touch her bosom—*put your hands down!* being the snap from the wolf bitch's bite. And then, I feel the warm tickling, trickling away from my smaller self, sliding serpentine into where the last part of me has come and gone—sliding firmly, forbidden up the path to this barrier, this barrier between sin and salvation; this barrier between carnality pushing, positioning her body to its final place above me—*open your legs all the way—pull 'em farther back and wider*—which I do with such reluctance as I am not accustomed, feeling as though something is inside me threatening to tear a hole in the space of who I am, to rip apart this place along the fabric of space-time, sliding further up into me where no demon hath dared go before, until the pain is laced with an icy fear unlike any I have ever known, until my arms are around this woman's neck unbenownst, and I exclaim with the last breath in my body a scream to the throne of God and Christ.

Whether or not it is the sound of my voice, or the feel of me dying inside, I will never know, but she suddenly lurches forward involuntarily, with a powerful shaking besides, piercing me with pain again, and the siren I hear in her weeps a pleading sorrow into the storm, and to the selfsame throne of the Almighty.

99

In our little world

In our place of isolation

There is no shame between us

Only pain

Pain caused by pressures of longing

Craving a life without fear and sadness

We are prisoners...two women

Living together alone

Bound by forces we cannot resist
Held captive in a prison
From which there can be no reprieve—
No escape from the pain of living

100

In the heart of memory, strolling through the field, I see the leaves of the White Forest, calling to me. Every leaf is as white as the petal of the rose, to decorate the trunks of ivory wood. And it seems that as I approach the forest of my youth, and the trees of days long gone, I can feel the grieving in every leaf and blossom, appearing as white as snow. I stroll through the fields of green, away from the hidden house of gray, feeling the breeze across my face, to dry the tears that threaten to flow.

When I stroll through the heart of memory, I can see the place where the White Forest grows, and I know that I must walk this journey, to find where the petal of the crimson rose is grown. In the forest, strolling the path to innocence, down the trail of my heart's desire, the white leaves are a blanket beneath my feet. High above me, from the tall trunks is the white leaf canopy, formed white as the clouds of Heaven. This is the Autumn of the White Woods, when the leaves are subject to cool breezes that flow.

The breeze whirls the wooded alabaster trail, and it blows my garment about me as a curtain in the wind, cloth born from the loom within, a soul of melancholy blue. My dress of deepest blue midnight contrasts the ground of ivory white, so that I am known as a creature fallen, who was cast down from days of purity. I am innocence lost. Strolling the heart of memory in midnight, in the woods of winter white.

The breeze blows again, to lift my hair with my flowing cloth. Leaves fall from the ivory wood, blowing down to where I stroll, falling like gigantic flakes of snow. These are carried in this otherworldly breeze, until they whirl about me, taken on currents as the whirlwind, until I am among a swirling mass of white leaves, blowing in the wind.

I continue. Hearing the tone of my piano in loneliness, calling me to fore. But I do not go to it on this walk, for I must complete my searching through the white woods, to where I know the crimson petals grow…

While I feel pain and suffocation try as they might, I breathe deeply this air of freedom, and my eyes catch sight of my melody in question. It is the single rose flower, on its lifeline made of white. I hurry in the motion of the flowing wind, and I retrieve the single red flower.

In the heart of memory, I stroll the path through the White Forest. To the place where love is crimson.

101

"*M*omma, please…"

"Hush up! Hush your mouth and do as I ask or you'll get worse."

"But why, Momma? Please tell me why you have to do this?"

"Put your arms down! That's right, put 'em behind you."

I lean back towards her, but she pulls away. So I face forward, and close my eyes…

"Momma, please don't do it. Please don't do it Momma…"

The stabbing pain rips through the front of my breasts, as Mother twists them without mercy. I scream my hellish noise, like one who is burning again in the Lake itself.

"Come back here!"

"No!"

"Get over here!"

"I said no! I won't let you do it!"

Mother hits me hard on the upper arms and shoulders, and on the top of my head, calling me a frigid, disobedient bitch, because I will not surrender to the Rule.

"Come here to me!"

"I can't! I can't take the pain anymore, Momma, I *can't!*

She stares at me, her chest heaving. Her flesh rises over the edges of her bra.

"Momma have mercy. Please Momma."

A frightening calm descends over her. Without another word, she reaches back, and removes her bra calmly.

"I'll stop it, Momma! I'll stop it. I swear to God and Jesus I'll stop it Momma!"

She grabs me by the hair, slapping me in the face harder than she ever has in her life. I stumble clumsily to the side, nearly falling, starry minded. Before I can raise my head, I feel another brutal slap, which knocks me against the wall. A jagged pain cuts the top of my head when I bump the wall. She slaps me over and over, until each blow brings a deep, begging scream from my mouth. After several minutes, she rips my bra and panties completely off. Several punches to the ribs double me over, reminding me of being hit with a hammer.

"I won't fight anymore! I promise I won't fight anymore!"

Her mind is elsewhere. She seems possessed as she trips me forward, throwing me down onto the middle of the floor. I feel her sit heavily on my back, grabbing hold of my arm, and bending my wrist up with all her might. I know that my deep, woman screams are beautiful to her, sending waves of pleasure through her strong body. Her movements are so determined that she must have done this many times in her imagination. But my wrist will not break. So she ceases the effort, then flips me onto my back.

"Put your arms to your sides!"

"I can't!"

She kicks me hard in the ribs. "Put your arms to your sides!"

"I'll do it! I will, I promise!"

All I can do is close my eyes, begging Providence, feeling the stinging, burning pain in my breasts, and the warm blood trickling behind my ear. But I wait. I wait for the twisting. The pulling.

But Mother is not concerned with that now.

She positions herself, bringing her knee down with full force onto my left arm. My body dissipates, reforming into something filled with more pain than I had thought possible. The pain shoots instantly through every muscle and bone, and I can hear my own screams to God and Christ, while she pins both of my arms to the floor. She spits full into my face, watching me writhe and tremble, shaking—babbling like a madwoman, teetering at the edge of sanity.

"You want the twisting back now don't you? DON'T YOU!"

Her voice trails off. The room is darker. The air is colder on my skin. My mind will not hold a thought. But the pain...the pain is going away....it feels wonderful.

Will she kiss me before I sleep?

"Does it feel better?" the nurse asks.

"Yes, thank you. It feels a lot better."

"Has it always been like this?"

"Mmm hmm, I've always been this clumsy."

The nurse gives me a knowing, but compassionate look. I saw my face in the bathroom mirror before I came here. It is badly bruised.

"Honey, if your husband did this to you, all you have to do is say so, and we can make sure it never happens again. It was only a bruised bone this time. Next time, he might break it."

"I'm not married. I told you, I fell down. I'm always falling down."

"We've seen it before, Ms. Coletti. Is he your boyfriend or your fiancee?"

"I've never been with anybody. I live alone in the country, with my mother."

The nurse's mouth opens, but she can't speak—

"I'll be alright. I've always been clumsy, and there's no telling what I'm gonna do to myself next time. I have to go now. Momma's waiting for me."

Outside, the clouds are a deep purple in the twilight. The nurse follows me through the exit, even though I asked her not to. But she can't resist following me to the old, gray taxicab. She'll give the old witch the prescription herself, she thinks. Perhaps, even a stern look. I watch her march toward the figure in the back seat, towards her window, ignoring my anxious gaze.

When the compassionate nurse looks inside, her heart leaps to her throat, and her blood runs cold…

The passenger is an older version of her patient, with large, piercing gray eyes. Her expression is friendly and cultured—possessing dignity, and nearly regal grace and humility.

102

*A*s it is written, for everything, there is a season. This is the revolution of the heavenly spheres, or the turning of a day, or the ticking away of a single hour. It too gives notice to the seasons of man, the comings and goings, hither and yonder, to and fro, to every place forward and back again. To encompass as well the seasons of activity, which are as the clock, which we use to mark the places along our journey through the universe, and our path among the stars of the second heaven.

This season is as the whirlwind. A storm of controlled rage and devastation, of wrath and fury so rarely seen upon the Earth, existing only to cause misery and destruction, fear and loathing in the hearts of women and men. This is the season of the whirlwind, which has blown above our isolated house without ceasing, blowing our doors off their unsturdy hinges, careening our barriers through the house like so much debris, shattering other parts of our lives into pieces, all of it being sucked out in the storms that pass, taken upward into the gray clouds, and dispersed to the four winds. These are the storms of what we know, which have visited themselves to us, which have destroyed us, and has whirled into the white serpentine, drawing itself up away from our eyes, and into the clouds of memory.

Our time in Desire's Field has finally come and gone, along with the sweetness and warmth I had come to know. Again, I feel the eyes of rejection stare. The cold, icy sting of contempt has returned. I suppose that guilt has combined with her boredom for me, and she has overcome her need to press herself to me warmly, or to grind my skin in a lover's burn. What burning I feel these days is that of her growing displeasure and intolerance, as the couple whose fire is long gone, and is left only with smoke and cinders, and ashes of regret. Her passion for me has been redirected through a mother's fervent distemper, and fevered desire to make me wish that I had never been born.

After so many months of such fire of want—such blazing, sensual heat and satisfaction, I am amazed to be in my room staring out the window, tears streaming down my face like wet air down a cold glass. This, because I endeavored to give her a kiss in the cool of the evening, after a day's work in the planting fields. As if I had cursed the name of God before her alter of prayer, she slapped me in a spirit of hatred and pure discipline, nearly knocking me off of my feet. I stood in the open field, staring at her in something beyond hurt, something greater than bewilderment, with my mouth open and my hand on my burning cheek. Obeying her command, I turn and stumble my *whorish backside* into the house, even running a little, feeling as raw and exposed as I ever have, while the sparrows whisper it to the red bird, talking of my humiliation in laughter and afternoon chirping. I stand in my room, watching the light of day give place to the blue of evening cloud bands, feeling the sting of her hand on my face, remembering the sound of it in her voice, and the sight of it on her beautiful features.

Mother! It was not love that we shared, then? It was the comfort of lust unbridled! The pleasures of sin for a season! What will I do, without the comfort of your embrace? What shall I do, but kneel before thy Throne?

Behind the trees of our world, I can feel the sun along the plane, somewhere above a deep blue horizon. It is there, beyond the setting sun that my Savior reigns, and where my Redemption draweth nigh.

103

Even though I had wished for Life
He did not wish for me—
From the beginning there has only been
An empty road to see

Life grinned a phony smile at me
Then beckoned me to ride—
Unbeknownst, I rode his chariot
My soul, I gave to pride

We drove beyond the Halls of Learning—
Expecting to know a way
Seeing other misdirected souls
Lost in their final day

In hope, I cruised the empty roads—
We passed the forest trees—
When I saw that they were skeletons
My heart raced ill at ease

But Life assured we travel on
Until our pace was done
Behind the Forest of Dying Leaves—
I felt the setting sun

We detoured away the empty road—
Across a Field of Green
We rode along the Grassy Plain
To where I'd never been

I gazed with hope toward my driver
With unbelieving eyes—
When I learned he was not Life at all—
But Death in brief disguise!

I grieved in fear for what I knew
Wishing for what I'd known
But he showed me the marker in the ground—
A place to call my own

104

*I*n these last days, beyond the passing whirlwind, I await the coming of a grander storm, from across the sounding sea. I am lucky that a part of me is pure dim wittedness, as I do not understand that my life should be different. Like a dumb lamb on the way to the altar of sacrifice, I always go willingly when she takes me to the summer woods at twilight, or sometimes in the middle of the night. Do I know better by now than to ask why? I do. But my prayers are answered this early evening, when I don't see the punishment stick in her hands. When it is the thick tree switch, I know I'll be stripped as naked as a jaybird. My hands will be tied above my head to a tree trunk, my back against the tree. She will stripe the front of my body from my chest to my legs, until my skin is stained red with blood.

We walk across the fields together as mother and daughter, as the early evening clouds are kissed by amber, in the glow of Apollo's Dying Light. The rope is a long, white serpentine in her hand. Again I can only thank the Lord God and Jesus that there is no stick this time. Though I try to be brave whenever she carries the stick, I still tremble inside at the thought. My mind is stupid, in that it will not allow me to believe I should fight or run. I move along like a dog on a leash, while she pulls me to the clearing close to my white tree. Every time she has the wooden rod, she grabs me by the arm and begins to hit me on the shoulders, the stomach, the back, the buttocks and the legs—whatever part of my body that is not covered in the flailing. She is uncompromising, hitting me very hard and repeatedly. In sorrow I try not to weep, but my breath soon flutters with my beating heart, and a scream will fly out of me in a long, deep wailing. Whether it is pain or fear, only the trees can tell. I often wonder if others in our world have heard this cry, the famous banshee of lurid and literary legend. It is only me, though. Letting the pain flow through my voice…as I have been taught so well to do.

In reality, she takes me by the hand and escorts me into the woods fully clothed. There, she ties me to my white tree in the dusk. The rope pulls tight around my throat, pinning my head against the smooth, white bark. I can swallow, and I think my breathing will be alright. She whispers a prayer to herself, devoutly, and then she leaves me there past sunset, under the Prairie Moon, beneath the journey of the Seven Sisters, until the early morning light. Many times I have awakened during the night or the morning, my back against the tree, to the sound of rustling leaves—either some unknown creature of the woods coming to laugh at me, or the footsteps of my captor coming to release me to cook and clean, while she sleeps her daily grief away.

What thoughts flash in her memory when she beats the blood out of me in the woods? When she binds me to the tree? Did Evelyn take her to the edge of the mountain woods in the snow and leave her there in the cold? I am blessed, however, that God has never allowed her to bind me in the woods when there is a north wind, or even in the rain. This is compassion, I think—as when a cat is brought into the house to escape an approaching thunderstorm. Not from love, but from pity.

In the dawn, on our return trip across the field to the gray house, I remember that there were no melodies last night, and no kitten in my dreams to brush against my leg, or sit nearby to keep me from being lonely. I should like to see it again. To marvel that it is as white as snow—with eyes the color of the ocean sky.

Whether it is real or a wishful dream, I do not know.

105

The forest leaves give voice to the trees, spoken by the breath of a fervent summer wind. A strong breeze blows a chorus through the woods, reaching through the open back door to my face while I stand at the screen. Mother languishes somewhere in the blue bedroom, waiting for our late Saturday afternoon dinner to be done. The house smells of the tender pork roast, which I will chop and season to what ability I have, until our southern barbecue dinner is made. I cannot help but gaze pathetically through the screen, across the field to the singing woods. Remembering my night against the tree.

In Holy scripture, even in my time, I have learned that unearned suffering is not always redemptive in this life, and that perhaps there is only Fate, Destiny, and the Will of God. Accursedness is very much predestination, and is a calling that must be endured. Moses! Oh, how didst thou suffer! From Egypt through the wilderness, to the Land of Canaan— to the Promised Land that thou would only see, but where you were never allowed to be! David! The Shepherd King! Thine desire for Bathsheba was beyond thy doing! From birth, you were going to murder her husband, so that God could put your son in the grave! How you suffered unredeemed, for the thorn He put in thy side! Dear Lazarus, at the rich man's gate, to not even be allowed to taste the crumbs from his table of plenty, and then to die in the same poverty in which thou wast born! Holy Apostles, for our Lord and Saviour Jesus Christ—glory in thy martyred selves! What evil hadst thou done?

Though I hear the melodies in the Chorus of the Leaves, I will only commit them to memory, and dwell upon it another time. Whether or not this chorus will be lost, I have not the strength to care.

My Dear Mozart! To burn the hottest flame of genius ever born, to be told over and over—no! No! You shall not rest upon the Hill, where your light would shine for the world to see! Burn in the wilderness, Amadeus, for a predestined few to gather warmth from thee! You will be consumed, and you will die in sorrow for this Heavenly Gift, this unearthly ingenuity! To retreat from endless toil, mindless composition for pennies? To cease having to cast your pearls before swine, to have them trampled in muddy fields of contempt and ignorant neglect? No! You will not rest! Thou shalt not taste the full fruits of thy labour! Your agonizing for the Opera Stage will blaze in your symphonies, your concertos, your sonatas, your quartets and beyond! Figaro! Giovanni! First fruits only… a taste of what feast you deserve! But Fret not, my Dear Mozart, your gift will light the fires of another, when your body is in the pauper's grave. The Opera melodies will unfetter their German bondage, to soar *Bel Canto* above the fields of Italy.

And what will he be?

The Italian Mozart—

Indisputably!

Emily! My dearest! I know the horror of this loneliness! I have sailed these same dark waters from my youth! I too, hear a cry from somewhere over the horizon of Amherst Lake, beyond where the eyes can see, but I know that I am carried on winds of his Will, and that these melodies are for my eyes only, to ease the suffering that I have to bear. I do not know thee! My verses are in the bars of music, but not riddles for the eye and the mind! I speak of Him in the bars of music, to send thanksgiving to His Throne! The Violin is a witness to this, it sings a poignant melody in the breeze! It conspires with the other strings, left on its own to sing when the bars have passed! Listening to the winds come together, to breathe Heaven's Melody upon the Earth—when the violin sings a melody, it knows. It grows—it flows Beauty into the world.

Oboes intertwine, upon the Harvest Trail! Tales of wind from another Time, another history! Another place of strings; cellos whisper velvetine tones, soothing the violin's apprehension, tensions for the viola's pain—

Basses booming, timpani's looming a stormy rumble! Tumbling trombones whirling through a brass ring of fire! Horns call from another place, coloring each key among them—saving grace from the ordinary in ambiguity. En masse, each voice in Tutti's Call, rising above the voices of chatterly, singing songs of Glory's Way; days of beauty and frolicking…rolicking times of grandeur, feeling across the Barrier Land, getting lost along the way to rhythmic perfection! Detection saves each waning section. Allowing seams to mend. Harmonies blend with the air itself, wishing. Longing for appreciation.

Hoping for a better time.

106

"izabeth!"

Torment has a voice. It calls me while I am in the evening field, looking at the stars begin to appear. I hear no malice tonight, so I pretend I don't notice her. I can be very stubborn.

"Elizabeth you come inside now. Elizabeth?"

"I hear you, Momma."

Suddenly, I feel an iron grip on my arm, and my body is whirled around as if it is hollow.

"Was that sass I just heard from you?"

"No, Momma."

I try to walk towards the house. But she yanks me backward, and glares at me.

"You think I can't hear it, don't you?"

My eyes are wide open in the dusk, while she stares at me. I would defy her if I could.

"My Momma taught me a hundred ways to beg for mercy. If you ever challenge me. I swear to God if you ever—"

"Never," I say. "I'll never challenge you, Momma."

"That's good," she says, nodding her head. "That's very good."

Her expression calms, and she steps close to me. Together, we look into the approaching nightfall.

"Sometimes," she says, her arm about my waist, "sometimes we have to be made to suffer, Elizabeth, despite our obedience. It teaches us humility. Some of us are meant for suffering."

She pauses, still looking above the treetops, into the beauty of our country eve.

"I think…I think that maybe the Lord has called me to make you suffer."

I look at her, wanting to ask her, but being too afraid to speak. If I open my mouth, I know that I will begin to stutter.

"Seven," she said.

"Wh-wh—"

"I'm going to bind you in your bedroom, and punish you for seven days."

We go back inside, while her arm is lovingly, but firmly around my waist. I feel as though I am being taken to a dungeon by a compassionate guard, who feels pity for me, but having no remorse for locking me away from the world, and making me wish I had never been born. I see a look come over her face, perhaps as one who has drank too much wine, and has given in to the depression it might cause. But she is in full possession of her faculties, and knows full well what she is going to do.

"D-do you want me to r-run your b-bath for you M-Momma?"

She ignores me while we walk through the kitchen, through the twilight of this day. When we get to my room, I see waiting for me on the bed a knife, a punishment stick, and a length of thin, new rope.

"Do you have to go to the bathroom?" she asks.

"Y-yes m-m-m…"

"Alright. Let's go."

I tremble and breathe and look pleadingly while she escorts me to the bathroom. She watches me sit there, and does not get angry when nothing happens. She only escorts me back to my room, which suddenly seems not like a refuge at all, but like a prison.

Leaving me fully clothed in my country flower dress, she picks up the knife, and cuts the rope into long sections. She is whispering bible verses about evil women. She binds my ankles and my thighs, then wraps a length of it around my wrist and arms, binding them together behind my back.

"Lie down, here, sweetie. Lie on your side."

The softness in her voice reassures me that I will not die. My legs are bent back, hogtied to my arms. Then, she gags me. Suddenly, it feels harder to breathe. I cannot move.

Mother retrieves the punishment stick, and my screams are muffled, as she hits my arms and legs very hard, until it feels like they are broken.

I wake up in the middle of the night, my arms and legs on fire with pain, wondering if I will be able to walk again. I really do have to go to the bathroom this time. What will happen, if she does not let me go? I am so completely tied, I do not think she will let me out again, until my punishment has ended. I glance out the window, grateful for a view of the full moon, beginning to count in my head the minutes it will stay in my view. In this light, I see that there is hope.

I am reminded of this past winter, the first time she alluded to this. It happened on a Sunday night, in the dead of winter, when the entire land seemed buried in a layer of snow. We had not walked to church that day, because of the thick snow. Whatever evil was present inside her had not been rebuked by our Sunday service, and the week's misery was compounded by the white winter cold. She did not speak to me that entire day, even at dinner time, and I knew better than to disturb her sensibility.

But sometime after darkness fell, I heard the soft patter of stocking feet coming towards my room, and I quickly put my music paper away, underneath my mattress, chastising myself for having been so careless. I shudder to think what she might have done to me if she knew I was writing music. I pick up my bible, and pretend to be reading a chapter. She comes into the room wearing her robe, and I get up from the bed quickly, greeting her with as much enthusiasm as I can. Truthfully, I think that she wants me to fix dinner, or check the kerosene fuel in the living room heater.

As soon as I approach her, she slaps me so hard that I lose my balance, and fall hard against my dresser. Already, I am screaming and begging her to tell me what I have done. She tells me to shut up, and to strip down to nothing, which I do without asking why, grateful that perhaps she only wants pleasure, and for me to help her through the night's depression and misery.

But she removes from her robe pocket a piece of white twine. I am not ashamed that I begged her to let me hug her. I did not want to be tortured, or perhaps even burned against the kerosene heater in the corner of my room.

After my wrists are tied behind my back, she stands in front of me, and does not make eye contact. She removes her robe, and she is as completely unclothed as I. In one smooth, fluid motion, she drops her robe upon my dresser, and swings the back of her hand full into my face. I stumble backward and she grabs me before I fall. She hits me again across the face, and throws me onto the bed.

She pulls me by the hair to the center of the bed, this very bed, and straddles me across the stomach. I remember a flurry of blows, striking me over and over across the face, while I beg her to let me hug her, to make her feel better. Her fury is controlled, but complete, and I wonder if she is going to beat me to death.

I remember waking up in the middle of that night on the cold bed, with my wrists still bound, and an aching in my head that seemed to penetrate the core of my brain. She had pulled me to my feet just before she was done, and had hit me hard enough to knock me unconscious, then left me there and went to bed.

I remember seeing myself in the mirror. There is dried blood under my nose and on the side of my mouth, and one of my eyes is slightly swollen. My arms are still bound, and I remember thinking how much I hate my body, and that I look like a freak of nature. I despise myself, for deserving to be beaten so badly. I deserve to die.

Even in the Land of Dreams, I know that I deserve to die.

107

There are rules to life and living, I suppose. I am learning to surrender to this, as the pain burns through my arms and legs, even into my back. Revelation descends as a reprieve, teaching me to relax, and to let the pain have its way. Struggling only invites fear, which makes the body tense. Tension makes it hard for the suffering to pass through. Pain cannot be fought. It must be surrendered to.

The days are merciful, moving swiftly along, until I am at the seventh day of my imprisonment. Early this morning I was awakened by the stick.

My body feels as though it does not work anymore. I am weak from the tiny amounts of food. Every so often, I can smell my own urine. I can hear her in the afternoon kitchen now, happily fixing herself a Sunday dinner. Her walk to church this morning must have been a lonely one.

The mind is a wonderful fortress, a refuge from the pain of living. Inside the mind is the imagination, wherein lies the keys to life. Even while I have lain bound these many days, unable to move, unable to keep my body from relieving, I am able to escape into another place, a world of beauty and song. Here in this lovely place, my mind is adrift upon the four seasons, and I stroll in a land where there is no suffering, beneath the branches of my Great Flowering Tree.

Upon a time long ago, in a Land beyond the Sea
Melodies sang from a Whispering Tree
Far away places near gathered 'round
To marvel this miracle in Heavenly sound

From Summer's hour, warm winds would whirl
To swirl precious harmonies in righteous pearl
Every eye did blink from wonders saw
While leaves played symphonies to wondrous awe

Pause ruled peaceful in the Land of Knee
Happiness because of their Whispering Tree

Through centuries they came in blade and fire
To slice with burning Wicked's Ire

    Not an inch of wood, nor a scrape of green
    No harm from witches or terror's glean
    Warlords and Beasts and Wizards flee
    From Summer's Leaves of Melody

    In Autumn's hour, enchanted hymn
    Silences by Nature's whim
    To colors flamed in every hue
    From Crimson Red to Harvest Blue

    Now Winter's gale through courses blow
    To bury their land in Ice and Snow
    Every leaf 'tis white as Luna's Light
    Bright until their Spring's Delight.

    As Winter claimed the Land of Knee
    The Queen did marvel her Whispering Tree
    From root to crown was white as Snow
    To guard her world from conquering foe

    When Spring interred fair Winter's cold
    Their snowy tree spun leaves of Gold
    Dear Legend cried both far and near
    Hear Splendor's season in Beauty's year

Now Creation breathed warm Summer's breeze
When life seeks shelter beneath the trees
The golden leaves hue green in glee
While their Tree of Life sings a Melody.

Four is a figure of completion. A number of Divine Resolution. The seasons, the Gospels. The intrepid winds, flowing from each of the four corners of the earth. There are even four sections to my beloved orchestra, and four main instruments which sing from the bow. Upon each of these are four strings to give voice, to soothe the troubled soul.

Beyond our little cropfield, just inside the forest wood is my white tree, my little tree, with its smooth, white bark. Some time ago, after the Evening, I tied a piece of twine to the tree, and I unraveled it westward, towards where I know the stream goes through the woods. I followed my white path, until I was lost in an unfamiliar world, a place thick with fallen leaves and dead trees. My nervousness would not let me extend the westward path, and I never did find the place where I knew the forest stream would be. Someday perhaps, I will return.

My mind begins my brief journey from my Southern Line String, my path in and out of the forest woods. It connects me to a tree deep inside, which is my conduit, my portal to three other lands of melody. From here, I travel upon the North Line, marked with a spot of blood, so I shall never be lost. Far north, away from the grieving land, is a vast world of ice and snow, populated by concertos great and small. They lie a great distance from one another, too small to see from afar, so I have to search this north land, hoping to find the Great Concertos, only a few of which I have yet found. The grandest among these are hidden inside crystalline forms with no color, the largest I will ever see, but blended into the field of white like diamond boulders, so that they are very difficult to find.

The crystal responds to my touch, glowing with the color of its key, and I hear every part in succession, until the entire piece is implanted upon my memory. Every note of music has its own distinct color, without variation. If I wish, the notes themselves appear as they should on paper, but three dimensional in the air, with their flags and stems, always in the hue of their sound, bright and pure and impossible to forget. The white crystal produces the greatest abundance of color and sound, and their melodic inspiration is always extremely high. They sing for the piano and orchestra. I have been lucky, for I have found one on this journey, and it is as big as an ocean, and as melancholy as the night. Here, in my ice world, the heat of pain is soothed in the cold, until I feel nothing but coolness upon my skin. I am a Snow Spirit, with hair the color of sunlight, who sees the music flow from the crystal shores of power. I cannot describe the tone of the piano I hear in this world, as it embodies all of Steinway's brilliant loveliness, and Bosendorfer's velvetine beauty.

My desert land lies upon the Eastern Line, with its ocean of sand, where symphonies hide in the golden rocks of color. I search this barren world, in hopes that over each horizon, there lies a great golden stone, a monumental work, that I may hear what manner of music it will be. I am blessed in that my inspirations are never dreary, even when they are somber or melancholy. When I travel the Western Line String, I find my beautiful jungle paradise, a shaded world of tall, green trees and exotic flowers every color of the rainbow. These flowers sing with tiny voices of every common and uncommon instrument imaginable, many for solo, but often in strange combinations, with mysterious harmonies, rhythms and modulations, but always pleasing; music of a type that cannot readily be composed by many. And still, what amazes me the most is my musical memory, which is so acute that I do not easily forget a single note of what I hear. Forever, I think I will associate sonatas, duos, trios and quintets with flowers.

Would that I were born in another century! I would meet a handsome young musician, a composer like myself, and I would give him the energy of my gift, and in his name the world would hear the beauty of these treasures I find. But I fear that they are mine alone, given to me for the twilight, that I may rest in the comfort that I am not alone. A gift, any gift, comes from the Almighty God.

A white dragon flew the Land of Dreams

From my homeland to infinity
I searched far and wide the Wealthen Stream
Grieving for the Land of Plenty

This dragon flew me high and low
In power of where I must command
I looked beyond the Azurean Glow
To the shores of a Fair and Distant Land

But no where among the dragon's flight
Did I see my Golden Harvest Loom
So I rode upon the winds of might
Drifting to my House of Doom

I grieved with hope from whence I came
From where the winged dragon flew
But I found my homeland just the same
The Land of Poverty I knew

Inevitably, the time arrives when I must again touch the Southern Line, which carries me back to my homeworld, the land of the dead, a realm of caves, a place of dark'nd silhouette. This place is inhabited by shadows that move, and among them hides blocks of light, speaking only with voices of the quartet for strings. In the quartet, the cello's brief voice is the most beautiful, whether pitched high or low. I should like for a block of light to whisper a cello's voice, with the violins and viola as its lighthearted accompaniment.

Answers conceal the blocks of light. Symbols reveal the meaning of life. From the caves of spite three wishes thrown, tapestries woven in Harvest Loom. Doomful promises disperse the night, when golden mysteries are clearly shown. This page turns upon the Thief of Blight— hearkened above this spirit strife. A foreshadow of destiny's enlightened shore, boldly near the crowning throne.

When answers reveal the blocks of light—

Symbols conceal the meaning of life.

Here, in the grieving land, I return to my house of isolation, where my body awaits in pain, bound by restraints bequeathed from ages before Eve.

The hours travel along at the speed of light, and this world is cloaked in darkness once again. Mother comes into the room without the punishment stick, and she unties my restraints. My neck feels as though it was not designed to move, as do my arms and legs. She helps me to my feet, and it feels like I have been bound for a thousand years, or for a single day. It hurts for me to walk, as she helps me through the living room to the bathroom. She helps me get undressed, and lays me in the empty bathtub. She disrobes down to her bra only, and squats above my nude body in the tub, urinating on me for the longest time imaginable, grunting very loudly from the relief it provides her. The house is filled with her voice.

She is unashamed.

As she draws my bath, I am amazed at the number of bruises on my arms and legs. Living things they are, black and blue with evil intention. Every part of me bears at least the edge of a sore or a bruise.

My body will heal itself.

But the truth will cut deep, and leave scars.

108

*S*ummer drifts in on southern breezes, swirling above our isolated house and garden field. Warm winds rush mightily through the forest wood, whispering of bygone happiness, and days of future sorrow. I return from the Land of Dreams, after a long, restful sleep. I hurry to get dressed, so that I may pluck the rose from the morning. The summer air is warm on my face. The dewdrops tickle the top of my feet as I walk through the grass. The doves coo their sleepy voices to the bobwhites, who happily return their cordial greeting call.

What I do, I do without fear. I must go boldly before her throne, to ask for the grace to live the rest of my life in blessed sanity. Beside my bedroom window grows this question, blooming with petals of snowy white. A single rose bush, inconspicuous, safe from her concern, the only promise to myself I've been brave enough to keep. Carefully, I clip the long stem from the bush, the lifeline to my prized flower, so that I may give it freely as a gift.

I wait bravely through the long morning, cooking the grandest breakfast, which does not serve to awaken her as I had hoped. But long after I eat, and even while I rest in my room, I hear the violin sing a Melody for a White Rose, above and below the keys of my piano, and I listen to the footsteps of origin echo from another part of the house. But now is not the time. When the haze of sleep, and memory of her nightmares is past, I shall step into the void, to rescue us from this life of misery.

But the sun climbs higher in the sky, until it reaches the zenith, and begins its descent towards the western gate. The rose sits afresh in its crystal water vase, waiting for its commission. It seems even more beautiful now, as if it knows what it was called to do. It watches the daylight soften, as the Earth turns toward the evening day, as the shadows draw nourishment from the coming twilight once again.

I lift the white rose from the water vase, and I go to the livingrooom where my life awaits me. Quickly I present my gift, and she stands up, bewildered, and takes it from me. The look on her face is a masterwork, a painted canvas of contrasting emotion. But I push through the tension, invading her personal space, and I slide my arms around her tightly. Breathing in the scent of her loveliness, the smell of flowers and crème lotion, and I tremble at the thought that this powerful woman has given birth to me.

"I love you," I say. "I love you."

I don't think she is frightened. She doesn't respond, but she doesn't pull away from me either.

"There's only one thing I want, Momma. It has to be, so we can live the rest of our lives here in peace. So I can take care of you. So all of me can be here for you without being afraid."

I raise my head from her shoulder, and look boldly into that winter gaze, those witch eyes, eyes of gray. Her strength, her beauty, they strike a fire in me. Even while I endure the memories of our life, I still hope for a time when our suffering will end. I have hardly spoken since that dreadful autumn Sunday two years ago, or hardly looked her in the eye before this moment.

"I want you to tell me you love me."

She studies my eyes, to see if I have gone mad.

"I want you to tell me."

Quietly, I begin to repeat it. Still latched on to her, hoping to break her resistance. This is the last of me, the only strength I have left. I hold on for dear life as she slowly, deliberately begins to pry my arms from around her. Fear takes hold of me, tearing through me like a twister.

"Momma. Momma you can beat me until the pee and blood run out of me, but we need to say it. Our lives depend on it Momma. Something's got us trapped. But we can get out right now. We can get out it right this second, Momma…"

Unbeknownst to the both of us, a struggle has ensued. A desperate clawing at one another for the strength of protection. Protection from the madness that has haunted us from birth. She claws at me to get away, lest I break down her wall of hatred, which has shielded her from the grief that seeks to destroy her mind. I grab at her like one about to drown in quicksand, about to choke in a mud bog of perpetual loneliness, seeking rescue from the floodwaters of her rejection and contempt.

I beg her through tears and soft, high pitched pleading as she slowly, deliberately uses her strength to pull away from me, while shaking her head in a definite *no*. But her face bears no bitterness, and though she does not speak, I can perceive her fearful cry to the heavens, calling forth my days of pain and agony.

"Momma please don't…please don't let it happen Momma. I beg you don't go. Tell me…tell me please… pleeeeaase… Momma you don't have to mean it, just say it to me, everything will be good when you say it to me…"

She moves toward her room, resisting her own fear as well as mine, still shaking her head in quiet, deliberate denial. She reaches behind her back, where my hands are locked, and with one last, wrenching pull, she unlocks my hug, and pulls my arms away from her. The motion is as painful as a hundred lashes, and it causes me to scream as if I am being burned alive. I grab her arm, trying to pull her, slipping in my usual clumsiness, as she drags me hopelessly begging to the doorway of her room.

She goes inside, with me pulling on her and screaming in the doorway like a child. Slowly, she begins to close the door, disconnecting me from her, as an ocean rising, separating me from the Living Shore. I pound on her locked door, still crying for deliverance, now understanding that there is indeed no salvation, nor deliverance from suffering.

Mother! Do not shut me away ! Withhold not the waters from the River of Life! If I drink of this living river, I shall not die. Woman of my soul. Daughter of Misery… give me this water to drink. Let me live, to care for you in the Twilight of Seasons. Give me this, so that I will not die…

Give freely of this living water, so that I shall not wither and die.

I sit on the floor in a frenzy of crying, which is familiar enough to these walls to be sure. But they are not tears of weeping, mourning for the pain of my battered body. These cry for the death of a human spirit. For the last flicker of light, that has now been extinguished. As I look through watery vision at the broken, scattered pieces of flower, which still lives, suffering the pain of its impending death, my mind sees her standing at the door of her bedroom with her ear pressed firmly against it, feeling it vibrate from the fury of my cry. From the pain of loss, I scream and pound on the door for an hour, more angry than afraid, but compelled by the pain of hope, praying that she will open the door, even if it is only to punish me.

But my strength is gone. I cannot scream again. I crawl away, rising to my feet just long enough to get to the sofa. I care nothing for the lying voice of the Flower, sprawled broken and dying across the living room floor.

I care nothing for myself.

I should have come into the world as a phantom. I would like to live in the woods, wailing my voice among the living. Having no earthly reason to mourn. Feeling no pain of lost love.

109

*I*n every life, there is a day of reckoning. A time when purpose is revealed, when the sum of days and years is tallied. But along the way, many false reckonings will appear, having every bit the persuasive power of reason, leaving a person wrongly convinced of what their future may hold. These can be exhilarating. Or terrifying.

I am learning the exhilaration of true terror.

Sometimes, she will lie on top of me, both of us fully clothed, with my arms pinned or tied behind me, pressing her hand over my nose and mouth until I almost pass out. Trying to squeeze the tears and the breath out of me.

But I will never fight back.

For many months, she has been making empty threats and promises, about the manner and severity of my death. I am scared to death of my own shadow, trembling at every sound, sometimes visibly shaking when she comes near, and even when she leaves me in the house alone to go into town. I am as dumb as a sheep, having lost the concept of what is a better life, understanding nothing except the fear and pain I have always known. I have no right to change the life I have been given. Who am I, to expect something better for myself? I live to breathe, and to serve the Mistress who cares for me.

It seems that every cross word, every fit of temper will leap into that horrific list she keeps well in her mind, and at the tip of her tongue. Hanging me nude upside down, and slowly cutting pieces out of my skin. Throwing alcohol on my wounds, and letting me heal, then throwing boiling water upon my face...

Letting me heal, and then tying me to a tree, and nailing my fingers to it. Driving nails into the bottom of my feet. Breaking my leg with a sledge hammer and setting it herself, giving me a permanent limp. Keeping me locked in my room forever, gagged and bound, seeing me only to feed me and treat my wounds, so that I can be cut slowly for many years...

Or to simply take me deep into the woods under the full moon, and lovingly rape me with a ten inch knife, or choke me, or whip me to death with her soft leather belt, and place my body in an unmarked grave, underneath the Harvest Moon.

This is the kind of fear that I have come to know.

It is the Fear of Death.

Her dark imagination has broken through. I don't know the truth of what she will do, but for her to even be able to imagine such horrible things is incredible to me. These thoughts are seeded by depression, but have been cultivated by hatred, and will perhaps be nourished by something resembling madness.

And now, my day is at hand. I know it, because her talk of death has become less venomous and threatening. She speaks of my end in casual conversation, even to the point of rationality, going back and forth on her decision as if she were speaking of a condemned barn animal. Months of this talk has begun to penetrate what is left of my feeble psychology, until I understand what it means to be afraid. The fear of pain cannot compare to the fear of having one's life taken away.

These fragments of forewarning, these prophetic pieces have come together, taking shadowy form on this sweltering hot Indian summer's day. It is very humid today. The rains will come soon, and wash away the summer's memory. I languish fully in my womanhood, a good month from my 22nd birthday. Our little chicken flock has grown again, and their clucking keeps me company while I feed them. The warmth of the afternoon sun is on my face.

Oddly enough, she has not punished me for weeks. It is the first time in years this has happened, and it seems that the fires of her lust have subsided. Sometimes, I think that I can see the end of the years of pain, when I hear traces of regret, and even apology in her voice. Maybe, she has spit all of her hatred out in those fearful words. I will tell her tonight, calmly, that I would like stay with her forever, so that I can take care of her for the rest of my life.

Soon, the Woman of Beauty drifts out the back door. She steps into the yard, wearing a lovely new dress, a shocking purchase, a beautiful white dress with pretty red flowers. Her hair is pinned in the pretty style of days past. Her face is absent of the bitterness of these dark years. My heart flutters with a new hope, as I watch her put her hands on her lower back and gaze above the trees, displaying the shape of her figure, so that nature may bow and worship. She has a calm, peaceful expression.

A spirit of relaxation flows from her. I think I can sense my freedom.

Is this a reprieve?

As I walk toward her from the chicken yard, she looks at me, and smiles. Her gray eyes are beautiful, but still having the power to unnerve me. I move quickly towards her, eyes wide with naivité, lips tucked in, ready to give her a hug that I know will not be returned.

But suddenly she moves towards me, frightening me at first, until I see the look of quiet happiness. She puts her arms out to me, and I run to her and nearly jump into her arms, hugging her tightly around the neck, listening to her comfort me with her soft voice. My body can hardly bear the feeling, as she hugs me in a spirit of purity, giving me the affection that I have craved for a lifetime.

"I love you, Momma."

"I know, sweetie," she said. "I know."

For the briefest moment, I think I am immersed in a dream, a vision of my heart's desire. If this is indeed a dream, then I pray that I will never wake up again.

"We're both gonna be fine, Momma," I say. "And I'm gonna stay with you forever, and take good care of you for the rest of my life."

She looks at me lovingly. Her grey eyes glisten, and her face bears the burden of compassion.

"At last, His love for you hath flourished," she says. "Your Day of Peace has come."

I look up at her in tears of joy, waiting for her to speak of our beautiful new life together.

"Last night," she says, "I had the revelation that I had been praying for. And now I know. I dreamed that there was blood, splattered on every wall, and splashed on every floor of the house."

Like a spirit, the fear takes form in the gray mist of her speech, and banishes the warmth from my body. Prickly needles tickle my skin.

"Yes," she says, nodding her head gently.

My lips quiver, but the power to speak is gone. She places her finger gently on my lips, shushing me quietly.

"There are no more words for you," she says.

Mother kisses me on the forehead, and hugs me lovingly once again.

110

I have gone to bed on this lonely night, remembering all the hugs and kisses and gentle looks, some of them replete with tears. I cannot rest in the heat, and the cold of my coming death. I think only of axe blades, and how it must feel to be chopped into pieces. I don't know when it will happen, but every little noise has become the call for me to sit up in bed, and listen for her footsteps.

My eyes are wide open as I lay in bed. I can see the room in front of me. But am I awake? Is this the room of my dreams? I hear a noise! The sound of frantic movement—hurried footsteps beyond my bedroom door, in the front of the house. But I cannot move. If I am awake, then why can I not move?

What is this I feel? This sickness, coursing through my body? Is this Death, stealing strength from my arms, drawing energy from my legs of power? Shall I not awaken from this dark place, to never again see the Light of Day? But the angel hath said *"Thou hast no infirmity…you shall not die."*

Though my body cries out for the grave…

I shall not die.

I sit up in bed with a start, gazing at the same room I peered at only a moment before in a vision. I am awake now, and still among the living. My clock tells me that it is too close to the witching hour. I think I can hear the night sounds beyond the door, as if they have moved into the living room. In my white cotton nightgown, I climb out of bed slowly, as quietly as the little mouse that I am, and creep slowly to my bedroom door. It feels like I am alone in the farmhouse. It think the house is empty. But how can that be?

The living room door is wide open in the dead of night. Mother's room is empty. Cautiously, I step through the dark'ned living room and out into this dense, black country night, calling to Mother in a voice that hardly rises above a whisper.

"Momma?"

I am familiar with these dark nights. But the blackness of this one is heavy. The Moon is hidden. I hear the voice of the wood devil, lurking through the air, low to the ground, stealing whatever unfortunate child that might happen to be out after nightfall. It was what mother told me back then, to make me afraid to go outside at night.

"Momma! Momma where are you?"

The air is very warm, even for Indian Summer. It is very humid. The rains will be here soon. I can feel the grass under my bare feet while I tiptoe around to the back of the house. Everything looks like twisted, blackened silhouettes. Like shadow demons.

Mother never leaves the house this late at night.

"Mommmaaa!"

My voice hangs still in the night air. It does not carry across the empty field into the thick woods. My vision adjusts, and the silhouettes transform before my eyes, becoming the tool shed and the chicken coop. I can barely see the pale glow of the dirt road. The tall woods loom around me, like a ghostly range of black hills, stretching to infinity.

Dear God...

Oh my dear God in Heaven

Why do I stare at the black woods? Why do I stand at the dirt road, blinking my eyes? Do I expect to see her drift to me out of the night, to hug me, and promise that we will live in peace? Is this my road to a better life?

Perhaps, this is her road to freedom.

Tears will serve no purpose. Turn away from the black woods, and stumble nervously back to the house! Walk quickly, to escape the oppressive dark! Deep despair has searched these back country roads, looking for a place to rest. Looking for a soul to torment. But take solace, *Elizabeth,* that you will not be slowly killed, and buried beneath the forest floor! Sing in your heart, dear woman, that there will be no death of melody, in this harvest season!

But you are alone.

"What's that you say, honey?"

"M-Momma's gone."

"For how long?"

"She's been gone for f-four days now."

"And she didn't say anything? She just up and left?"

"Y-yes sir."

He stands in awe, reeling under the force—the power of what is meant to be, unable to look me in the eye. My fear and uncertainty, my neediness are a weight upon him, and is too heavy for him to bear.

She has escaped, Mr. Shirley. Your kept woman has fled. Mr. Shirley, I am lost. I feel too stupid to do anything. What kind of animal am I, that will whistle melodies in the planting field, as I wipe the sweat from my face with my dirty hands?

What am I going to do?

111

My soul hath wrenched free
In agony she hath departed
Through misery I now go alone
Flailing in chaos and winter cold

No hope, no rest for souls in pain
From tortures laid at my feet
Woman with hair pitched in Ravenwood
In timeless beauty and despair

Lament for the Death of Melody
Greatness buried in cruelty
Wisdom breathed from Heaven's mercy
Lost in eternal Destiny

Words are given through Birth of Fate
Truth springs from Sorrow's Bosom
Her heavenly promises hath been delayed—
*A lifetime of futures is interred *

Now terror's regret is fulfilled
When Her soul hath gone from me
My spirit is in unbearable pain—
For all eternity

112

Mercy falls as gentle rain
Winds breathe from the Throne of Grace
Gray skies weep for lives of men
Grieving, longing for a day of peace

From far across the Eastern Sea
The wind whirls into a behemoth
A white cloud of soothing rage
Swirling bands of Beautiful Death

Moving gracefully above the crashing sea
Thrashing waves of gentle fury
The Great Cloud traverses the watery plain
Whispering promises of devastation

Now the waters of the sounding sea
Arise in Power of Benevolence
Nature seeks refuge from her embrace
From this storm of her Malevolent Beauty

Mercy falls as gentle rain
Grieving for a day of peace

113

From in the mists of high above
A woman fell to Earth below
As though she had nowhere to go
She drifted down to Earth

The woman fell from life above
Adrift with nowhere left to go
Drowned in waters of Hatteras
Found in waters of Evening Flow

As her children bereaved her soul in love
Her coffin lowered in the ground below
They grieved too great a grief to know
When their mother was laid to rest

They looked to a misty sky above
Knowing too great a pain to know
Wondering where it is they should go
As rain fell down to Earth

It rained in waters of Evening Flow
For the grieving down below

114

*W*hile these lonely weeks pass, Indian summer fades into memory, under the cold autumn rain. The radio blares constantly in the house for company. I have slept with every light on, when I *can* sleep, and I think that fear is now my constant companion. It feels as if a part of me has died, and drifted into space. I walk the dirt road like a grieving ghost girl, searching for where it is that her beloved mother could have gone.

O Indian Summer! Thy glorious departure! Colorful season of death, echoes of night and winter! Cold rains descend, through an autumn mist of gray. A wet, weeping world, frozen in regret. Days of mourning, tearful summer's passing. Eternal grief and sorrow. Gladness for nature's sleep.

I am thinking of her now, on this Sunday of Bereavement. The church feels warm on my skin today, but it cannot melt the fear—the constant dread that has grown inside me like an ice crystal. I watch Pastor Davis in the pulpit, with his fine gray suit and slick dark blonde hair, poking his finger in the air with righteous indignation, pointing it at some poor soul about one thing or another. Does he know that this place is my only hope? The only place in the world that I can go?

A few of them have already offered to help me. They even promised to visit. But they never did. I don't think that they ever will. The pastor talks to me every Sunday, asking me if I need help with anything, and if everything is alright. When he first found out that mother was missing, he was fervent in his enthusiastic announcement, and the church responded with many kind words and open arms, and even some money has found its way to me. Ms. Askew even brought me groceries last week, which answered a prayer I didn't even know I had prayed. I am dreading, with all my heart, the first day I will have to go into town alone.

Why did you leave, Mother?

Where did you go?

At least, Mr. Shirley says that I can stay. But I don't know for how long. How long will he tolerate me? How many seasons will he put up with me, before he has paid his debt to her memory?

I have nightmares every night now. Mother will visit me in my dreams, always with malice, chasing me down until she catches me. Her touch always fills me with a deep, cold fearfulness, that makes me wonder if my heart can endure the strain. And there are times when she will come to me disguised in sweetness.

One of these reveals to me her lovely image, with the two of us walking the road home from our country church. The skies will be the color of springtime, filled with the promise of summer's joy. She puts her arm around me, and we stroll leisurely through our freedom land, and she tells me she has made me a gift. In happiness and peace, we walk past our cottage of isolation, and my rosebush is in full bloom underneath the sunlight. When we get to the backyard, I see my gift, leaning against the back porch in burnished pinewood, in the unmistakable shape of a *coffin*. This dream has come to me more than once, with a variation or two, so that I am always surprised at the outcome, shocked into screaming myself awake.

I wonder if the dream means that I am going to die soon? Is this a living death that I'm in? Sometimes I will see shovels in my dreams, or I will hear phantom shoveling of ground even before I drift to sleep, or I will see an axe when I close my eyes, or hear the chopping of wood. Death haunts me now like a spirit, pulling at me, wanting to steal what is left of my mind. I am afraid of the whole world now, and everybody in it.

When I come to church, I seek refuge in community. I want to live in the safety of their loving kindness. But they are like creatures to me, eyes glowing with resentment, whispering among themselves about what they are going to do to me, now that my protection is gone. The young men leer at me more boldly than ever, and even some of the older ones, and so many of the women have unkind expressions, rolling their eyes and refusing to return my hopeful smiles. They think I am slow, with an addled mind and a feeble brain.

Is it that far from the truth?

The Truth stares at me from eyes of antipathy every Sunday. Pastor Davis' wife cannot hide her contempt any longer. As she glowers at me, I want to apologize to her. I guess I need to tell her how sorry I am for the trouble I have caused, that I do not mean to appear aloof and unfriendly. When she comes around me, the resentment flows from her in gentle waves, like a calm, winter wind.

For years, she has bided her time. Staring at the two dark-haired women who sit together in the back of the country church. Watching them closely. It is obvious they are mother and daughter. A shy, fearful girl, who apparently lives in terror and awe of her domineering mother.

Sometimes when they walk, the mother will push her along, hard enough to make her stumble. Once she fell, and her mother stood by, glaring at her while she picked her purse, Bible, and clumsy carcass off the ground. When the mother is in front, she might stop to adjust her shoe or to look behind her, and the daughter will slam clumsily into the back of her. The mother will turn around, even if people are looking, and stare at her with a look that can either melt ice or freeze fire.

They seldom speak. They don't have to. Their expressions speak volumes.

But every so often, they are less like tormentor and victim, and more like lonely companions. The mother will seem less impatient and contemptuous—the daughter, less awkward and fearful. They will walk a little slower, a little closer beside one another. A Great Protector, clinging for dear life to the one thing she has that matters. As a pair, the two of them are unsettling. Funereal. Gothic.

Every Sunday, they sit there. Acting like they need no one. Acting like they are too good to socialize. The dark-haired woman, and her weird daughter. The Witches. Where did they come from? Do they think they are beautiful? Now, the one with the cold, stern expression is gone, and her weird daughter is all alone. Why does she still come here? My husband watches her. Always going over to her. To comfort her. To smile in her face. To offer assistance. Dislike is not a strong enough word. I want to pull every black strand of hair out of her head. I want to tear the skin off her face with my fingernails...

"What a friend we have in Jesus. All our sins and griefs..."

Look at her. Too good to sing. Always acting like she's too good to sing. And she just sits and stares at that piano. Hate is not a strong enough word.

I despise her.

"How are you getting along sweetie? Have you got everything you need?"

As Mrs. Davis escorts me gently to her office, I can only nod my head, feeling apprehensive, but hopeful. Maybe, she will help me not to be afraid. When we get to her office, there are two women waiting for us.

They are much older than me. So much wiser. The door is closed quickly behind me. They are not regal like Mother.

My expression arouses no pity in them.

"Your Mother's been gone over three weeks now. She's not coming back is she?"

Mrs. Davis leans back against her desk. She is a pretty woman. Her blonde hair is straight, and stylishly cut. Her dresses are colorful. Ms. Wise and Ms. DeVane are both behind me, between me and the door.

"Your Momma's not here now, is she girl," a voice says in my ear, startling me. But what can I do? I can't run. They might think me rude or stupid if I run.

"We're so sorry for your loss, Miss Coletti," says Mrs. Davis, lowering her eyes, nearly smiling.

Out of nowhere, I feel a hard shove against my face. Before I can react, I feel my hair pulled. My unraveling is complete. My nerves are shattered. I stammer the word please, which is only a breathless puttering, like a motor which has no fuel. They have a tight hold on my arms, pressing so close to me I feel like I can't breathe.

"P...P..."

"I told you she was addled," one of them says. "Crow-headed *slut*."

"I d-d- I didn't-"

Mrs. Davis steps close in front of me.

"Listen," she says. "If we ever see you in this church again, we're going to drive you home, and finish what your mother started. And I know you understand what I'm talking about. I can see it on you."

"She smells like a strawberry whore to me," one of them hisses.

"What kind of a name is Coletti anyway for around here—"

"Those tears ain't foolin' us, slut, devil bitches can cry too—"

Words are trapped in my throat. A pleading voice, held captive. My tongue feels like its being pulled backwards in my mouth, and is going numb. I think I wet myself. I pray that I didn't.

"You've got my husband sniffing around you more than he ever did your mother. I want you to hear this, girl. If we see you again, we're taking you back to that house you live in *ourselves*."

"Oh you can believe that," Ms. Wise says. Deeply.

What kind of a person am I, who inspires such hatred in other people?

My mouth is open as I walk through the church to where my rain cloak is. Mother taught me to never leave my cloak or coat in the lobby, so that we could always leave quickly when services ended. I retrieve my black rain cloak, and march down the brick church steps for the last time. Holding back the tears as best I can.

While I drift alone, above this haunted road, the trees blur in my vision, and the River of Pain wets my face with tears. I think I shall never again see the Holy Place, the place where the Divine supposedly lives. But even as the cold, autumn rain sends my newest melody, I know that I am protected—because I know He lives in me.

115

*F*ar over distant places, the winds continue their journey. They could exact annihilation, were it not for the Hand of God. They travel to a place above the sea, to a land beyond the Sea, above the valleys and across the Open Plains. Forever seeking. Searching in vain for where to rest. Finding only places they have already been.

I can see the cold world through your gray eyes. And I can feel the curse of your life, coursing through my body. Perhaps, I am an accursed woman.

Mother—

Where did you come from? Into what world did you go?

Thine was a soul of grief. A melody of lost hope, and tearful promises unfulfilled. I know you did not want me to suffer. I know you longed for a day of happiness, when you would have no contempt, and could love me with all your heart. I pray you have found peace in the River Valley, along the shores of Azurean Sand.

I see the clouds of Heaven, as they close upon your Faith. Crushing your spirit to Earth, laying refusal upon your weeping cry. You could not love me, because you were bestowed none with which to give. From powers and principalities, you were compelled to wish me harm, and to keep your love apart from me.

Do not haunt my waking hours! Do not torture me in the fires of a dream! Do not drown me in fear, and the dread of each new night and day. Rest in your hour of peace, Mother! Hearken to the voice of your child. To the Daughter you bore. And to the Woman that you never knew.

The solitude, the isolation of my little house has grown upon me. As the wind whirls the rain against the house, I stand at the window of my bedroom, at one with this weeping world, listening to the quiet storm of melody and evening song.

The End

ABOUT THE AUTHOR

Jonathan Lovejoy is a graduate of the University of North Carolina at Greensboro, with a B.A. in Religious Studies, and a graduate of Liberty University with an M.A. in Theological Studies. He currently lives in Winston Salem, North Carolina.

For more info on the author's life and career, visit jonathanlovejoy.com

www.ingramcontent.com/pod-product-compliance
Lightning Source LLC
Chambersburg PA
CBHW071216250626
47163CB00001B/10